KING'S BLOOD

✳✳✳

KING'S BLOOD

Judith Tarr

A ROC BOOK

ROC
Published by New American Library, a division of
Penguin Group (USA) Inc., 375 Hudson Street,
New York, New York 10014, USA
Penguin Group (Canada), 90 Eglinton Avenue East, Suite 700, Toronto,
Ontario M4P 2Y3, Canada (a division of Pearson Penguin Canada Inc.)
Penguin Books Ltd., 80 Strand, London WC2R 0RL, England
Penguin Ireland, 25 St. Stephen's Green, Dublin 2,
Ireland (a division of Penguin Books Ltd.)
Penguin Group (Australia), 250 Camberwell Road, Camberwell, Victoria 3124,
Australia (a division of Pearson Australia Group Pty. Ltd.)
Penguin Books India Pvt. Ltd., 11 Community Centre, Panchsheel Park,
New Delhi - 110 017, India
Penguin Group (NZ), cnr Airborne and Rosedale Roads, Albany,
Auckland 1310, New Zealand (a division of Pearson New Zealand Ltd.)
Penguin Books (South Africa) (Pty.) Ltd., 24 Sturdee Avenue,
Rosebank, Johannesburg 2196, South Africa

Penguin Books Ltd., Registered Offices:
80 Strand, London WC2R 0RL, England

First published by Roc, an imprint of New American Library,
a division of Penguin Group (USA) Inc.

First Printing, October 2005
10 9 8 7 6 5 4 3 2 1

Rᴏᴄ Registered Trademark—Marca Registrada

LIBRARY OF CONGRESS CATALOGING-IN-PUBLICATION DATA:

Tarr, Judith.
 King's blood / Judith Tarr.
  p. cm.
 ISBN 0-451-46045-6
 I. Title.
 PS3570.A655K567 2005
 813'.54—dc22   2005011092

Set in Galliard

Printed in the United States of America

PUBLISHER'S NOTE
This is a work of fiction. Names, characters, places, and incidents either are the product of the author's
imagination or are used fictitiously, and any resemblance to actual persons, living or dead, business es-
tablishments, events, or locales is entirely coincidental.
    The publisher does not have any control over and does not assume any responsibility for author or
third-party Web sites or their content.

PART ONE

Inheritance

anno domini 1087

❄ CHAPTER 1 ❄

Spring came late that year, lashed with wind and rain and sharp-edged with hunger. In corners where the queen could not hear, people muttered of signs and portents, and said prayers that had nothing to do with the Lord Christ or the good God, although many of them called on Our blessed Lady.

Edith was small and quick and her ears were keen. When she went wandering, her nurses had long since given up trying to catch her. She might stay away for most of a day, but she always came back.

On the day the world changed, she had escaped to the top of the highest tower of her father's dun. The rain had stopped for the first time in days. The wind was fierce, but she was never cold. The people in the wind kept her warm: odd and insubstantial shapes and eerie voices, wrapping her about, singing her songs in their language and teaching her to see what their people saw. She was a blessed one, they said. She could see through the world.

Today she was feeling strange. It was not that she was hungry, although she had given her breakfast to a beggar at the gate. The wind was pressing on her, as if to push her down from the tower and out of the dun and away on the road. *South,* it sang. *South is your way.*

She clung to the wall, with the wind whipping tears from her cheeks, and glared defiantly northward. Beyond the roll of stony hills and winter-blasted heather, the firth was as grey as iron, flecked white with foam. The folk of the air swirled above her, shrilling their song. *You know the way. You know you must. It is fated.*

"I don't want to," she said, not particularly loudly. They could hear even if she said it in her heart.

They said nothing to that. She wished they had. Then she would have had someone to scream at. But the wind knew what it knew.

She could run away. But where would she go? Even if she could see what no one else would admit to seeing, and hear what no one else could hear, and ride as well as a boy besides, she was still a child. There was nowhere she could go, that her father could not find her and bring her back to face something even more terrible than himself: her lady mother.

She drew herself up, there in the wind. They were looking for her; she could feel them. Her mother had remembered her. It was time.

The queen inspected her daughter with a hard eye. She was beautiful, was the Lady Margaret, tall and fair, and royal to the core of her. She waged war for the Lord Christ as her husband the king waged war for Scotland: with heart and soul and a fierce, deadly sense of honor.

Edith did not have the sense to keep her eyes lowered in proper submission. Staring at her mother was like staring at the sun; it could strike a person blind. But Edith was fascinated. Wherever Margaret was, the world was overwhelmingly solid. Edith could not see through it at all.

Margaret reached from her tall chair, taking Edith's chin in firm cool fingers and tipping it so that her face caught the light. The queen sighed faintly. "Well, child," she said, "I see they did their best, but that you are a wild thing, no one could possibly mistake. It's time to make a Christian of you."

Edith very carefully said nothing. There were no folk of the air in this cold, still room; no creatures at all but the queen and her ladies and the pair of little bright-eyed dogs that crouched watchfully at Margaret's feet.

The dogs might have had something to say, but they chose not to say it. Margaret, who reckoned them dumb animals, paid no attention.

Having searched Edith's face, she let it go and folded her long white hands in her lap. "Tomorrow," she said, "you will go. The letters have been sent. Your aunt the abbess will be expecting you."

A shiver ran down Edith's spine. She could not help it then; she had to ask. "My aunt? You're giving me to an abbey? You're making me a nun?"

"We are offering you to God," said the queen. It was like a door shutting.

"But I thought," said Edith, not wisely at all, "that I was to be fostered, and when I was older, sent to be married. Not—"

"You are to be fostered." That was a voice Edith had not heard before. There were always maids with the queen, and nuns in veils. Edith had not been paying attention, not with her mother taking up all the light and air in the room.

This was a nun, or seemed to be. Her voice was soft. She seemed gentle and humble as a bride of the Lord Christ should be, but the small hairs on Edith's neck were standing straight up.

"Princess," the stranger said, "you will be tended and taught and shown the way to Our Lady's grace. Of that I can assure you."

Edith's heart was pounding hard. Her breath was coming short. She did not know why she should be feeling this way; there was nothing frightening about the lady. She was like the folk of air—even here in front of the queen.

That was why she was so alarming. Because she could be here and alive and speaking with her own voice. Nothing from the Otherworld could do that where Margaret was.

Which meant that this lady was very, very strong indeed. And she came from the place where Margaret wanted to send Edith. Which meant—

There was too much to think about. Edith's head ached with trying.

"Don't try," the strange lady said, so soft that only Edith could hear. "Just be."

That was exactly the sort of thing one of the folk of air might have said. It took the pain away, a little, but Edith did not object when her mother ordered her nurses to feed her a posset and put her to bed. "In the morning," the queen said, "if she is still vaporing, prepare a litter for her. She will go, whether it pleases her or no."

Edith did not know whether it pleased her or not. But even while she was carried off to bed, she knew that she would go—not because her mother commanded it, but because the lady was there.

The king was not there to see Edith off. Edith wondered if he even knew that she was going away.

If she had been a little younger she might have cried, but she was too old for that now. She blinked hard against the cut of the wind, and let her mother kiss her coolly on both cheeks and lay a blessing on her. Then she mounted her pony and waited while the guards took their places around her.

They were a strong escort. It was a long way to her Aunt Christina's abbey, all the way down into England. None of her nurses was allowed to go with her, though Nieve clambered on one of the packmules and dared anyone to stop her. It took three men to do it, but they did it. The queen had commanded. They would obey.

Once Nieve was dragged off shrieking curses, Edith was alone in the midst of all those armored men, except for the lady whose name she did not even know. But the folk of air came and swirled about her and sang to her, and she forgot to be either lonely or afraid. They would never leave her alone. That was their promise. She knew they would keep it.

Once she had ridden out of the gate, she did not look back. For all her determination, her eyes were pricking with tears. She set her chin and kept her eyes fixed on the broad brown rump of the horse in front of her.

That was all she would see for much of that long ride: great tall horses around her and armored men on their backs, and the folk of air swarming so thick above her that they almost hid the sky. They told her stories as she rode, and sang songs in their eerie voices, and taught her to feel the land as she crossed it.

That was a wonderful thing. This was all one island, and Scotland was only the edge of it. There was England, with all its old kingdoms, and Wales, and Cornwall where the magic was strong.

She was going to England, where her mother's ancestors had been kings. New kings ruled there now: gross men, bad men, whom her mother refused to name. She would only call them *those invaders* and cross herself fiercely as she said it, as if the blessing were a curse.

And yet she sent her daughter there, because it was her inheritance. The abbey was a safe and sacred place, where Edith would learn to be she hardly knew what. But maybe not a Christian.

The folk of air were wildly excited that she was going there. She would be so strong, they sang; so wise. There would be no one wiser than she.

"It's good to be wise," the lady said.

Edith started so strongly that her pony almost shied. For days the lady had said nothing. The guards walked wary of her, and spoke softly when they thought she could hear, but she hardly seemed to see them. Edith she seemed not to notice at all.

As soon as she spoke, Edith knew that that was not true. The lady had noticed every tiny thing. She could see the folk of air, and hear them, too.

She was wise. Britain was in her, or she in it—Edith could not tell which it was. She was very, very strong.

"I am a Guardian of the Isle," said the lady in her soft cool voice. "You will learn what that means—among many other things."

"Does Mother know?" Edith asked her.

The lady's brows lifted, as if she had not expected that.

"Mother thinks I'm going to Aunt Christina," Edith said, "to learn to be a nun."

"And so you are," said the lady, "but there is more to the world than some will admit."

That went without saying. Edith closed her eyes. She had not been counting days, but there had been more than five and fewer than twenty. They were very close now to the abbey—and to somewhere else, somewhere strong. She could feel it inside, ringing on a deep note.

Deep in the heart of her, a hard knot loosened. Much of it escaped her in a gust of air. Here was where she was meant to be.

The guards had drawn away for once, so that she could see where she was. The broad plain stretched to the edge of the sky. Clouds tumbled above it, full of glimmering shapes.

A ring of stones rose ahead of them. It was very old. Powers gathered to it, and all the roads led there.

They rode past it. The guards barely glanced at it, but the lady bowed her head as they went by.

Something in the way she did it made Edith want to do the same. One paid respect to the Powers. Her nurses had taught her that, although her mother would have been very angry to hear of it. Her mother had no use for any powers but the Lord Christ and his Church.

They passed the ring of stones at midmorning. By noon they came in sight of the abbey: a stone wall and a low square tower, crouched on a hill beside a river. The water was high, the current swift, running down toward the walls and roofs of a town.

Edith had not expected that. She had thought the Lord Christ's house would be far away from anywhere, like the ring of stones; but it stood not far at all from the town's walls. People were coming and going on foot or on horseback or in wagons. Voices were singing and shouting. She even heard laughter.

Within the walls was silence. Sounds from without were muffled; as she left the guards and the horses in the courtyard, they faded to nothing.

Even more than the silence, she noticed the smell. It was familiar. Her mother's chapel was the same, a mingled scent of stone and cold and incense, and something that she could not put words to, that made her think of a rabbit in a trap.

She turned to the lady, to take comfort in a familiar face, but the lady was gone. Edith had not even felt her leave.

The nun who led her away from the horses was an old woman, gaunt and stiff, with a face that had long since forgotten how to smile. Not that the lady ever smiled, either, but there was a lightness on her that Edith could not see anywhere in this place.

Only one thing kept Edith from turning and running: the glimmer of an inhuman face perched on an arch of the cloister above her. The folk of air had kept their promise. They were with her even here, in a place that racked their insubstantial forms with pain.

Edith gave the creature a bit of herself, a flicker of strength to take the pain away. It sighed in relief and fluttered above her as her guide led her on down the cloister.

✳ CHAPTER 2 ✳

The Abbess Christina surveyed her niece with a cold blue eye. She looked older than her sister Margaret, and taller, and much thinner. Years of prayer and devotion had made Margaret more beautiful, but Christina looked as if she had withered in the bud.

Edith did her best to seem harmless and humble. Maybe it worked. Christina sniffed audibly and said, "You look like your mother. I trust she has raised you properly."

"She hopes that you will make a Christian of me," Edith said, then added with care, "lady."

"I will make a Christian of you," the abbess said, "and a bride of God."

Edith kept her lips tightly pressed together. She knew better than to say what she thought of that.

"Sister Rotrude will take you to the mistress of novices," her aunt said, inclining her head toward the aged nun who had brought Edith from the gate. "Your mother, no doubt, has taught you the rudiments of obedience. You will be obedient always, and humble before the face of the Lord. Do you understand?"

"I will try," Edith said, and again: "lady."

"You will call me Mother Abbess," her aunt said. "Now go."

Edith could hardly have been happier to be dismissed. The air in the abbess' study had the same deadness that it did where her mother was. Even the cloister was easier to bear than that.

* * *

As her guide led her away, she found her wits somewhere. She remembered what her father had told her once, that a fighting man was wise to notice everything around him. He never knew when a small thing might save his life.

This was war in its way. She kept her head bent, but her eyes were alert, taking in as much as they could. She set herself to remember where they went: which turns, how many steps in each stair.

She did not know how well she did it, but she tried. It gave her something to think about, and it kept her from dissolving into tears. She was a long way from any home she had known, and from any human thing that she could call friend.

There was no one in the novices' dormitory when she came there—no novices, no dour nun to rule over them. Sister Rotrude left her without a word, all alone in the big bare room with its rows of hard narrow cots. Each had a thin blanket folded over a straw pallet, and nothing else to warm it or make it comfortable.

The only light came from high narrow windows. At night there must be lamps, but Edith did not see any now, while it was still midday.

What she did see was a flock of the folk of air peering through the windows. They tumbled together into the room, a whole babbling stream of them, scattering through the barren space and casting light in corners that had not seen such a thing since the abbey was built. They brought more than light: they brought beauty, and a memory of the world's splendor.

Edith sat on a cot that did not feel as if anyone was using it, and tucked up her feet and folded her hands. The folk of air explored every crack and cranny of the room. That did not take them very long. When they were done, they gathered in a flock, clustering along the beams and hanging head down, batlike, from the windowframes.

They made her smile. She wondered if anyone had ever smiled in this place. How she was going to live here, she did not know. She was tired, hungry, thirsty. She was terribly alone.

Someone was watching her. There was no danger in it that she could feel. She waited quietly.

After a while the watcher came round in front of her. She looked up along a length of black-robed body to a face that made her start.

The lady smiled. Even Edith's fierce glare did not make her stop.

"You went away," Edith accused her. "You left me alone."

"Some things are necessary," the lady said. As soft as her voice was, it had the ring of steel. "Come now. The rest of the novices are waiting to meet you."

Edith narrowed her eyes. "It's you. You're the mistress of novices."

"Here," said the lady, "I am Sister Cecilia, and you owe me obedience."

"You're not always here. Are you?"

"I am here while you need me," Sister Cecilia said. "For many reasons, you need this place. You'll learn those reasons as time passes. For now, study what you see; and remember. And cultivate obedience."

"That is my weakest virtue," Edith said.

Sister Cecilia looked as if she would have laughed, but even she did not dare do that here. "It's a virtue to know oneself so well," she said. She held out her hand. "Come."

Edith decided to be obedient. She was still angry, but it was hard to keep a grip on her temper with the lady smiling at her.

She had one question left to ask, even while she let herself be led out of the dormitory. "Who are you really? Besides whatever you told me?"

"In time you'll learn," Sister Cecilia said. And that was all she would say. She was like the folk of air: mysterious and rather wicked.

It was that wickedness which kept Edith from running away: that and the folk of air who followed her everywhere, even to chapel. It was not an unfamiliar life, in the end, with its daily round of offices and its constant duties and the long hours in the schoolroom learning to read Latin and write in a fair hand.

What was least familiar—and least bearable—was that the gates never opened for the novices. The walls were always there, the gates shut, the bonds of obedience compelling them all to live imprisoned.

Most of them did not seem to mind. They were quiet, milk-faced girls with a clear calling to this life, or else they knew no better. The few who did mind had learned to keep quiet about it. Edith could see it in their eyes, how they were trapped. But none of them had found a way to escape.

A few could see the folk of air. Some of the nuns could, too; and there was Sister Cecilia, who Edith was convinced did not belong there at all. She walked and talked like the others, prayed as they did, and her Latin was beautifully learned—and yet she made Edith think of a falcon shut in with a flock of ringdoves.

This was a Saxon abbey. Edith was half Saxon. In Scotland it was nothing terribly remarkable; people cared more that her ancestors had been kings.

In England it mattered a great deal. England meant Angla-land—Angle-land, land of the Angles and the Saxons. But years ago, before Edith was born, the Saxons had been defeated in a great battle. Foreigners ruled England now, invaders from Normandy, and the king was a Norman.

Edith had known all that before she left Scotland. She had known how much hate there was, and how much the Saxons yearned to be kings again. What she had not known was that the Normans let their worst enemies live together, shut in an abbey, too firmly locked in duty and sanctity to mount a rebellion.

There was Abbess Christina. There was Sister Gunnhild, whose father had been the last Saxon king; he had died in the battle at Santlache, and lost the kingdom for all of them. There had been another Edith, Edith the queen, who was the last king's sister; but she lay in a tomb in the cloister.

Edith was not entirely sure that her namesake was dead. A few days after she came to the abbey, when she was ready to fling herself over the walls and into the river, Sister Cecilia sent her on an errand to the infirmary. She was to fetch a jar of salve for Aldith's eyes.

Aldith was one of the younger novices, even younger than Edith, and she could almost see through the world. Maybe, once her eyes were better, she would be able to do it.

Edith had not been to the infirmary before, but she knew where it was. She had been studying as the lady advised her, and watching and listening. She found her way out of the schoolroom and through the whispering stillness of the chapel.

Beyond the chapel were the cloister and the tomb. There were others buried there, holy nuns sleeping under unmarked stones. Only the queen had the flat grey bulk of a tomb.

There was no effigy on it. That was somewhere else, the folk of air sang in Edith's ear. Mortals thought her body lay in another place far away from here.

It was here. This was not Edith's blood kin, not one of Alfred's line, but she had married Edith's great-great-uncle Edward. Her brother had been the last king before the Normans came. She had been royal twice over, and she had been something more.

The folk of air stayed well away from the tomb. It was as deadly to them as cold iron. Edith felt in it the same thing she had felt in her aunt and her mother. Where they were, the brightness in the heart of the world—the thing that her nurses called magic—shriveled and died.

It was very much stronger here, as if the body in the tomb had drawn great quantities of nothingness to itself. Edith could feel the bitterness in it, the long rankling of defeat. In her mother it was a fierce determination to rule again; in Christina it was a stone-cold sanctity. This was simpler as well as stronger. The name Edith found for it was hate.

She backed away, shuddering. She had to leave this place. She had to.

The sun beat down in the courtyard. The grass in it was fiercely green, flecked with yellow flowers, each as bright as a sun. The folk of air danced above it. The air sang with their glee.

The tomb was still there, heavy and dull. It tried to swallow the light, but it was not strong enough for that. It muddied the brightness directly above it, and no more.

Edith had slid through the veils of the world. She was in the Other-world, the world that most humans were too blind to see.

And it was strong—stronger than it had ever been in Scotland. The power of the stone circle was here, spreading in waves through the earth and singing in the air. Edith had only been able to see this world some-times. She had never walked in it before. And yet here she was, in both worlds at once.

She was almost afraid—but only almost. It was beautiful here. The sun was as sweet and strong as wine. She drank it when she breathed. It made her dizzy.

The folk of air were dancing around her, wild with excitement. There were greater beings nearby, but they did not make themselves visible to her. She could feel them as she felt the ring of stones, deep in-side her.

They wanted her here. They had something for her to do—not right away, maybe not soon at all, but someday. Meanwhile she was to wait and study, and learn all she could. Then when the day came, she would be ready.

Slowly the brightness faded. The sun was ordinary, the grass plain mortal green again. Edith blinked, trying to make herself see the Other-world, but it was gone.

It would come back. For now she had an errand, and Sister Cecilia was waiting. That was part of what she had come to learn: obedience, and patience.

She sighed, because after all she was very young, but she drew her-self up and stiffened her back, and went where she was bidden.

❊ CHAPTER 3 ❊

The old bastard was dying.

He lay like a bloated spider, half crushed and stinking, while his scattered realms shook themselves apart. No one pretended to grieve. He hated pretense, and he had never indulged in illusions, even when they would have made his life easier.

Ease had never been old William's vice. He had been sacking a city when the hand of God struck him: hurdling one of the earthworks thrown up against him, overbalancing his warhorse with his burgeoning bulk and catching himself against the high pommel of his saddle. His belly was crushed; the pain, for all that he would not speak of it, was brutal. He was rotting from the inside out.

It was a hideous death, and slow. He had lain for a month now outside of Rouen, in the hushed stillness of St. Gervais' priory. He was still lucid more often than not, although his memory tended to wander. Sometimes he spoke to people who were not there: old friends, old enemies, and above all his queen, his Mathilda, who had gone into the dark before him.

But then, thought Henry, maybe they were there—especially Mathilda. If anyone would come back from the dead to help her husband over the threshold, it would be she.

In the nights, when even the monks were asleep, Henry almost could see them himself. He had the gift and the eye, but not, in the end, the will.

The grief of his mother's death was still sharp, even after the passage of years. Now that his father was dying, too, he found that he wanted to see the world as simple men saw it. It was more bearable somehow, although his heart persisted in calling it cowardice.

That night, a month and more after the king's fall, Henry sensed a change. It was subtle; he almost thought that he had imagined it. The shadows were darker. The light was brighter. And his father looked, not transparent, no, but somehow less solidly there than he had before.

He was letting go. That was a mercy.

"If he'd been a horse or a hound, we'd have put him out of his misery weeks ago."

Henry had felt his brother come in. Young William, Red William, had no magic to speak of, but his presence sent a shiver along the edges of Henry's awareness.

William came to stand by the bed, breathing shallowly. His wonted high color had gone faintly green. "How long now? Can you tell?"

"He can hear you, you know," Henry said.

William's jaw tightened under the curling copper-colored beard. The rest of his hair was more gold than red, but the hair of his face was almost defiantly bright. He bent as close as he could bear, eyes narrowed, peering at the distorted mass of the once familiar features.

Henry saw the gleam beneath the eyelid, but even with the warning, he did not expect his father's hand to rise as swiftly as it did. It caught hold of William's shirt and fisted in it.

"You," the king said. His voice was thick, wheezing with effort. "Get out. Now. Get to England. Take the treasury. Get yourself crowned before the other can move."

"But," William began. "I'm not—you're not—"

"By the time you get there," the king said, "I'll be dead. Go!"

As faint as the word was, it carried such a weight of command that Henry found himself on his feet. William reeled back as his father let him go. His face was the color of cheese. He turned abruptly, with none of his usual honed grace, and ran stumbling out the door.

The room seemed empty without him. But there was still a presence in it, awake and aware.

Henry met the cool grey eyes in the ruined face. People said Henry had the same eyes, if not the same face. In that, he tended to favor his mother.

"So," he said. "William gets England. Robert gets Normandy. What's left for me?"

"Treasure," the king said. "And patience."

"No land? What's a lord without land?"

"Patient," the old bastard said. "You've got the sight. You'll get more than either of them in the end."

"Do you know," Henry said, quite calmly when all was considered, "I think I hate you."

There was no telling what expression that face wore, but Henry could feel the laughter behind it. "Yes," his father said. The tide of pain was rising again, squeezing the life out of his voice. "Of all my get, you're the most like her."

Like Mathilda, he meant. To the king there had never been any woman but that one. Henry had never understood, and maybe never would. So many flowers, so many fields—so sweet, each of them, in the plucking.

He was dizzy with lack of sleep and stink of death and sudden swirl of magic rising in the room. His father had used it seldom when Mathilda was alive, and never after she died. He found no comfort in it, and little enough profit, either, or so he always said.

Tonight it wreathed the king like smoke, pouring out of him with the life that, at long last, was freeing itself from the rotting flesh. Henry sat transfixed. If he had known what to do, he would not have been able to do it.

It was a spell. Even with his own gift of magic, which his mother had fostered and nourished and taught, Henry had never known how much was in his father. It had been buried so deep for so long, drowned in duty and in the mass of aging flesh.

William's spirit climbed out of it as if from the pit of a dungeon, crawling over the lifeless, all but faceless bulk and rising slowly to his full height. He was tall, as tall as Henry—much taller than either of his elder sons—and broad, but there was neither bloat nor fat on this inner-most self. He looked as young as Henry: nineteen summers, maybe, though hardened already and tempered by a life of war.

He glanced about. His eyes were keen, no sign of befuddlement in them. He arched his back and stretched, yawning luxuriously, as if he still had breath and lungs to savor it. His teeth were strong and white as he turned, grinning at the one who watched in mute astonishment.

"Ah," he said. Even his voice was different: lighter, stronger, younger. "That's better. What are you staring at, boy? Haven't you ever seen a dead man before?"

Henry caught himself shaking his head like an idiot. "Not . . . like this."

"Remember it," the ghost-William said, "for when it's your time. You won't be the fool that I was. You've no fear of magic, nor disgust for it, either. She made sure of that."

"Why—" Henry began.

The shade did not reply. It was fading even as Henry spoke, shrinking away from him, as if he stood on a dark shore and his father sailed away, riding a strong wind. The farther shore was out of Henry's sight, though he craned to see, stretching eyes and magic as far as they would go.

He was not strong enough for that yet. The cords joining body and soul had begun to stretch and fray. He quelled the rise of panic, work-ing his way back little by little toward the solidity of earth and life and the flesh.

Long before he lay gasping with relief, not even caring that he choked on the reek of gut-sickness and advancing decay, his father's spirit was gone. William of Normandy, duke and king, conqueror of the English, was dead.

Henry had no tears to shed. He sat in quiet still, the silence of deep night. All too soon it would shatter. Then his brothers would take their legacies: duke's coronet for Robert, king's crown for William, and for Henry, gold and patience—and whatever else he could win for himself.

"Bastard to the end," he said to the motionless bulk on the bed. "Robert's a layabout, William's a fool. I'm the last, but even you never reckoned me the least. Maybe you think I need the time and the tempering—but what will become of your domains with those two in charge of them?"

The king was dead and gone. The only answer Henry had, or could hope for, was the memory of a whisper in the air. *Patience,* it said. *Patience.*

❊ CHAPTER 4 ❊

William pressed his forehead against the wall and tried to remember how to breathe. The stink of his father's sickness clotted in his lungs, even here in the chapel, the length of the abbey away from the king's deathbed. He could still feel that hand, all but dead and yet ungodly strong, groping toward his throat.

He could hear the voice, too, and the words it had spoken, echoing and reechoing in his skull. *Go. Be king. Be king. Be—*

And why should that be such a shock? He had always known that he would get England. Robert never could keep his mouth shut or his temper in check around his father. It suited the old man's whim to let him keep Normandy. But England was a conquest, with far more to it than the world knew. England, he gave to the son who was obedient more often than not—though not to the youngest son, who was both obedient and brimming over with magic.

There was no fathoming the man. No arguing with him, either. Only Mathilda had ever been able to do that and win.

Abruptly William thrust himself erect. Candles flickered. Things danced in and over and through them: creatures of another world than the one he preferred to live in. It was a curse that he could see them, but it could be useful, too—as now, when their flutter and flurry warned him of another's coming.

William was kneeling when the monk trod soft-footed into the chapel: his head was bowed, his body bent toward the altar. But his eyes were alert, watching sidelong, and his hand was never far from the hilt of his sword.

The monk halted beside him. His skin shivered. Magic brushed at it.

"What, lad?" said a voice he knew well. "Hiding in plain sight?"

William suppressed a sigh. Whether it rose out of relief or long suffering, he was not entirely sure. "My lord archbishop," he said.

The Archbishop of Canterbury stooped and laid down his burden. It was threefold, wrapped in heavy silk: one part narrow and long, one narrow and shorter, and one squat and square.

William's hand stretched toward them before he had time to think. His fingers were stinging as if with the touch of a flame.

"Yes," Lanfranc said, sounding for once as old as he was. "Crown and sword and scepter. And the king's seal, too, wrapped close inside the crown. They're yours—if you ride for the coast tonight, and set sail for England at the turn of the tide."

"The tide's already turned," William said. "Why the hurry? Robert won't move in that direction until he's secured Normandy. Should I be afraid of Henry? Or my sisters?"

"England," said Lanfranc. "You should fear for England."

William's eyes narrowed. "Rebels again? Saxons? Danes?"

"Don't play the fool with me," Lanfranc said. His voice was mild, but the words were sharp. "There is more at stake than a mortal kingdom, and well you know it."

William shrugged with careful unconcern. "That was always Cecilia's worry. Or Henry's, lately—he's a fine little sorcerer. It's the waking world for me, and no witchery to taint it."

"That world is a delusion," Lanfranc said, "and the king of all Britain cannot afford to live in it."

"My father did."

"Only at the end," said Lanfranc, "and to his cost—and Britain's, too."

"Then why in God's name did he give the crown to me?"

Lanfranc barely blinked at the outburst. "You can refuse it. No one is forcing it on you."

William sucked in a breath. He was shaking as if with cold, although it was still the dead of summer, stifling even at night. "So that's the bargain, then? All or nothing?"

"That is the way of it," the archbishop said.

William stretched his hand toward the wrapped bundle that was the crown. The air was full of whispers and flitters, voices gibbering just on the edge of hearing, and minute gusts of air like the passage of wings.

If he had had any sense at all, he would have turned his back on it and gone to snatch Normandy from under his brother Robert's nose. Let Henry have this. Henry was a he-witch from the time he was born. He could stand it.

But even hidden, the crown called to William. To be king. To rule. To be more than either of his brothers, lord above lords. To lift his hand, and every man would bow and submit, and call him *Majesty*.

Power had its price. If William had learned nothing else in his life, it was that.

"What do I have to do?" he asked roughly. "Do I have to turn witch? Sacrifice a black cock at the dark of the moon? Shed my own blood?"

"That will come clear in time," Lanfranc said.

William could hardly have expected him to say anything else. "Just tell me what I have to do now."

"As your father commanded," said the archbishop. "Take these gifts. Ride for the sea. Sail with the tide."

William had had enough. If he was going to do this, best get it over. His mind was already racing, reckoning how many men he could gather, how fast they could mount, and how soon they could reach the sea.

"There's a ship waiting," he said. It was not a question. "You're riding with me. See that you're mounted and ready in an hour."

He had braced for resistance, but the archbishop bowed his head. "As my lord wishes," he said.

William eyed him sidelong, trusting him not a bit, but there was nothing devious there that he could see. He thrust himself to his feet. The world that had lurched dizzily the day his father took that ill-fated leap was rocking now like a ship in a gale.

He steadied himself as best he could. Lanfranc was behind him—threat or guard or both, who knew? The air was all aflutter, like a dovecote with a fox in it.

Not long now. The words came from nowhere in particular. Death was in this place. He could hope it would be satisfied with his father.

Cecilia lay motionless on her hard narrow bed. Outside her cell, the novices slept in their dormitory. They were noisy sleepers, as children could be: sniffling, tossing, murmuring. Some dreamed hard; some, the newest and youngest, wept with homesickness.

The newest of them all was quiet, but Cecilia could feel the deep warmth of the magic in her. She was wonderfully strong; none of her mother's bonds had constrained her, or weakened her in the slightest.

When she breathed, the earth breathed with her. Her spirit was woven deep within the fabric of Britain. Half a Gael, half a Saxon: born in two worlds, the world of the Old Things and the world of cold iron.

Cecilia, half a Norman and all enchantress, sighed against the rhythm of that breathing. Deeper even than Edith's awareness, the isle of Britain stirred uneasily in its sleep. Away across the sea, beyond the walls of air, its king was dying. The new king, the one whom he had chosen, had left Rouen; he was coming, riding as fast as swift horses could carry him.

Cecilia would have chosen otherwise. But the king was the king. Bloated and bitter, emptied of heart and spirit by his lady's death, closed off to his magic, he was still the trueborn king of all Britain. Even she, who was a Guardian of the Isle, had no power to undo what he had done.

They would all have to make the best of it. She rose and wrapped her blanket about her and trod softly through the dormitory. None of the novices saw or heard her, even those with the power to do it.

This was a difficult place for the likes of her to be. The one buried here kept still her malice, and her sister the abbess preserved it in the living flesh. The Old Things of Britain struggled within these walls. The earth beneath had begun, in parts, to leach itself of magic.

For five hundred years the Saxons had imposed their walls of iron on the old powers of Britain. The Old Things were driven out or hunted toward the edges of the isle. In the heart of England, magic was gone, the world all grey, and the rites of the Lord Christ perverted to the destruction of aught that was not of simple mortal flesh.

And then, one and twenty years ago, the walls of iron had broken. The walls of air had risen to defend Britain against invasion either human or magical. William the Norman, son of a Druid and a duke, had sailed in a ship full of Old Things, and with their help, conquered the Saxons.

But Britain was still full of them. There was no driving them out; they were too many and too deeply entrenched. William's best hope had been to dilute the blood: to marry Saxon noble to Norman knight or baron, and encourage his lesser troops to find Saxon wives and lovers. What he had made no great effort to do—and that was folly—was to see to it that his Normans were well endowed with magic, and their ladies and their lemans were properly corrupted with it.

Cecilia paused beside Edith's cot. The child shimmered softly in her sleep. She wore a cloak of night spirits, creatures of moonlight and gossamer, who wrapped themselves about her and defended her against the deadness that filled this place.

Such irony, Cecilia thought. This was the child of Saxon kings, bred to defy the Norman invaders and help win back the Saxon realm. And yet she was also a Gael, descendant of old gods and enchanters. In her the powers were delicately balanced: to raise great magic, or to suppress it utterly.

The Old Things were doing their best to shift the balance. So was Cecilia, for the matter of that. But there was old darkness laired in the heart of Britain, and stretches of emptiness where earth and water and air were deadly to anything made of magic.

It had grown worse since Queen Mathilda died. Now that the king was sinking down into death, the Old Things' enemies were waiting. Too few of them had died or been destroyed. Too many had found new life again, with no strong king to constrain them, and no queen to stand like a white pillar before the gates of Britain.

Cecilia straightened her back. It was aching as if with the weight of the world. The walls of air were in her charge: defense against invasion from without, and against destruction from within.

Three Guardians should have stood with her. But one was in Normandy near the dying king. One was walled in her Isle of old magic within the isle of Britain. And the third was four years dead, and none had come to take her place.

Cecilia was alone. The enemy was all about her. Here was the weapon it had made, brought here to be shaped and tempered.

It had seemed—not easy, no. But simple, in its way. She would settle herself in the center of the forces against her father, take the Scots princess in hand and bind her to the old ways, and in such moments as that left free, mend all that had been broken since the Saxons swarmed to this shore.

Simple. Arrogant. Profoundly foolish.

Now a new king came who had no understanding or sympathy for the old ways. The defenses were weakened, the defenders scattered. The kingdom that should pass from strength to strength was hardly stronger than it had been when her father took it from the Saxons.

The earth shifted beneath her. She swayed and nearly fell.

The dormitory had not changed. None of the novices was awake. Rain drummed softly on the roof, which it had not been doing before, but that was the perpetual song of England.

Edith's voice spoke, soft and blurred with sleep. "He's gone."

Cecilia stood in silence that had grown suddenly very deep.

"Was he a selkie?" Edith asked. "There was a thing without a shape, and a terrible stink. Then he climbed out of it. He talked to a man who looked just like him, but not as hard. Then he went away."

Cecilia shivered. She had felt rather than seen it: the spirit escaping the burden of the body. The earth of Britain sighed, and shuddered once more.

A great power had left it. In its place was void.

The walls of air stood firm, but their foundations had begun subtly to crumble. Across the breadth of the isle, the Old Things raised their voices in a long, soundless keen. *Gone! He is gone!*

"He will come back," Edith said. She was sitting up. Her eyes were open, but they were full of dreams. "When Britain needs him again, he'll come."

Cecilia had no doubt of that. The old powers were mourning him without reservation, but she was mortal and human, and he had been her father. There were no words for what she felt. No tears, either. Nothing but a kind of singing emptiness.

So much to do. So many battles to fight. His fault, most of them, or the fault of those whom he had trusted to hold power in his name.

"How like a man," she said, not caring how bitter she sounded. "Roar in, sack and pillage—and roar out again with it all half done, and as much undoing as doing for the poor fools who come after."

Edith seemed not to have heard her. Certainly the child would not have understood. Cecilia coaxed her to lie back down on her cot, and drew the thin blanket up to her chin.

The wide eyes closed. Cecilia laid a blessing on her brow, with a flicker of magic in it. Edith smiled in her sleep.

Even in the roil of grief and loss and bitterness, Cecilia mustered a smile in return. Magic delighted the child: that was well. Very well indeed. It almost gave her hope.

❀ CHAPTER 5 ❀

When William's riders had assembled—a solid handful of knights and squires and servants, all on fast horses—Lanfranc was nowhere to be found. Nor would anyone admit to having seen him in the abbey. "My lord," the abbot said when William got hold of him in the chapel—speaking carefully around the hand on his throat—"the archbishop is, as best any of us knows, safe and serene in his see of Canterbury."

William growled and let him go. Bloody bedamned wizards. He left the abbot to nurse his bruised throat, with a flock of monks clucking and fussing over the old fool, and all but ran back to his visibly patient men.

The crown and sword and scepter were still where he had put them, in an ironbound box on the back of a sumpter mule. He opened the box to be sure. They had not turned to leaves and dust like faery gold. They were real. And never mind how they had got there.

He snatched the rein from his squire's hand and swung into the red stallion's saddle, ignoring the stirrups that hung like an invitation to sloth. The boy, who knew him well, sprinted for his own sensible bay. Even before the squire's rear had struck the saddle, the lot of them were in motion. The gate barely had time to finish opening before William thundered through it.

*　*　*

They rode west as fast as horses could gallop. There was no moon, but William could see as clearly as if there had been. He had not remembered that the road to Touques was as straight as this, or as white. It shed its own light.

His men rode close behind him. The horses were calm, their strides steady. None seemed to mind the glimmering road, or the unnatural straightness and smoothness of it.

Magic. He spat past his horse's neck. A trick of wind blew the spittle back into his face. He cursed and spluttered, but he took no such liberty again.

Get to England. Get the treasury. Get himself crowned. He made it a litany as the leagues spun away.

They paused near dawn to rest and requisition remounts from one of the ducal estates. William took a certain pleasure in that; Robert did not know it yet, but he was helping his brother take England's crown away from him.

Just before the sun came up, they pulled themselves onto their new mounts and eyed the road again. William's skin was twitching. Something was odd—but not the road, now daylight touched it. It seemed as if one particular color had gone out of the world.

Old William was dead. Young William hesitated for an instant. Here he was in Normandy, in one of the duke's castles, with an arsenal and a bit of treasury that would do rather nicely. If he chose. If he would take a dukedom, and let the kingdom fend for itself until he went on to take it in its turn.

It was only a moment's lapse. The crown was calling, and with it a greater treasure than anything here. William's portion was the better one. Time enough later to take the rest.

The Abbot of Bec rubbed his eyes and sighed. It was ungodly late— past the Night Office, halfway to dawn. The letters on the parchment before him had begun to blur.

Time was when he could sit all night by candlelight, interrupted only by the summons to prayer, and every letter that he wrote or read was nigh as clear as if by daylight. Now he was not so young, and his eyes were not as steadfast as they had been.

The strain of thought had blurred with his sight and begun to slip away. He scribbled a few swift words before the last of it escaped, then straightened his weary back, and stretched and yawned. He was a little dizzy with the headlong return from the heights of theology to the reality of late night, stiff bones, and inkstains on his fingers.

It was still summer in this part of the world, but the air in the scriptorium was cold. Almost he fancied that he could see a puff of mist when he breathed.

He shivered with more than the chill. The creatures of the aether who crowded everywhere were gone tonight; he had reveled in the solitude. But that, rather insidiously, was broken. Something was there.

He knew the breath of the dead. There was no mistaking it. He looked up without either fear or surprise, into a face that at first he barely recognized.

Anselm had not known the king when he was as young as that. For a fleeting instant he wondered what Prince Henry was doing in Bec. Should he not be in Rouen with his father?

Then of course Anselm knew. He bowed his head. "Sire," he said.

King William's spirit seemed remarkably keen of eye and sharp of wit for one who must have died within the day.

"Just now," he said, reading Anselm's thought with ease, as the dead or the powerfully gifted could. "It's all done. Young William's off to England. The others will find their own way."

"It's kind of you, sire, to pause on your journey, to tell me this," Anselm said. He chose the words with care. Nothing about William alive had been kind; death could not have changed him so much. But Anselm judged it wise to pretend.

The dead king saw through it, inevitably: he laughed, a gust of chill wind. "Don't be a fool," he said. "You know what I need of you—what Britain needs. You have the power to do it, however little you may like to use it. I'm commanding you."

"You are dead," Anselm said steadily. "Your day is done. Mine is far from it—and my place is here."

"Your destiny is in Britain," the king said. "I've raised that boy to be king. He'll do it—he might even be good at it—but he can't do it alone."

"Surely not, sire," Anselm said, "But I'm a scholar, not a courtier. My gift is for the nature of God. The nature of kings eludes me."

"Don't lie to the dead," said the spirit. "Don't lie to yourself, either. I did, in the end—you've seen where it got me. Don't waste the power your God gave you. He gave it to you for a reason."

"There is some debate as to that," said Anselm. "If it were not God but the Devil—"

"Lies again," the king said. The air crackled with frost. "Use some of those famous wits of yours and face the truth. No one else has either the strength or the training to do what must be done."

"Lanfranc—" Anselm began.

"My old friend is *old*. He's not much longer for this world. The young ones need younger Guardians. My daughter Cecilia is where she needs to be, and the Lady of the Lake as well. Lanfranc does what he can. One more pillar has to be raised, and you are that pillar. Deny it as much and as long as you like—but the longer you wait, the harder it will be."

"Britain is no part of me," Anselm said. His teeth ached from gritting them.

"On the contrary," said the shade of that terrible king. "Britain is your destiny. As it was mine. As it is my son's."

He laid no spell, spoke no word of binding, and yet Anselm felt the force of his will. There was more in it than mortal wishing or a man's desire to smooth the way for his heir. He had been bound to Britain for life after life. Britain was in back of him, a great wall of inexorable power.

Fate. Destiny. Compulsion so strong that it buffeted Anselm like a strong wind.

"The dead may not command the living," Anselm said tightly.

The shade grinned—for a moment showing the skull that he had left behind. "The dead have no need. Fate is stronger than any of us."

"God is stronger than fate."

"God is fate," the dead king said, "and the gods are its plaything."

Anselm crossed himself. The shade laughed. "Take what comfort you can, father abbot. You'll give in in the end. You won't be able to help it."

"God will help me," Anselm said, but the dead king took no notice. He was finally, mercifully, letting go of what substance he had.

He left Anselm in deep disquiet and no little ill temper. Which was hardly fitting for a man of God, and an abbot at that; but William Bastard had never given a fig for what was fitting.

❋ CHAPTER 6 ❋

The cry went up in the early morning: a long howl more of anguish than of grief. It rent the air of Rouen and flung the city into a frenzy.

Henry had left the body to grow cold on its own and gone looking for something, anything, to wash away the memory of death. Even before he found a tavern that would serve him at such an hour, he was more than half out of his mind, and knowing it, too. If he had been sane at all, he would at least have told the monks that the king was dead. But he had walked away, and kept on walking, until he was out of the monastery and in the city and slumped on a bench in a dim and dingy place that stank of ancient ale.

Better that than the charnel stink of his father's deathbed. Some of that was still there, lingering like one of the spirits in the air. By the time one of the monks discovered the body, Henry had lost count of the cups that he had drunk. Maybe it was only one. Maybe it was a dozen.

None of it could shut the eyes of the mind. The monk had no need to touch the stinking thing to know there was no life left in it. He sketched a sign of the cross over it—good Christian cleric that he was— and gathered up his skirts and ran.

After that, there was a great deal of running. Shouting, too, and cursing—but no weeping. Henry was too blurred and bleared by then to recognize faces. They were all alike: human clods, no spark in them, and precious little soul.

They pillaged their king. They stripped the chamber of everything that had been in it, all but the bed—and that only because the body was too vastly repellent an object. They took the armor on its stand, and the stand with it; the chest of clothing and oddments at the bed's foot; the smaller but much heavier box of jewels and precious things; even the earthen jar of water, and the cup, and the table on which the two had stood, and the cloth on it, and the rug under it.

It was a madness, a passion of possession—and revenge, too, on a man who had taken and held everything within his grasp. Henry should have thought of it himself. But he had only been able to think of getting away from there and drinking himself into blessed oblivion.

That was not happening. He was drunk, there was no doubt of it, but his mind was all too clear.

He was the only waking creature in the tavern. There were sleeping ones enough, most of them snoring; the tavernkeeper had left a jar at Henry's elbow and stretched out on the bar and gone to sleep—snoring louder than any of the rest.

The jar was empty. Henry counted the steps to the cask, and the bodies he would have to step over or around to get there. It was a great errantry, but he was duty-bound. He was not unconscious yet. He must be unconscious. Otherwise there was no purpose in being here at all.

Past the bar and the casks of ale and beer and the jars of wine, shadows stirred. They were a curtain, Henry realized, and something moved behind them: a living presence. His ear caught the sound of a shod foot on a wooden stair.

His nostrils flared. Even through the fumes of ale, he could smell the ineffable essence of woman. It was a gift, a peculiar magic; one that Christians deplored. But he was only as Christian as need demanded.

She parted the curtain with a hand that, though hardly elegant, was round and well shaped. The rest of her, as it emerged, matched the hand admirably. Her hair was the color of newly planed oak; her skin was milk-white beneath a golden dust of freckles. She had the features that went with the coloring: short straight nose, flat cheeks, firm chin. Her eyes were dark in the dimness, but Henry was sure they would be blue.

He was in love. Love came easily to him always; it was a sin, the priests said, but he never had believed in that narrow view of the world.

She was barely awake, her hair loose down her back, with a cloth tied over it and her skirts kilted up, ready to face the long day. She paused behind the bar, taking in the sprawl of bodies and the remnants of the night's revels. Her face was resigned; she sighed.

Henry met her eyes, already tired with the weight of the world, and smiled. It was a pleasure as always to watch the smile take hold. Light dawned in her face. She had smiled back before she could have known what she was doing.

There were handsomer men than Henry in the world, and sweeter-tempered, too. But he had never found that to be an obstacle. Women loved to be loved. Henry loved to love them. It was a perfect exchange.

This one warmed to him as they all did, forgetting weariness and drudgery just as he forgot the horrors of the past days. When he rose and took her hand, she turned willingly and led him back up the stair.

She did not tell him her name, nor did she ask his. The heat of her body, the scent and shape of her, would stay with him. If he saw her again, he would know her, though she might long since have forgotten him.

For a little while she took away memory. There was only the moment, stretching as long as human flesh could bear.

But it was human and mortal, and the day was rising. The tumult in the city was beating on the shutters, piercing through it with darts of sound and light. A bellow from below brought her to her feet, slipping deftly out of his arms.

He made no effort to stop her. He could have stayed where he was; she had not ordered him out. But the world was calling. He made himself rise and find his clothes and put them on, taking more care than they strictly needed.

He was delaying the inevitable. She had asked for nothing, but he left a handful of coins on the table by the bed. It was her due; and however poor he might be in lands or titles, of money, thanks to his father, he had enough.

He drew a deep breath. Now, he thought. Face it; get it over. He made his way down and out of the tavern, into the glare of the day.

The king's body was gone. The bed on which it had lain was stripped, the curtains taken down, and the room scoured. Henry's eyes watered with the fierce stink of lye.

It was a far cleaner stink than had been there before. He found a monk at last, after too long a search, who would admit to knowing anything at all.

He was a novice, and somewhat simple. He babbled of angels and devils, and scourgings of sacred fire. Somewhere amid the nonsense, Henry gathered that embalmers had come, and a knight had overseen them. They had taken the body out of Rouen.

Henry was nigh as fuddled as the novice. He had been fighting his way through the city, with bruises and a cut or two to show for it; his mind was full of fog, as if he and not his father had wandered out of the world of the living.

The last of the ale had purged itself from him some while since. This was something else. Something . . .

For the second time in that endless day, he stumbled through the abbey's gate. Outside the walls, he was little less confused than he had been before.

There was no duke in Normandy, no king in England. Henry, who had been deprived of either, stopped short in the road.

The earth's spirit was in him. Its emptiness had crept into him; its confusion had swallowed him. He had been a fool not to strengthen the wards of his magic when he saw death standing close above his father.

His blood was king's blood, although he was not to claim the power that went with it. He was the youngest. He had no rights but what his father and his elder brothers gave him.

That way was bitterness. He must not indulge in it. He was perilously close to losing himself now, because he had given way to the shock of his father's sickness and all of its consequences.

He gathered the disparate parts of himself, the wits that were so terribly scattered, the magic that he had been in danger of forgetting how to wield. The cold of death seeped slowly away. He drew in the sun's warmth, feeding the power that was in him, as his mother had taught him to do when he was a child.

As his strength grew, his senses sharpened. He saw and felt and heard the confusion that reigned in this part of the world, now that his father's iron grip was loosed. Of his father there was nothing left.

And yet the body was still in the world, and powers gathered about it. They drifted on the winds of the spirit, knotting and tangling like threads of spider-silk. They laid a track for him to follow.

He poised on the edge of it. There was power to take, if he had the courage—if his strength was enough. If he had the right.

If he turned back, he could try to take one kind of power: earthly power, the rule of men and lands, maybe even the duchy, if he moved quickly enough. If he set foot on this path, his way would be longer and his victory less certain. But the prize would be greater by far—if he lived to win it.

Either way, he could lose it all. He was the youngest son. Nothing was his unless he fought for it.

He turned his back on Rouen and his face toward the old gods knew what. It was a road, but it touched only slightly on the earthly track. Men were in great disarray there: the last of the king's vassals escaping the city, riding hard for their own demesnes, to fortify them against a war they reckoned inevitable.

None of them spared a thought for the king who was dead. He was powerless now to help or harm them. They had to live in the world; and the world was turning cold.

Either they were fools, or Henry was. He entrusted himself to the straight track. The king was on it ahead of him, borne away by more than mortal hands.

❋ CHAPTER 7 ❋

The ship floated by the quay, down the river from the city. It was an old ship, its paint worn, the gilding faded from its high prow. Yet there was no concealing the lines of it, the swift deadly shape of a dragon ship.

A lantern hung on the tip of its mast, dim to invisibility in daylight. Yet at night it would blaze like a beacon, a great power of the Otherworld.

Henry's breath caught. He knew what ship this had to be. *Mora,* the ship made of Druid oak, shaped and fashioned for the conquest of Britain. His mother had given her as a love-gift to his father; when Mathilda died, the king had ordered her sunk in the sea.

She had risen again, somewhat worse for the wear, but with all her magic still intact. A great flock of spirits crowded about her. They cared at least that the king of all Britain had passed to the Otherworld.

"For a while," said a person perched just behind the dragon of the prow. He had the appearance of a bearded dwarf, thickset and massive for all his lack of height. But he was neither human nor mortal.

"Messire Turold," Henry said, bowing.

The boggart, who had been the king's friend and ally, grinned from ear to ear: a very literal and disconcerting thing. His teeth were numerous and sharp. "Prince," he said. "Will you sail with us?"

"That depends on where you go," Henry said. "I'm not ready to leave the world."

"Not yet," said Turold. "We're taking the rivers and the sea to Caen."

"Not Falaise where he was born?"

"Not by sea," said Turold. "It's what he wanted. We're bound to give it to him."

Henry bent his head. As light as the boggart's tone was, he could sense a grief so deep that it caught at his own heart.

No human thing had grieved for that terrible old man. These creatures of airy magic mourned with honest sorrow. He had belonged to them as much as to the children of Adam; although he had turned his back on them after his queen died, they had never forsaken him.

Henry understood a very great thing just then, standing on the quay in the plain daylight. Exactly what use he could make of it, he did not know yet. But he had seen a way through this riddle that his father had set him, and allies whom his brothers had neither the power nor the skill to call on.

The ship was waiting with a strong taste of patience about it. Henry swung over the side.

As he struck the deck, he staggered. He was light on his feet, trained and strong, as a knight should be; but the power in these timbers—the sheer force of magic that was in them—nearly flung him flat.

The crew were already casting off, lowering oars, dipping them in unison into the swift water. The ship leaped like a bird into flight.

Some of those who sailed the ship were human. Most were not. The captain seemed remarkably ordinary among them: a man of middle years and middle size, with a blunt plain face. But the eyes that rested on Henry were keen, and there was power enough in him to raise Henry's hackles.

While Henry found his balance and his wits, he saw Turold at the captain's back, watching him with a steady dark stare. He was being weighed and measured, and in a fashion tested.

He offered the captain the respect of a landsman toward a lord of the sea. That was well received. So were the words he spoke. "Messire. May I see my father?"

The captain stepped aside without a word.

The king lay on a bier under the deck's canopy. A heavy pall was drawn up over him, concealing the ruin of face and body. Nevertheless there was no mistaking that bulk.

Wards were laid on the body, suppressing the charnel reek. They guarded it against further decay, and protected it from evil both mortal and magical. There was great beauty in the shaping of them, and something very like tenderness.

Men had never loved this man, but the Old Things were not subject to human foibles. Henry found that his throat was tight. He did grieve after all, though a large part of it was anger.

He sat beside the bier as he had sat for so long beside his father's deathbed. There was a certain familiarity in it, and a certain finality.

The rest of those on the ship had drawn away, not in fear or revulsion but in respect. The ship was at midstream, the oars shipped, the sail raised to catch a wind that blew strong and steady down the river's length.

It was not a river he knew, exactly. Sometimes he saw familiar juts of crag, green clouds of woodland, or the stony bravado of a castle. But then the land would change, a mist close in, or the light dazzle so brightly that he could hardly see at all. Then the not-quite-human faces of the crew would change, and lose all their humanity; and flocks of otherworldly beings would crowd about the ship, singing a long, eerie dirge.

They passed from river to sea, then from sea to river again. Suns rose and set. Henry knew no hunger or thirst, nor reckoned the passage of time. He was outside of it, he and the body on its bier.

Somewhere in the dreamlike distance of that voyage, he knew that the calm sea and quiet sky were the work of great magic. Things moved without, coiling just beyond vision, surging beneath with the rise of the waves. Powers that had been held at bay through William's reign were stirring, growing restless.

The smell of death had roused them. Their hunger was sharp and their hate was strong. They would strike while they could.

Young William was still in Normandy, riding the straight track to the sea, but never as swiftly as *Mora* had. Britain was empty of a king.

With that thought, Henry half-rose. Britain was close, straight across this stretch of sea. He rode in the ship that had borne his father to the conquest. If he raised his powers, called on allies both old and new, bade them serve the blood of the last king—

"No."

Turold was standing beside him, balancing easily as the ship rocked and swayed. Henry had not noticed that the seas had grown so heavy. The sky was still clear, but the wind was wuthering, tugging sharply at the sail.

"It's not for you," the boggart said. "No matter how tempting it is— let it go. Or no good will ever come of it."

"Will any good come of William's taking the throne?" Henry demanded.

"That will be as it will be," said Turold. "It's his time. His fate."

"To destroy everything our father made?"

"What will be will be," Turold said. "Let it go."

The hot temper rose in Henry. Who did this creature think he was, to command the king's son?

But cold reason rose soon enough to stop the words before he spoke them. He was not in mortal realms now.

Turold nodded. "Good," he said. "You can be taught."

"What—" Henry began. But the boggart's glance stilled his tongue.

His father had bequeathed him patience. He was expending a great deal of it already. There would be far more, he knew in his bones, before this dance had ended.

They sailed by the straight way and the warded way, down to the river Orne and then, with the wind steady at their backs, upriver to Caen. Within the bounds of Normandy the sense of powers rising was less; this was a quieter land, less fraught with magic.

Yet there was magic here, deep beneath, and in Caen that both the king and his queen had loved, it bubbled up like a spring. The ship came to harbor in a windy morning, with a scud of clouds fitfully veiling the sun.

The crowd that waited was large enough: the whole city had come out, it seemed, with a company of monks and prelates in the lead. And yet there were startling gaps and absences. No lords of the realm were there. No workers of magic either greater or lesser, no embassies of kings either mortal or otherwise, had come to see the king to his rest.

Henry turned on Turold, to ask he hardly knew what—if this was a jest or a curse, or a simple oversight—but the boggart had vanished. Only the mortal crew were left, heaving the bier over the side and into the monks' waiting hands. Those were sturdy men, evidently chosen for their strength, but even they struggled to bear up that massive weight.

It seemed that no one recognized Henry. He disembarked unnoticed behind the bier.

As he set foot on land, once again he staggered—but this time not with the shock of power gathered in that place. Rather, it was the opposite: a sucking void, a perfect absence.

He stood at the heart of a maelstrom, in a zone of empty air. He gasped for breath, whirling in panic, tensed to leap back to the safety of the ship.

But *Mora* had already drawn away from the shore, receding far too swiftly for the natural force of wind or current. Even as he reached for her with hand and power, he knew that she was slipping out of the world. He could see her still, but her magic was closed against him.

He was all alone in the empty land, surrounded by people whose souls he could not sense at all. He was in hell, with no hope of earthly salvation.

He lashed out, still in a fit of panic—even knowing it was folly; knowing he hovered in delusion. Fire surged up out of the earth and poured down from the sky.

In the last instant he flung it away from the crowd, but he had neither the strength nor the speed to unmake it. It plummeted into the
midst of the city. Blood-red flames roared to heaven, then sank down
into mortal gold and blue and the black of smoke.

The crowd fled in a chorus of screams. The few with their wits about
them surged toward the flames. The rest scattered in panic no less mind-
less than Henry's, but far less perilous.

Only the monks were left with the king's body, and Henry with the
drawn and empty sensation of too much power expended too quickly.

The monks continued their slow procession toward St. Stephen's
abbey, which the king had built long ago to console the Pope for his
marriage to the royal and magical Mathilda. Henry followed even more
slowly. The fire was burning, too fierce to stop.

He sought inside himself for a glimmer of power, enough to raise a
bit of cloud, a brief fall of rain. But there was nothing. Only cold laughter under the earth, and things stirring that should never have been awake.

They were gathering beneath the abbey. There were old scores to settle, old battles lost. The great soul that had bound them was gone, but
the body it had inhabited was prize enough, all things considered. If
they could not devour his soul, they would dishonor his bones—and
that would be his remembrance.

Henry had been well and properly duped—betrayed by his own impatience and his foolish cowardice. He could only go on as he had begun. The monks were chanting, in part to honor the dead, in part to
shorten the way: a slow dirge in time to the rhythm of their pace.
Dirige, Domine, in conspectu tuo viam meam . . .

It was an incantation, if one chose to make it so. Henry joined his
voice to the rest.

Adorabo ad templum sanctum tuum in timore tuo:
Domine, deduc me in iustitia tua. . . .

The roil of darkness beneath the earth drew back—shrinking from
the power of that invocation. Henry drew a breath of relief. But he did

not leave off his chanting. The stronger the wards that the words could raise, the better.

The abbey's gate lay open before them. Gold and silks gleamed within: miters and copes of bishops, archbishops, holy abbots. The lords of England and Normandy had forsaken their king and duke, but the Church—in a grand irony for that son of an old goddess—had come out in force to bid him farewell.

To make sure he's well and truly dead, Henry thought. He could hear the words in his father's voice, with the familiar grim humor.

They steadied him, those words, as little respect as they had in them. His strength was trickling back. Here within the walls that his father had built, where magic had always been as welcome as prayer, there was sanctuary of a sort.

Not peace. Henry would not have that for a long while to come. But he would take what he could get.

It was a grand funeral, with so many prelates to celebrate it: worthy of a king. Henry let himself subside into the beauty of the words and the music, and the mist of holiness that rose over it all, turning the light in the abbey church to gold.

Henry woke with a start from a half-dream. The sermon had droned to its end. The choir was stirring, the bearers rising, preparing to lay the body in its tomb.

A voice rose above the murmuring silence, harsh and strident. A man was standing in front of the open tomb. He seemed prosperous: not a noble by his dress, but well enough off as townsmen went. He had a broad face, rather red, and a bristle of beard; and his fists were planted on his hips.

"Justice!" he cried. "I demand justice!"

The Mass lurched to a halt. The bearers paused with the bier half raised to their shoulders. People were gaping.

So was Henry, but he shut his mouth with a snap of temper and pushed to the front of the crowd. "Who dares disrupt this holy rite?"

The man flushed redder still, but his jaw jutted, and his beard stood on end. He had fortified himself with no little quantity of wine, Henry judged. "This is not your land! That one there—he stole it. It was ours. It *is* ours. And we'll not have him lying dead in it."

Henry opened his mouth to blast the fool, but someone behind him said with a hint of a quaver, "He is right. I remember at the time, we asked if he should investigate, and at least give the family a charter, but he said—"

Henry turned on his heel. The man who spoke was elderly, and wore the habit and tonsure of a monk. Although his eyes were clouded, there were still stains of ink on his fingers, and the calluses of long hours in the scriptorium.

"I did see the original charter," the clerk went on, innocently relentless, "and this man's father, whose name was Arthur, did own the land. And the king said to pay him no mind. God wanted it for Himself. The family should consider itself well paid by the honor of it."

Voices rose in outrage. "This is a mockery! To demand recompense here, now—how dare he—"

Henry's sentiments were much the same, but he had had a bit of time to think. The townsman was an innocent, but what lay behind his eyes was anything but that. It was laughing—mocking indeed. It would feed royally on contention.

Not if Henry had anything to do with it. It vexed his pride to say the words, but he knew he must say them. "You, Brother, since you seem so well versed in the matter—take whomever you need. Settle it. Pay him fair value for the land, from the abbey's treasury."

The abbot sucked in a breath to protest, but Henry stared him down. There were advantages now and then in having inherited his father's cold grey eyes. The man blanched and kept silent.

Henry did not look to see whether he was obeyed. He turned back to the bearers, who were wheezing with the weight of the bier. "Finish it," he said.

Their gratitude was palpable. The tomb lay open, waiting. Darkness coiled within.

It was only the slant of a shadow. The choir began the antiphon, blessing the body and the tomb.

The king had had it built not so long ago, made to his measure. It was a good fathom long, and nigh as wide: William had gone greatly to fat as he aged. It was more than broad enough to hold him.

The bearers lowered the bier as slowly as they could, with its great weight. Henry saw the tomb's walls draw in, closing like a mouth.

The bearers stopped perforce. The swollen mass beneath the pall bulged, overflowing the confines of the stone. Somewhere in the congregation, someone tittered.

One of the bearers must have acted without thinking. He set his foot on the body and thrust.

Henry held his breath. Others were not so fortunate. Fire from heaven had scattered the funeral procession. This stench from below sent the whole of the assembly, gagging and retching, toward the doors.

Henry drew his mantle up over his face and breathed as shallowly as he could. The run on the doors had had the inevitable consequence: people crushed and trampled, and eruptions of fists and curses.

The fool who had tried to wedge the body into its tomb like an overfull sack of meal had fainted. The body lay abandoned yet again, with a stain spreading beneath the pall, seeping from the burst belly.

There was a horrible humor in it, but Henry had no laughter to give it. This foulness made a mockery of a hard man and a strong king; nothing in his life became him less than this last vestige of it.

He could hear the sermons already, the priests preaching of pride fallen and pretension destroyed: the Conqueror conquered by the inevitability of decay. It was a gift of the old powers that had hated the king for so long, to the mortals who had hated him while he lived, but never dared speak until he was dead.

Let them enjoy their revenge, Henry thought. It would not last long. William's children were not all ingrates or fools. They would remember—and take revenge in turn.

✳ CHAPTER 8 ✳

The coast of England was suspiciously quiet. The sun was shining, the wind blowing soft, favoring the ship as it sailed for the harbor.

One or two idiots on board reckoned that an omen, declaring that William's errand was blessed by heaven. William was more inclined to regard it as the calm before the storm.

That cursed sight of his persisted in showing him a different country beneath the green swell of the isle. Parts of it were green, parts glimmering gold with magic. But wide swaths of it were grey, and parts were black, pitted with rot. Magic was dead there, or dying fast.

Which should have been all to the good, but it reminded him too vividly of his father on his deathbed: gross and moribund. This, he should want to rule? It would suck him in and kill him, too. That was the way the Old Things kept themselves alive: with kings' blood, and kings' lives buried beneath the green earth.

He thrust the thought down and set his foot on it. He was going to take an earthly crown and a mortal treasure—to rule men. Magic be damned.

They had sailed for none of the great ports, not even for Pevensey, where the elder William had made his conquest. William the younger wanted speed and quiet, and as clear a road to the treasury in Winchester as he could manage. For that, he reckoned, the quieter the better.

The ship was small and handy, and settled neatly into a fold of the coast, where a village barely big enough for a name clung to chalk and sand. Fishing boats hailed the stranger on her way in, calling out in broad Saxon, but few of the men on the boats were of that tall, narrow, fair-haired nation. These were people of an older breed, wiry and dark, like the common folk of Brittany and Normandy. William had an odd sense that among themselves, the language they spoke was neither Saxon nor Norman, but something of much more ancient vintage.

There was a man waiting for them on the strand. He was no fisherman, and no old Briton, either. His height and breadth and the cut of his clothes were Norman, and he wore fine mail under a mantle of deep green English wool. Up among the dunes, a handsome bay horse was grazing, with saddle on but bridle hung from saddlebow.

William raised a brow at that. There was a man who trusted his horse, to turn it loose in open country.

The man was young, not much more than a boy: seeming younger the closer the ship came. His waving hair was dark but with a hint of red, worn to the shoulders in the new fashion; it grew in a peak on a high fair forehead, above level brows and steady eyes that, William was sure long before he was close enough to see, hovered somewhere between gold and green.

He was a splendid young thing, and bold, too, to stand so comfortably alone in a world of strangers. As the ship slid within reach, he ran out with a gaggle of villagers and the ship's own crew, splashing through the waves, to catch and steady it.

William had had a thought that a king, even one as yet uncrowned, should stand in royal dignity and let his subjects sweat for him. But he could not be that kind of king. He vaulted over the gunwale and down into the sharp cold of the water, heaving and laughing with the rest.

He made sure that the one nearest him was the young lord, and equally sure that once they were all sorted out, the ship moored and the horses and baggage unloaded, they were side by side. Last to come off the ship had been Robert the clerk, carrying in his arms the wrapped bundles of crown and sword and scepter, and the king's seal guarded as close as his life.

Robert laid down his burden reluctantly and set to wringing out his skirts, while the rest of them found their feet and settled the horses. The boy from Britain stepped neatly around rather than over that most precious of the ship's cargo, just as one of the horses broke loose and charged him.

He stopped and stood quiet. As the big grey lunged, blind with God knew what passion, he caught the flying lead and shifted his weight from foot to foot. The stallion's leap turned into a spin, then a halt in confusion, while the man rubbed the sweating neck and murmured into the twitching ear. The long head drooped; the horse sighed. The wildness had gone out of him.

"That was well done," William said.

The young man smoothed the mane on the grey's neck and handed over the lead to a fiercely apologetic owner. "It's nothing," he said to them both. He bowed to the knight, then bowed low to William. "My lord," he said.

"You know me," said William. God: if he had seen this boy before, surely he would have remembered.

A smile hovered in the corner of the boy's mouth. It never quite escaped to fill the rest of his face, but William felt as if the sun had grown suddenly, notably brighter. "My name is Robert," the boy said, inconsequentially enough. "My father is sheriff in Kent."

"Robert?" said William, casting his glance across at least three of them on that shore, and God knew how many of the younger villagers might share the name as well; not to mention half of the Norman males in England. "Then you're what? FitzHaimo?"

"Robin," the boy said. "Robin will do. I came to guide you where you need to go."

"I know the way to Winchester," William said. He should have bristled, perhaps, but in that bright orbit, it was impossible.

"Surely you do," said the boy. Robin.

William's brows lowered. The light had darkened. His sight had cleared—enough at least to see what was behind that so-captivating face. "You're one of them," he said. "What was your mother? A nixie? A fey?"

Robin laughed. It was a robust, mortal sound, for all the shimmer that was on him, that he was deigning at last to let William see. "She was a perfectly ordinary child of old gods, a Lady of Avalon. She didn't corrupt me too badly. I'm not to turn you into a wizard or give you a devil's horns. I'm to stand beside you, no more, and be whatever you need me to be."

"That's a great deal," William said.

The boy lifted a shoulder in a wry half-shrug. "If you say so, my lord."

William gripped those shoulders. He made no effort to be gentle, but Robin did not even flinch. "I don't want your magic, do you understand? I want none of it."

"Not the crown or the throne? Not even England?"

"England I'll take," William said. "Britain can fend for itself."

"If you say so," said Robin again, "my lord."

William snarled and let him go. If he had had half a grain of sense, he would have knocked the young fool flat. But he could not bring himself to bruise that pretty face.

William glared into it. "Wherever you think you're taking me, it's Winchester I'm going to. You can follow or not. It's your choice."

"I am free to choose," Robin agreed amiably. He might have sounded like an idiot, if his eyes had not been so bright or so very aware. He knew perfectly well what he was doing, and just how far he could go.

He was good, that one. Too good to meet with anger. William cuffed him because he deserved it, but lightly, and said, "Tell your mare up there that we're riding to a crowning."

"She knows," said Robin. He bowed, both lightly and without mockery, and strode to meet the mare, who was trotting purposefully down the hill.

* * *

William would have known if they strayed from the mortal road. So he told himself, riding inland from the sea. The sun was still bright, the air warm and sweet; no rain threatened. In fields as they passed, folk were laboring: wielding scythes amid the gold of grain, gathering and binding the sheaves. Surely it was a trick of the eye that turned the scythes, like the grain, to gold.

It seemed night should have fallen sooner than this. Had they not come to harbor after noon? And had they not been riding for hours? The horses seemed fresh enough, and none of the men complained. Yet William felt the stretch of time in belly and backside.

The sun hung halfway between the zenith and the horizon. Shadow rose ahead of them: dark boles and woven branches of a wood. The road passed beneath the boughs.

It was dark there, and chill after the unremitting warmth of sunlight. William had ridden and hunted in the forests of Britain since he was a child. He knew the smell and the feel of them; he knew what grew there and what ran there, what chattered or sang or grunted in the undergrowth.

This wood was too dark. Its branches were bare but for a scatter of withered leaves. The mould underfoot was dank. When they came to the trickle of a stream, it was fouled with leaves and slime. The horses snorted at it; none would drink. Most preferred to leap over it rather than sully their hooves.

William reined his horse to a jarring halt. "Enough," he said. "Turn back. Whatever this is, it's not the road to Winchester."

"My lord," said Robin, "it is."

"I'm sure," said William, much too sweetly, "in time, through many turns and twists, it could be said to lead there."

"Oh, no, my lord," Robin said, "it's perfectly straight."

"I know all about straight tracks," William said with a growl in his throat. "We're turning back. If you won't show us where the ordinary winding road is, we'll find it ourselves."

If Robin sighed, it was not audible to human ears. He bowed and shifted his mare aside, so that William could lead the way back out of the wood.

William was not as sure of the way as he wanted his escort to believe. He could see the light ahead, and the track without turn or fork, but he had heard enough from his more willingly sorcerous kin to know that was no promise of easy or quick escape. Once magic got a grip, it hated to let go.

The road seemed quiet enough. No branches fell to stop them; the trees kept their places, as grey and lifeless as ever. As sure as he was that this was not an earthly road, William could see no magic here, not anywhere. The place was empty of it—dead.

He caught Robin's eye. The boy was riding beside him, apparently unperturbed by William's show of rebellion. "No bolts of lightning?" William asked him. "No armies of the Old Things to haul me back to whatever ritual I'm running out of?"

"No," said Robin. "Nothing. That's what's here. Nothing."

"It's not the way to Winchester."

"It was once," Robin said.

William glared.

Robin grinned. No one had been so signally unafraid of William since he learned to use a sword. It was not the fearlessness of a fool; the boy honestly was at ease, and undismayed.

The grin died. His face was suddenly somber. "You need to see," he said. "This is what the Saxons are trying to make of Britain. They don't know it; in half a thousand years, they never succeeded in killing the land, only in driving out the soul of it. But once we came, they had hate to arm them, and determination to undo all that we've done."

"That isn't my world," William said. "Can you understand that? I'm not the wizard-king they forced my father to be."

"He chose you," said Robin. "Now you've seen. If the Saxons win back England, this is what will become of it."

"The Saxons will not win back England," William said grimly.

"Good," said Robin.

The brightness had come back to his face. The plain light of day was on it, red-tinged with sunset. They had come out of the wood onto the mortal road.

It was not a straight track; it followed the curves of the land. And that was exactly as it should be.

William drew a deep breath as he surveyed it. He straightened in the saddle. "We'll ride as late as we can," he said. "The sooner we're in Winchester, the better for us all."

He did not look back to see if the rest of them followed. A king learned to expect it.

❊ CHAPTER 9 ❊

S acred offices in chapel made Edith think of a spider weaving her web. Abbess Christina spun each strand. The nuns' voices lifted it up. Where it rose, the world was a little greyer, the light a little dimmer. The air did not fill the lungs as thoroughly.

This trapped magic and wrapped it close and took it out of the world. Abbess Christina did not know that that was what it did. She thought she was praying—aloud for whatever the Church wanted her to pray for that day, and in her heart for the Normans' fall.

She had been praying harder since word came from Normandy that the king was dead. She had hated him with a true Christian hate; she had prayed not only for his death but for his destruction.

It seemed her prayers had been answered. Now she was praying that the new king would be weak and a fool, and would fall quickly. The spider-threads were so thick that Edith could barely sit through the offices. She kept getting dizzy and wanting to fall over.

Sister Cecilia was not doing anything to help. Her voice in the offices was sweet and clear, and the air was a little lighter for it, but that was all. Sometimes Edith thought she was helping with the web—making it thicker and heavier, until it sank under its own weight.

Then the rest of the abbey was cleaner, and the parts of it that were farthest away from the chapel glistened with magic. Everything was gathering in one place and closing itself off. It would eat itself, Edith thought.

It was a war. The whole of Britain was the battlefield. Parts of it were riddled with rot like a bad cheese, and parts of it were going bad. The parts that were still good were struggling.

And now the king was dead. Cecilia seemed calm. She was waiting for the new king to come, and taking care not to fret.

But Edith could feel deep underneath how Cecilia was afraid. Too much was changing. She was strong, but not strong enough in herself to shift the whole of the tide. The other Guardians were doing what they could, but they were far away, and there were not enough of them.

Edith wanted to help, though she did not know what she could do. She was too young and small, and all she had was magic. She knew very little about how to use it.

She could pray. But prayer was dangerous here. It could help, or it could do terrible harm.

In the end she decided that if she prayed in one of the sunlit cloisters far from the chapel, it might not turn all webby and twisted. She slipped away when the novices were given their hour of recreation. That was supposed to be something suitable and approved, such as reading from the lives of the saints or working on an altar-cloth.

If anyone asked, she would call it meditation on her sins. The sun was bright and the grass was very green. Bees were humming in the little orchard that grew along the wall, a row of pear-trees cut and shaped and tortured into lying flat against the stones. For trees so twisted out of their natural shape, they seemed remarkably happy. They were thick with leaves, and their fruit was round and sweet.

She breathed in the scent, but she was too well trained to steal a pear. Not that she cared about sin, but discipline was important. It helped her to keep her mind on what she was praying for.

The bees' song had words in it. It was not a language she knew, but there was no mistaking what it was. She had been praying as she was taught, kneeling on the grass, hands together and head bowed. Now she raised her head and opened her eyes to the brightness all about her.

She had slid sidewise out of the world again. Mostly she did it because she wished to, but sometimes, as now, it happened of itself. She was no more frightened than she ever was. Whatever world this was, it meant her no harm. The creatures who lived in it either paid her no mind or watched her in quiet interest. She could go where she liked and do as she pleased, and nothing seemed to matter.

Today she found herself on the edge of a wood. The wood was dark. The trees in it were all dead. There was a smell to it, a slow, cold reek that made her think of an opened grave.

There was light behind her. The grass was still green, the sun still bright. But what the abbess was doing in the chapel, someone or something had done to a great swath of the Otherworld.

She backed away from it. This was nothing she could help.

She nearly fell into a pool had not been there when she came that way before. It was round and clear and reflected the sky. Somehow she knew that it was very deep; it went all the way to the heart of the world.

Cecilia was sitting by the pool. She had not been there before, either. She glanced at Edith, but most of her attention was on the water. "Look," she said.

Edith followed her stare. The water was pure, clear blue. Then it began to shimmer. Shapes were moving in it.

At first she thought they were fish swimming below. Then she realized that they were men. There was a man riding with a company of other men—knights in armor on big strong horses. He was not a big man compared to the others, but he carried himself very straight. His hair was gold and his beard was red. He had no magic in him, but there was power—she could feel it even through the water. It made her think of her father, how he was king and knew it, and so did everyone else.

Then the vision shifted. She saw another man. He looked a little like the first, but where that one was red and gold, he was ruddy brown, and his face was shaven clean. He was younger than the other, though still much older than Edith.

He had magic. Great roaring tides of it. He might be even stronger than Cecilia.

"That is my brother," Cecilia's voice said beside her, soft and clear. "They both are."

"They're Normans," Edith said. She turned to stare at Cecilia. "So are you."

Cecilia nodded. "Does that disturb you?"

Edith frowned. "Does the abbess know?"

Cecilia's shoulders lifted in a shrug.

"She'll hate you if she finds out."

"She will," Cecilia said. Then after a pause: "Do you?"

Edith thought about it. "My mother would want me to," she said after a while. "My father might. Or he might not. My godfather is a Norman, you know. His name is Robert."

"Yes," Cecilia said. "That's another of my brothers."

"Really? Is everybody your brother?"

Cecilia laughed. "Not quite," she said. "But they do get about."

"Father says," said Edith, "that everybody has to live in the world, and Normans aren't going to go away. Better be friends with them than dead enemies. Mother says she'd rather be dead. They fight over it."

"I can imagine they would," Cecilia said. "So? Which of them do you agree with?"

"I don't know yet," said Edith.

Cecilia nodded. That surprised Edith. Everyone else tried to force her to one side or the other. Cecilia only said, "You have to choose for yourself. I can only guide you; I can't act for you. No one can. Remember that."

"That's not what Mother says," said Edith.

"Most likely not," Cecilia said.

The water rippled and shifted, then melted away. When Edith looked up, Cecilia was gone. Edith was sitting on ordinary grass under an ordinary sky, and a nun loomed over her like a standing stone.

"Mother Abbess would speak with you," the nun said. Edith did not remember her name. She was tall and quiet and rather old, like all the nuns.

Edith thought she might have to find her own way to the abbess, but Sister turned in the way they all had after they took their vows, as if she had no feet but instead ran on wheels, and glided across the grass toward the grey shadow of the cloister. Edith followed as quickly as she could. She still had feet and legs, and they were rather small still; she had to scramble to keep up.

Mother Abbess might not have moved at all since the first and last time Edith had been summoned to an audience. Her room was as cold and grey as it had been before. If the chapel was a spider's web, this was the larder, closed off from any glimmer of light or breath of living air.

Abbess Christina had kept Edith waiting in the anteroom for a long while. Edith was dizzy with lack of breath when at last she was ushered into the presence. She had to struggle to walk steadily, to bow the proper degree and then stand with proper humility: hands folded in front of her, head bowed, eyes lowered.

She could feel that cold scrutiny on her. The walls were closing in. All that saved her was memory of the brightness she had come from, and Cecilia's voice telling her that she was free to choose what she would do.

"It is time," Abbess Christina said, "that you begin the instruction for which your mother sent you."

That startled Edith into speaking without thinking. "But, lady, I already have. I've been studying Saxon and Latin and Norman and—"

The abbess cut her off with chill precision. "Additional instruction befitting your blood and breeding. Sister Gunnhild will take you in hand for an hour each day. She will teach you what a daughter of kings has most need to know."

Edith looked up under her lashes. The nun who had fetched her from the far end of the cloister was still in the room. Edith peered through the shadows, picking out white hands tightly folded, and a pale face framed in the black veil. The rest of her was wrapped in darkness.

Her eyes were lowered as Edith's should be, her lips pressed together as tightly as her hands. Everything about her was locked shut.

Edith's heart felt small and cold. Her stomach had drawn into a knot. She kept thinking of the ruined wood and the strangling web. Here were the hands that would guide her into them—make her part of them.

She could run. But where? She was too small. The world was too big. The time when she could have escaped, when she was on the long road from Scotland to this place, was gone.

It did not matter what Cecilia had said. She did not have a choice. No child did.

She bowed her head. She could feel that the abbess was pleased. Sister Gunnhild glided forward. Edith did reverence as was proper.

"You will begin now," Abbess Christina said. "Apply yourself well. Take heed of what you are taught."

"Yes, lady," Edith said. It was all she could say.

✳ CHAPTER 10 ✳

There was no angel with a flaming sword at the gates of Winchester, barring William from the city or the treasury. He rode in as one who had every right, and found the chancellor waiting, with clerks in attendance.

They were expecting him. The keys to the treasury were ready for him to take, the guards bowing him in.

His shoulderblades prickled. This could be a trap. But he had not come this far to tuck his tail between his legs and run. His own picked men were with him. He left half of them with the guards and told the rest to follow him.

William the elder had had a reputation for acquiring every scrap of wealth he could and keeping it as close he judged politic. His generosity had been calculated to the last groat and farthing.

Now William the younger walked where none of the sons had been invited to go. He had seen the treasuries in Rouen and Caen, and the train of sumpter mules and laden chests that traveled with the king. Those had been remarkable enough—and belonged to his brother Robert now, except for what the old king's will had left to Henry and the sisters.

This was William's own. Room upon room of it. Chests of gold, silver, jewels both loose and set in rings and brooches, armlets and collars. Bolts of silk and linen and wool, and cloth of gold and silver. Mantles and robes of ermine and vair and sable, packed away in strong spices. Armor, weapons, horse-trappings. Banners and tapestries. One enormous chest of books, which William could see little enough use in, except that they were bound in good leather and set with gems.

He had had no inkling that there was so much. England, he would wager, was notably richer than Normandy.

He found that he was grinning like a loon. His men were wandering through the rooms, peering into chests and boxes. Robert the clerk was deep in conversation with one of his English colleagues.

Robin FitzHaimo stood close by him, smiling that subtle smile of his. "Does it feel real now?" the boy asked.

It was a remarkably intimate question. William should have resented it to the point of a fist across the face. But he could not find any violence in him, not against this one.

His grin had died, but he had a smile to spare still. "It will be real when I have the crown on my head," he said, "instead of in a box on a mule's back."

Robin reached into the chest nearest him. In it was a crown of gold set with pearls. He held it up a flourish. "Here's a crown," he said.

"Are you an archbishop, then?" William asked him.

He laughed. "Not in this life."

"But in another?"

William did not know why he asked that. Nor did Robin look at him strangely. The boy shrugged, as light as ever. "Maybe." He turned the crown in his hands. "It's pretty."

"I think it's for a queen," William said.

"It does have the look," Robin agreed. He laid the crown back in its box and slid his eyes at William. "Have you thought yet about who might wear it?"

A swift flush ran through William's body. "No," he said. "No, I have not."

Robin did not press him, but wandered off down the row of chests and boxes.

The heat drained from William's skin. Robin knew. It was nothing he did or said. It was a quiver in the belly, a deep sense: he knew.

Well then; so did every man in William's guard, and a good number of his father's old court as well. William's father had known, he was sure. His mother had, for certain. His brothers? Probably. Most of his sisters, too. A man in this world, unbound to priestly vows, did not get past the age of thirty without a woman in his bed. Henry at nineteen already had a pack of bastards. Robert at nearly forty had his fair share—and women enough with or without them.

It was not a thing anyone spoke of, but it was there. Everyone knew it. There had been company in his bed—discreet, and well cared for when the flush of passion died on either side. William had been lucky in that. His line did tend to be.

This was different. He did not know why it should be. There had been other beautiful boys, and young men, too—some a great deal prettier than this. A few had even had magic.

Not like this.

God. Was he besotted? Was he—God forbid—in love?

He was a king, or nearly. If he had learned nothing else from his father, he had learned to bestow his favors carefully and to trust seldom. This boy made his flesh sing, but he knew nothing of the spirit behind the face. That could be treachery in the making, or a friendship he would cherish for his life long. At the moment he could not tell which.

There would be time—God and Britain willing. He turned amid the gleam of treasure and called his men together. "We'll secure this," he said, brisk and sharp. "Tell the clerks to carry on with their inventory, and keep a good accounting. I'll be on my way to London."

"Westminster," said Robin. It was not a question.

William nodded. "I suppose you have ways to fetch the Archbishop of Canterbury—and every other prelate in England. They'll be officiating at a crowning."

Robin bowed in all apparent seriousness. "It will be done, sire," he said.

* * *

It was done, and well done. With Robert the clerk in Winchester and Robin the knight in London, William was most well served. Within the fortnight, England prepared to crown its new king.

The night before his coronation, William could not sleep. All had gone well. Too well, he was thinking—though the thought alone might ruin the luck. He had a suspicion that certain powers of Robin's acquaintance had seen to it that nothing interfered with William's advance toward the throne.

That was a good thing, he tried to tell himself. He wanted nothing to do with such things. If others took on the burden, all the better for him.

But he was too well trained to let it be, and too ill-trained to know how to go about it. He paced instead, prowling through the palace that old Edward had built, who had named a Norman his heir and so changed the face of England.

Every human soul was abed. The things that flitted in the shadows were of no consequence. He knew the hum and flutter of magical wards: those were thick along the walls and above the roof. They let him by without trouble, apart from a brief, intense quiver in the skin, like an itch too deep to scratch.

The abbey of Westminster had lost the raw newness that William remembered from the early days, when it was just built and consecrated in time for King Edward to be buried in it and Harold the usurper to be crowned and then, a scarce year later, the conqueror from Normandy who had been Edward's true and sanctioned heir. It was settling now, the new-stone smell softening, the carvings losing their sharpest edges. Marks of feet were beginning to show on the paving.

In the night, by the light of vigil-lamps and the odd candle, it breathed like a living thing. Wards were here, too, but they were deeper, stronger. They thrummed like the notes of a great organ.

There was a figure standing near the entrance to the choir, thin and stooped and shrouded in black. Swirls of translucent spirits wreathed him and spiraled up to the vaulting.

William checked his stride. There was no reason for the stab of apprehension. It was only Lanfranc. He must be preparing for the morrow.

The archbishop was not alone. Two shadows stood behind him. William knew them both as well as his own skin. One was Robin in a dark mantle. The other was a woman in a nun's habit, but William happened to know that she was no Christian.

Her eyes on him were clear and hard. She had always weighed him light. From her expression, that had not changed a bit.

He knelt deliberately and kissed the archbishop's ring. Then he nodded to Robin, who seemed more amused than not. Only after that did he acknowledge his sister. "Cecilia," he said. "I thought you were in Caen."

"I've been in England since the spring," she said. Her tone was cool.

His brow twitched upward. "Premonitions?"

"Something of the sort," she said.

"You're not going to make a wizard of me."

Even to his own ears he sounded desperate. None of those three mocked him for it. His sister said, still cool, "We would not dream of it. But a king—it seems you will be that."

"That troubles you?"

She shook her head. "It had to be you. For all our objections, you are the one the gods chose."

"The gods?" William wanted to laugh, but he found he did not dare. "Not Father?"

"Our father did as he had to do. As will you."

"What—" William broke off. "Don't tell me. It's magic, I know it. I want no part of it."

"You want the crown," she said.

"Do I?"

She let the echoes of that fade into silence. The others were watching and listening, offering no commentary.

"Well enough," he said. "I want it. You're not going to force your wizardry on me. Do you understand?"

They did not answer that, either. They were trying to provoke him—and succeeding rather well.

He considered turning his back on them and walking away. He considered it thoroughly and in all seriousness. But he had never run from a battle yet.

He fixed his glare on Lanfranc. "Is that what this is? Are you going to refuse to crown me unless I swear to be your puppet?"

"Some would prefer the word 'disciple,'" Lanfranc said mildly. "I prefer neither. You will be what God has made you to be. My duty is to set the crown on your head, then try to guide you to the best of my ability. But I have no power to force you."

"No?" William put in the word all the doubt and suspicion that was in him—and that was a great deal.

"You have to take this of your free will," Robin said.

"Take what?" William demanded. "I've told you what I'll give, and what I'll have. If it's fated as you all keep telling me, then it doesn't matter whether I agree to be a wizard's familiar. I'll be king regardless."

"It would be better," Lanfranc said, "if you accepted the fullness of what you are."

"Yes, you've told me," William said: and if that was rude, then so it was. "You've had our minions show me, too. I know what you think I'm supposed to be. I can only be what I am. Either that's enough or it's not. You can kill me now and get it over. I'm sure my little brother Henry would be delighted to take my place."

"It is not his time," Lanfranc said. He sighed. He looked very old and frail, and impossibly tired.

William hardened his heart. Lanfranc was the strongest of them all. If he played at weakness, it was only to trap William—and William was not that much a fool.

Robin stirred as if to speak, but William saw how Cecilia's glance stopped him. She raised her hands, a flutter of white in the sea of black that was her habit. "So be it," she said. "You've made your choice. Another way would have been easier in the end, though difficult to begin; you might have lived longer. But you will do as you will do."

She was playing, too, at spells and subtle disturbance. William made himself impervious—and waited for Robin to strike the third and final blow.

The boy did no such thing.

Or did he? His silence, calm and without judgment, was a force of its own. He left William to his free choice—and that was a stronger compulsion than any other.

William's mind was made up. He knew what kind of king he had to be. No fear or force or niggle of guilt would shift him.

That was power. He felt it there, in front of these masters of magic. They could do nothing within the bounds of their law and the destiny they foresaw but let him do as he chose.

It was heady, that knowledge. If he was not careful, he could get cocky. Then they would find another way to trap him.

But not tonight. Not tomorrow, either. Lanfranc was going to crown him, and the other two were going to bless him. After that, what would be would be. He could bow to fate, too—as long as it went the way he would have it.

CHAPTER 11

Sister Cecilia had been gone for more days than Edith was old enough to count. She was supposed to be on retreat in one of the daughter houses, meditating on her sins, but the folk of air had told Edith she was in London. Sister Cecilia's brother was king now; she had helped to crown him.

The land did not feel any better because there was a king in London. It was still riddled with rot like a bad cheese. Maybe parts of it were not rotting so quickly, but that was all the good that Edith could find.

Here in the abbey, the greyness was spreading without Sister Cecilia to keep it in hand. Edith tried to stop it, but she did not know how. She had not come that far yet in her learning.

Sister Gunnhild's lessons were not as terrible as she had feared. Mostly they were in Latin—speaking and reading and writing—and most of them were about holy things: prayers and psalms and lives of saints. Sister Gunnhild had a particular fondness for fallen women who repented and turned back to God. She loved Mary Magdalene best, but there were many others—more than Edith had ever known existed.

Sister Gunnhild was only a grey, grim person in the abbess' presence. In the little cell in which she taught Edith, little by little she showed a softer face. She was actually pretty under the veil and the habit. She had a fair Saxon face and wide blue eyes, and her eyebrows were the color of wheat. Edith supposed her hair must be the same.

She had a beautiful voice. She sang the prayers and the psalms, and taught Edith to sing them, too. Edith loved the music, the way it put order in the world. The stars sang like that, and the folk of air when they came down near the earth.

"Aren't you supposed to teach me other things, too?" Edith asked her one day. Harvest was past and winter was closing in. It was nearly Martinmas, with grey rain and thickening of mist, and every morning was a little colder.

Sister Gunnhild paused. She had been setting out the scrap of parchment for Edith to write on, while Edith sharpened a quill for a pen. "Other things?" she asked. "What would those be?"

"I can learn Latin and psalms with the other novices," Edith said. "I don't need a special tutor."

She held her breath. She still was not entirely sure what Sister Gunnhild would think or do.

As Edith had hoped—and maybe prayed a little—she did not take offense. She finished setting out the parchment and the ink, but she set the book aside from which Edith was to read and copy. She was using the time to think, Edith thought, and find words to say that Edith might understand.

Edith did not try to help her. Grown people never appreciated that from a child. She waited instead, with her hands folded as she had been taught.

Sister Gunnhild's smile was surprising, because it was so warm. Edith would never have thought she had that much warmth in her. "You see a great deal," Sister Gunnhild said. "More than your aunt guesses, I think. Or your mother, too?"

Edith shrugged. "Old people don't see as well," she said. "Old people who are very holy—some things they don't see at all. They don't want to."

The fair brows rose. "Am I old, then?"

"A little," Edith said, though it might not have been wise.

Sister Gunnhild looked as if she could not decide whether to laugh or glare. In the end she chose neither. She asked instead, "Do you know why I was put in charge of you?"

"Because your father was a king," Edith answered.

"Indeed," Sister Gunnhild said. "And you know which king he was?"

"Harold," said Edith. "The last one who was Saxon."

"Yes," Sister Gunnhild said.

"He wasn't royal," said Edith. "Not the way my mother is. She goes all the way to Alfred. Whereas he—"

"He was still king," Sister Gunnhild said. Her tone was mild. She did not seem angry. "He had no Norman blood."

"We don't, either," Edith said. "That was Edward, who was king before your father. His mother was a Norman. My mother's grandfather was his brother, but *his* mother was Saxon."

"You were well taught," said Sister Gunnhild.

"Mother said I should know where I came from," said Edith, "and why it matters. I'm to help take England back. I don't know how. I think Mother Abbess does. Do you?"

"I don't think so," Sister Gunnhild said. "I'm to make a good Christian of you. And a good Saxon."

"Aren't they the same thing?"

"One would think so," Sister Gunnhild said.

"I think maybe they're different," said Edith.

She could tell that she had gone too far. Sister Gunnhild's face closed up. She reached for the book and opened it without looking. "I think you think too much," she said. "Here. Copy this page."

Edith had copied it only a day or two before. But she did not think it was a good time to say so. She set her lips together carefully and reached for pen and ink and parchment. Mutely, obediently, she copied Latin words onto scraped parchment, just as she would do an hour later when she went to lessons with the rest of the novices.

A little before Martinmas, Sister Cecilia came back. There was no great homecoming and no particular welcome. She was simply there again, singing the office in the morning—and with her presence, some of the greyness lifted from the chapel.

Edith felt as if she had been holding her breath for weeks and now could let it go. She supposed it should bother her that she needed a Norman here to feel as if she could breathe. But that was the way it was.

She had been escaping when she could. The Otherworld was very close here, except in the chapel and near Mother Abbess. Sometimes it was so close that she could see through to it even while she was with the other novices, at lessons or performing duties.

She had learned to be very quick and clean about passing back and forth. It was quiet on the other side, and peaceful. Folk of air flocked there, but she never saw any other human, or anything that troubled her unduly. Even the dead parts, the withered woods and blasted heaths, were empty and strangely clean. It was only in the mortal world that they were rotten and foul.

Now with Sister Cecilia back, Edith did not have so pressing a need to escape. She still did it because she could, and because she loved the quiet. As winter closed in, it went on being summer there, except in the dead lands.

She knew a place where roses grew, white as snow and red as blood. They had no thorns like mortal roses; they made wonderful and fragrant garlands. She had brought a single white rose back while Sister Cecilia was away, and kept it deep in her box of belongings, wrapped in a bit of linen. It did not wither or die like a mortal rose, but went on blooming. Little by little the scent of it crept through everything in the box, until it all smelled faintly of roses.

It was her secret, so perfect and so wonderful that she saw no need at all to look at it. Simply knowing it was there was enough.

It was the memory of that, and the ghost of its fragrance, that kept her breathing in chapel, and let her sing the psalms with the other novices when she might have been gasping and wheezing instead. Even after Sister Cecilia came back, she kept it in her heart, folded as close as the rose in the linen. It was a great comfort.

On Martinmas eve, the Otherworld was closer than ever. Even the chapel seemed less grey, and Edith thought she saw a glimmer beyond it, like stars through fog. The scent of roses crept out of the box and surrounded Edith's cot. The folk of air came drifting down to bathe in it.

She was strangely restless. She endured her lessons with less patience than usual. Those with the novices seemed intolerably dull. Her hour with Sister Gunnhild was simply intolerable.

The sky was heavy and weeping rain. Recreation today was in the cloister, for those who were minded to brave the damp and the cold. The less hardy stayed inside with lamps and candles and bits of lessons or needlework.

Edith eluded both. They each thought she was with the other, which suited her very well. She slipped out through the cloister, running through a brief downpour of rain, and slipped and darted and slid and halted in sunlight.

Warmth surrounded her. The scent of roses was dizzying. She shook mortal rain out of her gown. Where it fell on the grass, it turned to diamond and crystal.

She laughed, because she could only be here for a little while, but while she was here she was free.

Her laughter faded. Something was different. The sun was as bright as ever, and the air as warm, but it felt odd underneath.

The peace of emptiness was gone. Things were moving, stirring. There were powers in this place, stronger and more solid than the folk of air.

Much stronger. Much more solid. They were taking shape beyond the field of roses: tall people and fair, much fairer than any mortal could be. Even in the sun, they seemed to walk in moonlight and starlight. Their hair was long and shining, their faces white and cold and keen. Their eyes were like bright steel.

Edith was not afraid of them. She supposed she should be. They knew she was there: they knew everything that happened in their country. But they did not mind. She belonged there, too, in a way.

They were mounted on things like horses, if horses had fangs and clawed feet. They had swords and bows and heavy spears for hunting boar. Their hounds were as tall as ponies and as white as bone, with ears as red as blood.

One of the pale riders cast a glace at Edith. There was a mount for her if she would take it. It was more like a horse than some of the others, and its eye was not quite as wild.

As she reached for the rein, a firm and solid hand held her back. "Not yet," said Cecilia. She bowed to the pale lord and said to him, "Her time is not yet come."

The pale lord frowned slightly, but he bowed, giving way to her will. She bowed back, as a queen would.

The eerie hunt rode away. Edith stood forgotten. "That wasn't fair," she said.

"That," said Cecilia, "wasn't safe. They were hunting the black boar that feeds on mortal flesh and drinks mortal blood. Maybe they were sharing power with you. Maybe they were thinking of a sacrifice. Blood of kings, child: you have plenty of that. It's a potent magic."

"They didn't want my blood," Edith said.

"How do you know they didn't want your soul?"

Edith opened her mouth to answer that, but the words would not come. She did not know anything.

"You will," Cecilia said with a sudden shift from stern to almost gentle. "Come now. A day will come when you can ride with them. Today you belong in the abbey. Since you walk so well between the worlds, I have a gift for you: a bit of magic. You'll be warded when you come back. Then you'll be safe from temptation."

"What if I don't want to be?"

"When you have the knowledge to judge that," Cecilia said, "then you'll be free to do as you please. Now come."

There was a power in the words, a twist of magic. Edith had no power in her to disobey.

She thought about resenting it. But Cecilia had told her she would come back. She would have to be safer, that was all. She could understand that. Safe was good, if one was young and small and in great need of teaching.

She would grow up. Maybe not fast enough to suit her, but it would happen. That was as sure as the shift from sun to rain, from immortal garden to mortal cloister.

And when she was grown up—then things would be different. She would be much more powerful and much more wise. She would give the orders then, and lesser people would obey. Someday even, maybe, she would be a queen.

PART TWO

❊❊❊

JUDGMENT

anno domini 1093–1094

❊ CHAPTER 12 ❊

The wind wuthered across the empty land. There was a raw edge to it. Along the crumbling stretch of the Roman wall, patches of winter's snow still lingered.

Most of William's army had gone ahead to Carlisle. He had paused for a bit of hawking, trying the wings of a new gyrfalcon in this stark and forbidding country. The escort that rode with him was as hardy as he—he would not have kept the pack of them with him if they had not been—and as happily inclined to linger for a day or two, far away from the drudgery of the court.

He had spent the past year getting Cumbria firm in hand. That was done and well enough. A bit of court in Carlisle, then back to the south for another round of convincing fractious barons that he was, indeed, king.

There was never any end to that. He had seen it with his father, and every higher lord had to keep his vassals from erupting into revolt. It was the way of the world. A king never got to plant his backside on a throne and just sit. He had to keep fighting for it.

William grinned into the teeth of the wind. Kingship had turned out to suit him well. Once he was crowned, somewhat to his surprise, the Otherworld had let him be. Even his sister Cecilia had refrained from troubling him with what she perceived to be his less public duties.

Lanfranc had been less circumspect, but he had died soon enough. He had been in his tomb for four years now. William had never quite got round to filling his archbishopric, which was a constant vexation to the bishops, not to mention the Pope; but it was restful in its way not to have that particular gadfly buzzing incessantly in his ear.

There were other gadflies, to be sure, and plenty of troubles to occupy his mind and body, but taking all in all, he was quite satisfied to be king. And today, by God's blessing, he was free to do as he pleased.

They were riding down the line of the wall, on and beside the remains of the road that the legions had built. This was haunted country, full of the memories of old Rome. William had seen them marching as he rode, a shadow and a glimmer, and heard the distant tramping of booted feet.

He was not afraid of the dead. The vigor of life was in his body, and his blood ran hot and strong. Half the men he rode with had warmed his bed at one time or another—all but the one who rode closest, whom he had never quite pushed to it.

Robin FitzHaimo had made himself indispensable for many more reasons than that he happened to be part of the magical world. He was also notably gifted in the arts and skills of the world William preferred to live in. He had proved to be a good and loyal servant, a brave fighting man, and a surprisingly adept courtier.

A king had to be most careful of his friendship. But William considered Robin a friend. He had ambition—he was a lord's son, after all— but it did not blind him to either honor or loyalty.

He was also a splendid rider and a skilled huntsman. Today he rode neck and neck with William at whatever pace the king chose, laughing the more, the faster and harder they went.

They reined in as the sun touched the horizon, halting just below one of the castles that marked each mile of the wall. This one was more nearly intact than most: it still had a bit of roof, and the second story had not yet fallen in. Hunters and shepherds must use it as William planned to do; there were marks of fire within, and spoor of sheep and horses.

They had brought wood to burn, and gathered such of it as was to be had in this treeless country. By the fall of dusk, they had a rather pleasant camp made, with a fire burning and bread baking and a variety of wildfowl roasting on spits.

It was a rare, cloudless evening, with a distinct touch of frost now that the sun had gone down. William felt the cold away from the fire, but it was more invigorating than not. He wrapped himself closer in his mantle and wandered out of the milecastle into the chill twilight.

The legions were marching on the road below. Their faces were clearer in the gloom, the light of torches gleaming on their armor. Their cloaks were the color of blood.

One or two looked up and saw William standing by the castle. Their eyes glittered, but none of them spoke. He bowed to them. They turned eyes front and marched onward into the gathering dark.

The odor of roasting fowl made his mouth water. The men were laughing and singing, and Walter the jester was regaling them with wicked stories. Some of the squires were drunk already, and the wine had barely begun to go round.

William was hungry and thirsty. But he lingered in the cold, while the stars came out in their legions. The moon was new tonight, a thin curve, sinking already toward the horizon.

He was aware of the figure that stood watching him for a long while before it moved. If it was waiting for him to acknowledge it, it could wait until Judgment Day.

Even the dead had less patience than William had when he chose. The dark shape glided forward. Light of stars and campfire never quite touched it, but William's eyes needed neither to recognize the face. "Well, old man," he said. "Getting round to haunting me at last?"

The shade that had been Lanfranc sighed with the sound of wind in empty places. "There would be no need for that if you had got round to filling my place."

"Is that what you came for?" William shook his head. "I'd have thought you'd know better."

"I do know better," Lanfranc said. "Greater powers than I will take care of that."

"Then it's a social call, is it?" William wrapped his cloak more tightly about him and leaned against the wall. The dead had the unfortunate habit of draining heat from the air wherever they were—and there had been none here to begin with. He could feel his breath turning to ice in his beard.

"I came to warn you," said Lanfranc, "and to offer hope, if you will take it. You've eluded the gods' justice for rather longer than you should. You've escaped your duty and played at being king. Like a child you've been heedless, and happy in it. That is about to end."

William thrust himself erect. The flash of temper warmed him remarkably. "Playing? Heedless? I've been fighting wars, herding barons, fending off my brothers, seeing to it that the kingdom gets richer rather than poorer while I'm king of it, and you dare to call me—"

"You know what I am speaking of," Lanfranc said, almost too soft to hear, but it cut William off. "The Old Things are struggling. With but three Guardians left, the strength of Britain is at a dangerous ebb. You must take up the reins of the other kingdom. You must be king in all respects."

"Why?" William demanded. "The Druids are dead and gone. If magic is fading, isn't that the way of the world? This is a new age—a new kingdom. We bow to God and His Son, not the old forgotten gods."

Lanfranc sighed, a long exhalation of chill wind. "Do you think that God did not make Britain as well as the rest of the world? Or that magic was not of His making?"

"The Church—" William began.

"The Church is a mortal institution," said the shade that in life had been the Archbishop of Canterbury, "and subject to the failings of mortal understanding."

"Which is a long-winded way of saying it's a pack of fools." William spat just past the shade's shoulder. "I'll grant you that. But I'm not turning wizard for you or any man, living or dead."

"You won't do it for a man," Lanfranc said.

"Nor a woman, either," said William. "No one will force it on me. I am what I am. This is the kingship I'm fit to take."

"Maybe so," said Lanfranc, "but the gods care little for fitness and less for human desire. If you go on as you are, this land will die. You'll rule a wasteland, wracked with sickness and famine."

"Plagues and bad crops are in God's hand," William said. "We can pray they won't come on us, but they always do. They're our lot in this world."

"Not like this," Lanfranc said, each word distinct. "God will judge, my lord king. Have a care that you're not found wanting."

William opened his mouth to answer that, but a sudden wind had caught the shade and scattered it, turning it to mist and starlight.

Robin was standing in the doorway, wreathed in light and warmth. William reached for him with a hunger beyond words.

Somewhat to his surprise, Robin let him. He was taller than William but lighter built, supple and strong, steel blade to William's sturdy war-axe. After the cold breath of the dead, his living warmth was bliss.

William was not thinking at all. He had forgotten cold, fear, even anger. All that was here was a deep kiss that tasted of wine, and strong arms clasping him, and eagerness at least the match of his.

They slid together down the wall, unmindful of cold air or rough stone or half-frozen earth. Ghosts and spirits fluttered like moths toward the heat that radiated from them. Robin was like a hearthfire, a blaze of pure magic.

This kind of magic, William could stomach—oh, easily. It had some use and purpose. There was a spell on him, he knew perfectly well. It asked nothing of him but this hour in this place. What happened before did not matter. What happened after was in the lap of the gods.

Maybe Robin set out to take William by storm. William knew, none better, how to turn a battle to his own advantage. It was a fair fight, and a fair victory, too—on both sides.

* * *

When they rode out in the morning, William had forgotten the apparition and its warnings. He only remembered what had come of it. He made no effort to hide the grin that kept breaking out, though he was careful not to aim it too obviously at Robin.

They all knew. It would have been impossible not to, in those close quarters. But there was a courtesy among William's familiars, an honor of silence. Just as old lovers learned not to play at jealousy with new ones, they all knew better than to draw attention to any particular alliance.

There was a peculiar pleasure in circumspection, even out here in the wild. By evening they would be in Carlisle, in court where subtlety was an art and discretion a necessity.

William caught himself anticipating it with pleasure. Tonight there would be a warm bed under a roof, and a whole night to continue what they had begun on the old Roman paving under the stars.

Very far down in the deeps of his memory, apprehension hovered. He took no notice of it. He had had a bad dream, that was all. Robin had aroused him from it, and in more ways than one.

"This is a dangerous game."

Robin lifted his head from the king's breast. William was deep asleep. The fire had died; the room was cold. Robin drew the coverlet up over his bare shoulders.

Even good English wool was poor defense against the breath of the dead. He looked up into Lanfranc's shadowy face. "No more dangerous than yours," he said, "my lord."

The late archbishop sat on a stool beside the royal bed. He still moved like the stiff old man he had been before he died, as if he could not bring himself to lose the habit. "This heedlessness has gone on long enough. Why do you encourage it?"

William stirred and murmured. Robin slipped out of bed, reaching for the nearest covering, which was the king's great cloak of crimson wool lined with vair. The touch of it on naked skin was cold, but it warmed quickly. He laid a Word on the king, which deepened his sleep, and stood over the shade on its stool. "Surely, my lord, you noticed while you were alive that this man takes very poorly to compulsion. Preach him a sermon and you will most certainly lose him. Whereas subtlety—"

"Seduction is subtle?"

Robin flushed. "That . . . simply happened. I wanted him to forget his anger at your preaching. It wasn't supposed to—"

"Was it not?"

"No," said Robin, biting off the word.

"For six years," said Lanfranc, "you kept your distance. You watched him dally with every pretty fool between Scotland and Provence. You maintained a most Christian and admirable restraint. And now that it is nearly too late, now that there is no hope for this kingdom unless he wakes to the truth, you give way intemperately to the body's passion. Have you forgotten what you are? And what you are meant to do?"

Robin's back was stiff. "I have not forgotten."

"He may not forgive you," the archbishop said, "if he comes to believe that you seduced his body in order to seduce his spirit."

"Will you tell him?" Robin demanded. He was too furious, almost, to speak.

Lanfranc sighed. The ferocity had gone out of him, if not out of Robin. "You know I will not. But if he has an objection to sermons, what do you suppose he will think of seduction as a weapon?"

"I'll take the chance," said Robin, "if it saves both him and the kingdom."

"Even if you lose him?"

"Even so," Robin said steadily.

"I'll pray for you," Lanfranc said. He was already fading, melting into the grey light of dawn.

Robin sank down where the shade had been sitting. With its passing the air was noticeably warmer, but Robin had begun to shudder. Even for one of his arts and powers, it was no easy thing to converse with the dead.

❋ CHAPTER 13 ❋

William left Carlisle in high good humor. The north was secured, the fighting done for a while. He would spend Lent in
the south, where it was already spring, then at Easter consider the next
campaign. Scotland again, maybe. Or Normandy. Or God would send
him another battle to fight.

The road was open before him. His army marched in good order,
with a fine store of baggage, the wealth of the north riding on the backs
of strong mules. The wind was cold and edged with sleet, but he did not
mind that. It would be warm soon enough.

This riding was more haunted than usual—and worse, the farther
south they rode. William always had an insubstantial escort, a pack of
magical camp-followers, but this one outnumbered the mortal army.
Companies of skeletal warriors rode on bony horses, with packs of
fleshless hounds. Dim shapes skittered underfoot; dark wings spread
overhead. Far away on the edges moved a shadow and a shimmer.

The old Romans did not venture this road. These were older things
by far, nor had most of them ever been mortal.

The memory of Lanfranc's warning niggled at William's mind, but he
pushed it away. He was resolutely, stubbornly a part of the living world.
He rode on mortal stones over mortal earth. The mortal sky wept or
smiled overhead. Mortal wind cut through his armor with the last blast of
winter's cold, or wafted past his face with the first faint promise of spring.

He shut his eyes to the uncanny and made himself see only what was real to human eyes. It was harder than he had expected; it made his head ache. But it was worth the pain.

They had come safely out of the north and ridden down through the marches of Wales. The country for once was quiet, with no threat of war, and no raids across the border. William began to think he would reach Winchester without any more trouble than an occasional bout of rain and mud.

He paused for a day or two in Gloucester, resting men and horses and warming his bones in the midst of a sudden blast of winter. On the third day, though the weather was still chancy, he found himself too restless to sit in walls any longer. It was still a fair way to Winchester.

He set off rather later than he had intended. His bed was warm and Robin was in it, and his men were reluctant to leave comfort behind. It was halfway to noon before they passed the city gate.

The sun had been threatening to come out, but before they had been on the road an hour, the clouds closed in again. There were things in the air, shrill voices, and strange shapes that overcame even William's determination not to see them. A thin and bitter rain began to fall.

He set his jaw and picked up the pace. After a while, that cost him the baggage train and its heavily armed escort, along with the flock of priests and clerks who followed with the exchequer.

The horses would have to rest soon enough; then the slowest riders would catch him. For now he was glad to be moving—running away, it might be, but it was better than sitting still.

The road wound through fields as yet neither plowed nor planted, over and around low rounded hills, and past thickets of alder and hazel. Winter's grip tightened. The sleet turned to a squall of snow.

Darkness loomed ahead: the eaves of a wood. William had seen that wood before. It sat athwart every path, if that path was tainted with magic.

He muttered a curse. While he was priding himself on having kept the world real, the world beneath had lured him away from the bulk of his army and sucked him into itself.

This wood was not as dead as the one he had stumbled into years ago, before he was crowned. Its branches were bare and its undergrowth withered, but he heard sounds of life: whispers, chitters, brief eruptions of eerie laughter. Things moved in the shadows, flitting from branch to branch or creeping along the ground.

He had turned back from the dead wood. This one stretched as far as he could see. There was no way around it, only through it.

This time he refused to retreat. He was going to Winchester, and be damned to whatever tried to get in his way.

He hardly needed to look to know where Robin was: his presence was as distinct as a warm hand on bare skin. He knew that when he spoke to that presence, it would hear. "Give me wards. Get me through this."

"I'll do what I can," Robin said. He was riding beside William, where a moment before he had been well back toward the rear.

In this light he looked less human than William had ever seen him. The old blood showed through the mortal flesh, narrowing his face and fining his bones. There was a light in him, growing brighter the farther they rode into the wood.

"Be well advised," William said, "that I am riding through this place. I am not submitting myself to any test or judgment or any other magical nonsense. If anything in this place tries to do such a thing, you will dispose of it. Is that understood?"

Robin bent his head. His eyes were veiled beneath long lids. "Understood, sire," he said.

William eyed him narrowly. Robin kept his head down.

William decided to trust him. If that was a mistake, so be it.

They rode as straight as they could. The trees closed in until they had to ride in single file, bent over their horses' necks. Some of the men wanted to dismount, but William ordered them to stay in the saddle.

Now and then the trees drew back. There was even, once or twice, a clearing. The light was not much brighter there; snow was still falling, softer now but steady, covering the dead bracken and the withered grass.

The sun was hidden, the light so dim that there was no telling what time of day it was. Robin was leading them—rightly, William hoped, and not in endless circles.

God help them if they had to spend the night in this place. It was bad enough in what passed for daylight. He would wager it was infinitely worse after dark.

The hauntings that had followed the army out of Carlisle were back in force. They must have been herding William's escort—because surely they were not guarding it. As the day grew old, they seemed more solid; pallid flesh began to cover the naked bones.

Robin's face was white, his eyes shut as he rode. His lips moved. Faintly, almost inaudibly, William heard him chanting.

His horse stumbled. His voice faltered. The army of Old Things closed in.

As softly as he could, William drew his sword. Cold iron was deadly to magic, or so it was said.

None of the creatures that hemmed him in seemed perturbed by it. Still, he kept it across his saddlebow. It was something solid to hold on to; some hope of defense if herding turned to attack.

He looked over his shoulder. A moment before, twenty knights and squires had been riding there. Now there was no one. He was alone but for Robin. Darkness and mist shrouded the track.

There was a little light ahead. William pressed toward it. It might be a trap. He was not about to turn tail, not here—because for a certainty, what was behind was worse.

The light was a clearing. In a better season it might have been a rolling meadow with a stream running through it. Now it was barren and covered in snow, and the stream had gone dry. Only the meander of rounded stones told where it had been.

William paused on the wood's edge. He had prayed for the trees to part, but now that they had, he found that he was reluctant to expose himself to the sky. Things were up there watching. The clouds hid them, but he knew they were there—just as they knew where he was.

Robin was pale and shaking. He was out of his depth here. He had given up trying to control his horse; William reached across and took the rein, just as the beast made a break for it.

It fetched up short. Robin swayed in the saddle but kept his seat. There was one thing to be said for a Norman, even a half-breed with Druid blood: he could stay on a horse's back no matter what it did.

"Your father was a half-breed with Druid blood," Robin said. His voice was faint, but there was a hint of his old lightness in it. "Ride forward. Straight across the clearing. Don't look left or right, and don't turn, no matter what you see."

William swallowed. His mouth was dry. It was foolish—there was nothing there.

Straight across the clearing. He could do that. Robin's usually sensible horse had decided to be an idiot, but William's red stallion was as sane as ever. He kept a solid grip on the bay's rein and touched spur to his stallion's side.

It was not as easy to ride straight as one might have thought. The ground was uneven; there were stones under the snow, slippery and treacherous, and the stream's dry and rocky bed crossed and recrossed the line that William tried to follow. Robin's horse became more unruly rather than less as they moved out into the open.

After the idiot beast lunged sidewise, nearly pulling William out of the saddle and nearly casting Robin on the ground, William hissed in fury. He dropped his own reins on the chestnut's neck, trusting the stallion's sense and his own seat to keep to the track, and got hold of Robin's arm and heaved.

In mid-heave, he knew he had made a terrible mistake. He hung in the air between the two horses, with Robin's weight dragging him down. His stallion began to veer. Robin's bay, now completely mad, whipped about.

By God's good grace, it spun toward William rather than away—and

William's stallion checked and shifted and settled solidly under him. With a wrenching effort, he hauled Robin across the chestnut's neck.

The bay screamed and bolted. William should have known better than to look, but he could not help himself.

The ground rose up, or the sky came down. He could not be certain which. Robin's poor halfwit horse was swallowed, engulfed in nothingness.

Robin lay limp and still. He was breathing: William heard the catch and rattle.

Without him, William had no defenses. All he could do was keep to the straight track and pray.

Even prayer was a dangerous thing in England. The Saxons had turned it into a kind of weapon against magic. Their praying had made this place, sucked the life out of it and twisted what was left.

William did not want to understand why Lanfranc had so hounded him both alive and dead. He was ruling well. His kingdom was under control. He wanted Normandy, and intended to get it.

And yet here he was, alone but for a half-conscious witch-man, trying to ride straight on a track he could not see, through a wood and a meadow that did not exist on any mortal map.

It was always going to be like this. He could live a year, two years, six, and be free of it—but just when he thought he was safe, it would ambush him. Anywhere he went in England, he could stumble into a trap.

Straight ahead. That was the best he could do. There were eyes on him—watching, judging. He fancied that they were hungry.

So was he, but there was no stopping until he was out of this place. He did something he had promised himself never to do: he opened all his senses, especially those he least liked to admit to.

That, like his rescue of Robin, was almost a fatal mistake. He had not done such a thing in all the years since he became a man. The power of it—the sheer force of what he could see and feel and hear, smell and taste and touch—nearly flung him from the saddle.

The world was a far, far wider place than he had ever allowed it to be.

The sky was deeper, the shadows darker, the earth stronger. And every part of it was full of magic.

Except—

Once he let himself see what was there, he also could see what was not. The dead places; the places that were worse than dead.

Of which this was one. The Old Things here were warped and twisted. Not that they had ever been exactly safe for mortals to know, but these had turned poisonous.

William did not think he was supposed to be this deep in, or this defenseless, either. The lesson was not supposed to kill him, only put the fear of the old gods in him.

He was afraid, right enough. Any sane man would be. But he was not quite paralytic with terror—not yet.

His stallion's steps were slow but steady, even when the wind began to blow. It was only a breeze at first, though cold and smelling of graves. All too quickly it rose to a gale. It buffeted him, and rocked the chestnut on his feet.

The stallion lowered his head and pressed on against it, though a horse's instinct was to turn tail and hold fast. William bent as low as he could, shielding Robin's body as much as he might. He could not see where he was going. He had to trust that the horse could follow the track.

There were voices in the wind, shrieks and cries, but worse than that, a shrilling hum that shook William's bones. Snow swirled about him. Where it fell, it rattled like shards of glass. His horse twitched. Drops of blood sprang, scarlet on chestnut.

William had no power to turn aside that edged assault. Cold iron could do nothing against it.

He knew the way. It was the hardest direction and the most bitter: straight into the teeth of the wind.

He glanced over his shoulder. Not all the howling he heard was wind. Some of it was the hunt that rode on his heels. The skeletal horses, the pale hounds, were all too familiar.

Darkness waited ahead. It was full of eyes. What he had taken for trees were shadowy shapes. They crouched, waiting. The track ran straight toward them.

There was no way around or over or back. There might be no hope, either. William steadied his horse and his heart, and settled Robin more firmly in his arms. "Go," he said to the stallion, in hardly more than a whisper.

The lean ear slanted back. The horse picked up his pace from a walk to a soft, smooth canter.

Robin stirred and murmured. William tightened his grip and his legs. The canter stretched to a hand gallop.

That was faster than William had intended, but he did not try to slow it down again. With Robin's body for a shield and the Wild Hunt on his heels, he plunged into the forest of shadows.

❄ CHAPTER 14 ❄

There were trees in here after all, but where those before had been stark and bare, these were thick with needles so dark that they seemed more black than green. Their branches hung down low, hunched like the wings of vultures. Things moved within them, rustling and skittering.

William abandoned caution and began to pray. He knew better than to try fragments of childhood Saxon, though the temptation was overpowering. He held fast to Latin.

The wood did not like the sound of that. The trees shuddered and groaned. He caught glimpses of the things that lived in them: weird, pallid creatures with faces too close to human for comfort. They reminded him of the feys that had loved to flock to his father, but as strange as feys were, these were stranger—and not in any wholesome way.

Once he had seen them, they seemed to decide that there was no advantage in concealment. The trees were crawling with them.

Thick as maggots on a carcass, he thought, and immediately regretted it. Thoughts had power. As strongly as he had resisted any knowledge of magic, he had learned that much from listening to his mother.

Maybe, if he thought of the world he wanted to live in, envisioned it in every possible detail, willed it to take shape around him . . .

It was almost enough. For an instant he saw plain daylight and an open road and the green hills of Somerset.

The darkness came roaring in. The things in the trees shrieked and gibbered. His horse stumbled and went down.

William went off rolling, coiling his body around Robin, protecting him as best he could. Hooves flailed past his head. The red stallion's body crashed through trees.

The horse was already dead. In the whirling dimness, William saw a black dart in the red throat, and blood springing hot and bright.

Fear was far away, but William could hear it wailing to itself. He had landed easier than he expected: the mould of years was thick underfoot. He found he could stand, and drag Robin up with him, and heave him up over a shoulder and keep on walking.

Straight ahead. For he had noticed something while he rode. However thick the throngs in the wood, not one of them ventured the track. He was safe as long as he stayed on it.

God's mercy alone had kept him there. The horse had fallen astray, and the black dart had taken him.

There was no telling how far it was to any hope of safety. The best William could do was keep hold of Robin and keep walking.

Dark was closing in. Maybe it was night. Maybe it was not. The cold of it cut to the bone.

He was alone but for a dead but breathing weight, a coat of mail that made his shoulders ache, and the glimmer of the track ahead of him. With contemptuous ease, this perversion of old Britain had stripped him of everything that he had in the world, except this essence of what he was.

He stopped in the middle of the track. The darkness was nearly complete. He could still see the swarm of twisted fey; they were full of a sickly light.

"Enough," he said. "Kill me now and have done with it."

It was not the fey who answered. The voice came from behind, deep and cold and slow. "You will die," it said, "as all men do. But not tonight."

Gently William lowered Robin to the ground, circling as he moved, standing astride the slack body with sword drawn. He came to a halt facing the way he had come.

The Hunt was there: the great riding of the dead. The one who led it bore a stag's skull atop broad and bony shoulders, with a spread of antlers so high and wide that they mingled with the branches of the trees.

Deep in the hollow sockets of the eyes, a corpse-light gleamed. William met it full on with a glare as hot as the Huntsman was cold. He almost fancied that the creature rocked back a fraction; but that might only be his own exhaustion making his vision waver.

"We are not here for your life," said the Huntsman, "or yet for your soul."

"What then?" William demanded. He did not care if he was insolent. He would be just as dead whether he spoke softly or no.

The Huntsman did not seem to mind how William said it. "We owe you this," the apparition said. "What we are here, what Britain is becoming—those are your doing."

"Oh no," said William. "I'm not taking the blame for that. Saxons killed the magic, then my father brought it back—and dropped it flat the day my mother died."

"The blame is in the blood," the Huntsman said. "Only continue as you are, and all of Britain will belong to us. Then we will have your soul."

"Not," said William, "if I can help it."

"Ah," said the Huntsman, "but can you?"

William looked about. His horse was dead. His protection was half-dead at his feet.

He could think of nothing to do but what he had been doing. He heaved Robin up over his shoulder again, paused to balance the weight, and walked. Straight ahead. No flinching, no veering.

"Yes," the Huntsman said behind him. "Go as you have come. Every step you take, we grow stronger."

William set his teeth. He would not be provoked into turning back. The world of the living was ahead of him. He had to believe that.

Belief, like words, had power. There was no shadowed wood in front of him, no Wild Hunt behind. Robin had taken ill. His horse had had a fall and died. That was all.

"Yes," said the Huntsman, exactly as close as he had been before. "Feed us. Make us strong."

It seemed William had choices. Turn back and fail. Go on and fail. Die where he stood, of cold and starvation if the Old Things would not kill him.

"All that you do serves us," the Huntsman said. "By all means, live and rule and turn your back on your blood and breeding."

William did not stop or turn, but he said, "I got my fill of that when I was in the nursery. 'Don't do that,' my nurse would say—hoping that I'd do it. What do you want me to do? Put flesh on your bones? Make the woods green again?"

The silence behind him should have been a relief. Unfortunately for William's peace of mind, he knew better.

He kept walking. It was all he knew how to do. He wanted his world back, his people, his crown. He wanted never to be trapped like this again.

Maybe it was a dream, but it was a dream he could cling to. He squeezed his eyes shut and willed it into being.

Robin twisted and began to thrash, taking William completely by surprise. They went down in a tangle.

William was fighting for his life. The thing that had gone for his throat was not the Robin he thought he knew. This was red murder and strangling fingers, and teeth that snapped in his face, sharp as a wolf's.

He was at a severe disadvantage. This thing that wore Robin's body wanted him dead. He wanted Robin alive.

He kept the fingers from his throat and the teeth from his face, and pinned the thrashing legs and twisting body. It was taller than he was, but he outweighed it. He used that weight, and bound it to the earth.

The earth heaved beneath them both. The air was full of voices, shrieks and cries, and the flutter of wings.

He looked down into Robin's eyes. They were blurred with confusion, but they were sane. Between William's body and the earth, he was safe from the thing that had possessed him.

Those eyes shifted past William and widened. That was all the warning William had.

Could a bee sting through armor? It was a small pain, negligible, except that it grew so large. It burned and throbbed.

The strength went out of William's arms. He slipped to the ground beside Robin.

He had fallen off the straight track—into mortal daylight, mortal earth, and blessed Somerset. A mist was closing in, but it was earthly mist, with no terrors of the Otherworld in it.

Not that it mattered, he thought distantly. All the uncanniness that he needed was sunk in his breast above the heart: a black dart poisoned with a spell.

His hand scrabbled at it. His fingers had no strength to grip. He was losing the light. His body burned with fever. He tried to speak, but the words would not come.

This was the end, then. At least he got to die in the mortal world. That was a blessing, if a small one.

He let go of pain and fever, then words and consciousness, sliding down the long steep slope into the dark.

❊ CHAPTER 15 ❊

"Anselm!"

The Abbot of Bec lay motionless on his hard and familiar bed. His cell was protected by strong wards, set to keep out everything that hinted of magic. He had stopped short of swearing a vow never to wield his power, but in the years since Lanfranc died, apart from the wards that protected him from temptation, he had lived by a strictly mortal rule.

Nevertheless, a voice called to him out of the air, clear as the cry of a trumpet. "Anselm! Wake!"

He opened his eyes on lamplight and a face that could not possibly have arrived here by mortal ways.

The late king's daughter sat demurely beside his bed, gowned and veiled as a nun. Both the demureness and the habit were purely deceptive. This was a sorceress of enormous and unabashed power, a Guardian of Britain, a defender of all that Anselm had determined to reject.

"My lord abbot," she said, "it's time you woke from your dream and faced your destiny."

"My destiny is to be a man of God," Anselm said.

"So it is," said Cecilia. "And now God calls you to Britain."

"God has nothing to do with it," Anselm said.

She rose. "The king needs you now. The Old Things have turned on him; he's like to die of it."

"Why do you come to me?" Anselm demanded. "I have no arts to help him. That is your province, surely."

"He needs you," she said.

"I will not—" Anselm began.

He never finished. She had caught hold of his wrist and pulled him to his feet. She was stronger than a woman had any right to be. While he was still staggering, off balance in body and mind, she opened the wall between the worlds.

She must have laughed at his wards. This was magic so high and strong that there was no resisting it. He could only shut his eyes and suffer it to take him.

The king lay on a high and royal bed in Gloucester. Despite the heat of a room banked with braziers, and a heap of coverlets of both wool and fur, he shuddered with unrelenting cold. His skin was icy to the touch; his mind was gone, wandering where no sane man would wish to follow.

Anselm was a scholar, not a healer, but he was hardly immune to compassion. He bent over that white and shaking figure, and his heart softened in spite of itself. It did not matter if this was a king; he was a soul in torment, and Anselm was a man of God.

William's eyes opened. Anselm had recalled that they were blue, not this pale and wintry grey. Even they had had the color leached out of them.

They wandered aimlessly until they found Anselm's face. There, they stopped and held as if transfixed. William's hand gripped Anselm's with startling strength.

His spirit was still far away. Anselm could feel it drawing him into a cold and distant place, through white emptiness and a broad expanse of shadow.

William's sister had trapped Anselm and drawn him to this stifling room in Gloucester, on the other side of the sea from Anselm's proper place. Now William drew Anselm out of the world altogether into a kind of bleak damnation.

It did no good to resist. The harder Anselm fought, the lower he fell.

Through prayer and meditation and the lofty structures of philosophy, he had turned his back on everything else that he was. He knew what Lanfranc would have said to that: Lanfranc, whose only defiance of the Church's law in all his life had been to be both sorcerer and priest. As grim a thing as the Saxons had done to the Old Things of Britain, they had done God's will. Magic and the Church could not join together.

"God made you," William said.

They were standing in a field of ice, blank and bleak and empty of life. William with his red-gold hair and fiery beard blazed unnaturally bright here—and his eyes were brilliant and startling blue. He looked like a new-lit flame.

Anselm regarded him in no little surprise. "You were even more insistent than I that magic have no part in your realm."

"So I was," William said. "Maybe I still am."

"That is not logical," said Anselm.

"Maybe not," said William. "But I am practical. What I want and what is may have nothing to do with each other. Old Britain is doing its best to get rid of me. I'm not about to be got rid of. If that means magic—then I'll hold my nose and swallow it."

"That is practical," Anselm granted him, not happily. "Still, why am I here? Your sister is stronger than I will ever be, and she accepts that she is."

"She can't take the see of Canterbury," William said.

"Ah," said Anselm. It struck him, distantly, that this was a very strange discussion to be having in the landscape of a nightmare.

Or perhaps this was the perfect place for such a thing. If he had bad dreams, they were of being ripped from the peace of his monastery, flung out into the world, and forced to rule where he had wished only and ever to pray.

"I do not want Canterbury," he said. "You cannot force me to take it. Give it to one of the hundreds of men who want it."

"None of those several hundred is strong enough to do all the things that the Archbishop of Canterbury must do. Including," said William, "the things that no one talks about."

"That cannot be true," Anselm said. "The Church is full of sorcerers, some raised very high. Surely—"

"None of them is bound to Britain."

"I am not—"

"Believe me," said William, "I didn't want to be, either—not that way. But I am. So are you. Can't you feel it? It's like chains going down into the ground."

"This is all a lure and a trap," Anselm said bitterly. "Are you even ill? Is that a deception, too?"

"Oh, I'm poisoned," said William, "and I'll be lucky if I come out alive. Britain will need you even more if I fail. Henry's not ready yet. He's still reiving his way through Normandy."

"An heir of your own body—" Anselm began.

William looked him hard in the face. "Don't delude yourself," he said.

But Anselm was not going to listen to that. "Even a man of your . . . proclivities can force himself to stomach a woman for the sake of his line's continuance. Caesar—Alexander—"

"Not in this life," said William.

"That remains to be seen," Anselm said grimly.

"So. You're going to hang about and hope to see it?"

Anselm could feel the jaws of the trap closing on him. William had maneuvered him into them. And here he was, on the verge of accepting the one thing in the world that he wanted least.

"If you force this on me," Anselm said, "you may live to regret it."

"I'll be happy to do the living," said William. "Now bring me out. You know the way."

"I don't—" Anselm began.

"Then I'll die," William said.

It was tempting—so much so that Anselm crossed himself, here in the world of nightmare, and resolved to do penance when he was in the world of the living again. Even to save his own peace, he could not let a man die.

Years ago he had learned to walk the paths of dream, to find his way from the depths to the waking world. Some of that skill remained; he had made use of it in prayer, when he meditated on the nature of God. It was painful to turn it to this irretrievably secular use.

He made of this place a house of many rooms, a palace of memory. Down its familiar passages and its steps of reason and logic, he led the king. William followed in silence. What he saw, if he could see anything, Anselm neither knew nor cared.

The light drew slowly closer. Each door that opened, opened on a larger and airier room. William had begun to drag at Anselm's hand, weighing like a stone. Anselm set his teeth and trudged onward.

The outer gate rose wide and tall. Anselm had not built it so. In his memory it was a wall of glass that would melt away before the waking world. This was the gate of a stronghold, with portcullis and draw-bridge, and no doubt a moat.

Such sorrow it must be to be a king. Or was it simpler and more terrible than that? Was this what it was to be William Bastard's child?

Anselm was forgetting discipline and losing strength to distraction. He forced his mind into focus. William's weight of reluctance had slowed him almost into immobility.

One more step. One more, and they would both be safe. It was no great distance; the gate was already growing transparent, and he could almost see mortal light beyond it. And yet it was the most difficult step that had ever been. Even the thought of it was daunting.

William had turned to ice and stone. Anselm could let him go. It would have been terribly easy.

Ease had never been his virtue. He set his whole will and as much of his body as could reach into this place, and heaved William out into the light.

* * *

The king lay weak and pale, but he was awake and alive. He had not spoken in the day and night since he came out of his otherworldly fever.

Anselm was still there. People were not asking questions. The human will was an odd thing, and human understanding could alter itself to fit the world however it chose. For all Anselm knew, a shade of himself had shown itself in Bec, then departed in the direction of England. The Lady Cecilia was thorough and altogether ruthless.

He had found a place among the clerks, with decent light, ink, parchment, and freedom to do as he pleased. The nature of God that had so preoccupied him in Bec was slipping away here in Gloucester. Small weird beings kept flitting in through the window above his head and dangling from the rafters.

They were as pestilent as gnats. They fed on magic, and basked in it; the greater it was, the more of them there were to plague one's peace. Here in Britain they were larger and more solid than they were in Gaul—as if this troubled country bred them to be stronger.

He had no desire to study the nature of the fey. He was a theologian, not a magus.

As if the thought had brought him, one of the king's long-curled pages appeared beside Anselm's lectern and bowed extravagantly. "Good Father," he said, "his majesty begs that you attend him."

Anselm wondered how much begging there actually had been. He saw no purpose in refusal, although the fey were swarming about his head. The boy seemed oblivious to them, though how he could be, Anselm could not imagine. They were buzzing like bees.

He quelled the urge to swat them, tidied his lectern, pinched out his candle, and laid his pens away with care. The page shifted from foot to foot. An impatient servant of a less-than-patient master—Anselm sighed. Sweet heaven, what this world was coming to.

He was no more pleased by what he saw on his way to the king's chamber. Rain had set in before dawn; now, at midmorning, it was a drumming downpour. Courtiers who would have been out riding or hunting or practicing at arms were hanging about in the hall and the corridors. As if to mock the dimness of the day, they had put on their most extravagant plumage: silks and furs, jewels and gold.

The fashion for long curled hair had conquered this realm. So had another and even more pernicious madness. Anselm passed by it twice on his way to the king: lovers entwined in corners. One pair was kissing passionately. The other looked to be doing rather more than that. Which was not an uncommon sin among courtiers—but there was not a woman among them.

Anselm's teeth set. The sooner he answered the king's summons, the sooner he could win leave to go. Then he would shut himself up in Bec, with wards far stronger than those which Cecilia had penetrated with such contemptuous ease, and not even the Lord Pope would lure him out again.

She was there in the king's bedchamber, side by side with another black-clad woman. A tall young man stood by the bed—a guard, though ranked high. He was dressed like a nobleman of considerable wealth. That, thought Anselm, must be the notorious sheriff's son, fair Robin as rumor called him.

He was neither as effete nor as visibly dissolute as Anselm might have expected. He had the look of a fighting man, but the eyes that rested on Anselm were bright with intelligence—and something else.

They were all sorcerers here, all but the king. He was lying with his eyes shut, but Anselm could feel that he was awake. He looked like a well-preserved corpse: hair and beard unnaturally bright, skin greyish-pale. His cheeks were sunken, his eyes hollow.

Still, he was alive. He spoke clearly enough, a strong man's voice out of that image of death. "I owe you thanks. You saved my soul."

"It was my duty, majesty," Anselm said.

William's eyes opened. They were blue—not faded silver as they had been before. "You do your duty well."

"I am sworn to obedience," Anselm said.

The corner of William's mouth twitched upward. "Are you now?"

Anselm's back tightened between the shoulderblades. There was a purr in those words—a rumble of satisfaction. Anselm could feel the bars of the cage closing in, even as a pair of monks glided into the room.

They bowed low to the king and lower to Anselm. Anselm looked in a kind of despair at what they carried. Cope and miter and crozier, and on a silken napkin a ring that gleamed with gold and amethyst.

"My lord," the king said. His sister lent him her arm, shifting him and banking him with pillows until he sat nearly upright. "Duty calls. You will obey."

"I will not—" Anselm began.

The monks were large men, broad of shoulder, with muscles honed by long hours in their monastery's fields. Their grip on Anselm was light but firm. Soft hands laid the cope on Anselm's shoulders and set the miter on his head.

He clenched his fists against the crozier and the ring, but the monks were relentless. They pried at his right fist. He resisted with all his strength—though the pain of aging joints and merciless prying brought him near to tears. For a moment as he met those cold eyes, he knew they would break his hand if they must—but they settled for pressing ring and crozier to it. The metal of both burned his skin like ice.

He glared into the eyes of the two ladies. Cecilia he knew too well. The other he knew not at all—and yet he felt in her a deep familiarity.

"Another age," she said in a low sweet voice. "Another lifetime. You were always contrary, my old friend and enemy. But the gods will have their way."

"There is no god unless it is God," Anselm said grimly.

"What, are you a Saracen?" She was laughing at him. "That is their profession of faith, as near as makes no difference."

"I am a man of God," he said, "and I will not—"

"Duty binds you," William said.

"You cannot force this on me," Anselm said—struggling against his captors and doing his best to wriggle out of the cope. But even the miter refused to shift. They were bound to him.

By sorcery, he told himself. Not by his will. "Only Rome can give this honor. Only Rome has the power to—"

"I am the king," William said, very quiet—and that was alarming in that hot-tempered blustering man. "The Church in my kingdom is in my power and its offices are in my gift. I give you Canterbury. Lanfranc left it to you, more or less, and I was enormously remiss in leaving it vacant for so long."

Anselm went still, with a quiet that in its way was as ominous as William's. "Why? Why inflict this on me?"

"Because Lanfranc thought you were the best man for it," William said. "So do these ladies here, and this friend of mine. It's your fate, my lord. Live with it."

"As you are?"

William grinned. If Anselm had been a timid man or a superstitious one, he would have recoiled. The king's face, just then, looked like a death's-head wreathed in flames.

"I don't know if I'm living with it or not," William said, "and in any case, unlike a priest, I'm not necessarily bound to practice what I preach."

Anselm had known William since he was a boy. There had never been much in common between them. William was no scholar, and Anselm had little care for men of the world or men of war. Now, as he stood weighed down by the miter and cope of the primate of all England, he realized that he did not like William at all. Hate was too strong a word for it, and too un-Christian in any case. But there was no love there, and as for liking, however deep he delved inside himself, he could find none.

William laughed. Anselm had never taken him for a perceptive man, but it seemed he could read his new archbishop as easily as Anselm could read words written on a page. "Buck up, man," the king said. "You'll be good at it—and it doesn't take love to make a marriage work. Rather the contrary, your fellow priests might tell you. Love and lust are incompatible with the sacred institution and bondage between two well-propertied people."

"Bond," said Anselm with gritted teeth. "Not bondage. Bond."

"I know what I meant," William said sweetly. "You leave for Canterbury tomorrow. Your new see is waiting anxiously for you. Today, I'm sure, you'll want to do all you can to make yourself familiar with it."

"You will regret this," Anselm said. It was not a threat. It was a plain fact.

"Probably," said William with no sign of dismay. "Welcome to the Island of the Mighty, my lord. May your tenure here be long, prosperous and full of the gods' blessings."

Anselm bowed, stiff-backed. His guardian monks were still beside him, watching him with steady, implacable stares. So too were the silent ladies and the king's catamite. The lines of those stares shaped the dimensions of a cage.

There was no hope of flight. He crossed himself and laid aside, with grim effort, the anger that threatened to blind him. "Thy will be done," he said—but not to the ferociously grinning king, and certainly not to any pagan god.

✳ CHAPTER 16 ✳

Edith's knees were aching. She had been kneeling in chapel, it seemed, forever. All the novices were there, doing penance for a terrible sin: Aldith and Ethelfleda had escaped to the town, left their veils behind, and—most appalling on a fast day—indulged mightily in sweets and meat pasties. The sinners had been flogged as well as condemned to kneel on the stone floor between matins and vespers; the rest were held at fault for having failed to prevent the escape.

Edith would have been tempted to run away herself if she had not already been sinning—but no one had ever caught her. She slipped between shadows into the Otherworld, where only Sister Cecilia could follow. In fact she had been there for much of yesterday, while the sisters all thought her elsewhere being dutiful. She had come back to a great outcry and the capture of the culprits, and Mother Abbess' wrath upon their heads.

Aldith was weeping and shaking; she had always been a delicate thing. Edith was rather astonished that she had run away; she had never seemed rebellious. Ethelfleda on the other hand had been a difficulty ever since she came to the abbey the year before—dragged behind her father's horse, screaming and cursing every step of the way. She had no calling whatever to this life, and she openly hated every moment of it.

She was courting expulsion: she made no secret of that. Edith reckoned she would succeed—if not this time, then soon enough. She was stiff and erect now, far more proud than ashamed. Even Mother Abbess' rod had not been able to bow those shoulders.

It was a long day for thinking. Edith had been counting the years in days and weeks: six years within these walls, with a letter from her mother now and then, and from her father never. She was not as a young a child as she had been. Under the grey sack of the novice's habit, her body was changing: growing tall and long-legged like a yearling foal, and finding shape in places that had never had it before.

Other things were happening, too. Her magic was changing. It was rooting deeper inside her. Her body was waking as if from a winter's sleep.

If she had been a simple novice of the abbey, she would never have known what was becoming of her. But in the Otherworld, people were different. Those who were human or nearly were given to smiling when they saw her, and observing that she would be a woman soon. "Then you'll dance in the Beltane fires," they said.

Those were a thing that the Christians had forbidden with a great thunder of denunciation. They were most well versed in that. But the fires would burn in spite of them. The Old Things and the humans who knew them would dance the dances and sing the songs, and those who were minded would leap the fires and run away together into the welcoming dark, two by two.

Edith knew fairly sensibly what they did there. She had seen animals mating, and heard servants talking when she was small. She had heard them doing other things, too, up in haylofts or hidden away in corners.

Then she had been merely curious. Now, when she thought of it— even here in the stifling holiness of the chapel—her body felt strange. The place where breasts barely were was warm, and there was a most peculiar sensation between her thighs, as if she were melting from inside.

Her hands pressed together in the enforced attitude of prayer. They wanted to touch the warm places, to understand them better. It was a great struggle to pretend that she was praying.

Under cover of bowed head and lowered eyelids, she slid her glance from side to side. Everyone was kneeling in the same way, though some were swaying slightly. It was a terrible discipline to kneel all day without moving.

Mother Abbess was kneeling with them. Sister Cecilia was gone again on one of her supposed retreats. Mother Abbess had taken the fault on herself for losing two of her own to the lure of depravity. Edith could feel the anger in her, and the deep resentment of human failure—in herself as much as in others.

Edith squeezed her eyes shut and wished she could block her mind as she could her ears. She had been reading people too well lately—and she could not stop. She kept knowing to the last word how they felt, what they wanted, what they were thinking.

She wished Sister Cecilia would come back. No one here could help her. The people in the Otherworld laughed as they did at everything. *They* saw nothing to fret over. Magic was not simply in them; it was what they were. Nothing about it was strange or troubling to them.

"Not necessarily."

The part of her that was mortal substance was still kneeling in the chapel. The rest of her, all that was not needed to keep her body upright, had slipped right out of the world and come to rest in a place of leaves and green silences.

That had never happened before. She looked down rather desperately at herself, and she was there, or seemed to be: still in her fusty habit with the ragged hem and the stitches where the crooked-horned cow had caught it during a discussion as to the future of her calf.

There was a person in front of her. He was neither as tall as the fair ones who crossed the land in their ridings nor as small as the fey and lesser folk who populated both this world and the other. He looked quite human actually, if one disregarded the sharply pointed tips of his ears and the sharply pointed teeth, or the eyes as green and slit-pupiled as a cat's. His hair was as brown as oak-bark, and he was dressed in green and brown.

"Puca," she acknowledged him by name and kind.

He grinned and bowed. "At your service, lady," he said.

She was very careful not to twitch. No word spoken in this world was heedless, and service promised was service given. "Indeed?" she asked. "Have I earned it?"

"Your destiny has," said the puca, "and your magic. You're blossoming into it, lady."

"Like a nettle," she said.

He laughed. He was not mocking her, she did not think. But then he sobered. "We're not at ease with all of magic, either. Some of what's been breeding and growing in Britain is frightening. Even the great ones walk wary of it."

"The black places?" Edith asked. Even out of the body, the thought made her cold. "The places where it's all rotted and dead?"

The puca nodded. "It scares us. It's all wrong—and whatever it touches, it twists. It's caught the Hunt; they're even turning on their own, and feeding on magic."

"Won't the rites of Beltane and Midsummer help?" said Edith. "Aren't they supposed to feed the magic?"

"They do," said the puca.

"You want me to do something," Edith said.

The puca grinned. "Everyone said you had clear sight. Yes, we want something. We're not sure what, yet. Just . . . something. Because you have so much magic, and your blood is what it is."

"You want my blood," Edith said. She was very calm. "Do you think it will help?"

"Maybe not *that* kind of blood," said the puca. "We don't know. Fate swirls around you—time comes to a center in you. But we can't see how. Not yet."

Well, Edith thought. She was born to matter: king's daughter and descendant of kings. That she mattered to England came as no surprise.

"Britain," said the puca. "You matter to Britain."

"But England is—"

"England is a shadow. Britain was there before it and will be there long after it is gone."

"I was born to England," Edith said a little stiffly.

"Your mother was born to England. You are half a Gael, and all the magic is in you."

Edith set her lips together. She did not know that she was angry. He was saying things she had thought for herself. But part of her was still her mother's child, however little she loved the life her mother had meant for her. She had to defend it somehow.

"I won't destroy England," she said. "I'll never agree to that."

"We won't ask it," said the puca. Still smiling at her, he shrank and dwindled and shifted, until a sleek striped cat stood where he had been. His eyes were still the same, and his teeth not so different. He was purring loudly; his whole body shook with it.

Edith blinked. She had not expected that, even knowing he was a puca and therefore a shapeshifter. He crouched; she was prepared, somewhat, when he sprang to her shoulder.

His claws dug in, but gently. His purr was raucous. She caught herself smiling and stroking his fur. He was seducing her; but she did not mind.

She felt the tugging at her center. At first she resisted it, but it was stronger than she was. The mortal world was calling her back.

Greenwood and Otherworld and puca melted away. She was surprised, somewhat, to find her body still kneeling where she had left it, but the light had shifted considerably to the westward. The bells were ringing for vespers.

Aldith had fainted. One or two others were swaying dangerously. Edith felt a little weak herself, but her spirit had rested; she had strength left.

The nuns trod softly into the chapel, gliding in their dark habits. Their voices were ineffably sweet as they chanted the first verse of the evening's office. Edith heard it as pure sound without words.

The Otherworld was still in her. It shaped the sound, and opened it like a curtain. The grey pall that had always lain on the chapel was turned to mist and silver.

She forgot herself so far as to gape in astonishment. This, she had never expected. Something had happened to the nuns' prayer; suddenly it had stopped killing magic and started nourishing it.

It could not be her doing, surely. Sister Cecilia was nowhere to be seen. And yet there it was. The place that had stifled and horrified her for so long was suddenly—not comfortable, no. But far less wretched than it had been.

Only the abbess was the same. She seemed all the darker for the light that was around her. When her voice joined the antiphon, the clear sweet chant went dim and strange.

Edith was growing dizzy. She must not faint—which was pride, and that was a sin, but she did not care. When this was over, all the novices would be allowed to stand up. Then they could stagger together, empty and echoing and full of penitence, to their beds.

Music poured out of her, all without her willing it. It was in the air; it sang through her. It was a part of the nuns' chant, and yet it soared above it, weaving through it, lifting it up against all that Mother Abbess could do.

Edith had made a choice. She had not known she was doing it until it was done. It seemed perfectly natural and altogether inevitable.

CHAPTER 17

Mother Abbess surveyed Edith with a cold eye. Edith had not been summoned into the presence in a long while. A year? More? It had been a respite—but like all such things, it had had to end.

All the novices, even Aldith, had recovered from their day's penance. Aldith was pale and quenched and more attentive to her prayers and duties than ever, but Ethelfleda was brewing another rebellion—Edith could taste it.

At the moment Edith would do better to consider her own position. Her rebellion was years long and much more insidious than Ethelfleda could have dreamed of. She stood in the abbess' workroom with her hands folded and her eyes lowered, doing her best to seem humble and obedient.

She was stronger than she used to be. She could breathe in this room, if with difficulty. She was less tempted to panic and run. But it was still not a pleasant place to stand in.

At last Mother Abbess deigned to speak. "Sister Gunnhild tells me your studies progress well."

"Yes, Mother Abbess," Edith said without lifting her eyes. She had left the rest of the novices' lessons some years since; Sister Gunnhild was her only tutor. That was a happy enough arrangement, all things considered; they had been studying theology together of late, and were working through whatever the library had. Sister Gunnhild had even got hold of a new book on the nature of God, written by a very holy man named Anselm.

Edith said none of that. She did not think Mother Abbess would approve. Theology was the highest of all the arts and the queen of sciences, but Edith was quite certain that Mother Abbess did not want any of her nuns to think. She wanted them to pray, and to be blindly devout.

Mother Abbess let the silence stretch again. Edith continued her study of patience. Then the abbess said, "I have been taking thought for your future here. You are somewhat young for this decision, but your preceptors agree that you are well grown and unusually wise. If the lord bishop will agree to a dispensation, you may take your final vows."

Edith so far forgot herself as to raise her eyes and stare. Of all the things she would have expected, this was the last. Foolish, too; she should have known it would come. She was an oblate, an offering to the abbey. It was inevitable that she should be admitted to full orders.

She had been refraining from thinking about it—avoiding it, for a fact. She had a calling, that much was true, but the longer she lived here, the more sure she was that it was not to the veil. Certainly not here, if she was to take orders anywhere. She could not be what the abbess wanted her to be.

Someday she would have to say that. Maybe it was cowardice, but she told herself that it did not have to be today. She swallowed, because her throat was dry. "When?" she asked—trying not to choke on it. "When would that be?"

"When the lord bishop has responded to our petition," the abbess answered. "I would hope to welcome you among us on the feast of the Virgin's assumption into heaven."

Edith shivered. Beltane had come and gone—and she had watched the fires from afar, but something had kept her from coming closer. The Virgin's feast day was in August; that was hardly more than three months away.

Three months to find an escape. Or maybe, she thought with sudden hope, there would be more time. Bishops were notoriously busy men.

Maybe Sister Cecilia could help. The king was her brother. Or she could find a way to send the abbess' message astray. Or Edith could do that herself. If she could think how to begin. If —

She was panicking. Her mind was babbling, leaping from thought to thought like a bird dashing itself against the bars of a cage.

She could run away. She could vanish into the Otherworld and never come back.

She knotted her hands together in the full sleeves of the novice's habit and did her best to still her wildly flailing thoughts. There was time—not much, but not too little, either. First, she had to get out of this room without betraying herself.

"I don't think I'm ready," she said. She hoped it sounded humble and not desperate. "When I'm older—when I've studied more—"

The abbess smiled. It was a chill, bloodless smile, but it was as genuine as she was capable of. "Your humility becomes you," she said. "Trust your elders' judgment, child. You are well suited to this calling, and it would please your mother greatly to see you consecrated so soon."

Edith could easily believe that. Aloud she said, "Will Mother come? Would she be here for the ceremony?"

The abbess' smile was gone as if it had never been. "Now those," she said, "are the words of a child. We forsake worldly bindings here— among them the bonds of family. We are your family now. I am your mother in spirit. Your mother in the body will know from me that you have become Christ's bride."

Edith bowed her head. "Yes, Mother Abbess," she said, as low and yet as clear as she dared.

"Go now," the abbess said. "Meditate; pray. This is a great thing, not to be undertaken lightly. You are ready; be sure of that. But there is much to do to prepare for the final vows."

Edith knelt in respect, then rose and backed out of the room. Each step she took, she dreaded that the abbess would call her back—but she had been properly dismissed.

Once away from there, she knew a powerful temptation to slip side-wise out of the world. But something held her back. Not fear of discovery—she never had been caught—but a deep reluctance, and a voice far down that said, *Not now.*

Anyone with magic learned to listen to that voice. Sister Gunnhild was waiting for her in the library, seated at the table that had become theirs as a matter of course. No one else was there; Sister Librarian was ancient and doddery and more inclined to find a warm corner to sleep in than to play chaperone to the abbess' favorites.

There were books open on the table and parchment and ink laid out, but Sister Gunnhild was neither reading nor writing. She sat with her cheek resting on her hand, and such an expression on her face that Edith's steps slowed to a stop.

Edith had never seen her other than serene. But she had never surprised her before, either. Sister Gunnhild was always ready and waiting for her, with her face a cool mask and her self walled behind a barricade of words. Such passion as she would ever show, she kept for the books she read with Edith.

This was a different person altogether. For the first time in a long while, Edith realized that Sister Gunnhild was pretty—maybe even beautiful. Nor was she nearly as old as Edith had first thought. If she had been married or had children, she might have been wrinkled and toothless already, but in the sexless quiet of the cloister she had kept her body's youth. She was a young woman, or nearly, and in that un-guarded moment, Edith saw a part of her that she kept hidden as rigor-ously as Edith concealed her escapes out of the world.

If Edith had not had such a shock as she had just had, she might not have understood what she was seeing. But the thoughts that had been running through Edith's mind were mirrored in that face—without the possibility of escape. Sister Gunnhild had taken her final vows long since. She was bound to this life, whether she would or no.

In twenty years, this could be Edith.

No, she thought. It was quite clear and quite uncompromising. She was not going to let it happen. No matter what she did or how she did it, she was not going to take those vows.

She shuffled her feet and coughed, as if she had just come into the room. Sister Gunnhild started slightly. The mask came down; the living woman vanished. She was the holy nun again, with no thought in her but what turned toward God.

There was no solution to Edith's dilemma in the books of theology, unless one believed that they encouraged every Christian to seek the life of the soul. She found theology interesting enough, but it seemed bloodless to her. Magic was a much realer thing.

Probably that was blasphemy. But still, had not God—or the gods who were His many faces—made magic, too? And all the beings that came of it?

Sister Cecilia would have relished such questions, but she was not there to ask. Sister Gunnhild would have been appalled. None of the other nuns, and certainly none of the novices, could have understood. Edith was alone with her troubles.

Days passed in the endless round of duties and holy offices—either comforting or stupefying, depending on whether one was meant for this life or no. Edith had been tolerating it well enough. But with every day it was clearer: she could not live with this until she died. She was not made for it.

The feast of the Ascension passed, then Pentecost with its hints of an ecstatic sanctity that had scarce been dreamed of in this chill and proper place. Edith felt her soul closing in on itself. To walk out the gate and brave the world, or to walk between worlds and vanish into the Otherworld, both were beyond her. It was as if, after she had discovered in herself the capacity to scatter the abbess' web of unmagic, she had fallen prey to it herself.

Even in the cloister, rumors from the world crept in. Some of the older nuns were allowed to walk abroad, to bear messages to the bishop—

one of which must be the petition for Edith's vows—and travel to sister houses. They brought back word that the king had taken ill, and on his sickbed had compelled the most holy abbot Anselm to take the archbishopric of Canterbury.

That woke Edith slightly—enough to ask Sister Gunnhild at lessons the next day, "Is it the same one? The Anselm whose book we read in the spring?"

Sister Gunnhild nodded. They were back to Augustine again—wrestling with that angelic intellect, and losing more often than not. "The very same. He fought it, they say, so that they had to hold him down for the consecration."

"And yet he was consecrated," Edith said.

Sister Gunnhild shot her a glance. "It was a terrible thing to do to so holy a man—and thoroughly Norman. Seize, compel, overwhelm. They know nothing of subtlety."

Edith thought of Sister Cecilia, whom she reckoned deeply subtle, and wondered. But she held her tongue. "Will it hold?" she asked. "His consecration? Because it was against his will?"

Sister Gunnhild frowned. They had been studying canon law, too, sometimes neck and neck now, because Edith was very quick. "That depends on the Lord Pope," she said. "Yes, such things are supposed to be freely chosen, but as with marriage, reality is not always in accordance with the law."

"What is real?" Edith asked—then stopped, and startled herself with laughter. "Oh, no! I'll be a theologian in spite of myself."

Time was when Sister Gunnhild would have laughed, too, but Edith had not had even a smile from her since before she had that brief glimpse of the woman behind the mask. Today Sister Gunnhild simply said, "You do have a talent for it."

Clearly that was as far as that would go. Edith suppressed a sigh and turned back to the book she was supposed to be studying.

Somewhat to her surprise, Sister Gunnhild said, "It's not an easy lesson: that free will is so often subject to the whim of those in power.

That's why we take vows of obedience. We're supposed to take them willingly—but if we're ordered to take them, and disobedience is a sin, what else are we to do?"

That was as complicated in its way as anything in Augustine. Edith wondered if she dared ask the question that came immediately to mind.

Best be silent, she thought. In all these years, she had learned little of Sister Gunnhild but that she had a very clever mind and very little pride. She was willing to learn as well as teach; she always listened when Edith had questions, and she always found an answer, even if that answer was, "I don't know. Why don't we find a book that does?"

Sister Gunnhild shook her head. "I'm talking nonsense. Here—where were we?"

In Augustine, she meant. Edith could not remember, either. "Does he say anything about monastic obedience?"

"Shall we look and see?"

"That's a great deal of looking," Edith said.

"Then we'd best begin," said Sister Gunnhild.

✳ CHAPTER 18 ✳

Midsummer's night was a great festival in the Otherworld. The gates between the worlds lay open then, and the Old Things danced under the moon.

In other years, Edith had danced with them, slipping out after the Night Office and slipping back in before dawn. This year she was all confused. She wanted desperately to vanish out of the world, and yet she could not muster wits or magic to begin.

It was not the abbess who had done this to her. That struck her as she knelt in the Night Office, chanting the responses with no thought for them at all. It was her own body, growing and changing, and her magic transforming into God or the gods knew what.

Abbess Christina had sensed something—perhaps she herself hardly knew what. She sought to bind and compel it.

Edith was suddenly so restless she could barely stand it. The rest of the office was a torment. She held herself still by main force of will. When the office ended, it was all she could do not to bolt for the door.

If her gait was stiff in the slow procession to the dormitory, it seemed no one noticed. They all lay down for what remained of the night. Most of the novices were asleep even before they dropped to their cots.

Edith was painfully, irretrievably awake. The moon taunted her, sending a shaft of light down into the dormitory. Folk of air slid up and down it, chittering with glee. They loved Midsummer.

So had she, once. She could feel her heart tugging at the moon. One thought, one sidewise slip of the mind, and she was there, in the world where magic was all there was.

No—there was something more. Something . . .

She rolled onto her face, away from the moon. Her skin quivered. Her body was now hot, now cold. The rough linen of her shift was excruciating—unbearable. Then somehow that shuddering discomfort shifted and changed, melting into pleasure.

The moon was in her, filling her. The folk of air swirled and sang. Magic shivered through them. The rhythm of their dance was in Edith's blood.

Her eyes were squeezed shut, and yet she saw the green country, and the dancers in a shimmer of mist and enchantment. There were visions in those dances, dreams and prophecies, and wild fancies given flesh and substance.

And temptation—oh, by the old gods, such temptation. To see what was to be; to know what would become of her. Whether she denied it all and bowed her head and took the veil—or whether . . .

She could become one with those dances; be part of them forever. Or . . .

So many unfinished thoughts. Not only her body was a stranger to itself; her mind was slipping its moorings, too.

Dawn found her still awake and in her bed. The folk of air had followed the moon to the Otherworld, bored with her refusal to follow. It was still early; the morning office would not begin for yet a while.

She rose softly and put on her habit over her shift, and slipped out of the dormitory.

The air in the cloister was cool and smelled of rain. Clouds had chased the moon away. There would be no sunrise, only a slow swelling of light through a mist of rain.

It suited Edith's mood perfectly. She stood in the shelter of the cloister near Queen Edith's grave. Her late namesake was as angry as ever, blighting the earth beneath her tomb and the air above it.

One moment Edith was alone. The next, Sister Cecilia stood beside her—slipping out of air as Edith had so often done herself.

Edith was barely startled. She had felt something coming, but although it made her spine shiver, it was not an evil thing. Nor was Sister Cecilia, even if she was a Norman.

Sister Cecilia looked tired. Her magic was as bright and strong as ever, but the many threads of it were spread far and thin. Without thinking, Edith reached toward it and made it brighter, the threads thicker.

Cecilia drew in a sharp breath. "You are remarkable," she said.

"I was born to live in two worlds," Edith said. "I don't think Mother knows which they are."

"Nor Mother Abbess," said Cecilia. She drew a bag from the depths of her habit and held it out. "This is yours," she said.

Edith studied it for a moment. It did not look familiar. It was a plain leather bag, like one of the satchels in which she had seen clerks carry their pens and parchment.

Cecilia waited without impatience. She always had understood Edith—and not many people did.

Slowly Edith took the satchel. It was light in her hands, and yet she felt the weight of importance in it. She opened it.

There were letters inside. One or two she recognized. Those had her mother's seal. She knew what was in them, too: exhortations, instructions, commendation of Edith's life and soul to the abbess and the abbey.

But others she had never seen, though she knew the seal perfectly well. It had been broken on each letter. Each had her name written on it.

She smoothed one broken seal with the tip of her finger. "These are from Father," she said. "For me. I never saw them. I thought—"

Cecilia nodded. Of course she knew what Edith had thought. Edith had told her often enough. Her father was a king, he was busy, he sent greetings through his queen on the infrequent occasions when she wrote to their daughter.

It had hurt at first—a great deal. Then she learned, as she thought, to be a rational person, and put aside the hurt. What did a king care, after all, about a daughter, when he had sons to inherit his kingdom? She was safely stowed. He could love her from a distance, when he remembered. That was all a mere female either needed or deserved.

There were twelve letters. Two for each year Edith had been in the abbey. She almost could not bear to open them.

When she looked up, Sister Cecilia was gone—melted back into the mist. Edith slid sidewise and inabout for herself.

There was mist in the Otherworld this morning, just as there was on the other side. The place she had slipped away to was a dolmen in a grove, serene and quiet, and sheltered from the soft rain that had begun to fall. She made a light with a thought and set it to hover above her head, and with hands that shook a little, took out the letters and spread them on the mossy stone, and read them one by one.

They were simple letters, mostly. Malcolm could read and write, and he had written these in the old language, which they had loved to speak between them—though the queen did not approve of that at all. He asked after Edith; he added a bit about this or that—a foal born, a book found that he had thought she might like, a story about one of the people they both had known.

There was no book, of course, or any other gift that he spoke of. Edith was surprised that the abbess had kept the letters, and not burned them.

It had been Abbess Christina who kept them—not Sister Cecilia. Her presence was heavy on them, like thick grey dust. So was the weight of her disapproval.

They were all terribly worldly letters. There was nothing about religion in them, and no exhortations to Christian behavior. Malcolm had always left that to his wife. They were little bits of Scotland, so clear and present that Edith could smell the heather.

She had to stop halfway and choke down the tears of homesickness. When her eyes were clear of tears again, she read the rest one after the other. They were all much the same—until the last one.

That had come in—Edith read it three times to be sure—the day before the abbess called on her to take her final vows. There it was in his sharply angular hand, smudged here and there and marked with hatchings and corrections. He was not a frequent writer or a practiced one, but in his way he was fluent.

My heart, he wrote, *while your letters to us both have pleased your mother and me, this is for you and you alone, and I ask you to answer me only. I know what your mother wants for you. It's a high and holy thing, and no doubt a very good one, but even those stiff Latin exercises you call letters are telling me you're not made for that life. I would be happy if you were, never mistake that, but if I'm guessing rightly, I have an alternative to propose.*

You're nearly grown now, daughter, or so they tell me. They say you have beauty—you take after your mother there, God be thanked, and not your old wreck of a father. Even in the cloister I'm sure you've learned enough of the world to know what a daughter can be to her family, if she and her family are so minded.

I'm coming down to England, daughter, before the summer's out. Red William's been sick and nearly died, and he's having a fit of setting his house in order. Since we have a certain disagreement as to borders in the north, I'll be on my way to settle things with him. I'll come by your abbey afterwards, and it's possible I'll have a gift for you—one you might be pleased to take.

That was all there was, except for his name: *Malcolm King of Scots.* Edith smoothed the parchment over and over, until the ink began to fade from the page and darken her fingers.

Her father did not want her to be a nun. He was not forcing her to be a bride of Christ. His ambitions were far more secular. He was going to bring her a husband—that was what he promised.

Her mother must know of this by now, since the abbess had intercepted the letter. Clearly Edith was not to know. She would be bound and sworn before her father came, snatched away out of his reach.

Did she want a husband? Did she want anything but to be free to work her magic?

That, she could not answer. Maybe she was too young. Though princesses married in infancy often enough, and no one ever asked them what they thought of it.

She had almost rubbed the words from the page. She folded the parchment carefully and laid it with the rest—years' worth of damnation for Abbess Christina, if God chose to be just.

Edith found she could not be as angry as she should. Her mother and her aunt only thought they were doing what was best for England. Edith in the cloister, her wings clipped and her magic bound, was worth more to them than Edith in the world, married and making sons for some lord or prince.

What was Edith worth to herself? That was what she had to decide. In the way of the world, she was not really her own person. She belonged to her family, who could dispose of her as they would.

But how they would dispose of her, neither her father nor her mother could agree. That was a choice she could make, if she had the strength. But which? If she wanted and was ready for neither, how could she choose?

Beyond the shelter of the dolmen, the mist was thinning. Light glimmered through it. As she sat staring, the veils of the world grew transparent. She looked down as if from a lofty height on a steep promontory, a high domed rock above a level country and a river. On the rock was a castle. In the castle, as she spiraled down like a bird on the wing, was a great crowd of people.

Most of them were men—knights and men-at-arms. The few women did not look like ladies, and they certainly were not nuns.

In the castle's hall, a man sat on a high seat. He was not a child, but neither was he very old. He wore a cotte of crimson silk; under it, visible at throat and wrists, was the grey gleam of mail. His hair was ruddy brown, his face strong-boned but fine, and his eyes were as grey as rain, cool and distant as they rested on the people who drank and feasted and caroused in front of him.

He was not a king, but he was no commoner, either. He had magic. A great gleaming tide of it, brilliant and beautiful.

She had seen him before. Somewhere—in a place deep down in memory—he was there. But she could not grasp it. It almost seemed that it willfully eluded her.

The mist quivered. The hall shifted, brightened, grew. The man in the high seat shrank in height and breadth and much brightened in hair and beard: fair-haired, red-bearded, blue-eyed. The other man was earth and water and the powers of air. This one was fire: hot, hasty, change-able, and inescapably powerful.

That one she knew. This was the Norman king, the one they called Red William. He had no magic, but his eyes could see between the worlds. He did not like that: she saw how he tried not to look when folk of air danced among the rafters of his hall.

The mist blurred again; again she saw a hall, smaller than the first two, and this time there were two men: grey and old, black-haired and not so old. Father and son, she thought. They had the same face, hawk-nosed and wild. They were not as magical as the brown man, but there was power in them, and the ferocity of birds of prey.

And then came the last vision, the last hall, the only one she knew for herself: her father's dun on Eidyn's mountain, and her father in it. She had never thought of him as old, but it struck her with a small shock that he was. His hair was still mostly dark, but his beard had gone white.

She shut her eyes. When she opened them again, the world was closed in with mist and rain, and the visions were gone. What they meant, she could not be sure. She could not be marrying all of them, and certainly not her father. But fate had shown them to her. Somehow their destinies were twined with hers.

Time would tell. That was a favorite saying of her father's. Malcolm was an old fox and a sly one. He knew the uses of patience.

She could learn them. She was young, but she was a woman, and women needed patience.

She was almost at peace, thinking that. She still did not know what she was supposed to do, but she would. In time. When she was ready.

✳ CHAPTER 19 ✳

Fornicators! Sodomites!"

William had come to Gloucester Cathedral to hear Mass on this bright Sunday after Midsummer, as he had been doing more or less devotedly since his illness in the spring. He told himself it was only prudent. Cold iron was no use against what stalked him—but he still had some hope of good Norman Christianity.

He liked a good sermon, too: a little brimstone was good for the soul. A rousing chorus of damned souls, an angry God, a voice duly thundering from the pulpit, was almost as entertaining as a troupe of mountebanks.

This priest of Gloucester, speaking in the bishop's stead, was in splendid form. But William had not expected to be taking the brunt of it.

Oh, it was veiled in the Bible and a pack of parables, but the man's eyes were on William and his escort, and when his long white finger stabbed the air, it stabbed toward the king. "Lost in lust," he intoned in a melodic snarl, "wrapped in one another's arms, bearded kiss to bristling bearded kiss—bodies locked that never were meant to fit together so—"

William's teeth gritted so hard they ached. One or two of his squires blushed furiously. The rest of them either looked bored or slumped against one another—body to body as the priest so vividly described them—snoring unabashedly.

If the king walked out on the sermon, there would be a scandal. He did his best to shut his ears to it—not easy considering the strength of the priest's voice. He should have been a herald: that clarion call would have carried across a battlefield.

"Rise up!" the priest cried. "Rise up against the children of Sodom! Cleanse the earth of their sin! In God's name, in the name of holy purity, let their foulness be scoured away!"

"It seems he's put a great deal of thought into it," Robin observed. Good if quiet pagan that he was, he had been elsewhere during Mass, but William had regaled him with the sermon's more telling points.

"I'd say there was more than thought in it, myself," William said. "There's a man who's made a thorough and no doubt intimate study of his subject."

William was mostly dressed and pacing the floor of his bedchamber, still incensed after a full day of chewing it over, but Robin was in bed and at ease. He stretched out naked on the coverlet and yawned. "Pity you couldn't have shown him for what he is."

"One of us?" William spat. "I'd disown him."

Robin yawned again and stretched. William stopped short. That was a very fine body, lying there—no longer a boy's, but lean still and beautifully drawn, and as supple as an eel.

William was not in the mood to be seduced. He was too bloody angry. "They have no damned right to preach against me. I'm the king— and I am what God made me."

"Priests have never been noted for practical logic," Robin said, "particularly when it comes to matters of the flesh."

"I'll give them sin," William said. "I'll sell them to the Saracens. They think they know what debauchery is? There's a lifelong study for them."

"Now there's a dream," Robin said. He propped himself on his elbow. He was more awake than William had thought, and more serious, too. "You know, you should be thinking. It's not only the Church that needs a king to perform certain duties. The kingdom needs it, too.

King's blood is more than what he sheds when he bleeds. He's bound to pass it on—to get an heir."

"I have an heir," William said. "I have two. There's Robert—who I admit is a sluggard, but he has the blood—and Henry, who's a sorcerer, too. Henry's been populating the earth with bastards. Robert's been a bit less diligent, but there's no doubt he's a man for women. There's more than enough of the Conqueror's blood to keep old Britain happy."

"You are the king," Robin said. "King's blood is the land's strength."

"It's got as much of that as it's going to get," William said. He hoped he sounded grim rather than desperate.

"You should think," said Robin. "There's more to the rule of a kingdom than the king. A queen is its strength, too. Your mother stood beside your father over the land of Britain. When she died, the land suffered. It's still suffering."

"That's no fault of mine," said William. "It's not mine to mend."

"You know better than that," Robin said.

William scowled at him. "What would I do with a queen?"

"Share the rule with her. Get sons on her."

William shook his head. "No. Oh, no. I'm not sharing my power. And I certainly am not—"

"Think," said Robin. He kept saying that. William was going to hit him the next time he said it. "A queen who is also an enchantress, who is prepared to do her duty, who can stand beside you and stare down the priests and the scandalmongers—"

"Well," said William, "if that's all I need, I'll call on my sister. I don't need to marry her, do I? Wasn't there an old kingdom that had brother and sister sharing the throne?"

"No doubt," said Robin, "somewhere. But the Church would still thunder against you—maybe worse, if it can add incest to the count of your sins."

William hissed through his teeth. "God! Is there no end to the prurience of priests?"

"I would say not," said Robin. "Since they can't have it, they dream endlessly of it, and with great invention, too."

"I'm not going to take a queen," William said.

"You may have to," said Robin.

"Why? Do you have one in mind?"

If William had hoped to catch Robin off guard, he was disappointed. "In fact," Robin said, "there is one. Would you like to meet her?"

"Who is she?"

Robin smiled. Then he shook his head. "No, no. You're not interested."

"You're teasing me," William said, and not pleasantly, either. "Tell me who she is."

"She's in a convent at the moment," Robin said. "Her lineage is doubly royal. She goes both to Alfred and an old royal line of Britain. She has great magic."

"Her name," William said with the rumble of a growl. "Tell me."

"Edith," said Robin. "Her name is Edith."

A bark of laughter escaped William. "What! Old Edward's queen? She's years dead."

"Hardly," Robin said. "That Edith was no descendant of Alfred. This one comes from the old blood."

William's eyes narrowed. People said he had more brawn than brain, and thinking was not his greatest strength. But he was not quite an idiot, either. "What, old Malcolm's daughter? My brother Robert's goddaughter? She must be all of seven years old."

"Twelve," said Robin, "and growing fast."

"No," William said flatly. "I don't rob cradles. I don't lust after little boys, and I won't take a girlchild from her mother's tit."

"Meet her first," said Robin, "before you refuse altogether. She has magic to burn—and wit and skill to go with it. Your sister has been tutoring her since she was a child. She's been raised to stand beside kings."

"One of whom will not be me," William said.

"Will you at least look at her? For me?"

William rounded on Robin. "That was a low blow."

"All's fair," said Robin lightly, "in love and politics."

William raised his hand to box the boy's ears, but lowered it before he began. Robin's smile never wavered. "You'd risk losing me to a woman? You'd do that?"

"There's no risk," Robin said.

"Then what of her? Is it fair to any woman to bind her to a man like me?"

"This is a queen," said Robin. "She knows her duty."

"Duty is a cold thing," William said.

"If it saves your kingdom," said Robin, "and saves you, then it's worth the price."

"Is it?"

"Look at her and see."

William started to shake his head, but something made him stop. "You could find yourself regretting this."

"I'll take my chances," Robin said. He opened his arms.

William should have turned his back on them. It would have served the conniving fool right. But he had no sense when it came to Robin FitzHaimo. He sighed, he growled, but he let those arms draw him—however briefly—away from the world and its troubles.

❈ CHAPTER 20 ❈

Edith almost failed to come back from the Otherworld once she had read all her father's letters. She left them there, safe in a place she knew, with words of guarding on them and folk of air to watch over them. It took all the will she had to pass through the worlds again, and go back to the cloister that had been set to trap her.

Knowledge is power. Her father had taught her that. So had Sister Cecilia. The abbess did not know what Edith knew. Nor would she, if Edith could help it.

Always since she first began, she had taken great care to reappear in hidden places: a dark corner of the cloister, a forsaken bit of garden, the far end of the orchard. On that day of revelation and confusion, she was not as careful as she should have been. She sent no scouts ahead, and did not look first to see where she was going.

She fell out of air onto the paving-stones of the cloister, far enough and hard enough to drop her bruisingly to her knees. The cloister, mercifully, was deserted—until she heard the gasp of breath behind her.

She scrambled up and spun. A nun in black had been sitting on a bench in that distant corner. Her face at first was a pale blur; then Edith's sight cleared enough for recognition.

Sister Gunnhild stared at her as if she had done exactly what she had: appeared quite suddenly out of thin air.

Edith's whole mind and body went still. A babble of excuses ran through her head, but none of them reached her tongue. Some of the nuns might have chosen to believe whatever story Edith could think of to tell. But not Sister Gunnhild. Her sight was too clear and her mind too logical.

Even so, Edith had to do something. "Sister—" she began.

Sister Gunnhild closed her eyes. "You are not here," she said. "You were never here. I saw nothing and heard nothing."

Edith opened her mouth, but closed it again. Sister Gunnhild's fingers were in her ears. She was setting Edith free—though with what perturbation of mind, Edith could too easily imagine.

She took the gift. She fled away down the cloister.

Edith kept her head down and her magic to herself for the rest of that day. Every time someone coughed, she jumped like a cat. But no summons came from the abbess.

The next day after morning office, she had her daily hour with Sister Gunnhild. She almost refused to go—but she still had not been ordered into the abbess' presence. If there was a trap waiting for her, then so be it. And if there was not . . .

Sister Gunnhild was sitting in the library as always, walled in books. Her face was no more or less easy to read than it ever was. She said nothing of what she had seen, and showed no sign of having remembered it.

Edith bit her tongue and sat where she always sat. It was hard to focus on the page in front of her, but somehow she managed.

And that was how it was. No summons from the abbess. No word from Sister Gunnhild. After a week she began to believe that she was safe.

Then the summons came.

That had been a strange day. When Edith went for her usual lesson, Sister Gunnhild was not there. Sister Librarian did not know where she was. Edith spent the hour reading, despite the temptation to slip away elsewhere.

After her hour in the library, she went to the kitchens for her morning duties. It was never quiet there; not only the nuns and novices and
the abbey servants had to be fed, but there were the pensioners and the
not infrequent guests as well. But this morning the kitchens were more
than usually frantic.

Edith caught one of the undercooks as she flew past. "What—"

The girl spun them both full around. "The king! The king's coming
here!"

For a wild instant Edith thought she meant Malcolm of Scots.

But this was England. England's king was William—Red William,
whom Edith had seen in a vision in the Otherworld.

"What does he want with us?" she asked.

The undercook shrugged free. "Does it matter?" she flung over her
shoulder.

Probably not, Edith thought. Except that nothing a king did
lacked consequence. For him to come here to this house of holy
women, full of Saxons who had been raised in secret rebellion against
all that was Norman—it was not a casual visit. There was no way it
could be.

She rolled up her sleeves and set to work kneading bread. She always
had loved that part of her duties: digging deep into the yielding dough,
rolling and folding it, beating it into submission. There was more of it
than usual today: enough for the royal party, and made with the finest
flour, too, and not the coarse brown meal that the nuns were given.

She was deep in it, well and truly floured, when Sister Gunnhild
came to fetch her. She brought the summons Edith had been dreading
for a week and more: "Mother Abbess would see you."

There was nothing about her that warned of betrayal. Edith searched
hard for it, too; but Sister Gunnhild was the same as she had always
been. She was bringing a message, no more.

Edith set herself in such order as she could, brushed off as much
flour as she might, and followed Sister Gunnhild. She was somewhat
surprised not to be taken to the abbess' study. Instead they went where

the novices were not to go, out through the cloister toward the guest-houses.

There was a great crowd there of men and horses, hawks and hounds and all the appurtenances of a hunting party. Most of them had found places to settle and were dicing or talking or tending the animals. They all had eyes that tended to wander, and not many of them seemed to care that the women they stared at wore nuns' habits.

They had a distinctly pagan air, though they were no worse than Edith's father's men had been prone to be. Men were men, unless they were clergy—and even there, Edith had heard enough to know that not every priest or monk was devoted to his vows.

Edith knew better than to meet those bold stares, but she could see quite well sidelong; she had had enough practice in it. Normans, she already knew, were human enough when they were not raping and pillaging. They were big men in the main, red or brown or fair; not many of them were small or dark. Their ancestors had been Vikings, ruthless raiders from the north. Normans—Norsemen. She could see it in them, a hint of wildness beneath the silk and linen and the finely woven mail.

As many as they had seemed to be, there were no more than two dozen altogether. That was a small escort for a king. Edith wondered if the rest were in the town, or if this William really had come to the abbey with hardly more attendance than a minor baron.

The king was in the hall where noble guests were used to dine. It was open now to what air there was on this breathless summer day, the trestles laid away and the benches lined against the walls. There were chairs by the hearth, which was clean and swept of ashes, but no one was sitting in them.

In her vision, Edith had seen this man as a creature of fire. Certainly he was as restless as that.

Even in Abbess Christina's presence, clouds of the folk of air surrounded him. They shrank and shuddered near the abbess, but they could not stay away from the king.

And yet he had no magic. That was perfectly clear. It was because he was the king, and because he was old William's son, and Mathilda's.

William was very much out of place here in this stronghold of holy women. Women were not to his taste at all, Edith thought. She was not sure what she meant by that—it came into her head, whole and complete. William and women were not comfortable together.

The abbess was not making anything easier for him. She had to suffer his presence—however much she hated him—because he was the king. She would give him all that duty demanded, and be sure he knew why she did it.

William prowled the room. Half a dozen of his men stood by: guards, most of them. One was brimming over with magic, carefully damped now and walled against the abbess.

That one watched Edith from the moment she passed the door. She could feel that scrutiny like the heat of a fire on her skin. She raised wards against it—quite like those that he had raised against the abbess.

His eyebrows had gone up. Bemusement? Respect? Both, she thought.

He was like her: half of the old blood. The rest of him had to be Norman. He was dressed like one, and carried himself like one, too. No one else was that arrogant.

Except, of course, for descendants of Saxon kings.

Sister Gunnhild bowed in front of the abbess. So did Edith. The king was across the room just then, scowling at the tapestry that hung on the far wall. One of the pensioners had brought it as part of her offering to the abbey. It was meant to depict the Last Supper, but the ladies who embroidered it had transformed the Lord Christ into a Saxon king and his apostles into earls and thanes, and behind them were scenes of hawking and hunting and even a battle against Vikings in longships.

"So Harold's still king here," William said.

Edith understood Norman. She even spoke it. Her father had made sure of that, as little as her mother had approved of it.

It had been a long while since she needed it, but it came back easily enough. She knew what William was saying. She could even answer, "That's the Lord Christ, my lord."

William turned. Behind the scowl his face was not bad to look at.

He seemed to find her even less to his liking than the tapestry. "That's Harold, fighting Normans."

She shook her head. "No, really. It's the Last Supper. See. There's the chalice. And twelve Apostles."

His scowl sharpened to a glare, then drained away. For the first time he seemed to see her. "You're Malcolm's daughter," he said.

"Yes," said Edith.

"You can go now, Mother," William said to the abbess. And to Sister Gunnhild: "You, too."

"That would not be proper," Mother Abbess said, "lord king."

"She'll stay," William said, tilting his head at Sister Gunnhild. "You, Mother, have many duties crowding on you, I'm sure. I won't take any more of your time."

Edith had been thinking that this king had no grace. Now it was clear he did—when it suited him to use it.

Abbess Christina knew herself dismissed. Edith waited for her to fight it, but for whatever reason, she chose not to. She nodded coldly to the king, and said to Sister Gunnhild, "Remember what we are."

Sister Gunnhild bowed. Her face was expressionless within the veil. Edith thought she seemed a little pale—but maybe that was only the way the light struck her, with her fair skin that looked so ill in black.

Mother Abbess took her leave with stiff dignity. William watched her go. He did not like her at all, Edith thought.

When she was well gone, the king turned back to Edith. Much of his bad temper had vanished, along with most of the shadow that had lain on the hall. He looked her up and down. "So you're my brother's god-child. You've grown up well."

"Thank you, sire," Edith said. "How is my godfather? Is he well?"

"He was the last time I saw him," William said. "I'll remember you to him when we meet again."

"That's kind of you," she said.

There was a silence. Edith could not find anything to say, and neither, it seemed, could William.

She took the time to consider whether she liked him. She did not think she did. Whether she hated him . . . no. Nothing as strong as that. Aside from a mutual dislike of the abbess, they had nothing in common. They were quite literally worlds apart—she with her magic and her learning, he with whatever he did without either. Hunt, she supposed. Fight. Preside over banquets.

When William spoke, he startled her. She had been content with the silence. "There are those," he said, "who think I should be making a royal match, and royal sons. What do you think of that?"

"I think you don't want that at all," she said.

The words had come out on their own. If she had had anything to do with it, they would have stayed buried where they belonged.

His glare was back, more sulfurous than before. "What makes you say that?"

"It's true," she said.

"Does it matter what I want?"

He was amazingly angry, and yet she was not afraid. This man was no danger to her. "You're the king," she said. "No one can make you do anything unless you allow it."

"Duty can," he said. "The Church may."

"It can try," she said.

"Do *you* want to marry?" he demanded.

She blinked. That was so close to what she had been thinking that she had to wonder . . .

Her father might have considered such a match, but he would have made it clearer that that was what he meant.

"I don't know," she said.

"Would you want to marry me?"

"No." That was altogether unpremeditated and completely honest. "We're not meant for one another."

"There are those who say we are. Your bloodlines, mine—we match like blooded horses."

"You can't just breed blood to blood," Edith said. "Any breeder knows that. You have to consider the animals, too. We wouldn't match well. We'd hate each other—and nothing would come of it."

"Even the worst marriage can produce sons," William said.

"This one wouldn't." Edith met his bright blue stare. "I do want to marry. I think I'm meant to. But you, no. God made you as you are. When you see my father, will you tell him something for me? Tell him I'm to be bound with final vows on the feast of the Virgin."

William might be no scholar, but his wits were quick enough. He followed all of that, and barely blinked at it. "I'll make sure he knows," he said. His eyes narrowed. Then, astonishingly, he smiled. "I see why they made me come here. You're not for me, no—and that's a pity, taking all in all. You'll make someone a remarkable queen."

"I would hope so," Edith said, "unless God gets me first."

"Then we'll hope He doesn't," William said.

CHAPTER 21

"W as that a disaster?" William asked. They were back in Gloucester, and it was late: well past midnight. But William could not find it in himself to fall asleep.

Robin arched a brow at him. "Does it feel like a disaster?"

"No," said William. Then, less quickly, "No. It feels as if something happened, something important—but I don't know what."

"You'll find out soon enough," Robin said.

"That's the trouble with this world," muttered William. "Too damned much of it is waiting and watching and trying to see what will happen next."

"I rather think that's part of the pleasure," Robin said sleepily.

"You would." William flung himself on the bed. Robin was already asleep, gone far away from William and his fretting and his memory of the clear-eyed child with the face that would, in time, be beautiful.

She reminded him of his sister Cecilia. Even if women had been to his taste, he would have found her too witchy for him. But that she could and indeed would be a queen, he had no doubt. A king would find her someday, and set her as high as she deserved to be.

Which of course did nothing to solve his problem—but then nothing could. That was the lesson he had learned in Wilton abbey. She had said it. He was what he was. There was no changing it.

* * *

The king's visit left a strange scent in the abbey's air—as if he had flung open the doors on something new and as yet unfathomed. Edith's mind was clearer. She had come to a decision.

Once William was gone, she had to face the abbess. She had expected that, and rather oddly, she did not dread it. For the first time since she read her father's letters, she was calm inside herself.

Sister Gunnhild was interrogated first. Edith had to stand in the hallway. The time for dinner came and went; the bread she had worked so hard to make was fed to everyone else while she went hungry.

It was a sacrifice. Perhaps spitefully, she chose not to offer it to God. She gave it to Britain instead, to the earth beneath her and the air she breathed, and the folk of air who shrank from coming so close to the nullity that was the abbess' presence.

Maybe it was spite, but once she had done it, she knew it had been the right thing to do. She leaned against the wall, and the stones held her in a cool embrace. It was like a long draught of clean water, or a deep night's sleep.

When Sister Gunnhild came out of the abbess' study, Edith was almost sorry to leave the place of rest she had found in herself. She was ready, she thought, to face whatever the abbess had in store for her.

Sister Gunnhild's face gave her nothing to hold to: no warning and no reassurance. The walls were high and the gates barred.

Edith took a deep breath and mustered what defenses she had, and stepped through the door.

She almost lost her resolve when she saw the abbess' face. The abbess was not smiling, but there was an air about her that Edith had never seen before. It was approval; gratification. "Come," she said as Edith hesitated. "Sit."

She had never said that before, either. Edith had not even known there was a chair in the corner, or that the privileged might sit in it.

She sat very carefully, knees together, hands folded in her lap.

Abbess Christina regarded her with a notable lack of coldness. Edith would never have called it warmth, but it was warmer than anything she had shown before.

"Sister Gunnhild tells me," the abbess said, "that you dealt most adeptly with the king."

Edith kept her eyes on her interlaced fingers. That had always been the safest course during these audiences, and she saw no reason to change now. "Sister Gunnhild is very kind," she said.

"Is it not the truth?" said the abbess. "He demanded that you be his queen. You rightly and properly refused him."

That was not all that had gone on, but Edith was hardly inclined to say so. "Yes, Mother Abbess," she said. "I told him I am to take full vows. He accepted that."

"Did he indeed?" said the abbess.

Edith shot a glance at her. She was much more gratified than Edith might have expected—in fact she sounded almost triumphant. "Was that a mistake?" Edith asked. "Should I have said something else?"

"No," said the abbess. "Oh, no. That was excellently done."

"Then what—"

"Child," said the abbess with a return of her old, grim manner, "you have done well. That is all you need to know."

"Yes, Mother Abbess," Edith said as meekly as she could force herself to be.

"Good, then," said the abbess. "Go; continue your studies. Be assiduous in your devotions. It will all be done soon enough, and you will rejoice to be the bride of Christ."

Edith bit her tongue until the pain made her eyes water. She rose and genuflected, and kissed the ring that was presented for that purpose. The stone was cold under her lips, with an odd tingle, as if some spell lay on it.

Whatever it was, it could not pass her wards. She was safe—though from what, she was not exactly sure.

The next morning, when Edith went to her lessons, she found only a single book on the table in the library, and no Sister Gunnhild.

The book was one she had often read from before: a collection of bits from old philosophers. There was a scrap of parchment in it, and on the parchment a handful of words in Greek: *In the orchard, by the oldest tree.*

It looked like a fragment of poetry, and there was no doubt that was what it was meant to seem. Edith raised her brows at it. Notes and secrets were not like Sister Gunnhild at all. But who else in the abbey could either read or write Greek, except Edith?

It could be a trap. If it was, Edith had wards, and the folk of air were flocking thick today. She tucked the scrap of parchment into her sleeve, closed the book neatly and left it exactly where she had found it and made her casual and unconcerned way out of the library and the cloister and through the orchard.

The day was glorious: warm, bright, sweet-scented. The grass was almost as green as that of the Otherworld; the sun was nearly as splendid. Apples and pears were swelling on the boughs. Some had begun already to blush with ripeness.

Such a day reminded Edith more vividly than ever that the life of the cloister was remote and cold, and her body was young and beginning, itself, to ripen. She was powerfully tempted to cast off the heavy bindings of her habit, but she was not that far gone—yet. She did slip out of her sandals and dangle them from a finger, and if the wind chose to pluck the veil from her hair, well then, she could catch and carry it, but she did not have to put it back on—not yet.

The sun was warm on her uncovered head, the wind playful, plucking at the tight braid of her hair, teasing out random curls. She almost hated to go on, but the sooner it was done, the better.

Sister Gunnhild was waiting deep in the orchard, near the wall that divided it from the open downs. The apple tree that grew there had been planted when Rome ruled in Britain, or so the story went. Edith sometimes wondered if it was older even than that. Its roots were sunk deep, and it drank the power of this earth—drawing up strength from the great stone circle that was not so very far away at all.

Edith seldom thought directly of the circle, the Giants' Dance as people called it in the Otherworld. It was there, drawing in power and radiating it out, but it had never seemed to have much to do with her.

For some reason, today it was strong in her awareness. Things were stirring. The king had come here, and brought with him more maybe than he knew.

While Edith's awareness leaped suddenly wide, Sister Gunnhild rose from where she had been sitting. *Her* veil was still in place, but her feet were bare, too. Her face was guarded as always. Still, Edith could feel gates opening under it, and walls crumbling that had stood for years, maybe all her life.

When she spoke, the words came tumbling out—strange, because her tone was still so composed. "Ever since you walked out of air, I've been gathering courage to ask you something."

"Ever since I—" Edith began.

"Please," Sister Gunnhild said. "I know you have no reason to trust me. I was set over you to be your watchdog, to shape your mind and bind your spirit. I was supposed to empty you of everything that was not perfectly Saxon."

"You never even tried," Edith said. "We were learning philosophy, theology, Greek, but not—"

"Not what I was supposed to teach you," Sister Gunnhild said. "I know. I lied to the abbess. For years I told her you were learning prayers as she instructed, and histories of your ancestors, and invocations of their memory. I let her believe that you were perfectly prepared to be what she wished you to be. There are great sins on my soul, and I will atone for them."

"Why?"

Sister Gunnhild's shoulders tightened, then eased. She drew a long sigh. "Because I loathe this life. Because I was never made to live in walls, constrained in a cage. Because I saw from the beginning what the queen your namesake would have made of this isle, and what the abbess still labors to make it. I have no love for Normans, but I believe God has given them this kingdom for His own good reasons. I also believe the abbess has let her hate for them overcome her acceptance of God's will—and I will not be a part of it."

Edith did not know what to say. Some of it was not so surprising, once she thought about it, but the rest had taken her off guard. It had been a while since she felt too young for anything. Just now, she was making up for it.

"Can you help me?" Sister Gunnhild asked. "Can you send me away? It doesn't matter where. Wherever you go, I'd far rather be there than here."

"Even if it costs you your soul?"

Sister Gunnhild never even flinched. "If I stay in these chains, my soul will die."

Since that was how Edith felt, she could hardly argue with it. But she said, "How do you know I go anywhere?"

"For years, I've watched you," Sister Gunnhild said. "You're never at recreation with the others. You're always gone—vanished. I've seen you slip through air as through a curtain. Wherever you go, it must be better than here."

"It is," Edith said, "but not for a long time. Not for mortals. We can't eat or drink there, or we'll be bound forever."

"That," said Sister Gunnhild, "I could well bear."

"I can't do it," Edith said. It was hard, because Sister Gunnhild was so desperate, but Edith could never have forgiven herself if she had given way. "I am sorry, really I am. But I hate it here, too—and I haven't vanished forever. There's no place there for a mortal soul."

Sister Gunnhild lowered her eyes. Edith knew that gesture all too well. She refused to waver because of it, but it did make her heart twinge.

"Please," said Edith. "Don't do something you can't get out of."

"Such as take vows in this abbey?" Sister Gunnhild did not sound as bitter as she might, all things considered—but Edith was little comforted. It was even less comfort that she sighed and said, "I'm desperate, I suppose. And cowardly. I could run away and trust to God to keep me safe in the world. But would God do that? I'm supposed to be His bride. How angry will He be when I repudiate Him?"

"I'm not sure God minds," Edith said.

"That's heresy," said Sister Gunnhild, but she sounded more bemused than appalled.

"Heresy is what old men in Rome say it is," Edith said. "What do they know of women in Britain?"

Sister Gunnhild stared. Suddenly she laughed. Edith had never heard her laugh before. It was a remarkable sound, light and young. "Sweet saints! What would the abbess say to that?"

"Are you going to tell her?"

Sister Gunnhild shook her head. "Not a word. Did you think I would?"

"No," said Edith. "We have a bargain, I think."

"I believe we must," Sister Gunnhild said. "I hope you can escape before the vows bind you. I wouldn't wish my fate on anyone."

"I never knew," said Edith. "I'm sorry for that."

"Don't be. It means I've played my part well—and I'm still safe. The abbess still believes me to be her ally."

"Were you ever?" Edith asked.

"I wanted to live like a real woman," Sister Gunnhild said. "I wanted a husband. Children. A household to manage and a life to live. Not this living death."

Edith found that her fists were clenched. She knew better than to ask why Sister Gunnhild had not refused to take vows. She was the daughter of a conquered king—enemy by blood and breeding. What could she hope for in the world but dishonor or worse?

Or so the abbess would have told her. The truth would have been less simple. Maybe she could have had the life she wanted. Now . . .

"I can't help you," Edith said. "I don't even know that I can help myself. But if I can, I will."

Sister Gunnhild spread her hands. "You have a generous heart. Don't fret for me. I've burdened you with more than you need to carry. If you can get out of here, by all means do. Don't hobble yourself with trying to save me."

"I will try," Edith said. "I promise you that."

CHAPTER 22

The world was heavy on Edith's shoulders. All the deceptions, the games she had to play, the preparation for vows that she hoped—even prayed—she would never be forced to take, weighed her down until she could hardly bear it. Her only hope was the message she had asked the Norman king to give her father—and there was no surety that he would do any such thing.

She began to think that she should slip over the wall and find her way to her father—wherever he was. Or if the wall was guarded, she might venture the Otherworld. It was not so perilous if one merely passed through it on one's way between mortal place and mortal place. Maybe Sister Cecilia could help her. Or maybe . . .

But Sister Cecilia was nowhere to be found. No one knew where she was. Sister Gunnhild had returned to her veiled and shrouded self, and the instruction that both she and Edith knew was, in its way, a lie. The rest of the nuns and novices went on as always.

A fortnight before the feast of the Virgin, while Edith was still wavering over what to do, Ethelfleda vanished. This time she was alone, and this time she made good her escape.

Edith envied her bitterly—both for her cleverness and for her courage. But more than that, Edith was furious. Any hope she might have had of mortal escape was gone, now that Ethelfleda had so effectively tested the abbey's defenses. The nuns and novices were under strict discipline, and all the doors and windows were watched.

The only way out, such as it was, was through the Otherworld—and even that would not be easy. None of the novices was allowed to go off alone. They were to do everything in pairs, and there was a nun watching over them always—even in the garderobe.

After a week, Edith was ready to go mad. Another week and she would be bound. She was going to have to resort to the Otherworld, and do it in front of her watchers—there was no other way that she could see.

Each morning she woke and told herself that today she would do it. Each night she went to her bed as desperate as ever. The folk of air had fled; she could not ask them if they had seen her father in England, or if they knew how far away he was. They were all gone, wise creatures, escaping the strangling clouds of unmagic that were swallowing more of the abbey with every day that passed.

Six days until her binding. Then five. That was the day when she discovered that the Otherworld was out of her reach. The magic had drained out of the abbey. When she tried to part the veils, there was nothing there.

She had waited too long. Even the magic that was in her was starting to fade. She felt like a cracked jar with water seeping slowly out of it— and she had not even noticed until she was all but empty. It had been going on . . . how long? Years?

It was a spell in its way, a sapping of will and sense until there was nothing left but to do what she was forced to do. Sister Gunnhild had succumbed before her. Others would after her—unless by some miracle this destruction of magic could be stopped.

No wonder Sister Cecilia had fled. This must have been deadly for her; and she needed all her power to be a Guardian of Britain.

Four days. Edith could barely bring herself to get out of bed in the rainy dark before dawn, to wash her face and hands in the basin and pull on her habit and shuffle to chapel with the rest. They were all subdued this morning. Even their prayers were dulled, and their plainsong seemed muffled and flat.

Sister Gunnhild had no stomach for lessons, either. She set Edith to copying lines in Greek—trifles and bits of poetry, and a passage from the Greek Gospel of John.

Somewhere between the entry into Jerusalem and the Last Supper, a commotion brought Edith somewhat awake. People were shouting—men's voices, and women remonstrating. The men were winning, from the sound of it.

That was unheard of in this house of holy women. Edith glanced at Sister Gunnhild. She sat stiffly upright. In her face was something terribly like hope—though for what, Edith was almost afraid to wonder. Death? Rape? Worse?

Edith was not afraid. Maybe she was too numb. The shouting was coming closer. The women were not screaming as if in terror. They were arguing, loudly. Edith could almost make out words.

The door to the library burst open. There were nuns, fluttering and squawking like a flock of jackdaws, but the men in mail took little notice of them.

Malcolm of Scots had changed little since Edith saw him last. There was a new scar seaming his cheek, and as in her vision, his beard had gone completely white; but she would have known him in the dark by the rough sweetness of his voice. "I've come for my daughter," he said, as he must have been saying since he thrust his way through the gate.

"Your daughter is here," Edith said. Her voice was steady. That surprised her. She did not throw herself into his arms, though the urge was almost irresistible. She stood and faced him, and let him see what she had grown into.

He did not seem too terribly disappointed. He looked hard at her, searching her face until he must have memorized every line of it. "You're safe?" he asked at length. "I'm not too late?"

She nodded. Her throat was too tight for words.

He held out his hand. "Come, then. Get your things. We've a fair way to ride before nightfall."

As easy, as simple as that. Cold iron, she thought, and colder steel; and a king's will that even here, so far from his own country, was strong enough to turn the abbess' will aside.

Or so she tried to tell herself. He had taken the abbess by surprise. She could never have expected anyone to dare what he had: to bring weapons into an abbey and snatch away one of its novices.

She ran as fast as she could. The novices' dormitory was deserted. Her bag of belongings was where it had been all along, packed and ready to go. The scent of roses wafted around her as she snatched it and spun and ran.

Her father was in the corridor, running to meet her. He caught her hand and drew her with him, pulling her in his wake. Speed, yes—that was their best defense. They had to be out of there before the abbess gathered her wits and the terrible bindings of her will. Edith would not put it past her to bind Malcolm as she had his daughter; and all his men, too.

They had to go back past the library. Sister Gunnhild stood at the door. As they passed, she fell in with them, close behind Edith. Her face was white and set.

Malcolm nodded sharply to the man nearest him. It was hard to tell through helmet and mail, but Edith thought he was an older man, too, though quick on his feet and strong. There was something familiar about the scrap of face that she could see: the sharp tip of a nose, the fierce gleam of eyes.

He caught hold of Sister Gunnhild and braced to thrust her back toward the library.

She braced and thrust against him. She was as tall as he, and even with armor to give him bulk, she was nigh as broad. When he firmed his grip on her, she cried out, "Majesty! I beg for sanctuary!"

Malcolm checked his stride. "What—"

"Let her come," Edith said. It was not wise at all, and it certainly was not safe, but she had to say it. "She hates it here. Besides," she said with belated intelligence, "she might be useful as a hostage. She's old Harold's daughter."

Malcolm's eyes narrowed. "Is she now?"

Edith held her breath. That could have been completely the wrong thing to say, but she had cast the dice. Now it was for him to make the choice.

He nodded abruptly. "Bring her with us. We've already kidnapped one nun. Why not two?"

The knight barked laughter. "As well hang for two sheep as one. Or is it a sheep and a lamb?"

"It's mutton either way," Sister Gunnhild said sharply. "Are you going to stand here nattering or can we go?"

That took both men aback. Edith was gaping, too. This was a side of the good sister that she had never seen.

It was rather terrifying. She decided she liked it. So, from the glint in his eye, did the knight who had captured Sister Gunnhild. He let her go, except for a grip on her hand. They all ran together through hall and cloister, past wide-eyed staring nuns, out into the courtyard where, a bare ten days ago, another king's men had waited as Malcolm's did now.

Those had been, if neither invited nor welcome, at least tolerated. These were invaders, and they were mounted and ready to ride.

They had a horse for Edith. There was none for Sister Gunnhild, but her abductor pulled her up behind him on his big-boned bay. The beast barely seemed to feel the doubled weight.

Already Edith could feel walls of the soul closing in. Some of the men were wavering, their horses starting to wander. She forced her mind to clear, and turned her horse's head toward the gate. It needed no more encouragement than that. It was a fine and sensible creature, and the open air, in its mind, was infinitely preferable to a crowded courtyard. It sprang into a gallop.

They were well out of sight of the abbey when at last Edith's horse consented to slow its headlong gallop. Her father and his escort were strung in a long skein down the road, which on this day of mist and rain was happily deserted.

She had not even noticed the rain. It fell out of a sky without walls, onto earth untainted by empty holiness. And nowhere was the abbess' presence. Those walls enclosed it.

Edith had escaped. As she turned her face to the dripping sky, folk of air came flocking, leaping and swirling, singing in their eerie voices. She spread her arms wide and laughed for joy.

Malcolm had not been jesting when he spoke of a long ride before nightfall. Edith continued to delight in her escape, but within the hour she was reminded all too forcibly that she had not sat on a horse since she was six years old.

She gritted her teeth and endured it. It was no worse than a day's penance in chapel. The mare she rode had soft paces and a level head to go with them; Edith had little to do but let her find her own way down the long road.

For all her father's joy in the rescue and her own far deeper joy in the escape, Edith became aware soon enough that this was not a victory ride. Her own rescue had gone well, but Malcolm's embassy had not gone at all.

"He wouldn't see me," Malcolm said that night. They had stopped in a manor that owed fealty to a Norman lord, but the lady of the manor was Saxon, and her sons, though half Norman, spoke Saxon with a pure accent. The king of Scots, whose queen was Alfred's descendant, was sincerely welcome there. That queen's daughter, once it was known who she was, was greeted as if she were a queen herself.

Edith could grow to like that. But once dinner was over and the Lady Aelfgifu had gone to bed, Malcolm still sat in the hall, drinking mead and snarling at the dogs. Edith should have been in bed, tucked away in an alcove off the hall, but she was wide awake, drunk on freedom. She listened at the curtain as her father talked to the man who had captured Sister Gunnhild. Alain, his name was—and he was Breton, which rather surprised her. Bretons ran in a pack with Normans, and shared the Conquest. It was a Breton, or so it was said, whose arrow had killed King Harold.

This man's son's name was Alain, too, and he was equally Breton. Yet they were clearly good friends to the Scots king.

"He let me sit like a beggar at his gate," Malcolm said, growling into his mead. "He turned my messengers away. When he rode out hunting, he ignored my very existence. What does he think he's trying to do? Has he gone out of his mind?"

"William's preoccupied these days," Alain the elder said. "That illness of his in the spring—it addled his brain. I don't think even he knows what he wants of the world, now he's back in it. I'll wager he wasn't ignoring you, exactly. He just couldn't make up his mind what to do about you."

"What he's going to do," snapped Malcoolm, "is give me back the lands he wrested from me. I'll give him something to think about. I'll give him a bloody war."

"Do you reckon that's wise?" Alain asked.

"Wise? What's wisdom got to do with it? I'm his brother king. He shamed me in front of the world."

Edith peered through the crack in the curtain in time to see Alain spread his hands and shrug. "As you say. You're a king. You'll do what a king must do."

Malcolm bared his teeth at him, but Alain only broadened his shrug. He had no fear of royal wrath.

He looked old, with his white hair and lined face, but he felt young. His teeth were still good—maybe that was part of it—and his eyes were keen. He drained his horn of mead, adept with it as foreigners almost never were, and rose with none of the stiffness one might expect in a man of his age. "I'll leave you to your reflections, sire. If you take time to pray, add a bit for me."

Edith distinctly saw him wink. Malcolm flung a gnawed bone at him. He danced aside lightly and went off laughing.

❈ CHAPTER 23 ❈

When Edith went to bed, Sister Gunnhild was there already, asleep on a pallet by the wall. After Alain took his leave, Malcolm gnawed his grievances for a while, as the fire died in the great hearth, but in time he rose—creaking a great deal more than Alain had—and made his way to his own bed.

Edith was still awake. She could not seem to fall asleep. The air was too free, even in this small and firmly enclosed space. She did try: she lay on her own pallet and closed her eyes, and thought drowsy thoughts.

A stir and a rustle put them hopelessly to flight. She cracked an eyelid. Sister Gunnhild had risen. There was no more sleep in her face than there was in Edith's.

She peered toward Edith. Edith shut her eyes quickly and tried to breathe long and slow.

It seemed the ruse succeeded. Sister Gunnhild sighed. "Good," she breathed. "Sleep till morning, and may God bless you."

That was kind of her. When Edith peered beneath her lashes again, Sister Gunnhild was already through the curtain.

She must be going to the privy, no more. But Edith could not help herself. She slipped out of bed and made herself a shadow, flitting in Sister Gunnhild's wake.

It was a brief chase. The ordinary ranks of men were bedded down in the hall, but the higher ones had alcoves like the one the women shared. Sister Gunnhild passed by several, then paused. Her hand trembled as it rose to the curtain. Edith watched her waver back and forth in her mind: the body reflected it, now leaning forward, now half turning as if to go back.

Abruptly she slipped through the curtain. Edith should have fled then. But she had always been a curious creature, and she was lastingly astonished to find Sister Gunnhild so different than she ever suspected.

She crept closer, hardly daring to breathe, and craned her ears to hear.

"Sister!" That was Alain the elder. He sounded surprised, but not unwelcoming. "Is there trouble? Have you lost your way?"

"I was lost long since," Sister Gunnhild said.

There was a slight pause. "Where do you need to go?" Alain asked. "The privy? Your chamber?"

"I am where I need to be," said Sister Gunnhild.

"Sister," said Alain, "this is hardly—"

"Messire," Sister Gunnhild said, "you are being deliberately dense. What should I do? Ask for sanctuary?"

"I'm not a church," said Alain, "and certainly I'm no churchman."

"Precisely," Sister Gunnhild said.

This pause lasted considerably longer than the one before it. "Ah," said Alain at length. "So. Why me?"

"Because," said Sister Gunnhild, "I take you for a man of sense. And also of property, and courage. You're a good son of the Conquest, yes? Would you spite a Saxon abbess?"

"That depends," said Alain. "Are you a spiteful woman?"

"Not by nature," said Sister Gunnhild, "but after a lifetime in that woman's care, I would be more than happy to cause her grief."

"I hear she's a hard woman," Alain said. His tone was musing. "Having met her sister of Scotland, I can believe she's not easy to live under. But this that you do, breaking your vows, proposing to sin mortally—I won't have it said that I corrupted a bride of God. I won't have you taking me as the lesser of great evils, either. I've never yet raped a woman, nor have I been accused of it. It's a matter of pride."

"It would not be rape," Sister Gunnhild said steadily. "I do not ever wish to go back to that life."

In the third pause, Edith heard the rustle of cloth on cloth, and a soft slither, as if a habit and then a shift slid to the floor. There was an intake of breath; then Alain said, "Ah, lady. Who would dream that a few yards of wool and linen could hide so much?"

"Does it please you?" Sister Gunnhild asked. Her voice was not so steady now. She was breathing hard.

"You are a rare beauty," Alain said.

"I will belong to you," said Sister Gunnhild, "and be faithful to you, because you have freed me from a trap that, before the God who made me, I thought I would die in."

"There's faith," Alain said with a touch of dry amusement. "Come here. If it's mortal sin you would commit, who am I to refuse such beauty?"

Edith wrenched herself away at last. She knew well enough what was happening: she had spied the servants more than once when she was small, wriggling and scrabbling at one another in dark corners or in the hayloft. It seemed a terribly undignified thing for a holy nun and an elderly lord to be doing.

She should have been either laughing at it or deploring it. But her body was warm all over, and little shudders tried to run through it. She was not appalled—she was, God forgive her, just a little bit jealous.

She escaped to her bed and pulled the blanket up over her head. It was not that she was a coward, and she was certainly not afraid. But this was nothing that she could help, and she had no desire to hinder.

Even as hard as she tried to ward herself, she could feel the dizzy delight that radiated from Sister Gunnhild—Sister no longer, maybe, with her vows so thoroughly broken. And it was thorough. There was no doubt of that. Alain was as strong in that capacity as in everything else.

* * *

Morning dawned bright and clear. All the rain was scoured away; it was a fair summer's morning, dawning warm and growing warmer as the day advanced. They were on the road by full light, pressing the pace still, but without the urgency that had driven them the day before.

Sister Gunnhild had been in her bed when Edith woke from sleep she had not expected to get, and had risen and put on her veil and eaten her breakfast as if nothing had ever happened. But Edith knew it had not been a dream. There was something in her: a gleam that had not been there before, and a way of moving that spoke of tightness well and truly released.

There were no glances exchanged between Sister Gunnhild and the lord Alain. Both were too wise for that. Edith did her best to follow their example: she kept her eyes to herself, and said as little as possible.

She wanted to hope that Abbess Christina had chosen to accept God's and the Scots king's will—that she would let her two prized prisoners go without a fight. What could she do, after all? The abbey had no army, and no earthly power to command a king, especially when it came to his own daughter.

But Edith could not settle to complacency. She was glad they rode so fast still, though it was torture to a body already sore from a day's unaccustomed riding. She would have suffered worse, if they could have gone any faster.

They stopped at midday to rest a bit, and to water and graze the horses. There was bread to eat, and meat and cheese, and a napkinful of figs, ripe and honey-sweet. Malcolm brought them to Edith as a gift, and smiled at her unfeigned delight. "I remembered," he said. "You were wild for figs when you were small."

"I still am," Edith said. When he was close, she was not so uneasy. He was warm and strong, and though the magic in him flowed so deep it was barely perceptible, it was there. It made her feel safer.

They had paused by a bit of wood, where the shade was cool and there was a stream. Up on the hill the wind was blowing as it always did in this country; the leaves were rustling with it. But here below, it was warm, and the air was almost still.

Malcolm sat on the grass and shared the figs with Edith, biting into the sweet, rich flesh and savoring it almost as blissfully as she did. When the last one was gone, after they had both washed their faces and their sweet-sticky hands in the stream, they sat for a while in comfortable silence.

Malcolm broke it, speaking softly, hardly to be heard above the sound of leaves. "Do you know, I haven't told you what your gift is, yet."

"I thought it was my freedom," Edith said.

"That," he conceded, "and something else." He tilted his head toward the men who were sitting together some distance away, and particularly toward one. Alain had propped himself against a tree and gone peacefully to sleep. Edith had been thinking, in fact, that he must be short of rest, after the night he had had; Sister Gunnhild was heavy-eyed, too, though she seemed determined to cling to wakefulness.

Edith doubted that her father was aware of any of that. He had another thing on his mind. "What do you think of him?" he asked her.

That took her aback, somewhat. "What? I hardly know him. He seems pleasant enough."

"You think so?" Malcolm asked. "What would you say to him as a husband?"

Edith opened her mouth, then shut it again. Her first thought—that he should ask Sister Gunnhild—was not anything she could say aloud. The best and most harmless response she could find was, "He's older than you are."

"He's rich," said Malcolm. "He's kind enough, by his lights. He'd cherish a royal wife, and keep her safe on both sides of the border."

"Are you telling me it's done?" Edith asked. "Is there a priest waiting, and a contract all written and signed?"

Malcolm frowned. "No," he said a little testily. "No, of course not. There have been discussions, well enough. Negotiations. All the usual sorts of things."

"I don't know," said Edith, "if I know what is usual. I was supposed to be a nun."

"Do you want to be?"

She looked into his face. He wanted to know—honestly; and not with anger or annoyance, either. "No," she said, and that was the truth, from the heart. "I don't want to be a nun. I'm not meant for it."

"So you want something younger." Malcolm's eyes were glinting. He was not angry. He sounded more wry than anything else. "I can understand that. Though if it's Red William you're wanting, I'll tell you now, even if he bent that way, I wouldn't consent to it. I am not in charity with the King of England."

"I'm not terribly fond of him myself," she said. "And since I've already told him I won't marry him, I don't think you need to fear on that account."

"You've told—" Malcolm glared. "When in God's name did you see him?"

"A little while ago," she answered. "He came to look at the merchandise. We agreed it wouldn't be the wisest match."

"You agreed—" Malcolm shook his head as if to clear it. "So that's why he turned me away from the door. He was afraid I'd try to trap him into taking a queen."

"I'm sorry," Edith said. "I wasn't thinking."

"Well, how could you? You never expected all this marriage-brokering. You were supposed to be shackled to God."

Edith startled him, and herself, by hugging him tight. "I've missed you," she said.

"And I you," he said. "You didn't go away with my consent. I hope you've understood that."

"I do now," said Edith.

"Good," he said. "I was afraid . . . I love your mother, girl. Never doubt that. She was supposed to be a nun, too, and I took her away and led her into sin. She never quite forgave me for that—or herself, either. She wanted you to be what she thinks she failed in."

"Does she know?" Edith asked.

"She will," said Malcolm. "She might not forgive me for it, either—

but that's as God wills. I won't see you walled up in a convent, unless you're clear about wanting it."

"Believe me," said Edith, "I don't want it. I was going out of my mind trying to find ways to escape."

"And now you have," he said, hugging her to him and kissing her forehead as he had when she was small. "So then. If yonder prospect won't do, we'll find you another. There's time. You can learn to be a lady."

"That's well," she said, "because I know very little of that."

"You'll have time now," Malcolm said. He grinned and thrust himself to his feet. "Come, then. Let's get on our way."

Edith rose more slowly. Each time he spoke of having time, she felt a shiver in her bones. She tried hard to ignore it, but it refused to go away.

He felt it, too, she thought. The pace he set was just as fast as it had been before. He was in a right hurry to get out of England, and he made no secret of it, either.

✳ CHAPTER 24 ✳

On the third day, Sister Gunnhild took off her veil and rode with a hood over her head like a laywoman. She spoke to no one, and indicated by no sign that she had spent the previous night, like the one before, in Alain's bed.

And yet there was no mistaking that she had changed. The colorless creature in the nun's habit had transformed into a woman, and even with her eyes lowered and her body covered as thoroughly as it had been before, she was beautiful. Men noticed the purity of her profile and the whiteness of her skin. Those who were allowed a glimpse of her eyes found them to be deep blue. The curls of hair that showed themselves beneath the hood were gold.

She was opening like a flower. Edith wondered if she was doing the same. She felt as if she were shedding scales of time and frustration and holiness, slipping her skin—more like a snake than a rose.

That morning as they rode past a town, a grey-striped cat made his way through the stream of people coming to market. There were animals enough on that road in that hour: horses and mules of course, and donkeys, and dogs, and pigs and cattle and sheep being driven to market, and here and there a quick-witted cat. But this one came direct to King Malcolm's riding, lofted weightlessly to Edith's saddlebow, and yawned in her face.

The puca seemed quite as much at ease in this world as in the other.

What he was doing here, she did not know, but from the way he curled on the pommel of her saddle, he was not about to leave.

Some of Alain's Bretons slid eyes at him. So did a few of Malcolm's Gaels. They knew what they were looking at.

The puca met their glances. They looked away in haste. It was never wise to question the whims of the Old Things.

Edith took comfort in this one's presence. There were folk of air enough, some of whom had followed her from the abbey, but a puca was a stronger power by far. A power for mischief, yes—but also a faithful ally who had sworn to her his service.

For the moment he seemed content to ride purring in front of her. They passed the market town without stopping, and the next one, too, on their swift ride northward.

Toward evening there was a debate. Malcolm wanted to stop in an abbey that he declared was safe. His Breton allies spoke in favor of camping in a wood a league or more past the abbey. "If the abbess has sent word out," Alain the elder said, "we'll have the Church on our necks, and no easy escape come morning."

To which Malcolm replied, "Look at the sky, man. We'll be drowning in rain by nightfall. Even if we push the horses, they won't get past the abbey before the storm hits."

"I'd rather get wet than see these two ladies bound in orders again," said Alain.

"They won't be bound," Malcolm said. "My word on that. We'll keep them close and keep them veiled, and tell the monks they're your lady and her maid, and both of them are taken ill."

"There's no safety in deception," Alain muttered.

"Safer for them and drier for us than sleeping wet in a cold camp."

Alain shook his head, but Malcolm's will was stronger than his. Neither of them so much as glanced at the ones they claimed to be thinking of.

Edith did not want to spend the night in an abbey, no matter how safe her father thought it was. But the clouds were hanging low, and Gunnhild's shoulders drooped. She was not as far from being ill as maybe Malcolm hoped. It was a long ride and a hard one for a woman who had spent her life in a cloister; and she was perilously short of sleep.

Much against her better judgment, Edith held her tongue. The puca was there, and she was no weakling herself. She could manage to protect them for one night.

Hubris was a favorite word of the Greeks: arrogance that provoked the gods to anger. Edith had cause to remember it as she lay wide awake in the guesthouse of Saint Grimwald's abbey. The abbot and his prior were Norman, but the monks were mostly Saxon. The chapel had a distinctly Saxon air: grey and much too still.

Female guests, one of them demonstrably ill, received the best room, with a fire in its hearth, and heated ale to drink. Gunnhild gagged on it. Edith did not try to drink hers at all. She choked down a little bread and a bit of cheese, and fed the rest of the cheese to the puca, who seemed unperturbed by the chill holiness of the place.

The puca's calm did not reassure her as much as she would have liked. He was not sleeping, either—maybe pucas did not sleep, but cats did, and a cat awake was a thing worth watching.

She kept her mind focused and her heart as steady as she could. The Otherworld was far away; these walls were thick and cold with Saxon sanctity. As in Wilton, the earth was tainted. Greyness sank deep beneath her feet.

Once night had fallen, with rain drumming hard on the roof and wind rattling the shutters, the puca rose. The flick of his tail bade her follow. He padded soundlessly to the wall—the east; though how she knew that, she could not have said—and blurred and shimmered and grew. And there stood the brown youth of the wood, with his sharp teeth and his gold-green eyes. "There are words," he said. "Speak them with me."

She did not know the language of those words, but she could feel the power in them. Her skin shivered; her bones thrummed. Slowly, she repeated them exactly as he had spoken them: rhythm and intonation as well as the shape of the words.

He grinned. "Wise student! Now follow. And when I stop, say the words again."

This time the shift barely surprised her. When he was a neat-footed, grey-striped cat again, he began to walk at a measured pace, circling from east to south. There he stopped.

Edith's mind was a perfect blank. It was all grey, all empty. There was no magic in it.

The puca's eyes caught and held her. The words were in them, as if written on a page. They were harder to say than they had been before. There were more effort in them; the air was heavier. The greyness dragged at her feet.

It was fighting her. She pushed against it. As the puca circled toward the west, she felt as if she were wading through sand. This time she could remember the words, but it was all she could do to chant them as the puca had instructed. They kept wanting to go flat.

After she sang them, she had to stop and breathe. The air could not seem to fill her lungs. What there was of it smelled strange, like old stone and damp wool and aging flesh. It almost had a shape to it, and a face: Abbess Christina, reaching to drag her back.

The abbess was praying for the lost ones, the one who had fled first and the two who, she permitted herself to think, had been snatched away by evil men. Her sense of that evil was strong, her anger deep. It bound itself to the powers of Britain, twisted and crushed them. Even with the wards all but made, Edith could feel the power of it, reaching through her defenses to unmake the wards and destroy her magic.

The puca pressed against her leg, purring so strongly that the sound and vibration of it pierced the spell that was creeping to bind her. She clung to the sense and the sound, and to the wall, and pulled herself toward the north.

The north was her place: the land in which she was born. South and east and west had bred her blood and bone, but the north had bred her heart. She would be strongest there—but so also was the power raised against her.

It was waiting, heavy and dark and slow. It sapped the strength from her. She had enough magic, just, to complete the circle—if the thing that sucked at her did not overwhelm her.

So much for arrogance, and for pride in what she was. She could dream of escape, and fancy that an army of mortal men could take her away from the life that her mother and her aunt had ordained for her. But they were too strong. Her father's insistence on bringing her to this monastery—that had been their doing, the result of their prayers. They would have her back, and bind her until she died.

A sharp pain brought her reeling back into the world. She gasped. The puca extricated his claws from her ankle, in no haste at all.

She was standing at the northernmost point of the circle. The words were in her to close it, to guard herself against the thing that sought to drag her down. Whether she had the strength . . .

The puca's claws flexed, gleaming like steel. On the end of each was a droplet of blood.

Edith sucked in a breath. The first word came out in a squeak, but the rest were more as they should be. She had to breathe between each one, because she felt as if she were running up a mountain, and the air was thinner with each staggering step.

Her eyes were growing dark and her voice was faint, but she finished the spell. The circle closed.

The silence was beautiful. Wonderful. Full of peace. The greyness lurked beneath, but it could not pierce the walls.

The puca's purr rose to a raucous chorus. Edith slid down the wall to the miraculous softness of the stone floor. With her head on the puca's soft side and his purring in her ears, she slipped into sleep.

Edith woke exhausted—and yet her heart was lighter than it had been since she could remember. When she left the guesthouse, both the wards and the puca went with her. She found that she could extend the wards to the whole of her father's escort. It was not easy; it cost her some effort, but no more than she thought she could spare.

She was careful to remember the meaning of hubris. This was a great magic, but she had only worked it because the puca showed her how.

She had been thinking herself well educated because of all her Latin and Greek and her smattering of theology. Magic had been simply what she was; it was her escape from the confinement of the cloister, and her secret that she shared with no one but Sister Cecilia. None of the Old Things seemed to need any teaching in magic. They willed, and it was so.

Well, so had she; but she had not known what to set her will to or how, until she was shown. How much more was there? How much did she not know, or did she not know she knew?

She lifted her eyes to the roll of hills into which the road was winding, but she did not see either the earth or the sky. She was seeing a world she had not known to look for: a world in which magic, like theology, was both art and science. Could it be? Was it even allowed?

The puca, riding on her saddlebow as before, watched her with a sardonic eye. To him, no doubt, she was a profoundly silly creature. Of course magic was a thing that one could learn—if one were mortal. Where else did one get sorcerers and enchanters, and strange ladies who guarded lakes and springs and looked after enchanted swords?

Was that what Edith wanted to be? It was better than a queen, maybe. She could dress in white and sit on an enchanted stone, and ask riddles of knights who happened to pass by.

She was maundering, and the day was passing. The land was changing. The softness of southern England had begun to give way to a harsher landscape: starker hills, broader sky, and bones of the earth thrusting through the green.

There was less greyness here—more brightness of magic. The land was not so terribly scarred. Scotland was drawing closer.

Her mother had laid the Saxon spell on it, to be sure. But it was only one woman and one lifetime—not half a thousand years of concerted effort. There was still hope for Scotland.

Edith had made her choice. She had no regrets. No fears, either—or so she told herself, safe within wards, riding under guard into the north.

✳ CHAPTER 25 ✳

They left Sister Gunnhild still within the borders of England: in Alain's lands in Northumberland, where he was a great lord—greater than Edith had known. Gunnhild had done well for herself, as the world measured it.

She seemed happy. Her farewell to Edith was warm but distracted. Only at the last, as they parted at the gates of York, did she bring herself into focus. Then she embraced Edith, and held on tightly, until Edith wondered if she would ever let go.

She did at last, holding Edith at arm's length. "I'll miss you," she said.

"And I you," said Edith. "Maybe we'll meet again. If you're a great lord's lady, and I'm a queen . . ."

Gunnhild laughed. "If! No, when. When you're a queen. We'll dine at each other's table and embroider tapestries together, and lament the follies of our children—including the great babies we're married to."

"May it be so," Edith said, making it a prayer.

Gunnhild kissed her on the forehead. "God keep you," she said.

She seemed to see no strangeness in that: a blessing from a woman who had fallen willingly into deep sin. But then Edith could not believe it was a sin. Not this happiness, or this joy in freedom.

No doubt they were both heretics, and hell would take them—if they chose to believe in it. Edith turned reluctantly to mount her horse. The others were waiting with deliberate patience. Scotland was close enough to taste. She was all that kept them from it.

Gunnhild stayed in the gate as they rode away. Edith could feel her there long after the road had carried them out of sight. She was more alone than anyone Edith had known: separated from kin and family, turned against the vows that had bound her. And yet she was happy. She had sought this; she felt that she had won it.

Edith hoped that she could do as well. Scotland was calling her; her father was with her, and that was a wonderful thing. But her mother was waiting in Edinburgh. Edith might have done no more than flee from darkness to darkness.

Anything was better than the cloister.

And for a few days more, as she rode into autumn and the wild hills of Scotland, she was as free as mortal could be. The Bretons were gone; they were all Scots on this riding. They sang their own songs, that were as strong as stones and as fierce as the wind in the Highlands. No Saxons here, and no conquerors from Normandy. Every one of them was a Gael, native born of this black earth.

They came to Edinburgh in the teeth of a storm, laughing at the wind that carried them through the gates. The lash of rain was exhilarating; the cold only made them livelier. As for the sleet that edged the rain as the sun went down, they reckoned it a spice, sharp enough to be interesting.

Edith had lost more hardihood than she liked, living in walls for so long. She was cold and wet and shamefully glad to get out of the rain.

Her father's hall was warm and dry. A fire roared in the hearth. There was brown ale waiting, and bread fresh from the baking, and a whole ox roasting on the spit.

Her mother was nowhere to be seen. Edith had been tensed against her presence, closed within the wards that had come with her all the way from England, but there was no sign of her. Folk of air flocked in the rafters, which they would never do in the queen's sight, and the fire was full of dancing spirits.

They welcomed her with headlong gladness. Her father's people were pleased enough to see her, but the Old Things of this place were ecstatic. She was theirs, their beloved, their princess.

The puca who had ridden with her for so long had taken station on her shoulder, from which he dared anyone, mortal or otherwise, to dislodge him. None of them was fool enough to try. He rode easily there as she drank from the welcoming cup and walked with her father through the hall, seeing faces she knew and faces she had never seen before, all bright with interest.

Some she had been looking for were not there: her nurses, Nieve in particular, and one or two of the guards who had been kind to her when she was small. Everyone whom she did recognize had been familiar enough, but not a friend. She had no friends here, and none but her father who loved her.

It was home nonetheless, or so she told herself. Here was where she belonged. Her father kept her close until they came to the far end of the hall, where servants—some new, some old—took her in hand and brought her to the room she remembered surprisingly well. It was much the same as she had left it, with the bed and the chest for clothes and the pallet for the nurses, but the hanging on the wall was gone.

It had been very old when she had it, threadbare and faded, its design too blurred to make sense of, but she was sorry to see blank stone in its place. She would have to find or make something to put there.

Tonight it was enough that there were dry clothes—which did not fit her too badly—and a warm bed ready when she would need it. There was a maid, a wide-eyed and silent young woman hardly older than she was, who helped her out of her travel-stained clothes and into the new ones.

She barely remembered dinner, except that it passed in a haze of warmth and repletion. The only clear thought she had was that her mother had not come down for it. Lost in prayer, most likely, and in no way pleased that her husband had abducted their daughter from the abbey.

It did not matter, she told herself. She was safe here. Her father would make sure she was never bound again in the walls of a convent.

The puca's purring woke her, grinding in her ear. Grey light crept through the shutters. The rain was still falling, but its drumming had faded to a hiss. Through it she could hear the roar of the sea.

The maid was asleep, snoring softly. Edith would have to learn her name.

There was someone else in the room. She shivered inside her skin. The folk of air were all gone; there was only greyness, thick as mist, and a dark figure in the center of it.

She sat up. The mist scattered. There was no one there but the maid on her pallet. The only memory of what she had seen was a faint scent, like old stone and cold incense.

Abbess Christina?

She shivered. Even that power for nothingness could not reach across the whole length of the isle. It must have been her mother. Maybe she had been praying for Edith, and the prayer had come to watch over her.

Edith slipped out of bed and dressed with trembling fingers, taking great care not to wake the maid. If she had been wise, or even sane, she would not have contemplated what she was doing, but she had had enough of waiting and cowering and being helpless. If she destroyed herself, so be it.

Which was a rather overwrought way to look at it, but she was worn out. She needed to be free of this—one way or another.

This early in the morning, Edith would expect to find the queen in the chapel, having heard early Mass and then lost herself in prayer until the Mass at midmorning. But there was no one in the chapel. It was cold, and dark except for the vigil lamp over the altar.

Queen Margaret was here in Edinburgh. Edith knew that as she knew where her own body was. She followed the queen's presence like a scent out of the chapel and down a maze of passages and through the hall. People were awake there, beginning the day's duties and pleasures. She slipped through them unseen.

The puca was waiting for her beyond the hall and up the stair, in front of the door that led to her mother's rooms. He sat with his tail stretched out behind him, flicking it lightly, restlessly.

She had to stop and breathe for a while before she set her hand to the door. She had never gone to her mother. She had always been summoned.

She was older now, and bolder. She gathered up her courage.

The door opened to her touch. The air within was thick with the mingled smells of smoke and incense. A fire burned strongly on the hearth; a maid, dressed as somberly as a nun, fed it with twists of dried herbs.

Beneath the pungent sweetness, Edith caught a quite different reek. Sickness: old, cold, and set deep.

Her mother lay on her bed that was as narrow and hard as a nun's. The thin blanket was drawn up over a breast that had shrunk terribly since Edith last saw her.

She was still beautiful. She could still swallow any magic that was in the air. Even the puca came no nearer than the door.

The wards that had been with Edith for so long were straining. They were made to protect against this, but the strength of it left her gasping. It wanted to suck the life and breath out of her; to drain her magic away and transform her into a shadow, like the shadows of priests and bishops, monks and nuns who hovered near the bed.

It was a kind of hunger, not of the body but of the spirit. To be holy for holiness' sake. To take life and beauty out of the world, because no world mattered but the next one.

Edith stood by the bed. Her mother was awake, but her spirit was far away.

Edith waited for it to come back. She would not have called it patience. She emptied herself; she drew the wards closer about her and went still within them.

It did not matter how long she stood there. The light changed little, but the clouds were thick; the rain had closed in again. The air in the room grew chill as well as dark.

The queen's attendants were praying, some silently, some in a murmur that rose and fell. Its cadences were Saxon, not Latin. The strongest prayers, her mother had always insisted, were in the language of her birth.

"Rome is far away," she used to say. "England is close and alive. When the Normans are gone, we will raise it up, stronger than ever."

Edith could hear her voice, low but clear. She spoke in Saxon. It was so near and so distinct that she started a little.

But the queen had not moved. Her lips were still. Her breast barely rose with her breathing.

Her eyes were open. Edith had forgotten how blue they were. In her memory they had been grey, like the shadow of the queen's presence.

They had come to rest on Edith's face. She tried to read their expression, but they were as blank as stones set in a reliquary. What they saw in her own face, she could not tell. Sin, probably. Rebellion. And white fear.

The fear did not last long. It was old habit. Edith looked into those eyes and asked, softly and respectfully but without flinching, "Does Father know?"

The queen sighed faintly. Her head shook just visibly.

Edith could well see her father letting himself be convinced that his queen was engrossed in one of her sieges of prayer. Whatever their differences, he still loved her with all his heart. And love, the poets said, was blind.

"So that's why you let him bring me back," Edith said. "I'm more use to you here."

"You are what you are," the queen said, "wherever your body finds itself."

"And what is that?" Edith wanted to know.

"God knows," said the queen.

She meant it quite literally. Edith bit her tongue. When she spoke, she did it with care. "I have no call to the veil. That I am sure of."

"Your abbess assured me otherwise."

"My late abbess has dreams on my behalf," Edith said.

The queen sat up with an effort. Several of her shadows leaped to assist her. When she was banked in pillows, paler than ever but upright, she said somewhat breathlessly still, "It is for the best. As blessed as that life would have been, you were bred to wear a crown. For as much time as I have left to me, I will teach you what you need to know. Then when I am gone—"

"Don't talk like that," Edith said. "You'll get well again. I'll pray for it."

"God is calling me," the queen said. "I will stay for you—for a while. But my soul is yearning to go."

Edith astonished herself with grief. She had been afraid of her mother for as long as she could remember. She hated the greyness that surrounded the queen; the death of magic wherever she was. And yet this was her mother. There was love there after all.

"Come now," the queen said. "Remember your training. When a nun dies, the convent never mourns—it celebrates. The bride has gone to the Bridegroom at last. So too shall I."

Edith countered that fiercely with one of her father's sayings: "Grief is for the living. Grant us a little, who have to stay in the world when you're free of it."

"That is an indulgence," her mother said.

She was making it all too easy to remember why Edith had been so glad to escape her. Abbess Christina had ignored Edith for the most part, and given her a tutor who had proved to be as little suited to the cloister as Edith herself was. Queen Margaret was unlikely to make the same mistake.

Edith had gone from trap to trap. And yet she could not make herself feel the panic that she should have felt. Her mother was dying—she grieved for that. But it meant that whatever trap she had been brought into, it was finite. It would end.

"You are young," her mother said. "Life will teach you. Death, too, when it comes. Sit with me. Pray."

Edith could sit. She had no intention of praying in the way her mother meant.

She sat on the edge of the bed. The queen's hands gripped hers, as thin and cold as if they already belonged to a corpse. "Pray," said the queen.

Edith prayed. She prayed for a swift death, free of pain. She prayed for an end to the greyness that was trying to swallow the world. She prayed to be strong enough, wise enough, skilled enough to do what she must.

While she prayed, the puca crept into the room, flattened to the floor, as if the touch of the queen's glance would render him to nothingness as it had all else of magic that was in that place. He pressed against Edith's foot, warm and soft, trembling but steadfast.

He gave her strength. That was what he was for. He protected her against the powers that would have turned her against him and all his kind.

CHAPTER 26

King Malcolm might have returned to Scotland, and he was clearly glad to have his daughter back, but he could not stop chewing over his anger at the English king. It rankled more, the longer he was in his own country. He paced his hall in the evening after a long day of hunting, ruling, or occasionally fighting, and cursed Red William with mounting fury.

It was the temper of the Gael. It burned hot and long, and it never forgot a slight. "Am I not a king even as he is? Am I not his elder? Do I not deserve at least a moment of his notice? What right had he to shut his door to me? He summoned me! I came like a servant, I who am a king. And he treated me like a beggar at his gate."

His people knew better than to get in his way when he had a fine rage going. But Edith was still too young to be sensible.

She had been in Scotland for a month now. Her mother was no better, but Edith's presence seemed to have given her strength: she was no worse.

Edith was holding on. Sometimes it was hard. Sometimes she woke in the night, strangling in greyness. But her wards were holding. The puca was feeding them, and the earth of Scotland, when she could escape from her mother, helped to keep them strong.

She had come down to the hall this evening to hear a singer of songs who had come across the sea from Ireland, and found her father in full cry. The singer, a nondescript little man with a sharp fox-face, was listening enthralled. He was setting the rant to music, Edith thought.

She should have faded back toward her mother's rooms, but she was hungry and there was food on the tables, and wine that her father had already been into. She could smell venison pie; she had a passion for venison pie.

Like a fool, then, she sat at the high table. The king had paused for breath, and maybe for inspiration. Edith said, "Maybe by spring he'll have decided to listen to you."

Malcolm rounded on her. "Oh, he will indeed," he said. His smile showed a flash of teeth. "He'll be hearing me by Martinmas, I'll lay wagers on it."

"War?" Edith asked. "Again?"

"If war is what it takes to get his attention," Malcolm said, "then war I'll give him."

"Can you fight him? Are you strong enough?"

She had not meant to bait him, but the words kept coming and she kept speaking them. She could not seem to stop herself.

"I'll harry him like a pack of hounds after a boar," Malcolm said. "I'll eat away at his borders until his kingdom is the size of a farmstead—and then I'll teach him how to treat a king."

"Then you are a fool," said a voice Edith had not heard so sharp or so clear since she was a child.

Queen Margaret was standing in the door that led to the women's solar, slender and tall in a gown as blue as her eyes, and a mantle the color of the sky at dusk, and a great collar of gold and pearls, and the crown of a queen.

Edith found that her mouth was hanging open. The hall had fallen silent. Even the most boisterous revelers were struck dumb.

If Edith had not known that her mother was dying, she would have sworn that the queen was as strong as she ever had been. Her voice certainly was. "What possesses you, my lord? Your people are worn out with fighting. Surely you can give them a winter's rest."

"It's not winter yet," Malcolm said. He was smiling, but it was not a pleasant smile at all. "Come down, my lady. Drink a cup with me. Wish me well; I'm going to war in the morning."

"If you go," Margaret said, "you will die."

The king's eyes gleamed as he looked up at her. "Will I then? Have you had a vision?"

"God speaks to me," said the queen. "Your death is out there. Stay home; be sane. Let the Normans think you cowed. When they least fear you, then is the time to strike."

"They don't fear me now," Malcolm said. "They laugh at my name. I'll turn their laughter to pain."

"The pain will be yours," the queen said.

"On your head be it," said Malcolm, "both you and your ill-wishing."

Edith tasted blood. She had bitten her lip through. Her father was quite out of his mind, and her mother was no better.

"I forbid you to go," the queen said.

"Do you, lady? Isn't this your dearest desire? Haven't you urged me to do exactly this?"

"Not in a fit of temper," she said, "and not for simple spite. My desire is victory, not the shame of defeat."

"I will give you victory," Malcolm said.

The queen looked at him. She must have seen what Edith saw: that he would never yield for strength. Her face softened as much as it ever could, when softness was no part of what she was. "My heart, I go so far as to beg. Stay here with me."

"My heart," said the king, and there was a snarl in it, "I will not."

The queen had to have expected that. She pressed harder—with softer weapons. "Not for me? Not for your sons and your daughter? Not for your very life?"

He wavered not at all. "For my soul and honor, and for the honor of my kingdom, I must go."

"You will die," she said. Her voice was flat.

"So you persist in saying," said Malcolm. "And I say to you, my lady, that if I shrink from this, Scotland will rue it for a thousand years. The Normans will invade us, hound us and hunt us, and trample us into the ground."

Edith shivered. There was power in what they both had said: truth so strong it made the stones of the hall shift subtly under her feet.

Neither seemed aware of it. This was the worst kind of war: war born of love. Pride fed it, and fear—not of death, but of things that were worse than death.

"Go, then," said the queen, letting go her grip on a temper as formidable as his. "Go and feed your pride, and die in sin."

"If I die," the king said, "and believe me, lady, I do not intend to, then I die in honor, for my kingdom's sake. I cannot do otherwise. It is not in me."

"Nor is plain common sense," she shot back in the passion of despair.

He flung down the cup that he had filled for her, splashing dark wine over her blue hem. Then he whirled. "Out!" he roared to his startled men. "Up! To horse and ride!"

"Father," Edith said—it was futile and she knew it, but she had to try. "Father, don't go."

He never paused, not even for her. She doubted that he even knew her. His back was turned already, his men scrambling up from the tables, abandoning food and drink and comfort. His will was strong and they were trained to obey.

"The sun is nearly set," the queen said, cold and clear. "Will you ride in the dark? Where will you sleep?"

"Anywhere but here," the king snarled at her. "Better cold in a hedgerow than warm under a Norman thumb."

"If there were a drop of Norman blood in my smallest finger," she said with gritted teeth, "I would cut it off."

He bared his teeth. "I'll bring you Red William's head, and a sack of Norman bones for the dogs. Isn't that what you've prayed for?"

"I pray that you come home safe," she said.

"From your lips to God's ears," said the king.

Edith ran after him. But he was too quick. When she would have stretched her stride to catch him, a soft furry body tangled her feet.

She fell headlong. Hands reached to catch her, but she struck the floor hard enough to knock the breath out of her. By the time she had been lifted to her feet and had made a hasty count of her bruises, with a hearty curse for the puca who had barred her way, her father was gone, and the whole of the royal warband with him.

Her mother too had vanished. But that, Edith could act upon. She was as polite as she could be to people pressing wine and tidbits and poultices on her, and escaped as soon as she could.

The queen had exhausted her last strength. Her maids were still tending and folding her royal garments, cleaning spatters of wine from the hem. Margaret had returned to her bed, and lay barely breathing. A gaggle of priests and nuns surrounded her. Their prayers mingled into a dull confusion of sound.

It was like a thick smoke, a cloying incense. It made Edith dizzy.

They were praying for the king as well as the queen. Edith struggled through the fog to her mother's bed.

Margaret was conscious. Somehow Edith had not expected that. Her lips moved: she prayed with the rest, in silence that in its way was more powerful than her servants' voices.

They were making matters worse. It was like a curse on them all. Even the puca seemed to have succumbed to it.

Edith could do nothing here. She would not have said she fled, but her retreat was rapid.

If it had been daylight she would have found a way to escape to the open air, but the dark had closed in. Her father was already too far away to catch: he had pressed his men and horses hard. They would make a hunting camp, she supposed, and sleep on the ground under the fitful stars.

Her only refuge was the room in which she slept. It was as bare as it had been when she came, but with the puca's help she had warded all its walls. Its door was protected against intrusion; its window was open to folk of the air, but ill spirits and mortal invaders could not pass through it.

The puca was curled tightly in the middle of the bed. He wore his human shape, which was rare; but he was drawn into a knot like the cat he most often was. He shivered in spasms.

Edith had been troubled. Now she was honestly afraid.

When she touched him, he erupted. She recoiled from a flashing nightmare of wings and fangs and claws.

As abruptly as he had moved, he was still, as human as he was ever going to be, shuddering and gasping. It might be absolutely foolish, but she touched him again, this time to set her hands on his shoulders and hold him still.

He quieted slowly. "Tell me," she said.

She wondered if he had forgotten human words, it took him so long to answer. But in the end he did. "Too much," he said. "Too many things all at once. Taking magic out, pouring magic in—death, rebirth, war and gladness, everything all tumbled together and no sense in it. No order. I am mischief, lady, but even I could not have stirred this pot into such confusion."

"I don't understand you," Edith said.

"Nor do I," said the puca.

She shook her head. "No. That's not what I mean. I don't know enough. I can feel things. I can do a little. I know Latin and Greek and grammar and theology. I don't know anything that matters."

"No," said the puca.

He was not going to help her with that. He was not human enough. She needed humanity—magical humanity—to teach her what she should know.

She should have stayed in the abbey. It was a horrible thought, but there, close by the Giants' Dance, where Sister Cecilia could come and go, she would have been within reach of what she needed. She could have found a way around the vows, surely. Sister Gunnhild had. Or she could have been granted rescue or escape. Something better than what she had here: one warded room and a frightened puca, and no one to help or teach her.

Almost by instinct she reached for the part of her that could pass into the Otherworld. But the puca flung himself at her, babbling words that only slowly came clear. "No. No! Not now. Not here. Too much—too dark. Too many. The Hunt rides. The Black Hunt, the Hunt that eats souls. It will eat yours."

"I'll go to a safe place," Edith said. "I know where—"

The puca thrust his face at hers. She had an eyeful of wild cat-eyes and sharp cat-teeth. "It is not there! Everything is dark now. Nightfall—starfall—"

"It *is* there," Edith said. "I feel it. You're feeling my mother, that's all. She swallows magic. The bright place, the safe place—it hasn't gone."

"For us it has," the puca said starkly. "She swallows magic, yes. And places that are magic. And doors that open on them. Souls, too. Her own. Her king's. You are safe, but for how long—I can't—"

"I have to get out of here," Edith said. She was suddenly, perfectly calm. "I can't stay."

"You have to." The puca was calm, too, but it was not the same kind of calm. "This room is safe. Nowhere else is. Outside is fate. It drives us all."

"I can't stay in this room," Edith said.

"I can make the dun safe," the puca said, "if—"

Edith waited, but he did not go on.

"If?" she pressed him.

He shrank almost into cat-size. His lips had drawn back from his teeth. "If there is no queen."

Edith stared. Sometimes, she thought distantly, quick wits were a curse. "You mean . . . ?"

The puca nodded.

"I can't," she said. "I can't kill my mother."

"No," said the puca. "Not kill. Enchant. Make safe. Take out of the world."

"Into the Otherworld? Where the Black Hunt rides? Where souls are swallowed?" Edith sat on her hands. They wanted to wrap themselves around that half-human neck. "That's worse than killing her."

The puca hissed. "She did it. She and the others. They made this. They twisted the Hunt and opened the darkness. If the darkness swallows them, it will not be so hungry. And you can go where your fate is. Your good fate, not the bad one."

Edith shook her head. "I can't. No."

"Then you are a fool," said the puca.

"Like my father?" Edith almost laughed. "So that's what he meant. That's what honor is. Even when you know what it will do to you, you can't stop yourself. I can't murder my mother—body or soul."

"This will bring great grief," the puca said.

"Maybe," said Edith. "And maybe good will come of it—in the end. I'll have to hope for that."

"Hope has wings," said the puca. "We who walk on earth, we can't catch it."

"We can try," Edith said.

CHAPTER 27

In spite of the puca's doomsaying, when Edith emerged from her sanctuary, she fell prey to neither darkness nor the Wild Hunt. She was still protected. The world was still quiet—more so for that her father had taken most of the men to his new war.

Her mother was still dying. The grey pall of prayer still lay over her and threatened to spread through the dun.

Edith did what she could to keep it contained. That was not very much: she knew too little. No one in this place could teach her.

The puca, who knew more than he admitted, was not choosing to impart it. The weight of foresight had crushed him down. He shrank into cat-shape and stayed there, hunting mice and sleeping in the middle of Edith's bed.

He was hiding. So, in her fashion, was she. She was waiting again, and lying low, and letting the world pass over her.

This time she did not feel quite so helpless. Something was coming. What it was, whether it would come to her or she would bring it about, she did not know. But the time for waiting and hiding was nearly over.

On a fine but blustery day, a fortnight after her father stormed out of his hall, she appropriated a pony and went for a gallop through the heather.

The pony was shaggy and unlovely, but he was fresh and sturdy, and he was as glad to be out as she was. He showed a surprising turn of speed, and a flash of heels toward the grey walls that had kept him confined through a week of rain. The road was muddy but the turf beside it was solid enough, and the pony was sure-footed.

The blight in the earth had spread far since Edith was small. It showed itself in the dying of heather along its track, and the stunting and twisting of the lesser greenery that grew there. Where the greyness met stone, it dissipated; but she could see where the stone was beginning to crumble.

This land was both stronger and weaker than the earth of England. Saxon power had not ruled here until Margaret came, but neither had the Old Things been as potent in this heath and highland as they had been for so long in the south. This was raw earth, where magic lay close to the surface, and was all the more easily disposed of.

Edith was looking for a place she remembered. The memory was half a lifetime old, and she had been much smaller and the world much larger then. But she had ridden the same pony on those escapes, and his stride had not changed since she went to England.

He was wise, that pony. He knew where she wanted to go. She let him pick his own way off the road, following a track too faint for her eyes to see. Streams crossed and crossed it again; it bent and doubled and twisted.

Edinburgh's grey bulk vanished quickly, but the firth came and went: a tumble of waves, a promise of endless sky. Folk of air danced in the wind, swirling like leaves and then scattering in sudden gusts.

Between the pony and the flocks of Old Things, Edith found her way at last to her old hiding place. It had been a hollow hill long ago. But time and the earth's shifting had broken the roof. Now it was a green bowl with a spring in it, and a tumble of fallen stones, and magic bubbling up like water from the earth.

She had more than half dreaded that the stream of magic would have dried or been corrupted. But it was as clear as the spring, and as strong as ever. It rose from deep wells, and it was as pure as any power in Britain.

She drank the magic with water from the spring. It was cold and clean, and it filled her stomach and spread through her body.

She lay on the grass that was still green, here in this sheltered place. She could feel her heart healing. Grief was there still, and fear, and old pain, but the longer she lay there, the more able she was to bear it.

That was what she had hoped to find here. But there was more to this place than a healing spring. Just before she turned the pony loose to graze, she rummaged in his saddlebag for a napkin of barley bannock and strong cheese, and a silver bowl that she had stolen—quite shamelessly—from her father's treasury.

She was not exactly sure what she was doing. She had read a little, heard a little. It might be a terribly foolish thing to do. Or it might break the spell of inaction that had been on her for so long.

She filled the bowl with water from the spring until it trembled just on the brim. Carefully she set it down on one of the fallen stones.

It was the flattest stone, and maybe had been part of the roof once. There were carvings on it, faint and all but worn away, but she could still trace their intricate, coiling shapes.

Once she had set the bowl down, the shapes seemed somewhat clearer. It was almost as if they had reached to twine about the bottom of the bowl.

She paused, listening hard with mind and ears. There was nothing evil nearby, nothing dangerous that she could sense. The magic bubbled as clear as ever. The folk of air danced as they always did. Their whole existence was the dance.

When she first set the bowl down, the water had quivered, perilously close to overflowing. Now it was still. It reflected the sky: scudding clouds, intermittent flashes of sun.

Nothing was going to happen. Edith knew no words to say, and nothing to do but let the magic flow, and wait.

Little by little she began to feel that the magic had diverted; that it was flowing not through the spring but through her. It was a strange sensation, more pleasant than not, as if she were hollow and empty and clean.

It came to her that she could direct the magic, turn it toward the bowl and the water. It fluttered like a moth, trying to escape, but she held it in a soft firm grip.

Its fluttering eased. It sank into the water and filled it. The surface rippled as if with the touch of a breath.

Edith was suddenly very tired. Her eyelids drooped; her body swayed. Just as she caught herself, the water changed.

She was looking down, not through a reflection of clouds to a silver hollow, but into a place she had seen before: a nobleman's hall. She knew the nobleman sitting in it, too. He was the grey-eyed lord— Henry, that was his name: she could almost see it written in the air of this place. Cecilia's youngest brother, who was so full of magic.

It was not magic she could use, though something told her that he knew a great deal more about it than she did. She needed to see another face, a face she held in memory, becoming more distinct the longer she pondered it.

Henry did not vanish easily. Either he wanted to stay, or the vision wanted it—she could not tell which. She had to call on her fading strength to dismiss him.

Then, at last, the one she wanted was there. Eyes as grey as the young lord's looked into hers. They saw her; knew her. "Edith," said Sister Cecilia. Edith heard her as clearly as if she stood in the hollow, clear and present beside her. She did not sound surprised at all.

Edith stumbled over the words she had planned to say, caught between startlement and urgency. "Sis—Sister—I can't—I don't know how—"

"Hush," Sister Cecilia said. "Be calm. Focus. Breathe."

Her voice eased Edith's confusion. Edith did as she bade, trying a little too hard, maybe, but not so hard that she failed altogether. After a while she could speak more or less coherently. "I need help," she said.

Sister Cecilia raised a brow. "Do you?"

"I don't know anything," Edith said. "I don't know what to do, or how, or where or when or anything else that I can think of."

"You know more than you know," said Sister Cecilia. "Be patient. Sit still and wait. When the time comes, you'll know."

"But how—"

"Patience," Sister Cecilia said.

Edith raised her hand as if to strike the water, but Cecilia had vanished. Edith felt no better than before. In some ways she felt worse.

No one was going to help her or teach her or show her the way out of this trap she had thrown herself into. She had no one to rely on but herself.

She moved to cast the water away, but some wild impulse made her drink it instead: raising the bowl to her lips and draining it in long gulps. The water was cold and clean, with a faint taste of silver. It met the magic in her and melded with it.

She was no wiser for it, and certainly no more patient. She dried the bowl and wrapped it in the napkin and thrust it into her saddlebag.

The pony snorted rebuke. Her temper was not his fault.

She was too deep in it to be contrite. She flung herself into the saddle and wheeled the pony about, clapping heels to its sides. He grunted, squealed and bucked her into a clump of bracken.

She lay winded, too busy struggling for breath to feed any more of her temper. The pony had been kind. He had not thrown her into the rocks—though maybe she had deserved it.

Slowly, still wheezing a little, she got her feet underneath her and pushed herself erect. The fall had shaken the wickedness out of her. Though her eyes were blurred with dizziness, her mind was clearer than it had been in a long while.

It was not thinking of much but getting back on the pony—more politely this time—and riding back to Edinburgh. Maybe that was patience: this clarity, this emptiness waiting to be filled.

Before, she had been waiting because she knew no better. Now she knew that something was coming. What it was, how it would come, she could not see. But Cecilia had said it: she would know.

❋ CHAPTER 28 ❋

The Day of the Dead passed in careful Christian observance. No one within reach of Queen Margaret, however near she might be to death, dared mention that great pagan rite and festival.

Edith stayed in the mortal world despite powerful temptation to go wandering elsewhere. It was not her mother she was afraid of. Something felt wrong. Even the desire in her to walk between worlds seemed to have come not from her heart but from outside. That made her more than wary. She was almost afraid.

She lay in bed that night, doubly and trebly warded, with the puca warm against her side. It was a wild night, full of wind and storm, and with the sun's setting, rain had turned to sleet and then to snow. The Night Office was already sung, deepening the greyness that had sunk through the castle's walls into the earth below. Any magical thing that passed it withered and died.

Tonight, that was not the sorrow it would have been at any other time. What rode the wind was deadly. Even through walls and wards and three heavy blankets, Edith could hear the baying of hounds and the eerie cry of horns.

She hoped her father was safe, raiding away in England. Letters had come in from him only that morning, most meant for his clerks and the commander of his guard, but there had been one for Edith. It was a hasty scribble, with nothing much to say but that he kept her in his heart.

She had laid it under her pillow, a silly, sentimental thing to do, but she made no apologies to herself or anyone else. An answer would go back to him tomorrow, written in her careful scholarly hand, saying as little as his and meaning as much. She had laid a blessing on it, a prayer for his safe return home.

The wind was howling. Sometimes there were words in it, but none of them had anything to do with comfort. They were hungry words, words that yearned after blood and souls.

She slid into an uneasy sleep. Dreams stalked the edges. She kept seeing her father, and the English king, and her mother—or maybe it was Abbess Christina—prostrate before an altar. Then the dark shape shifted and took wing, flying through a tumbled heaven: an army of skeletal horses bearing shrouded riders, in the wake of skeletal hounds.

They were hunting mortal blood. High blood, royal blood. Their thirst was for kings and princes. The earth cried out to them, begging for a share in their quarry.

King's blood could heal this earth, bring back the magic, put the greyness to flight. England's king refused to rule as the Old Things believed he should. But there were other kings in Britain.

Edith tossed in her sleep. She had king's blood, too, though she could never be a king. So did her mother, and her aunt in England. The Hunt bayed outside her window. It could smell her; it lusted after her.

Her wards held. They strained; they tattered in places. But they were strong enough—just—to keep the Hunt away.

Her spirit reached out across the dark land, through the wind and the storm, to a camp in a storm-tossed wood. The tents rocked and swayed, but like her wards, somehow they held. Dark shapes huddled under trees: the horses, heads down and backs to the wind.

She could feel her father in the middle of the tents, a surge of warmth in her heart. The Hunt had not found him yet. The earth was quiet beneath him.

She should have left him to his safety. But she had seen the Hunt; her heart was cold with terror of it. She did the only thing she knew to do, which was to try to set wards on him.

It was one thing to set them while she was in the body, with the puca to give her the words and the ritual. Bodiless in a dream, she had words and magic, but no more. There need not be more—she knew that in the core of her magic—but what to do, how to do it, that was a quandary.

Magic, in dream, had substance; it glowed like mist in moonlight. Tendrils curled about her father's tent, shaping the elements of the wards. It was reassuring to see that they were set properly—for a little while.

Not only Edith could see what she had done. The heavens had eyes, and the earth had bones to sense the shifting of powers above it. The Hunt wheeled, following the track of fresh and delectable magic—and finding the scent of royal blood.

Edith spun in her dream, now impelled to shut down the wards that had so betrayed her, now reeling back before she destroyed her father's only useful protection. She had made a terrible mistake—and it did no good to tell herself it was only a dream. It was real. On the boundary between waking and sleep, she heard the muting of the wind. It was still blowing hard enough to rock the towers, but the eerie howling was gone.

She had banished it from Edinburgh—but sent it straight to her father. She woke sitting bolt upright, her back rigid, hand outstretched as if to pull herself back into the dream.

But it was gone. Nothing that she did could bring it back. Nor was the puca there to help her. He had vanished.

She had no doubt that her stupidity had put him to flight. The one bit of magic she knew had turned on her. She could think of nothing else to do but get up, dress as warmly as she could and venture her last resort.

It was very late, and the chapel was dark. The vigil lamp had burned low. The air was perfectly still, and seemed colder even than it should. Greyness suffused it.

Edith drew a deep breath. This might make matters even worse. But she could not think of anything else to try. She clasped her hands and stilled her mind.

The prayers and psalms that came to her were in Latin and the beautiful lilt of Greek. She was very careful to keep her mind away from Saxon. The words poured through her, taking shapes as notes of music: pure clarity of chant rising to heaven, up and up to the limits of her strong young voice.

The walls caught it and sent it echoing back. The chapel rang like a bell. Edith's body resonated with it.

She had sung her heart out and exhausted her voice, until even her silence poured upward to Whoever was there to listen—God, old gods, she hardly knew. She crumpled onto her face and lay there, perfectly empty. There was nothing left in her—not even enough to know whether she had succeeded in what she tried to do. She had given it all away.

Edith opened her eyes on daylight. She lay in her bed, and the sun was well up: it streamed through the window. She had no memory of coming here—unless she had never left at all.

If it had been a dream, then it had left her remarkably spent and ill. When she tried to get up, dizziness sent her reeling back down again.

The maid who had been looking after her, whose name was Myrna, was outside the door. Edith could hear the girl chattering to another of the servants, greatly excited about something.

With dizziness came an unnatural clarity of hearing. The words rang in Edith's skull. "Oh, yes! Angels, for a fact—they sang in the chapel all night long."

"Did you see them?" the other girl asked. She sounded skeptical and rather bored.

"I was asleep," Myrna said regretfully, "but my brother Dougal, who works in the kitchen—he was up to bake the bread, and he heard them. The chapel was full of light, he said, and wings and eyes and voices—he never heard such singing. It sent him a little mad, I think."

"Oh," the other girl said. "Well. That one was addled long before this."

There was a sharp sound like a slap. "Don't you speak so of my brother! Dougal sees a little differently than most, I'll grant you that, but this he did see. I saw the light in his eyes."

"Angels in the chapel," the other servant said, with a shrug in her voice. "Where else would you expect to find them?"

"Angels are everywhere," Myrna said, "and you are a fool, and if you don't stop lagging about and bring my lady her breakfast, I'll see you thrashed right good and proper."

Even as sapped of magic as Edith was, she could feel the other girl's indignation, and hear her loud sniff and the thud of her feet as she flung open the door and stamped into the room. She was young and very sulky, and she dropped her armful of plates and bowls onto the table from a palm's height above it. They crashed down with what must have been utterly gratifying emphasis.

The noise bade fair to split Edith's skull. She buried her face in the pillow and tried to stuff it into her ears.

Even through that, she could hear Myrna knocking the idiot girl down and laying her out with ferocious—and sickeningly loud—words. None of them made any sense. Edith was not well at all. In fact, as far as she could shape the thought, she was very, very ill.

And very, very foolish. That was the last thought in her head before she sank into greyness.

"Foolish child." The voice was Sister Cecilia's, but the place in which Edith lay was too bright and beautiful to be mortal. It seemed to be a bower in a wood, under an arbor of roses.

Roses. There was something—Edith should remember—

She was outside of memory. The people who bent over her were not human, except Sister Cecilia—no nun here; her gown was white and shimmering and clung to her body—and one other, likewise in white, whose eyes on Edith were deep and quiet.

The rest were the oldest of Old Things, the great ones, tall and fair.

They were all women, or creatures like women. "Folly is every mortal's way," said the tallest of them, whose hair was like a fall of silver, and whose face was almost too beautiful to bear. "Yours no less than hers, child of men."

Cecilia bent her head, but she was not cowed. Not even close. "You know better than I what will be. I did what I had to do."

"That may be," the great Lady said. "Now you may lose her before she fulfills her destiny."

"We won't lose her." Cecilia said it softly, but the edge of it was fierce. "Help us!"

That was imperious, and impossibly impertinent. But the Lady chose not to take offense. "Once and once only," she said, "will I give this gift. Have a care you do not squander it."

Cecilia held out her hand. It was very easy just then to remember that she was a king's daughter.

But the Lady stood above any mortal king. She passed by that outstretched hand to rest her palm on Edith's forehead.

The touch was warm and cold at once, calming and troubling, comforting and deeply disturbing. "You will be what you will be," the Lady said. "First patience. Then endurance. At least, perseverance. Then destiny will hold you in its hand."

Edith did not know what that meant at all. But she would. That was the Lady's promise, sunk deep in the silence beneath the words.

Patience she had had. Now she must endure—what?

"Patience," the Lady said. If she had been mortal, Edith would have said that she smiled. She drew back, taking both warmth and terror with her.

The light whirled away, and the vision with it. The last of it lingered in an exchange of voices. One was Cecilia's. The other was a stranger's, but something about it was incontestably mortal.

"I will take her," the stranger said.

"Are you certain?" Cecilia asked. "After this, the gods know what will happen."

"I have faith," the stranger said. Like the Lady, she seemed more amused than not. "The child needs teaching. Who better to instruct her?"

"No one," Cecilia conceded. "But—"

"You have troubles enough," the stranger said. "Go, attend to them. I'll keep watch. When the time comes, I'll do what is necessary."

"As you will," said Cecilia. She sounded reluctant, but not so much that she would keep resisting.

Edith stored that exchange away in her memory, keeping it there until, like the Lady's words, it should begin to make sense. She lay for a while then in her own body and her own bed, until the world was steady around her, and she could trust herself to open her eyes.

She felt like herself again. Her body was strong. Her magic was safe in its place. Her wards were even stronger than she remembered.

She had been given more than restoration of strength. Her magic was more solid somehow. At the same time it was more supple. She could lift it like a hand and make a light in the dark room, and open the window on wind and starlight. But it would not let her see where her father was, or if he was safe.

That was part of the burden that was laid on her: to be patient and endure. She had not been given a choice.

Someday, she vowed to herself, there would be choices. Someday soon. She was not a child any longer. When she was fully a woman, she would act as she judged best—and nothing, mortal or otherwise, would stop her.

❊ CHAPTER 29 ❊

King Malcolm had been feeling strange since the eve of All Hallows. That was an unchancy night in any age or place, but as he lay in his tent, struggling to sleep, he had thought he heard the Wild Hunt in full cry above him.

It had not touched the camp or taken anything from it, man or beast, but the raiding that until then had been almost carefree had gained a wild edge. The blood they shed was redder, and their weapons thirstier for it. The earth drank it greedily, but gave nothing back.

"There's a haunting on us," said Connall. He had been Malcolm's squire years ago and still looked after the king's weapons when it suited him. It had, lately—he had demoted Malcolm's squires to cleaning armor and tending horses, and taken the royal armory into his personal charge.

Connall was of the old blood—so old that people whispered he was part fey. He was small and wiry and dark, with quick eyes and quicker hands. No one could catch a fish in a running burn faster than Connall, with only his hands and the light of his eye. That eye could see farther through a stone than most, and make good sense of what was on the other side.

Today, the day after Martinmas, they had taken a little cesspit of a castle outside a market town. The market had retreated before a torrent of rain, but the castle was surprisingly well provisioned. Malcolm's men had found ways to warm its drafty keep, mostly having to do with tanned hides on the floor, bolts of wool fashioned into makeshift tapestries, and a decent supply of firewood.

The garrison that had supposedly been left to defend the place had buckled easily once the Scots overran the town. Malcolm had stripped them of horses and arms and let them go. They were on the road to Newcastle the last anyone saw, trudging glumly in the rain.

Connall's commentary on the supernatural came in the midst of a council. To stay in the castle and hold it, or go on raiding along the river—that was the decision Malcolm had to make. He was inclined toward the raid, but too many of his captains found the lure of warmth and walls too tempting to resist.

Connall was not helping it. "Haunted?" said Rhodry, who was superstitious at the best of times. "What do you mean, haunted?"

Connall shrugged. "We've had company since All Hallows. Things watching us. Other things hunting our trail. We're not raiding alone."

Rhodry shuddered and crossed himself. Dougal the Huntsman, who happened to be his brother, cuffed him until he reeled. "Idiot! Stop your quaking. It's no more than Norman spies sniffing our arses. I'm for leaving a garrison here and storing our loot, and seeing what else there is to raid."

Now that, thought Malcolm, was what he wanted to hear. But Rhodry was no coward when it came to facing down his brother, whatever else he might be afraid of. "If there is something out there," he said hotly, "whether it's a mortal ambush or the Wild Hunt its very self, then I say we stay here where the walls are more or less solid and we can hold off whatever it is."

Dougal snorted. "What, be caught in a siege with winter coming on and barely enough provisions for a week? If you have to die, wouldn't you rather do it fast than slow?"

"I'd rather not die at all," muttered Rhodry.

"Nor would any of us," said Malcolm's son Edward, entering the fray somewhat late but with welcome good sense. "If I'm to be listened to, we'll ride out tomorrow, and trust in God and our wits. If anything is following us, I'd rather meet it under the sky, in a clean fight."

Of the dozen of them, less than half even troubled to nod. The rest were frowning or shaking their heads. The men in the hall, who could see and hear them on the dais, grumbled in response.

They were getting out of hand—and they were all blinded by comfort to Edward's eminent logic. Malcolm slammed his cup down on the rough planks that passed for a table, spraying bad ale over half the captains. "Damn your eyes! If it's death in bed you're wanting, don't you think we can find beds with a smaller stock of vermin? There's bigger castles upriver, and downriver, too—with more loot and better beds, and by God, women to warm them."

That raised a shout. This castle had presented one vast disappointment: not a female to be found, except for the mangy cow in the stable—and she was dry. But for the rain and the wind, Malcolm had no doubt that a good portion of his army would have crept off to the town in search of consolation.

Tonight they were all here. He felt the strain in them, the resistance that came to armies when they had lost the fire and begun to think too much of home.

He was not ready yet. His rage against the English king was still hot. These raids had drawn out a few defenders, but nothing notable yet. He wanted William's notice—and William's fear.

But a king was only as strong as the people who followed him, and these were losing heart. They had fought a winter campaign last year and lost. None of them was eager to do it again.

Bad luck to them, then, he thought. He was king, and he had suffered enough insults. This war he was going to win.

He bent his head to his son. "We're riding in the morning," he said. "And now I'm for bed. Sleep while you can. I'll draw Red William out, and then we'll have a battle that will get our blood running."

"Inside our skins rather than out on the ground, one would hope," someone muttered. Malcolm's glance darted, but whoever it was had hidden himself well.

No matter. These men were still his. They would obey. And he would give them a battle, if he had to take them all the way to Winchester and break down the gate.

Temper was a fire to keep him warm. He needed it that night. The air was colder than it had a right to be, even on the threshold of winter. He would never give Connall the satisfaction, but lying in his conquered bed, with no conquered woman to bear him company, he knew that Connall had told the truth. There was a haunting on them.

Tonight it was quiet, like watchful eyes. He could not help but think of a cat stalking prey, crouched outside its door, waiting for it to come out.

A mouse did not boast an army. Malcolm took that thought to sleep with him, dropping off like the soldier he was. No fighting man worth his weapons let himself lie awake fretting when there was a battle to be won.

There was bright sun come morning, with clouds blowing away toward the sea. The roads were muddy but passable, and Malcolm's men were in much the same condition. They were still his, in spite of their evening's lapse.

The fine weather roused them somewhat. Malcolm had in mind to take the next market town as he had the last, and hope the loot was better and the accommodations less drafty. If that did not draw out the king's men, he would have to gamble for higher stakes: attack a castle and hope the siege was not too long. Not too likely a prospect at this time of year, with the harvest just in, but if the gods of luck were with him, who knew? He might carry it off.

He was in a surprisingly cheerful mood, all things considered. Whatever had been haunting him had drawn back, if it had ever been there at all. He shook off the brief suspicion that it was hovering, watching and waiting for something that he, idiot mortal that he was, could not foresee.

He grinned at the sky. If there was a battle ahead of him, so much the better.

To be prudent, because after all he meant to win, he sent scouts down the river. The day passed and the army advanced, but the scouts did not come back.

He was not alarmed, not yet, but he gave the order to ready weapons. The line had drawn out somewhat; it came together in something more like battle ranks.

There was no warning. Crows had been cawing, and were suddenly still. That was all.

Edward was riding beside Malcolm, having just come up from the rear, where nothing had been happening or seemed likely to. "River's high," he said, nodding toward the flood that nearly lapped the road. "Let's hope the bridge isn't out, or we won't be getting across this week."

"Then we'll raid on this side till there's a ford we can use," Malcolm said.

Edward opened his mouth to answer. For a blank instant Malcolm wondered why the boy suddenly had a mouthful of feathers. Then the wide eyes and the sudden passage of life from the body brought the world back into focus: sharp as the arrow's point, fiercely bright as the sunlight on a thousand spears.

Malcolm had done it. He had brought out the king's men. A whole army of them lay in ambush at the river's bend, where a copse of trees and the steep hillside had hidden them. They had the heads of Malcolm's scouts on spears, and banners of great lords of the north: Mowbray and Bamburgh, earl and baron, come to drive the Scots back across the border.

Malcolm snatched at his son as he fell, but their horses shied away from one another, and Edward's body tumbled under the hooves of the men behind. There was no grief yet. No time for it. Malcolm's heart had gone cold as it always did in a fight.

The arrows were as thick as rain. The enemy had archers on the hilltops, admirably placed.

Malcolm took an instant to admire them. Normans always had known how to use a good troop of archers. It had won England for them, and might win this battle, too.

Or it might not. Malcolm was old and wily and he had a fire in his belly. He wanted Red William's head on his spear. He felt the rage building, rising up to fill his body, until it burst out in a great bull-bellow.

His ranks drew in, weapons flashing to the defense. The Normans had chosen a fine place for an archers' ambush, but a wretched one for that other and most potent weapon of theirs: the charge of armored knights. With steep slope on one side and river's flood on the other, the heavy horses had no room to maneuver.

Malcolm's smaller, lighter, faster cavalry, even here, could dart from the line in twos and threes and dozens, hack their way through the line of attackers, then draw back to charge again. His knights, such of them as there were, made a wall around him, while his foot resorted to the shieldwall that they had learned, not from the late-come Saxons, but from old Rome itself.

The enemy kept coming, and kept coming—ahead and behind. It was a trap, and beautifully laid. There was no escape to either side—only forward or back, against two armies.

Flights of arrows were not limitless. Quivers emptied; archers gave way to spearmen and swordsmen fighting in close. The shieldwall bristled with spent arrows as it pressed forward step by step. When a man fell, his mates closed in, and the ranks behind stepped over him, steady and relentless.

The Normans had no need to drive from behind. The Scots advanced of their own will. They would break through the ranks ahead—or they would not. That was in God's hands.

Malcolm had no more use for despair than he had for grief. He should have been more wary, chosen another road, given himself more room to maneuver. He had not done those things. And the Hunt, swirling above him, laughed the wild laughter of the Old Things gone mad.

He howled back at them. They might be great powers of air, but he was a king of the Gael, and long before his ancestors had been kings, they had been gods. He swept out his sword and spurred his horse through a gap in the wall that defended him, and set to work slaughtering Normans.

CHAPTER 30

Edith stumbled and fell.

She had been walking down the passage to the stillroom with instructions to fetch a potion for her mother, when the vision smote her. Such a thing had never happened before. It was like one of her magical dreams, vivid and immediate, but much stronger: so strong it brought her to her knees.

It was a soft day in Edinburgh, with a mist from the sea, but the sun was shining brightly in the vision. There was a river, swollen into flood, and a steep hillside, and a road running between hill and river.

Armies were fighting on the road and up the hill and falling into the river. She had never learned to make sense of a battle—an important skill, the men always said—and to her eye it was a confusion of men and horses, banners and weapons. Still, even she could see that some of the men were trying to push forward, and many more were before and behind and on the hill, either trying to kill them or trying to drive them into the river.

There were more than men in that place. The spectral Hunt was there, in the mortal world and under the mortal sun, well outside of its proper time and place. It circled in the air above the battle, poised to catch souls as they fled. The skeletal hounds rent them; the fleshless hunters devoured what little was left.

All but the Huntsman. He sat motionless on his bony mount, with his long stag's skull bent on the scene below, and the pale ghost-fire of his eyes followed one mortal out of them all. That was his prey, and he was waiting with terrible patience for it to fall into his hands.

Edith hovered in the air above both mortal men and Old Things. As she bent her focus on the battle, she seemed to swoop down toward it, until she drifted directly above it. Then she saw whose soul the Huntsman waited for.

Her father was fighting hard, his sword a blur of steel. He never seemed to tire. He was making headway—driving the enemy back, and rallying his own men to charge after charge. She could see that, once she focused on him: how some men fought with him, and a great number of others fought against him.

So that was how men saw a battle. She did not like it any better now she understood it. Because once she did, she could see that the Scots were terribly outnumbered, and the enemy—Normans, she presumed—could send men in waves, so that a good number rested while the others did the fighting.

This was her fault. She had shown the Hunt where to go. Now men were losing their souls because of her, and her father was like to lose his.

Somehow, far away from all this, her body staggered into the still-room and collapsed onto the bench by the door. No one was there to stare or ask questions.

It was almost too strange, being in two places at once. Tempting, too, to leave the vision behind and try to forget it—but guilt and anger were too strong.

She pressed her hands to her face, squeezing her eyes shut. The still-room vanished. There was only the battle, and her father fighting for his life and—though maybe he did not know it—his soul.

She saw the spear that struck for his heart. It was an ordinary spear in an ordinary man's hand, but it came from beside and below while Malcolm fought off a knight on a giant of a horse. He never knew it was there.

The Huntsman's face was a skull, and therefore lipless. Yet he smiled.

She cried out. She tried to muster magic—anything, spell or cantrip or sheer force of will—to turn that spear aside. But her power would not reach so far, not with the Huntsman to bar the way.

With appalling inevitability, the spear thrust through mail and padded gambeson, upward beneath the ribs to the heart. Malcolm continued the stroke that killed the knight—struck the head clean off his shoulders—and turned to find another man to kill. His stopped, eyes widening, surprised that he could not finish the turn.

Then he knew that he was dead. It did not seem to trouble him. He shrugged; laughed. Clove another Norman in two. And fell to the bloodied earth.

The spear wrenched loose as he toppled. Heart's blood sprang from the wound.

A sound like a long sigh ran through the Hunt. The Huntsman stooped out of the sky, reaching with a bony hand.

Edith had done nothing but grieve or rage—she could not even tell which. And yet abruptly she was there, between her father's body and the Horned King.

The soul was rising out of the broken flesh. The Hunt bayed. "No," Edith said.

Her voice was much clearer than she had expected. It drew power from the earth below and the sky overhead. Her father's blood was in her, and her mother's that went back to Alfred: blood of kings twice over.

She looked into the hollow sockets of the Huntsman's skull, where a corpse-light gleamed. She was not afraid. The soul behind her was still struggling, like a snake slipping its skin. It was taking a terribly long time about it, while the earth fed on the blood that drained from the body.

"Britain has his blood," Edith said to the Huntsman, who loomed over her, threatening her with sheer size. "You've no right to his soul."

"Nonetheless," the Huntsman said, "we will take it."

"No," Edith said as she had before. "You have what you came for. Now go."

The horned head lifted. It was so close that she had to tilt her own head back to see it. "You dare command us?"

"In the name of Alfred," she said, "and Arthur, and Bran the Blessed, I bid you begone. Blood of a king has fed you. Blood of a king will banish you. Turn away from the sunlight and return from whence you came."

The Hunt had gone still. Souls drifted up past it, for once forgotten.

The Huntsman laughed, a deep bay. That sound beat Edith down. Somehow she fell across her father, as the last of him slipped free. But as she looked up, she saw the Hunt waiting, spread out across the sky.

He was befuddled as souls were when the body let them go, unless they were powerful mages. Like any newborn thing, he was weak and helpless: easy prey for their hounds and their masters.

She flung her arms about him. He felt like a memory of his old sturdy self. "Take me," she said to the Huntsman. "Let him go."

The Huntsman stooped over her, peering into her face. "You are a great power still to come," he said. "Would you sacrifice it all for an old man whose time is past?"

"He is my father," she said.

The Huntsman bent lower. But the soul in her arms said, "Wait."

Edith was startled almost into letting him go. The Huntsman paused with his hand half-outstretched.

Edith did not recognize the being she clung to. He had been grey and old when she was born; she had never known him when he was young.

He was a fine young thing, upright and strong, with thick ruddy hair and a bright blue eye. The grimness that had been so much a part of him in age was barely beginning; the lines of care were not yet there at all.

He was still her father, and he stood up straight and set her gently but firmly aside. "So, old horror," he said to the Huntsman with boldness that made Edith's breath catch, "what's this you're up to now? Shouldn't you have a scrap or two of flesh on those bones?"

"We are what fate has made us," the Huntsman said.

Malcolm's eyes gleamed with the same cold light as the Huntsman's. "William has made you. So I'm the sacrifice that saves him. Was it you who drove me to this? And now you'll eat my soul?"

The bony shoulder lifted: half of a shrug. "We do what we must."

"I would think," said Malcolm, "that you would be glad of this. You're riding in daylight, taking souls when it should never be your time. Your power is greater than ever."

"We are Britain's own," the Huntsman said. "We do what we are destined to do. But if Britain dies, in the end, after we have devoured it all, we ourselves shall die, last and most terrible of all."

Malcolm tilted his head. "You are complicated," he said. "I'll make a bargain with you. Let my daughter go. I'll ride with you—and I'll help you hunt down Red William."

Edith opened her mouth to protest—because that was a terrible thing he was doing, a ghastly thing, sealing his own damnation. But neither he nor the Horned King had any care for her.

"What help can you give us?" the Huntsman asked. "A mortal soul is of little use except to feed the Hunt. Why should we make you one of us?"

"Because," said Malcolm with a death's-head grin, "I'm a king of this land and now my blood is in it. Who better to hunt a king?"

"And if we choose not to hunt him? If we pursue other quarry forever, and let him be? What then?"

"I'll risk it," Malcolm said.

"You can't do that!" Edith burst out.

Malcolm brushed his hand over her hair, light as a breath of wind. "Go back now. Live well, and remember me."

Edith could feel the magic tugging at her, the bonds of mortal flesh drawing her back. She fought, but they were too strong for her.

Everyone was too strong for her. She was sick to death of it.

"Not death," her father said. "Not yet. Go."

She whirled away like a leaf in a strong wind, straining and twisting to break free. Her father was mounted already on a beast like a horse, clothed in pallid flesh over the stark bone.

All the hunt had lost somewhat of its skeletal quality: it seemed lighter somehow, and less hideous. They had fed well, and regained a measure of their old substance.

Her father had done that. It was a great sacrifice, and a great damnation. Her heart wailed in sorrow, even as she opened her eyes on daylight.

Tears were running down her face. Her throat was raw as if she had been keening aloud as well as in spirit.

For a long moment she gave herself up to it. But cold sanity was creeping in. No one here could know what had passed far away in England. They still believed their king alive, well, and raiding Red William's towns and castles.

She wiped the tears away as best she could. There was still no one in the stillroom. The potion for her mother was made; she knew where it was, on the third shelf on the back wall, in the jar with the blue lid.

As thick as her head was with crying, she could barely smell anything, but this was pungent enough to make her sneeze. It cleared her head, too, inside and out. She measured it into the vial she had brought with her, lidded the jar and stoppered the vial.

By the time she was done, she was as calm as she could expect to be. Her first, childish impulse, to run crying through the dun, was gone. The messenger from the south would come soon enough. Until then, let Malcolm's people live without grief.

It was a fine resolve, and she was strong enough to keep it, too. She could feel her heart turning to steel. She was not a child any longer. She was going to learn how to use what she had, and how to make herself stronger.

The queen lay exactly as she had been before, hovering between life and death. Her priests had debated fiercely whether to give her the Last Rites. That would come soon, Edith thought.

There was no room in her for any more grief. She could be cold and dispassionate as she gave the vial to her mother's physician and went to stand by the bed, looking down on that wasted figure as the Horned King had looked down on her.

Had he felt powerful? Edith did not. She felt nothing.

She knelt beside the bed. Queen Margaret lay very still, but her breast rose and fell. Edith laid a hand on her forehead. It was cool. The life in her had retreated to her center.

Not long now, Edith thought dispassionately. She drew back for a moment as the physician dosed her mother from the vial. The queen struggled faintly, but her strength was nearly gone. When she lay still again, Edith returned to her side.

People came and went: priests and nuns mostly. Sometimes a man, uncomfortable in that thick, close air, came to assure himself that the queen was still alive. One or two of those were her brothers—strangers to her when she was small, and no more familiar now. She had to search her memory for their names.

She doubted that they were any more familiar with hers. They hardly seemed to see her: yet another female in black, hovering over their mother.

One of them must be king now, since Edward was dead, too. It little mattered to Edith which of them it was. She was growing out of Scotland, or Scotland had grown out of her.

Night fell as she knelt there. She hardly felt her body. Someone brought food that she ate and a cup of something that she drank. She was the only one who stayed so long. The rest took watches like guards.

In the deep night, when life even in the young and hale burned low, Edith started awake. She had not been asleep, exactly, but she had been dreaming: a dream that fled as consciousness recovered itself.

The queen's eyes were open. In lamplight they were dark, already fixed far beyond the world. But they saw Edith; they knew her face.

The cold gaunt hands gripped hers. Flesh covered them still, but she could not help but think of the Huntsman's skeletal fingers, and the terrible power that was in them.

He had never touched her. The queen held her fast. The black eyes bound her. The voice was a whisper, but it filled her skull. "I must go. My Lord, my beloved—He calls me home. But you I bequeath to England. You will restore it as I could not. I sinned—I loved a mortal man. You will turn from that path."

"But—" Edith began.

"I see," her mother said. "I know . . . You are more even than I hoped. You must go back; take vows. Give yourself to God."

Edith bit her tongue. What she did not say, she could not be forced to unsay.

The queen's grip tightened, grinding bone on bone. Edith hissed with pain. "Your father will try to force you into sin, as he forced me. Resist him."

"My father is dead," Edith said.

The pain did not stop. The queen had gone so still that but for her burning eyes and her agonizing grip, Edith might have thought that she was dead.

"He died yesterday," Edith said, "in an ambush. Edward died before him. Your sin and your hope are dead. You will be gone by morning. Will you let me go, or must you break my hands?"

The queen barely heard the last of it. "Dead? Malcolm is dead?"

Edith set her teeth. She was not going to say it again.

Nor did she need to. Margaret was breathing hard. "He cannot be dead. He was to live. He was not to—"

"You should be pleased," Edith said. She did not know that she meant to be cruel, but the truth was not often kind. "A Norman spear killed him. The Old Things took him. Now he rides with them, because he thinks they can give him revenge on the Norman king. But all they can give is damnation."

The queen's eyes flicked from Edith's face to God knew what, back and forth. "I prayed," she said, "for him to see—to understand—and turn away from the Normans. And he did. But he was supposed to live. It was the Norman king who should have died."

"Didn't you teach me," said Edith, "that prayer is a dangerous weapon? 'Be careful what you pray for. You might get it.'"

"I did not pray for this," the queen said, fierce even in her dying. "God would not be so cruel. This was the Normans' doing, they and the devils who serve them, and on their king's head be it. He will pay. Oh yes. He will pay with blood and soul, to all eternity."

Edith could not move to avert the curse. She could not honestly have said that she wanted to. It was William's fault in the end, and William's failure, that her father was dead. Let him pay as God and the gods willed.

She was almost content with that, until her mother's eyes fixed on her face. "Daughter," the queen said, "you are our legacy. Through you shall this be fulfilled. Take what I have to give; cherish it. Destroy the reivers who seized our kingdom."

Edith should have warded herself while she could. It was too late now. Greyness swirled about her. Death of magic, destruction of all that was not Christian and Saxon; deep hate and longing for vengeance overwhelmed and all but drowned her.

Her mother's life, all that was left of it, was pouring into her. She was everyone's vessel: her father, her mother, her aunt, the Church, her blood and lineage, the as yet unknown king whose sons she was meant to bear—yes, even her magic and all the powers that either depended or preyed on it. There was nothing anywhere for her, for her soul and self.

She dug in her heels. The greyness shrank. She wrenched free of her mother's grip, not trying to be gentle. Gentleness would destroy her. Her hands ached and throbbed.

"I will do what I am destined to do," she said, "but I will do it in my own way and in my own time. Your time is done. Be glad; go to your God with a soul that has only and always done what you believed was His will. Maybe you can intercede for Father, and save him."

The queen's eyes were all but empty. Edith wondered if she had heard a word of it.

It did not matter. The spell was broken. Queen Margaret was near to death, sinking low with the last of the night. When the sun rose, she would be gone.

And so would Edith. She had come to the moment when truly she must choose: whether to go on being everyone's instrument, or to make her own mark on the world.

It would have been terribly easy to turn coward, to give up and let it all roll over her. She would stop resisting after a while, even by instinct. She could recite the prayers by rote, take her vows under compulsion, shrivel away into a simple weapon for someone stronger and surer and much wiser to take up and wield.

Perfect submission: the purest of Christian virtues. Utter meekness, that would inherit the earth. She had only to surrender.

The greyness was there, waiting. Whatever part of it had been her mother was gone, slipped away while she maundered. If she opened herself, it would fill her, and she would be all that her mother had been—and more, because she had magic, and the power of the Gael. She could transform not only this earth but the Otherworld, too.

She was more than her mother or her aunt had ever dreamed of being. Even her terrible namesake, Queen Edith whose presence drained the earth of its strength, had not been what she could be.

She turned her back on it. She gathered what belongings she had— so few they fit into a small purse—and raided the kitchen for a loaf of barley bannock and a wedge of cheese. In the dark before dawn, she set out on the southward road.

dith walked alone until she was well away from Edinburgh. The sun came up; she turned off the road, making her way across the open hills. She was aiming for the place of stones.

It was not an altogether mad thing to do. She knew this country. If what she had in mind turned out to be hopeless, there was always the mortal road. She could make her way from monastery to monastery, as pilgrims did. This was a pilgrimage after all, though none that the Church would acknowledge.

Deep inside her was a great emptiness, far emptier than these stark hills. Her father and her mother had been there, alive and in the world. Now they were both gone: one to a fate quite literally worse than death, the other securely and blessedly dead.

She set that aside to grieve over later. For this moment she had to be focused. The greyness was still haunting her; she had to be rid of it, or it would taint everything she touched.

The fallen barrow had a guardian. The puca sat on the edge of it, wearing his cat-shape. He had been gone for long enough that she had thought he was driven away. But he seemed as insouciant as she remembered, springing down from his rock to coil mewing about her ankles.

That was approval. It warmed her heart a little.

Someone or something else was waiting in the green bowl. It seemed as if it had grown in the earth until it moved, rising: a figure in a hooded mantle the same color as the stones. Something in the way it carried itself told Edith that it was female.

The face in the hood was smooth and ivory-pale and of no age in particular. Edith would have said it was young, but something about it made her think of the Old Things: unimaginably old. Yet it was human, and presumably mortal.

When the lady spoke, Edith knew her. She had been with Cecilia when Edith taxed herself to her limits. She had promised something. Edith could not remember what.

"Good morning," the lady said. A very ordinary greeting, in a pleasant but distinctly mortal voice. "You come in good time."

Edith's brows went up. "Were you waiting for me?"

The lady smiled. "My name is Etaine," she said—not an answer, but not a refusal of one, either.

"Edith," said Edith, bowing slightly. "I think . . . I may have been looking for you."

The smile deepened. "You may," Etaine conceded.

"I heard you," Edith said. "Talking to Sister Cecilia. Making promises—about me. Should I be sure I want to know you?"

Etaine laughed. It was much brighter laughter than the Horned King's. Edith did not find it particularly comforting, but it did not make her skin creep. "You will have to make your own decision about that," Etaine said, still laughing. "Come, are you hungry? I have honey mead and apples, and there's water from the spring."

"I have bread," Edith said a little slowly, "and cheese."

Etaine's eyes danced. "A feast! Shall we dine?"

Whatever Edith had expected, it was not this. They sat on the grass and shared their provisions. Etaine's were clearly of earth, as she was, but also like her, they had an air of something altogether different. The apples were gloriously sweet, and the mead tasted of sunlight and flowers.

Edith's bread and cheese were terribly ordinary beside them, but there was something to be said for ordinariness, too. There was strength in it, and nourishment. It satisfied hunger admirably.

When they had eaten their fill, the sun was visibly higher, transcribing its low arc across the threshold of winter. And yet in the hollow the air was warm and sweet, the grass as green as in summer. They were not in the Otherworld, not quite, but neither were they precisely in the world of grey and grief.

The puca had shared a bit of Edith's cheese, then drunk from the spring. Edith knew well what that water could do: she watched him swell and arch and gleam, and gain back the brightness that the queen's presence had leached out of him.

She moved on impulse to follow his example. Almost she thought Etaine might stop her, but the lady watched without a word. She bent over the water, and paused.

At first glance she thought it was her own reflection there. But that should have been a narrow oval face and a long fair braid and wide-set blue eyes. This was a man: Cecilia's grey-eyed brother whom she had seen so often before.

She could not tell where he was. He was simply there, in the water. He looked up as if he had heard or seen something, directly into her eyes.

She could almost have sworn that he saw her. His eyes widened, then narrowed slightly. Suddenly he smiled.

That smile transformed him. Without it he was pleasant enough to look at, not handsome particularly, but what the servants would call a comely man. With it, he made her breath catch. It lit his whole face, and made him—yes—beautiful.

She had never seen a smile like that before. It made her want to touch him. But of course, as soon as her hand touched the water, the vision rippled and shattered. She looked into her own face, wide-eyed and startled, and the tumble of stones on the bottom of the pool.

She tried to bring him back, but he was gone. She sighed with regret and filled her cupped hands with water so cold it numbed her fingers, and sipped slowly.

Somewhere in the middle of that, she knew a stab of fear. One did not eat or drink in the Otherworld—that she had known since she was small. But here between the worlds, what would the cost be?

Whatever it was, she thought, it was worth this: brightness, calmness, strength. And if the man in the vision had helped with that, so much the better. What her mother had taken from her, this at least in part restored.

She laved her face, gasping with the cold, but it invigorated her wonderfully. Then she turned.

Etaine was on her feet, the remnants of their breakfast hidden away, and the puca sitting upright on her shoulder. "It's time," she said.

Edith had a fleeting thought of asking Etaine why Henry FitzWilliam kept appearing in her visions. But she had a long habit of silence and ingrained mistrust. She found she could not break it now.

She nodded instead, not sure at all what she was agreeing to. Maybe something terrible, but she trusted the puca, and the puca was purring raucously.

Etaine nodded as if Edith had spoken aloud, and said, "Come."

Then she walked into the hill.

Edith stood flat-footed. The barrow was still fallen, the ground green and hollow, and stones scattered in the grass. And yet there was a door that should have been flat on the ground, but was upright as it must have been while the barrow stood. On the other side of it was a shimmer that Edith knew very well: the light of the Otherworld casting a reflection on mortal earth.

She was less glad of that than she might have been, after the things she had seen: blighted land, corrupted Hunt. But the light seemed as bright as ever, clean and pure. She took a deep breath and stepped through the door.

She almost leaped back out again—but the door was shut. There was only more of the Otherworld behind her.

Ahead of her was a great crowd of people. They were all Old Things, high and terrible, dancing to the tune of pipes and drums. It was a weird and potent music, shivering in the skin and throbbing in the blood.

She had never been so close to it before. Always when she was in the Otherworld, she had seen it from far away, or hidden in hedges or along the edges of thickets, peering out at the Old Ones in their revels.

Etaine led her straight through them. The lady was almost as light on her feet as they were, and she seemed unperturbed to find herself there.

They gave way before her. Edith told herself they were simply eluding the passage of a solid and mortal body, but it was clear soon enough that they knew the lady. They were bowing as they dipped and whirled and spun away, bending low before her: Great Old Ones paying homage to a mortal woman.

Edith began to think that she was a fool and a child. Then she stumbled in confusion, because the Old Ones swayed like grass in the wind, bowing to her as well as her guide. She could find no mockery in it.

"It is a great thing," Etaine said in her ear, "to be one of earth's children."

"It's more than that," Edith said.

"Maybe," said Etaine. She was not a person who liked to answer questions, Edith thought.

Or else she only answered them in their proper time. That would be a fine thing, if somewhat exasperating.

They came through the dance to a green level, with the shadow of a wood beyond. It was green shade, living shade: no greyness or creeping blight that Edith could see or sense. Folk of air were thick in and above it.

The pipes skirled in the dance. Edith almost turned back and vanished into it. But Etaine said, "Come."

It was not that Edith was obedient. It was that she knew better than to let the dance ensnare her. Wherever Etaine was leading her, with the puca still upright on her shoulder, was safer for Edith's soul than this beautiful and treacherous place.

The wood was not as deep as it had seemed from the edge of the dance. The trees were tall and the growth beneath them low and thin, ferns and creeping vines that fed on dappled light. Folk of air shimmered through the trunks and danced on the ground.

There was no track that Edith could see, but Etaine walked unerringly, as straight as she had since she entered this country. She seemed utterly at ease. This might have been her own garden for all the wariness Edith could sense in her.

The wood thinned to a long roll of downs and a green marshy country. Light glowed on the horizon. A sea, Edith thought, or a broad lake.

Her nostrils twitched. She smelled no salt, but of wet and richness there was enough.

Lake, then. And beyond it the steep loom of a tor. A tower rose there, high over the lake.

Edith sucked in a breath. She had heard legends of such a place. "Is this . . . ?" she asked, too faintly maybe to be heard.

Etaine's ears were keen. She smiled over her shoulder. "Yes," she said. "Then you are—"

"Yes," she said again. "And you are, too, if you will."

Edith stopped. They were moving too fast; the wood had retreated with unnatural speed, and the lake was drawing closer as if of its own accord. She could see green along the shore: trees.

Apple trees. Orchards. It was after Martinmas; the branches should be bare and the trees asleep. And yet they were in full leaf, and a whole rank of them were laden with blossom. Others bore green fruit, and yet others, closest to her, were heavy with ripe apples, red and gold.

This was mortal earth and not the Otherworld—and yet it was steeped in magic.

"This is the oldest of Old Britain," Etaine said. "Here it has always been as it was in the dawn time. The rest has faded and too much of it has died. Here, the land is still whole."

Edith stood still, closed her eyes and breathed deep. This must be what it was like to be a tree in the spring, drawing up strength from the deep roots. "I never knew," she said, "that it could be like this. Even the Giants' Dance is sick and faded—and I thought it was so strong."

"That is the strength of stones," said Etaine: "deeper and colder and less clearly evident to the living. Here is the strength of green and growing things. It calls to you."

"I feel . . ." Edith said. "I feel healed."

She could feel Etaine's smile, too, warm as sunlight on her face. "It's a good beginning. Yet again, come. We're almost home."

Home, Edith thought.

When she was small it had been wherever her nurses took her, following her mother and sometimes her father. Wilton abbey had never borne that name in her heart, though she lived half her life within its walls. When she came back to Scotland, the earth had known her, but the dun at Edinburgh had not been home. It was old stone and creeping greyness, and grief that grew sharper until at last, with her father's death and then her mother's, it had cut her to the bone.

This place was a legend, a tapestry of old stories: Avalon, Ynys Witrin—Isle of Apples, Isle of Glass. On another side of its coin it was Glastonbury, a town and an abbey and a quite mortal existence, but the Isle lived somewhat out of the world.

It was a lake and an orchard and an island to which the elder ladies went by boat at times of need or festival. They all—ladies of all ages, from postulants or novices or whatever one wanted to reckon them, of whom Edith was one, to the great Lady herself, whom Edith was only mildly startled to discover was Etaine—lived on the eastern shore of the lake, in a circle of round houses of a style so ancient that the rest of Britain had utterly forgotten it. The center of the circle was a larger house, almost as large as the bailey of a castle, where the Lady and some of the elders lived.

There were dozens of ladies—more than a hundred, and certainly more than there had been in the abbey. Two dozen of these were not yet initiate. Edith made two dozen and one. They shared a house beside the lake, which though round and peak-roofed and redolent of smoke and thatch rather than stone, reminded Edith of the novices' dormitory.

That first day, Etaine led Edith to the acolytes' house and left her there with a blessing and a smile. "You'll know where to go next," she said before Edith could ask.

Edith knew nothing better than to walk through the low door—she had to stoop beneath the lintel—and find herself in a circle of faces. They were all curious. None was surprised. A few were smiling.

"We've been expecting you," one of those said.

"We were waiting," another said helpfully. She was very young, no older than Edith had been when she went to Wilton.

Some of the others were nearly as young as that, but Edith was rather relieved to see that one or two were older than she was: almost grown to womanhood. The oldest, who was one of the smallest—truly of the old blood, bright-eyed, black-haired, and quick to move and speak—took Edith's hand in warm firm fingers and drew her into the center of the room. The roof was open there over the round hearth, where a fire burned, warming the heart as well as the body.

They took Edith's clothes away and bathed her in a copper basin that looked as old as Rome, and dressed her as they were dressed, in a plain linen shift and an equally plain grey gown, with soft shoes on her feet and no veil for her hair. They all went bareheaded here, with their hair plaited and either left down or coiled around their heads.

Clearly they were not nuns. Some of them had Saxon blood: fair hair, blue eyes, slender height. None was as tall as Edith. Most were of older lineage, dark and small. They all had magic, every one.

They were nothing like the quenched children in Wilton. Edith looked from face to face and sighed inside. These were her own kind. Was she home? That, she did not know yet. But she thought, at least for a while, she might be.

PART THREE

King's Blood

anno domini 1099–1100

✳ CHAPTER 32 ✳

Henry had been patient—in his fashion. He had taken the treasure his father left him, and parlayed it, one way and another, into the title of count and a shifting pattern of power that sometimes left him empty-handed, but more often than not put him ahead of where he had been before. His brothers played their game around him and occasionally over him: a grand tug-of-war that had gone rather strange when Robert took it into his head to go on Crusade, and mortgaged his duchy to William while he was gone. Robert got money to pay his troops, and William got Normandy—for three years. Then he had to give it back.

Henry had not done badly out of that: he expanded his lands and therefore his resources, and fed his patience on a rich diet of power. It was satisfying in its way, and amusing, too, to wonder how much of this his father had foreseen.

For himself he had occupations enough: war, politics, and the deepening and strengthening of his magic. Robert had never had even a glimmer of it, and William was as obdurate in refusing to face it as he had ever been. The interlude of his sickness had passed soon enough, and William's spate of repentance had gone with it.

Britain had found ways to preserve itself. But the patches and the mended places were wearing thin. Even in Normandy, Henry felt the powers shifting.

* * *

William had been invading France—chiefly for the game of it—but just before Easter, a dozen years after old William died, he came back to England to be king for a while in his own kingdom.

Henry came with him. He was no stranger to England; he had been there often enough in this long game of princes. But this was different. England was calling him for the gods knew what purpose—though what he could do, being prince and count and most assuredly not king, he did not know.

He felt it from the sea: a deep ringing like a bell beneath the waves. When he set foot on the chalky earth of Dover, he staggered. The world was shaking itself to pieces, and he was caught in the middle of it. He had felt the same when he set foot on *Mora*'s deck after his father died: the same deep summons, the same power.

No one around him seemed perturbed, least of all William. The one who was always so close to the king, whose face said *lord* and *courtier* and whose spirit was pure power, never missed a step.

Maybe he was used to it. This land was so often broken and so haphazardly mended; it would be torture to have magic and live in it without strong defenses. Henry was used to land that was whole, that was not being eaten alive.

It had never been so bad before. People who saw him thought he had lost his land legs; then they decided he was either sick or drunk. Their rough sympathy carried him through the day. Night had its own compensation: a warm-hearted woman who brought the world back into balance.

And so it stayed, through the feast of Easter and onward into a wet and storm-tossed spring. Toward the beginning of May, William had brought the pick of his court to one of his manors, a hunting lodge under the eaves of the forest that his father had made by law and seizure. The New Forest, people called it; it was a work of men's hands as much of the gods' will, and all of it belonged particularly to the king.

It was a great monument to Norman arrogance, but it was also a great sanctuary for the Old Things. Henry wondered if William knew how welcome they had found it, or how thoroughly they had taken it for their own. William held to a steadfast disregard for matters magical—and the more so, the older he grew.

Henry had his own protections, some of which relied on closing his eyes to what did not directly concern him. Here in Brampton, where the manor was, a blind yeoman lived with his three daughters, each more beautiful than the last; and they had all cast their eye on the king's brother. They were a thorough and pleasurable distraction.

The forest's powers did not trespass within the borders of village or manor. Henry was safe enough even in the dark before dawn, making his way from the yeoman's house to the postern gate of the manor. The starlight was fitful, clouds scudding across it; wind whispered in the leaves of the trees that nearly overhung the manor's walls. The air smelled of damp and leafmould and of spring.

Someone was leaning against the postern when Henry came round to it: a man somewhat taller than he, with a too-familiar glimmer on him. Henry set his teeth. "FitzHaimo," he said. If there was a snarl in it, then so be it.

He did not need to see the man's face to feel the smile. "Count Henry. Out sowing the royal oats again?"

Henry flushed. He did not doubt that the grinning bastard wanted him to whirl to the attack. But he had more self-control than that. He mustered a smile, with a great number of teeth, and said sweetly, "Someone has to do it."

The other's smile vanished. "We are not enemies," he said.

"Are we not?" said Henry.

"For my part," said Robin FitzHaimo, "no. I was Britain's long before I was your brother's."

"I'm no threat to either of them," Henry said.

"Did I say you were?"

"You don't approve of me."

Robin grinned: a white gleam in the starlight. "When did we exchange sides in the game? I should have said that to you."

"It's not my place to approve or disapprove," Henry said.

"Nor mine, either, I suppose," Robin said. He straightened, stretching like a cat. "Whereas it is my place to invite you to a dance."

Henry stood flat-footed. He had been prepared for any number of oddities, but this was not one of them. "A—"

"Tonight," said Robin, "at sunset, be ready."

"What—" Henry began.

Robin was gone—vanished, as if he had been one of the Old Things. The postern was open, the light of a torch shining out, dazzling Henry's dark-accustomed eyes.

Henry shook his head. The man was mad if he thought Henry would trust him, even if he was incontestably loyal to both Britain and William. He owed nothing to Henry—and God knew, he might have decided that Henry's existence boded ill for one or the other of the powers he served.

Henry was not that kind of fool. He went to bed for what remained of the night, and slept well enough, all things considered. His dreams had no meaning; nor should they have. He was warded.

He rose with the sun, reasonably fresh and clear of mind. The day was mapped out for him: morning Mass, king's court, brisk if brief hunt through coverts nearby the manor—and a lady or three who cast eyes at him. Ladies were as fond of Henry as he was of them.

Maybe he smiled at one or more of them. Maybe he was circumspect. Those who had husbands, he knew better than to encourage. Those with troublesome fathers or brothers were no safer to touch, but there was something to be said for his ancestry. It gave pause to all but the most blindly outraged; and those usually ran headlong into the wall of their saner kin.

There was one lady here who might reward closer inspection. She was a widow, young but no child, deep-breasted and wide-hipped, with hair so fair it was nearly white, and wide dark eyes. Henry took note of her, aware that she was doing the same for him.

Tonight, he thought, perhaps. Or perhaps she would welcome a leisurely hunt. That would be a pleasure.

He was well over his weakness, and feeling rather full of himself. It was a bright day, warm with spring; there was talk of going a-Maying tomorrow, if the weather held. Today there was a feast in the king's honor, and dancing, and priests frowning and muttering of pagan rites.

Henry whirled out of the dance, breathless and laughing. The fair-haired lady with the dark eyes had given him her name: Rosamond. The singers were making a song of it. *Rosa mundi,* rose of the world: fairest of ladies, well fit to be queen.

Few enough of William's favorites had any eye for her, though they took up the tune with a good will. From across the hall, she arched a brow at Henry. It was half irony, half invitation.

When he moved toward her, he found his way barred. Robin FitzHaimo, resplendent in green and gold, bowed before him and said, "The sun's setting. Come."

"The dance is here," Henry said.

"And there," said Robin. "Follow."

Henry's eyes narrowed. He should turn on his heel and walk away. But there was no danger here. No hostility. There was something . . .

"Come," said Robin.

"May Eve," Henry said. "It's May Eve."

Robin nodded. "Beltane," he said. "When the dark falls, the fires will be lit. Come; we shouldn't be late."

Henry looked about him at the dance of the court, the jeweled splendor, the music, the wine flowing; the lady Rosamond, who waited for him. This was mortal beauty. It was no danger to anything but his heart, and maybe his head if he drank too deep of the wine.

What Robin would lead him to, the old gods knew. The strangeness that had felled him by the sea had risen again, stronger than ever. It made him dizzy and drowned his mistrust.

Two things he trusted, as he had since he was a child: the magic that was in him, and his mother's teaching. There was danger here, but only because all power was dangerous.

Britain was calling him, on this night of all nights. He chose to answer.

❈ CHAPTER 33 ❈

E very year at Beltane, one or more of the young women in the
acolytes' house passed through darkness and fire. Then they were
Ladies of the Isle; or they were gone.

Edith had long since begun her women's courses. She had studied
more deeply than any, and done well at it, too. But the summons never
came for her. She did not even care if she failed, and was sent away or
even died. The testing came to everyone, except her.

She felt as if she were suspended between heaven and earth, unable to
advance or retreat. She was the oldest of the acolytes who were left. Even
Grania, who would have fled even before she was tested if Edith had not
nurtured and tutored her, had passed the ordeal and taken the white robe.

On the eve of Beltane, six years after she came to the Isle, Edith went
looking for Etaine. It was not a thing any of the others would dare;
Etaine was the Ladies' Lady, the highest one, born and reborn from life
into life. She was a great power and a great mystery.

She was also a mortal woman who had taught Edith the first begin-
nings of the high magic. Edith was not afraid of her. This morning she
was too incensed to care whether she was overstepping her bounds.

She found Etaine where she usually was at this hour: stirring a pot in
the kitchen. The cooks had been preparing the Beltane feast for days;
every dweller in the Isle had taken a turn with the spits or the baking.

One might have thought that now the feast was nearly ready, the pace might have slowed; but it was as frantic as ever—except for the curve of the wall where Etaine was, where a fire burned on one of the lesser hearths, and a pot bubbled over it. As many as the mingled fragrances were, Edith could still smell the scents of rosemary and thyme, marjoram and bay, and the rich undertone of mutton.

Etaine was the calmest living thing in that place. For all the excitement around her, she was as serene as ever. She looked up as Edith approached, and smiled; then tasted the stew that she was making and made a slight face.

She dipped the spoon again and offered it to Edith. "Taste this," she said. "I still think it needs something, but I can't tell exactly what."

Edith had learned the habit of obedience. She pondered the savory mouthful, reflected on its subtleties, then said, "Pepper. It needs pepper."

Etaine reflected on that. Her face brightened. "So it does." She sprinkled in a pinch of the costly spice, tasted yet again, and smiled in great contentment.

It was beautifully done. The edge was off Edith's temper, though she was still in no charitable mood. As Etaine moved to knead one of the loaves that were rising in a long row by the hearth, Edith settled beside her. Side by side, they beat down the loaves: Etaine with grace, Edith with gratifying force.

After a while Etaine said, "You've flattened and reshaped my face admirably—six times now. Have you killed me yet?"

Edith looked up from the seventh loaf, which was dying an even uglier death than its sisters. "Should I want you dead?"

"Should you?"

That was Etaine's way: take a question, fling it back, compel an answer. In the world of magic, where so much could be indirect, subtle, allusive, Edith had found that sometimes it was useful to be direct. "I'm here," she said. "I'm not on the Isle. I'm older than anyone else in the acolytes' house. I have the magic; I have the knowledge and the skill—the whole of the Isle has done its utmost to make sure of it. Why am I still in the grey robe? What is wrong with me?"

"Nothing is wrong with you," Etaine said.

Edith wanted to shatter that composure. She attacked the bread instead, until it wheezed in protest. "Then why?"

"Do you want to go to the Isle?" Etaine asked.

Edith stopped. She stared. Etaine's expression was calm as it always was, except when she was laughing. "Are you playing me for a fool?" Edith demanded.

"If you insist," said Etaine, "I won't stop you. But consider this. There is more to the initiation than testing in magic. Would you perform the full rite? Would you do that, daughter of kings?"

That gave Edith pause. A noble lady had one thing of her own—apart from her blood and wealth, which belonged to her family—to bring to her husband. That was her virginity.

But she said, "In the old time, a bride brought her fertility, not her ritual barrenness."

"Indeed," said Etaine, "and in these degenerate days, would a king understand it?"

"A true king would."

She was being stubborn. Etaine let Edith know she knew it, without a word or a gesture. "So," she said. "You would lie with the Horned King, and dance in the fire."

Edith shuddered. Even her temper could not warm her in the face of that vision: skeletal man-shape on skeletal horse, crowned with the skull and antlers of a stag.

It did no good to tell herself that the Horned King of the rite was another power altogether: living flesh, hot and potent, such as the Huntsman had been before the blight came over him. And in strict truth, it would be a man in a mask—young, one hoped, but wise, and rich in magic.

No use. The corrupted king had seized her soul, twisting himself into it; when she thought of him, that was all she could see.

Etaine broke the silence. "I relieve you of your duties for today. Go, rest, do what you please. Tonight, come to the dance."

"Have I ever failed to do that?" Edith asked sharply.

"Come to the dance," Etaine said.

* * *

Edith finished what she had begun, which was a small disobedience but rather satisfying. Then she washed her hands and brushed the flour from her skirt and did as she was told.

Or rather, she tried. In half a dozen years, she had had precious little leisure. There was so much to do, to discover, to learn. Even her dreams were full of instruction.

And now she was free to do—what?

She wandered for a while, but everywhere she went, people were busy: preparing for the night, studying their magic and their history and lore, performing the rites that were as constant as the passage of hours in a monastery. There was no place for Edith in any of them, by the Lady's order—though she supposed she could have joined in, since she was given leave to do as she pleased.

She ended by the lake, wading in the water. The air was warm, but the water still remembered the winter: it was icy cold.

She welcomed it. It helped her focus. When her toes were blue with the chill, she sat on the shore and let the sun warm her.

The puca came stalking toward her, sleek striped cat with his tail at a jaunty angle. He came and went as he pleased, but he was always some-where nearby, mindful as ever that he had sworn to her his service.

Even in her odd mood, she was glad to see him. He sprang into her lap and made himself comfortable there, kneading her thigh with needle-sharp claws.

He was waiting for something. She began to wonder . . . maybe . . .

But no boat came across the water. No summons came to the Isle. When noon had come and gone with nothing more to say for it than a flock of swans come to feed in the lake, Edith rose, dislodging the puca, and continued her wandering.

She found herself, in the end, in a circle with the youngest acolytes, teaching them cantrips that she had learned when she first came there. Their voices were light and young, and they looked to her with awe, too young to understand that she was old enough to be dressed in white in-stead of grey.

230 • JUDITH TARR

It was a surprisingly calming exercise, and useful in its way. It reminded her of why she was here, and how far she had come. It passed the time admirably.

By the time the sun began to sink, Edith's temper was much improved. She was calmer, certainly, if not exactly resigned.

At Beltane the Otherworld lay open, and the great Old Ones could pass through. The blighted Hunt would be riding, and it would be a terrible night in the darker corners of Britain. But here, where the magic was still pure, the powers of light passed freely back and forth.

There were mighty guests at the feast, beings of power and splendor, great lords of the Otherworld. They mingled with the Ladies, and with mortal guests who in the outer world were lords and ladies, wealthy folk of the towns, even a priest and an abbess or two. They all had magic in common, and a love for the old ways.

That was nothing out of the ordinary. All the great feasts were so attended. But there were fewer of the great ones than Edith remembered from her first years there. The blight had spread wider; the magic was weaker. Her father's sacrifice had strengthened it for a while, but it was losing ground again.

Even here, even tonight, she could feel it. Deep down below the magic of this Isle, the greyness was creeping. Through the music and the dance, she almost thought she could hear the baying of the Hunt.

Her anger was gone, but her mood was dark again. What use after all to pass through the fire, if there was nothing to hope for in the end? Britain was crumbling underfoot. She had been deluding herself, blinded by the magic of this place.

The feast was done, the tables cleared away. In the great circle beyond the circle of houses, a slow drumbeat rose, calling them all to the dance. Its pulse quickened; a pipe skirled. With clapping of hands and stamping of feet, the gathering streamed into the circle.

Edith trailed behind. Her feet that usually could not resist the rhythm were dull and leaden. She was ready to turn and walk away, and keep walking until she had left the Isle altogether, when something made her pause.

The lords of the Otherworld were beautiful, and their dancing was the essence of grace. Gods knew, she had danced with them often enough, and a great pleasure it was. But she had always had a predilection for mortal men. Their beauty was rougher, their grace far more earthbound, but they were her own kind.

Some of them had old blood: they ran taller and fairer than the rest. Others had so much magic that they shone in the dark, and trails of light followed them. They drew Ladies as a lamp draws moths, and as often as not, one of them would dance until he was reeling on his feet. Then one or more of the Ladies would bear him off into the dark, and there celebrate rites that were older even than this dance. And maybe when winter came, another daughter would be born to the Isle, another acolyte to serve the Ladies.

There were mortal guests in plenty, whirling in the dance. But two looked to have just arrived: a man in green and gold, dressed like a courtier, and one in crimson so dark it seemed black in the firelight.

The man in green had the look of the old blood: tall and fair, and he was smiling, leaning toward the dance. The man in crimson was standing perfectly still. His face was in shadow, but Edith could see the wariness in him, in the set of his shoulders and the turn of his head as a skein of dancers flitted past, trailing streamers of pale fire.

The man in green seemed familiar. His magic was very strong indeed. Edith had seen him somewhere, long ago.

Quite in spite of herself, she had slipped into the swirl of the dance. Her body had a mind of its own. It had learned to dance as the Old Ones did, as if it had become the dance. That was a kind of magic, and a great joy, even when she was most troubled.

Someone, whirling past her, crowned her with flowers: the sweet pungency of hawthorn, that of all blossoms was dearest to the old gods. She spun until the world blurred, flower-scent and wild music and pounding of the blood all bound together into a single great enchantment.

❋ CHAPTER 34 ❋

It had been a long while since Henry saw a dance of the Old Ones, and longer still since he had been on the Isle of Glass. His mother had taken him there when he was small, to be blessed by the Lady and stared at by the Old Things. Maybe they had laid a destiny on his head, too, but if they had, he had not been permitted to remember it.

There was a most peculiar sense of homecoming tonight, even stronger than when he had come over from France. This was the heart of Britain—and he belonged in it.

He glanced at Robin FitzHaimo. The elaborate clothes and the long curled hair marked him the king's favorite, but in this place, under these stars, he was much more than that. He was a Guardian of Britain and a great enchanter, descendant of old powers and ancient lineage.

So then: what was Henry? Whatever his father's soul might have been—and there were those who said he was Arthur and Bran and Caswallon come back again—Henry's body was offspring of a Norman duke and a Flemish sorceress. There was no blood of Britain there, though of Druid magic there was quite enough.

Nevertheless, here was Henry, and here was, however unexpectedly, home. The dance that had begun slowly was swifter now, with a pounding pulse-beat that crept under his skin.

Many of the dancers were crowned with flowers: hawthorn mostly, a scent that to his senses was almost too pungent, and yet it stirred him strangely. There was nothing Christian about this dance, at all. It was purely pagan. It celebrated that least Christian of all rites, the union of god and goddess, flesh and flesh.

Henry loved women. He had never loved a single woman—how could he? They were all beautiful. Young or old, sweet young thing or sour old harridan, every one of them was a wonder of creation.

In the old time, he would have called them incarnations of the great Goddess. In this Christian and constricted age, they were temptation, and he was a great sinner. But ah, such a sweet sin.

Every woman here, whatever her age, was beautiful—truly; marvelously. Every one shimmered with magic. They danced life; they danced desire. They dizzied him with their sweetness.

He had barely eaten before he came here, and never touched the wine—and yet he was gloriously drunk. It was a giddy drunkenness, a surge of happiness such as he had never felt: a pure and unalloyed delight in the world and its beauty.

At the height of it, the dance paused. Or maybe the world stopped.

She was tall—nearly as tall as he—and fair. Saxon-fair, part of him thought: gold and ivory. But the power in her had nothing Saxon about it.

As fair as her face was, and it was very fair indeed, her magic was so beautiful that he stood in awe. The strength of it, the brilliance, and the perfect order of it, trained and honed like a fine weapon, moved him to tears.

In one way or another he had loved every woman he had ever lain with. A good number had borne his children; and he had acknowledged as many as came to him, and provided for them, because he was an honorable man. Some had had magic, and a few had even known what to do with it. But none had been as glorious as this.

It was the place and the dance and this night of all nights, and the sheer beauty of her. He knew that; he was sane, and rational enough when the sun was in the sky. But tonight, it did not matter.

She was staring at him as if she knew him. Her eyes were wide, her lips slightly parted.

He had to kiss them. There was nothing else he could do. Lips, then eyes—the lids trembling, but no resistance in her. She smelled of hawthorn, and of something sweeter beneath: roses, and a hint of herbs. Her hair was soft, slipping like silk through his fingers.

Most women, when he did that, closed their eyes and gave themselves up to him. This one raised her hand to stroke his hair.

Her touch made him gasp. The sheer, simple, casual power in it—the strength that hardly even knew itself—all but drove him to his knees. This was no wanton widow or hot-blooded farmgirl. Nor was she a goddess, although tonight there was that power in her.

He had no words for what she was. That disturbed him remarkably little. For this, there was no need of words.

The dance had moved away from them. They were alone on the edge of the grassy circle, some little distance from the lamps and torches, but not far from the outermost of the fires. A moment ago it had been a mound of woven withies filled with tinder. Somehow, while eye met eye, the flames had sprung up.

That was the first. The rest caught one by one in swift succession. The Beltane fires were lit.

The lady seized Henry's hand. He was already seeking hers. Their fingers met and wove together. They leaped in a broad exuberant arc.

The flames leaped high. They leaped higher. The lady laughed. Henry grinned. They tumbled together onto sweet and yielding grass.

They lay in fitful light, a flicker that now brought her face into sharp relief, now cast it into shadow. His court dress was much more intractable than her simple linen gown: no more than a long tunic, which slipped off as if meant to do exactly that.

He struggled and cursed at his own clothes, until her hands relieved him of the fight. She seemed to find it amusing to unfasten laces and slip odd bits of silk and fine linen free, uncovering him little by little.

He relaxed slowly and gave himself up to her. She rose over him, bare white body and smiling face, and fingers that lingered over him in places tender and not so tender, making him shiver with pleasure.

She stooped. Her hair streamed down, veiling them both. Her kiss had been warm before. Now it burned.

The music that drove the dance had changed. It was wilder now, its pulse more urgent. It beat in the earth, up through Henry's body into hers.

She was a maiden. That took him aback. But when he recoiled, her thighs tightened, holding him fast. If there was pain, she offered it to whatever powers she worshipped.

She was the goddess, he the god. They celebrated the rite in the heart of Britain, naked flesh on naked earth beneath the open sky. Her maiden blood fed the land. She drank deep of him, drained him dry.

Henry lay utterly and perfectly spent. The lady lay atop him, breathing hard. After an exquisite while, she lifted herself slightly and slid to the ground, but she did not try to escape his arms.

Somewhat to his surprise, he could speak. "That," he said, "was the most . . . astonishing thing I ever . . ."

Her lips stopped his, but the kiss did not linger. Her eyes were shut. She traced the shape of his face, slowly, as if to commit it to memory.

Just as he began to wonder if, after all, she was blind, she opened her eyes. They were clear in firelight, taking him in as carefully as her fingers had.

"Henry," he said. It was very important, suddenly, that she know that. "My name is Henry."

"I know," she said. Her voice was low and sweet. Her accent . . .

He waited to hear more, but that was all she said. Before he could move or speak, she rose and turned.

"Your name!" He called after her. "I don't know your name."

She was gone, back through the fire into the swirl of dancers.

* * *

Henry looked for her. He danced himself into exhaustion, hunting for that one tall, fair-haired lady—but every time he thought that he had found her, the face that turned to his had the eerie otherness of the Old Things.

She had been mortal. He was absolutely sure of that. No Old One had that particular warmth, or that wondrous humanity.

Dawn brightened over the dancing-ground. The Old Things flickered out one by one, vanishing like mist and moonlight. Mortal dancers reveled for yet a while, all who had not gone to celebrate the rite in the orchards and the hedgerows, or stumbled off to more humanly comfortable beds.

Even as sunrise limned the horizon with fire, Robin FitzHaimo picked his way across the field. Henry barely trusted his tired eyes, but he thought he had seen the king's favorite arm in arm with a lord of the Otherworld, before the light swelled and the Old One melted into it.

Robin seemed content. Henry wished he could have said the same. His body was melting with satiety, but whenever he closed his eyes, he saw her face. She had no name, but he knew her. Down to the marrow of his bones, he knew her.

He would have gone on hunting her across the Isle, but the sun was up and his guide was waiting. There were women in grey and brown and some in white, moving slowly across the field, raking and clearing and carrying the lingering sleepers off to their beds.

None of them was the lady of the night. They bowed to Robin, with glances that found him familiar. To Henry they bowed much lower. Some bowed to the ground. Sometimes they murmured in a language he did not know: the same words, as far as he could tell.

"What are they saying?" he asked Robin.

FitzHaimo was going to be coy, Henry could tell. Then of course he had to do the opposite. "They are saying," he said, " 'There is the blessed one, the year-king.' "

Henry stopped short. "The year-king? What—"

"You know what that is," said Robin.

"What, will I be dead in a year?"

The sky was clear, the air already warm, but Henry felt as if a cloud had passed over the sun. So apparently did Robin: he shivered and made a sign against ill luck.

Henry shook off the cold and the clenching of fear. "Then we're lucky, aren't we? It's a Christian world. Kings die in battle or they die of old age—but after the One died on the Cross, there's been no need for the rest of it."

"No?" said Robin. He looked as if he might have said more, but he turned instead and went on across the field, back the way they had come—a night or an age ago.

Henry could have stayed. But there were things he had to do, and people waiting, his brother among them. Women, too. Though when he thought of them, he could see none of their faces. Only hers.

CHAPTER 35

William's world was a glorious place. He was king; he would have to give up Normandy soon, if his brother came back alive, but meanwhile he was duke in all but name; and he was casting an eye on France. Why not? His father had taken a kingdom that no one believed he could take. Was his son any less a man than he had been?

He could rule it all. God was with him. After that strange sickness of his, with its eerie visions and its inducements to panic, his star had risen steadily higher.

He had even got rid of Anselm. Bloody mistake that was—he had been drunk on terror at the time. The man had proved to be a worse stick even than William imagined, and intransigent in maddening ways. He would not accept a secular lord's authority. Everything had to come from the Pope. And never mind that there were two of those more often than not, each claiming to be the one and only heir of Peter.

Ah well, William thought on this Whitsun morning, while a bishop of his own choosing—and a much better choice, too—sang the Mass in Westminster. Anselm was in Italy, or maybe France. It little mattered to William, as long as he was not in England.

William could hardly stretch and yawn loudly and shout his pleasure in the world, not in front of the whole court, but he could smile as he bowed before the altar. William was a happy man.

* * *

After Mass came the feast, the first in his new hall that was grander than anything that had ever been in Britain or Normandy or France. He had had it built higher and broader and longer, and made sure it would stand for a thousand years.

People were suitably in awe. "So high," they said. "So big. We never saw the like."

William laughed for the pleasure of it. "It's not half big enough for me," he said. "You wait—I'll build another twice as high. It will be a wonder of the world."

"Aren't you getting a bit above yourself?"

Henry had been alternately sunk in gloom and drifting in distraction since he got off the boat from France. He had a place of honor here, but William had half expected him not to appear, or else to go wandering off halfway through the first course.

But there he was, surveying William's splendid new achievement with a jaundiced eye. William cuffed him not quite hard enough to knock him down, and laughed. "There, puppy. You're jealous, that's all. If you're ever a king, you'll raise yourself higher than I could imagine."

"I doubt that," Henry said sourly. "You know what they say. The higher you fly, the farther you fall."

"My wings won't give out," William said. "I've paid a price or two. Now God loves me. He favors everything I do."

"When He drops you," said Henry, "He'll drop you hard."

"He's not going to drop me," William said. He reached for the pitcher, snatching it from the hands of the page who stood vacant-eyed and useless, and filled Henry's cup brimful with wine. "Drink up. This is a feast, not a funeral. Put off your gloomy face. You used to know how to laugh. Didn't you?"

Henry glowered at him, but drank the wine. William decided to be satisfied with that. He turned to the royal guest on his other side, the young king of Scots, who at least remembered what a smile felt like.

* * *

Henry drank his cupful, then had another, because the first might have been water for all the forgetfulness it gave him. He had been trying, night after night, to forget the lady on the Isle. Night after night, when his only thought should have been pleasure, he could only see her. He had not taken a bedmate since Beltane, because none of the women who cast eyes at him was she.

And he had never learned her name.

His brother was trading banter with young Edgar of Scots, who was not too dour as his people went—surprising, since half of him was Saxon, which should have soured his disposition even more. But Edgar was lighthearted enough, all things considered.

It was a calculated lightheartedness, Henry could see. Soon enough he came to it. "My sister," he said, "is of age now. An alliance—our two kingdoms—"

That brought William up short, Henry was pleased to see. But not for long. "What, that again? They trotted her out in front of me years ago. She agreed with me, it wasn't a match."

"She was a child," Edgar said. "She's a woman now. She's been in the abbey all this time, but I remember when she came back to Scotland, before our father died, she declared that she had no calling to the veil. She was meant to be a queen."

"I don't think—" William began.

"Do consider it," Edgar said. "You've heard the rumors, surely. Your brother the duke is contemplating marriage. He has a prospect or two; he'll be considering them once he finishes his Crusade. He's what, fifty?"

William grunted.

Edgar's fist struck the table, clattering plates and bowls, and sending a cup or two flying—lucky for him, none flew into William's lap. "Exactly! He's ripe for it—and so are you. Would you have him making heirs when you have none? What if one of them decides to make a move on England?"

"If any of them has a brain in his head, I'll make him my heir, and he'll get it honestly," William said.

Did he glance at Henry? It was hard to tell. Henry found he did not particularly care. Whatever happened—if Henry even survived to see it—William would go on for years. He would take no queen, either. Of that, Henry was as sure as if he had cast a spell of foreseeing. There would never be a child of William's body.

He thought of enlightening the young pup from Scotland, but Edgar should have known it already. Maybe he simply could not imagine a man who could not bring himself to bed a woman. God knew Henry had trouble with it, and he had seen it all his life.

Pity the poor princess, wherever she was. Some abbey in the Midlands, was it? She must sincerely hate it, if she had told her father she had no vocation. But Malcolm had died in an ambush, and his queen had died the next day. The girl must have been shipped back where she came from, whether she would or no.

There was a reason to be glad Henry had not gone that way himself. Youngest sons often did. In Byzantium they were even gelded, to keep them there. But Henry's mother had refused to send him into a life he was not fit for. "You have too much magic," she had said, "and too much spirit. You'd die there, in soul if not in body."

Maybe it was easier for a woman. Their arms were weaker, and they did not fight as well—but they had more endurance. They could suffer more, and stand it longer.

And *she,* the nameless one—did she even remember him? Had he been any more to her than a convenient partner in the rite?

He brought himself sharply to order. He was supposed to be thinking about the Scots princess, not the lady on the Isle. She was everywhere, in every thought that came to his mind.

He was possessed. He must be. But who could exorcise a memory?

William had sidestepped Edgar's eagerness at last. But the boy was not about to let it go. When the king went down into the hall to join the dance, Edgar leaned toward Henry. "Can you talk him into it?"

Henry was hard put not to burst out laughing. "No one talks William into anything," he said. "Marriage least of all."

"You could do it," Edgar said. He was a very Saxon-looking creature, tall and blue-eyed and fair-haired. The milk-and-water coloring gave him a look of guilelessness that might after all be deceptive. "Or maybe, if he saw her now, he'd be more inclined to consider her. She was a gangly thing when she was younger. She must have grown up decently—our mother always said she would."

"Your mother the saint?" Henry asked.

"Well," said Edgar, "she did deplore it. 'Cursed with beauty,' she said."

"Beauty to my brother," Henry said, "is not exactly—"

"It doesn't have to be, does it? This is for heirs, not for love."

"So they say," Henry said.

Edgar leaped up. He staggered but kept his feet. He had been into the wine, and deeply, too. "Come with me! Let's go to—wherever she is. Walham, Wilham—Wilton! That's it. Wilton. It's not too far. We can be there in a day. Or two."

More like three, Henry thought, or four or five if the roads were bad. But he held his tongue. Edgar was tugging at him. "Up! Let's ride. If we start now, we'll be there all the sooner."

What was it with royal familiars dragging Henry hither and yon? He should most probably have dug in his heels, but there was nothing of interest happening in London, except a great deal of intrigue and gossip. It was getting into summer, and the roads would be decent, and maybe there would be hunting.

And who knew? He might meet another mysterious and wonderful lady, but this time she would tell him her name.

Henry was not known as a creature of impulse. England was doing it to him, changing him, making him do things that he would never have thought of before. One of them no doubt would kill him, but he had no premonition here. This was a harmless adventure, with no worse cost than miles and time.

On the morning of the fourth day after their drunken sally forth from London, they came in sight of Wilton abbey. Edgar had rallied his

Scots guard and a pack of wild souls from the king's court, and Henry had his own handful of knights who had followed him since his father died. It was a small army, and it could have ridden faster, but with the sun shining and summer burgeoning, they had made a holiday of it.

But Edgar had not lost sight of what this ride was for. "I barely know the girl," he said to Henry as they approached the abbey's walls. "We hardly had a word to say to each other when she was in Scotland. Either she was too young to be worth noticing, or later, when she came back, I was out campaigning and she was tending our mother on her deathbed. Then she went away again. But blood calls to blood. We'll know each other when we meet."

Henry murmured noncommittally. In his experience, strangers of the same blood were strangers nonetheless. Some of his sisters he knew well—notably Cecilia. Others he hardly knew at all: they had been nuns or wives for years before he was born.

Edgar was still young enough to know everything there was to know. He was not notably younger than Henry, but he made Henry feel ancient.

He approached the abbey as innocently as he seemed to do everything else. For Henry it was no pleasant place to be. It was thick with the kind of miasma that beset other places of old Saxon power: a sucking emptiness that ate away magic.

Edgar had no magic to miss. Henry, who had too much, mustered his protections, strengthening them until the emptiness retreated. It was still there, but endurable—just.

It even distracted him from that other thing which had been tormenting him as much as ever. In a house of holy women, however brief his time there, surely he would be able to forget the Beltane fires.

This abbey had been wealthy in its day—somewhere about the time of Ethelred. It was still well founded, but the guesthouse was showing its age. The hall to which the heavily veiled portress had taken the Scots king and half a dozen of his escort was dark and low, the beams gone black with years of smoke from the hearth.

It was clean, at least—almost painfully so—and the bread and ale that they were given was not of bad quality. They were waited on by a pair of elderly nuns, one half blind and the other half deaf, who were, one would suppose, immune to the temptations of young men.

Somewhat after Henry had begun to wonder if they would be sent away without speaking to anyone of consequence, a slightly younger nun than the rest brought word from within. "Mother Abbess will speak to the king and to one other," she said.

Henry did not ask to be the other. He followed when the nun turned back the way she had come. Edgar, somewhat slower to react, trailed behind.

The air of the cloister was stifling. Henry struggled as if up a long and grueling hill. But the floor was level and slightly worn, and when they ascended a stair, it was neither steep nor high.

Edgar passed him there, eyeing him a bit oddly but keeping any questions to himself. Their guide had never once looked to see if they were with her. If they paused or slowed, they had no doubt that she would go on without them.

The stair ended at last. Then was a door and a passage and a second door; and there the nun said, "You will wait," and vanished within.

Henry used the time to focus on simply breathing. Edgar leaned against the wall, humming to himself. It was a secular tune—very. Henry wondered if he was aware of it.

The humming stopped. A moment later, the door opened. Their erstwhile guide peered out. She did not seem overjoyed to find them still there. "Come," she said.

✳ CHAPTER 36 ✳

The abbess was very tall and very thin—gaunt and grey, with eyes as pale as water under ice. Years of prayer and abstinence had worn away all softness, and leached the warmth from her.

Edgar greeted her as if there had been nothing disconcerting about her. "Aunt!" he said with every evidence of pleasure. "Well met at last. Mother told me a great deal about you. Are you well? Is all well with your abbey?"

The pale eyes blinked slowly. Maybe she was taken aback. Edgar was everything that she was not: bright, young, full of life and laughter.

And yet there was a resemblance. The height; the long oval face. The narrow hands with long fingers—stiffened with age or supple with youth, they had the same shape and quality of movement.

"Nephew," the abbess said. "You are welcome here—but you have a purpose, surely, other than to pay your respects."

Directness could be a weapon. Henry knew it very well. Edgar should have: he had been in William's court long enough. But he blinked, caught off balance. "What—I don't—"

"You have been in and out of England for a number of years, dancing attendance on a Norman king," his aunt said. "This is your first visit to this abbey. What do you want of us?"

"My sister," Edgar said—blurted, rather.

The abbess raised a brow. The air, which had been almost too warm, grew suddenly cold.

When she did not answer, Edgar hastened to fill the silence. "My sister Edith—did she take another name in religion? She came here when she was small."

"She was here," the abbess said. "Her father abducted her before he died."

"Then she went back," Edgar said. "We've had letters—Bishop Osmund has assured us—"

"Has he?" The abbess seemed to find that illuminating.

So in his way did Edgar. "Are you telling me she isn't here? That she never came back from Scotland?"

The abbess inclined her head.

Edgar's brow wrinkled. "But I've had letters from the bishop. They talk about how she studies, how she devotes herself to her calling. How can she not be here?"

"She is not here," the abbess said. "She was taken from us. We prayed for her return, and called down God's vengeance on those who took her. He granted us the latter but refused the former. Surely He knows what has become of her, for most assuredly we do not."

"But the bishop—"

"Perhaps," the abbess said with formidable gentleness, "you should seek audience with the bishop."

Edgar blinked, then nodded. "Yes. Yes, of course. Please forgive us for troubling you."

"You have done nothing that requires forgiveness," the abbess said. "Come, kneel. Accept my blessing."

Edgar knelt all too willingly. Henry was much more wary. This terrible old woman had had news that pleased her not at all. What she would do with it, he could not tell—and he did not trust her.

She laid her hand on Edgar's head. Henry, standing behind him, felt the drawing of power, whirling away into a grey void. He almost fancied that the walls of the room crumbled ever so slightly, wearing away as if with the passage of years.

His wards were barely enough. As Edgar accepted his aunt's blessing with becoming devotion, she raised her eyes to Henry. She had taken little notice of him before; he was a guard, that was all. He had hoped that she would continue to see him as nothing and no one.

But her eyes sharpened. Surely she did not recognize him. He did not look Saxon, no, but there were Normans enough with his height and coloring.

He did his best to seem harmless: lowered his eyes, folded his hands, shrank as much as he could. There was no hiding the bulk and trained strength of a knight, but there were half a hundred of those waiting outside the abbey. Henry prayed she would see no more than that, if manifestly no less.

It seemed he succeeded. She turned away from him to finish the blessing. Edgar had no magic to lose, and so much youthful strength that he did not seem to notice the life that had been drained out of him.

The abbess seemed less gaunt, her face less pale. Henry suppressed a shudder. He had heard of creatures like this, but never seen one. He was more than glad to escape from her.

They were not invited to stay the night in the abbey, nor would Henry have agreed to it if Edgar had tried. But Edgar seemed as eager to get away from there as Henry.

One or two of the men would have been happy to turn the abbey inside out in hopes of finding the missing princess, but Edgar shook his head. "If my aunt says she's not here, then she's not here. Maybe she's in Salisbury. Now I think of it, the bishop never did say she was in Wilton. He'll know where she is. We'll ask him."

Henry wondered if he had ever been that young or that impervious to the darker side of the world. Edgar was a little pale, that was all, and a little less lively than usual. It was Henry who felt as if he had had the soul sucked out of him.

The bishop was not in Salisbury. None of his clerks was particularly helpful about either his whereabouts or that of Edgar's sister, although the bishop's palace was pleased to offer hospitality to King William's royal vassal.

Henry barely noticed what he was fed. He fell into the bed he was given and slept hard and long—with dreams that fled before his eyes were fully open, leaving him with a sense half of foreboding and half of incongruous joy.

He had slept through Mass, but Edgar was not about to leave Salisbury until he had spoken to the bishop. Henry could rise at his leisure, foray to the kitchens for a sop of bread in wine, and work through the dregs of the dream.

He had been a child in this house. Some of the servants were still there, greyer and older but delighted to see him. They plied him with dainties and insisted that he tell them all the news—which for them meant all the gossip from the courts of England and France.

He owed them a great debt. They made him forget the abbess of Wilton, and the trap he had fallen into without any hint of warning. He was smiling when he left the kitchens, full of bread and wine and sweet cakes and honeyed fruit, and he had a napkinful of cakes and tartlets that they insisted he must save for later.

He took the long way back to the alcove he had been given to sleep in, by way of a cloister far brighter and more pleasant than he had seen the day before. The apple trees were in bloom in the cloister garth, and the apricot in the shelter of the wall was already setting fruit.

His sister was sitting under it, at ease as if she belonged there. Instead of the nun's habit she usually affected, she was dressed in a white gown under a blue mantle.

It had been a while since Henry had seen her, but she had not changed at all. She had looked the same for as long as he could remember: slender, tall, beautiful in a way that was not cold but neither did it invite a man to ravish her. Henry could not imagine her as anyone's wife or lover—and he had a very good imagination.

It struck him rather strangely on this morning of May, that she was older than William, but she did not look even as old as Henry. She was ageless, like one of the Old Things.

"Good morning," Henry said with what he thought was remarkable composure.

She raised a brow. "So it is," she said. "You look a little thunder-struck. I gather the Abbess Christina was more than you bargained for."

Of course she would know where Henry had been. Cecilia made it her business to know everything. "You've met her," Henry said. It was not a question.

"Often," said Cecilia. "I was mistress of novices under her for half a dozen years."

That set Henry back on his heels. He took time to sit on the grass near her, setting the napkin of cakes between them. Her eyes lit at the sight of them. She helped herself to a berry tart, biting into it with an expression of unself-conscious bliss.

"So," he said as she licked crumbs from her fingers. "How did you do it? Why weren't you eaten alive?"

Her eyes narrowed. "She's that bad?"

"She sucks the soul out of a man," Henry said. "I was warded, and I nearly couldn't stand it."

She frowned. "As strong as that? Gods; she must be drawing the old queen's malice. I never thought—" She glanced at him as if she had suddenly remembered he was there. "If I had known, I would never have let you go there."

"I'm not a child," Henry said testily. "I don't need you looking af-ter me."

"Certainly," she said. "But I was remiss, and I owe you an apology. I should have come before, and spared you that."

"Why?" Henry demanded. "What are you up to? Do you know where the princess is?"

"She is safe," Cecilia said. "Much safer than she would have been in Wilton."

"Clearly," said Henry. "Where is she, then?"

"Do you need to know?"

"I want to know."

"Ah," she said.

She was being deliberately maddening. Henry refused—with considerable effort—to let her bait him. "Edgar's trying to marry her off to William. You know how much chance there is of that—but she's a valuable commodity. Especially if she hasn't actually taken vows."

"Vows would be a difficulty, yes," Cecilia said with suspicious neutrality.

"So she hasn't taken them," said Henry. "But if she's been living in sin with a lord of the Otherworld, or has put on armor and a man's face and gone to fight in the Crusade—"

Cecilia laughed. Henry glowered, which only made her laugh the more. It was a long while before she could say, "Have no fear, little brother. The lady of Scots is as safe as she can be, and whatever sins she may have committed, none of them will bring her to harm."

"You don't reassure me," Henry muttered.

"No? I did mean to. Your young king has nothing to be afraid of, though he'll not find his sister here or anywhere else he may be allowed to look. When the time is right, she'll come where she is needed."

"You want me to tell him that," Henry said. "Why not tell him yourself?"

"Because," she said, "he knows you."

"But what can I tell him? That my sister the sorceress is hiding her away in a place where no man can go, and he's to be patient and put up with it?"

She shrugged. "If that's what he'll listen to, then yes. If not, you'll find another way."

"Not unless you tell me the truth. Where is she? What have you done with her?"

"If you don't already know that," she said, "I'm not the one to tell you. Patience, child. You'll know it all in time."

Henry opened his mouth to declare that he wanted to know it *now*, but her expression stopped him. She knew exactly what he was thinking; and she was laughing at him.

There was an instant's warning: a flicker, a shift. By the time Henry moved, it was too late. She was gone.

He struck the wall with his fist. She would have laughed at that, too, and called him *child* again. He refused to care. She had left him with a duty he was too royal a fool to shirk.

Her voice came out of air, sounding faint but very clear. "Do you trust me?"

No! he should have cried, but that would have been false. However sorely she tried his patience, he did trust her—or at least, he believed her. If she said the princess was safe, then it was true. Whatever else Cecilia was prone to, she never lied. She might obscure the truth in some delusion that she was protecting him, but that was as far as she would go.

✷ CHAPTER 37 ✷

The French were at it again—provoking William into taking the whole kingdom and setting it to rights. This time it was an irruption in Le Mans: the Count of Maine was sacking it, for mockery of William's claims to the city.

The news came to William a fortnight after Pentecost. He had had a bellyful of courts and clerkery, and had been thinking to rest his mind with a good hunt. But war was a far better diversion.

He rose up from his dinner and went straight to the stable. People were yattering at him, bleating about preparations, arrangements, armies. He laughed at that. "I'll have an army. All I have to do is ride—and my men will follow me."

That set them to squawking like a flock of broody hens. He did not stay to listen. His horse was ready—and sure enough, there were twenty men struggling into armor and yelling for sumpter mules. "Never mind that!" he said to them. "God will provide. To horse, now. Ride!"

It was glorious, that ride to the sea, galloping into the teeth of a storm. And a ship was waiting, as William had known there would be.

The sea was high, the waves tossing, but William grinned into the spray. God loved him. The ship's captain did not, but William showed him a judicious handspan of swordblade and an edged smile. "Did you ever hear of a king whom the sea dared destroy? No? Well then. God may rule the heavens, but the sea is mine—and I say it will carry us across."

The captain crossed himself at this royal blasphemy, but he had only a sea-knife and the knights who surrounded him had an arsenal of weaponry. He cursed and spat, but he gave way.

William had expected nothing else. The crew, by God's grace, were obedient to their captain; they readied the ship to sail, while William's men found places to stow themselves and what baggage they had.

Not the horses—this was not a horse-transport. The beasts would have to stay in England. They would find fresh mounts when they came across the sea.

"I'll see to them," said Robin FitzHaimo. He had been at William's side from start to finish of this ride—but now he met William's glare with unruffled calm.

William should not have been surprised. Robin was a Guardian, one of the sorcerers who claimed to keep the isle safe from untoward magic. He was not supposed to leave the bounds of Britain. But that had not kept him there before. "What's stopping you now?" William demanded.

"I'm needed here," Robin said.

William checked for an instant. "Something bad?"

"Nothing that need keep you," said Robin. "Go on, rescue Le Mans. The count will raze it to the ground if you don't."

"Come with me," William said. "Britain can spare you for a month or two."

"Not now," said Robin. He smiled, but there was no moving him. He set hands on William's shoulders and touched forehead to forehead. "Be safe. And be careful. Watch your back—and be wary of strangers. Not every man who courts you will wish you well."

"Now there's a lesson I learned when you were in swaddling bands," William said. "I'll come back to you—and you'll wonder why you ever stopped to fret."

"You'll come back," Robin said. "Come back safe—and come back alone. Any friend you make on this journey, he'll bring you ill luck."

"What," said William, grinning, "jealous of a man I haven't even met? Don't be. There's no one like you in the world."

"Be sure you remember that," Robin said.

William shook his head at the foolishness of the man, and slid out of his clasp. The captain was calling, in no very patient mood.

Even a king had to defer to the master of his ship. William darted in quickly, snatched a kiss to remember Robin by, and left him standing on the shore, whipped by the wind, with the horses in a docile line behind him.

War was war: mostly ugly, often tedious, and at times no one could even be sure who had won. William got Le Mans back, but the bloody Count of Maine dived for a bolthole that was more trouble than it was worth to pry him out of.

That was a sour victory, but William decided to take it. He would rather have had the whole of Maine and the rest of France, too—but that would come in time. William had to be patient, that was all.

It had not been a bad little war, he decided as summer rolled toward autumn. The apples were ripening in the orchards of Normandy; honey was rich in the comb, and the sheep and cattle were fat. England was waiting, but Normandy wanted a bit of him, a dispute here and a squabble there, and the touch of a ruler's hand.

He found he welcomed that. It was easy work, and less tedious than some. People were reasonably pleasant, too. Priests in Normandy were not as straitlaced as their brethren in England, or else they were better at keeping their thoughts to themselves.

There had been a boy in Le Mans—a young knight, supple and delightfully inventive—but he was the head of his family, and it needed him to oversee the harvest in their demesne. William could have commanded him to stay and sent a seneschal in his place. But when the time came, he let the boy go.

He regretted that for a night or two, but he had to admit, sleep was a useful thing. Maybe he was growing old. Young enthusiasm was losing its allure.

He missed Robin: familiar presence, familiar calm, the gift of sharing silence. Robin always knew what he needed and how to give it to him. There were no rough edges.

Yes, he thought as he led his escort down the old Roman road between Aumale and Amiens, in war and kingship he was as strong as he had ever been—but when it came to lovers, he wanted his comfort.

Time to go back to England, where that comfort was. He almost turned then and there and rode for the sea, but there were people waiting in Amiens. He could give it a day or two, finish what needed finishing, then go.

A town and castle stood where two of the old roads met, not far from Amiens. The town's name was Poix; its lord was highly regarded in these parts, but William did not recall having met him. No doubt he should, sooner or later.

Maybe he would summon the man to Amiens. A king could never have too many allies.

Some distance outside of Poix, William paused by a little river to rest and water the horses. On one side of the road, a wood stretched away in green gloom. On the other, fields and orchards rolled toward the horizon. The river ran alongside the road on the forest side before curving away under the trees.

Old Romans had camped here. William could just make out the shape of one of their earthen walls—and the sense in him that was never quite under control recognized those walls for what they were. He could almost see the gleam of helmets and hear the tramp of feet.

They were long gone. William's knights and men-at-arms dismounted, stretching and groaning. Some went off to see what fruit was left in the orchards. Those came back in a little while with a sackful of apples and pears, enough for them all.

William bit into a pear that tasted the way sunlight felt. Juice ran down his beard. He fed the core to his horse and bent to wash his face in the river.

As he knelt there with water running from his cheeks and chin and the sweetness of the fruit still vivid on his tongue, his ears caught a distant belling. As it came clearer, he recognized the baying of hounds, then beneath it the pounding of hooves.

Someone was hunting in the wood. The hunt seemed to be coming toward him. He considered pulling his escort out of its way, but the hunters would not cross the river, surely. It was shallow but swift, and its bed was stony: not impossible to ford, but not easy, either.

He saw the quarry first: a stag with a wide spread of antlers, leaping through the underbrush. It was a marvel how it kept from tangling itself in the branches of the trees. Then behind the stag, William saw the hounds, and after them the huntsmen winding their horns and baying with the hounds.

The stag ran straight for the river. Either it was too blind with panic to see the small army on the other side, or it preferred dismounted men and idle horses to a pack of hounds in full cry.

It paused on the bank, gathering to leap. Its wild dark eye looked straight into William's. Just as it left the ground, soaring over the water, an arrow appeared as if enchanted, plunging deep into its heart.

The stag hung in the air. Death took it there; it dropped.

Almost too late, William scrambled back from the water. The stag's body fell heavily where he had been. The broad tines of its antlers pierced the soft ground; one hind hoof, flailing, brushed William's cheek.

He felt the sting of a cut. His hand, lifting quickly, came away stained with blood.

"Good God, sire!" said the captain of his guard. "If you hadn't moved, it would have fallen right on top of you."

So it would have—and the antlers would have sunk into his body instead of the earth. William found that he was shaking—not with fear with a kind of crazy elation. Did not God love him? Was he not born lucky?

He looked up, grinning crazily, into a row of shocked faces. The hunt had tangled on the far side of the river, hounds milling and baying, men reining in their horses hard before they fell over one another. Only one in front, with a bow still in his hand, seemed to have kept his wits about him.

Young, William thought, though by no means a boy. If he had Viking blood, he did not show it: he was wiry and dark, with curling black hair and wide black eyes, and a nose that could have come straight from old Rome.

"Messire!" he called across the river. His voice was clear and rather high, with a strong music in it. "Your pardon, I beg you. I didn't see you. Are you hurt?"

"It's nothing," William said. The cut was shallow and had bled out quickly. All that was left was the sting.

"Take the deer at least, messire," said the young lord, "as recompense."

"Surely," said William, "if you'll come across and share it with us. We're on our way to Amiens."

"Poix is closer, messire," the young lord said, "and it's mine. May I offer you my hospitality?"

William might not have been inclined to delay, but if this was the lord of Poix, then God had delivered him into William's hand. It was worth a drop or two of blood and a night in his castle, with fresh venison to sweeten it.

Maybe there was more sweetening than that, too. The dark eyes reminded William of the stag's, but where those had been purely wild, these softened on him.

Ah, so, William thought. Indeed. He stood back as the hunters crossed the river, picking their way with care. None of them attempted the stag's leap.

When they were all on the nearer side, their lord sprang from his horse and dropped to one knee in front of William. "Messire," he said. "Walter Tirel at your service—and humbly, after what he nearly did."

William pulled him to his feet. "It's nothing," he said again. "I accept your service—and your hospitality. My name is William; I come from England."

Walter Tirel tried to kneel again, but William held him too strongly. "Majesty! I should have known—I should have recognized—"

"No more apologies," William said. His tone was mild, and he smiled, but the young lord shut his mouth with a snap.

He was well trained, and well mannered, too. He not only did as he was told; he did it with lightness and grace. William had been wary, thinking him too obsequious by half, but that proved baseless. He was polite, that was all; it was a shock be out hunting in all innocence, and find oneself face-to-face with a king.

They gutted and dressed the stag and loaded it on one of the horses, rounded up the hounds and set off down the road to Poix. Walter Tirel's men were as lively as he was, but William found they did not wear on him as the boy in Le Mans had. They made him laugh; better yet, they made him feel young again.

It was a fine feast. Walter Tirel had a lady, it seemed, but she was safely stowed on her own manor, with two sons fostered out and a third coming.

"She does her duty," Walter Tirel said over wine, when the last of the venison had gone to feed the dogs, and the rest of the feast had been taken out for the poor.

Night had fallen some while since. Most of their combined escort had gone to bed in the hall, or fallen asleep where they sat. King and count had gone up to the solar, where a sleepy page kept their cups filled, and half a dozen hounds sprawled across the floor.

William was half inclined to join them, but the chair he was in was comfortable, and the wine was good: strong and sweet. Walter Tirel sipped at his own cup, eyes on the flames in the small hearth. Autumn was coming, though the day had been summer-warm: there was enough of a chill in the air that the fire was welcome.

"She's a good wife," he said. "Quiet. Easy to talk to. Mind you I fought it when the marriage was arranged, but her dowry was too good to miss. I'm not sorry I gave in."

He was easy to talk to, too, William thought. Amazingly so, considering they had only met a few hours ago. It could have been disturbing, but William found it remarkably comfortable. This was meant. There was a blessing on it.

He caught himself rubbing his cheek where the stag's hoof had scored it. He lowered his hand and rubbed it on his thigh. "You had no difficulty, then. Considering two sons, and the third on the way."

Walter Tirel shrugged without embarrassment—and without cockiness, either. "She's a good wife: better than I have any right to. But there it is. God has blessed me."

"You almost tempt me to try it myself," William said.

Walter Tirel smiled. "Heirs are useful. They silence the preachers rather conclusively."

"My people are pushing a marriage at me," said William. "She's a child—well, not so young now, she must be eighteen, give or take a year. Raised in a convent. God knows what good she'd be."

"She might surprise you," Walter Tirel said.

William peered into his cup. Somehow it had emptied itself. The page had fallen over among the dogs. They were all snoring in unison.

Walter Tirel rose lightly and plucked the winejar from the page's oblivious grasp, bending to fill William's cup. William felt the heat of him, and caught the scent of clean young male, that was better than flowers. Flowers were a woman's vanity.

It was perfectly natural and inevitable that they should kiss. William always had his guard up—he never let it down. But here, with this man, he felt no fear at all, and no mistrust.

The kiss lingered. Just as it began to fade, William lifted them both to their feet. They picked their way through hounds and sleeping page, through the door that led to the top of the tower.

No lamp was lit in the lord's chamber, but the high window was open, and the moon shining through. Things were dancing in the light: gauzy beings, all but transparent. William told himself they were harmless.

He let himself fall to the bed, taking the young lord with him. Walter Tirel was as limber as a boy, but strong as a grown man should be. He fit wonderfully into William's spaces.

William woke in the dark. There was warmth beside him, breathing gently. His hand brushed thick curling hair and smooth plane of shoulder. Walter Tirel murmured and burrowed into his side.

William sighed. His body was still singing. His cheek stung. He would have to find a salve for that, come morning.

The moon had set, but the stars were bright. The spirits that had crowded the moonlight were gone. But something was there, watching.

Whatever it was, William could not see it clearly at all, but he felt it keenly: a deep chill. Almost he thought he saw a skeletal body and a stag's skull with a corpse-light in the sockets of its eyes, hovering in the air above the tower.

It was waiting. Watching. Against his will, he remembered Robin's warning. *Any friend you make on this journey, he'll bring you ill luck.*

William shook off both the memory and the bony apparition. It was an attack of night terrors, no more. This beautiful and perfect creature, whom God Himself had cast into William's lap, had no stink of ill omen about him. He was born as lucky as William. They were meant for this; for what William knew, thoroughly beyond doubt, was love.

❄ CHAPTER 38 ❄

I t's begun."

Edith looked up from kneading bread. The puca was perched on a stool in his least-favored, most nearly human form.

"The last dance," he said. "It's begun."

"What—" Edith said.

The puca shrank into his much more familiar and beloved cat-shape and sprang down from the stool, trotting off toward Brigid the cook, who always had a bit of fish for a cat who seduced her properly.

Edith stared after him. It was like a puca to utter something incomprehensible, then leave her to baffle herself with it.

Of course when he spoke of a dance, she would think of Beltane — and flush hot down to her center, though that dance and its aftermath was close on half a year past. She had spoken to no one of that night, and no one had asked. It was her secret, cherished close, to remember and dream about through the whole of that spring and summer and into the autumn.

Henry did not even know her name. She wanted it that way. What had been between them was a great magic, Beltane magic. It did not even matter if he remembered her—and chances were he did not. Henry was a lord in the old way; very old. He sowed his seed far and wide.

Mostly she accepted that. In ancient days she would have taken many lovers, too, and a king every year, to be sacrificed when the old year died. Now the world was different. Christians had a dream of fidelity, of one man and one woman, through life until death.

It was a dream more often honored in the breach than in the observance. Kings were worse sinners than any, and priests of the Church were not known for chastity, either, regardless of what their law might say.

Still there were times when Edith was ferociously jealous of any and all women who might have shared Henry's bed since Beltane night. She wanted him to remember her; to think only of her. To—

What? Come riding to the Isle and sweep her away? That would be all well and good, but he was a mere count. She was meant for a king.

He was the year-king—her year-king. Maybe she should sacrifice him on the Day of the Dead, or wait until Beltane came round again. Then he would be hers utterly, and no one else would ever have him.

She was a little crazed. No doubt of that. And now the puca had spoken his words that made very little sense at all.

She was supposed to remember them. She finished what she was doing, slid the finished loaves into the oven to bake, and went on to the next of her duties. Whatever was coming, people still needed to eat.

"There now," said the blue-eyed girl. She was not laughing, which was merciful of her. "Don't look so shocked. It happens to everyone."

"Not to me," Henry snarled. "It never happens to me."

"I'm sure," the girl said. She might not be laughing, but neither was she trying very hard to pretend she believed him.

It happened to be true. Henry rolled out of bed and snatched up his clothes, pulling them on so sharply the seams bade fair to give way.

They were well sewn. They held. The girl lay where he had left her, pale gold hair tumbled over her shoulders, taut breasts mocking him with their impudence. Her face was hardly more than a child's, but her eyes were old. "You'll get it back," she said. "You'll forget her—or she'll come back to you. Maybe both."

Henry stopped short. "I don't even know her name," he said.

"That matters?"

He stared at her. His eye had fallen on her because—God help him—she looked like *her*. He had not had a woman since that night in the hedgerow—the longest he had gone without since he was a beardless boy. He should have been a rampant bull, not this useless, cursed thing.

"I know a charm," the girl said. "Give me a penny and I'll get one for you."

"What, you're a witch now?" Henry said. "You have a charm to make me a man again?"

"That's not what you want," she said. "You want *her*. I'll get you something to bring you back to her."

"If that could be done," Henry said bitterly, "I would have done it."

She looked hard at him. Her eyes widened slightly. "Ah," she said. "So. Still—men don't have the art, not this kind. Either it's beneath them, or it's too high for them to see."

She held out her hand. Henry was a fool, but he thrust a silver penny into it. She tested the penny with her sharp white teeth, and made it disappear—though where, since she was naked, he could not imagine. "You wait here," she said.

She pulled on her shift and gown, plaited her hair quickly, and slipped out of the room.

Henry had no intention of waiting for her, but he had to admit he was curious. If she came back with an army of bravos intent on robbing him of the rest of his silver, well, he had defenses against that.

He sat on the bed. It was clean, which was not always the case in such places. It smelled of herbs and a faint, sharp tang of magic. Outside he heard people passing on the street, going to and from the market of Gloucester. The tavern downstairs was almost quiet. It was an odd time of day for drinkers: too early to carouse, too late to sleep.

He had found the girl in the market. Whatever she had gone there for, she had seemed pleased to forget it in return for a brisk hour with a charming knight. The owner of this tavern was a friend of hers; she had slanted a glance at the woman as she led Henry up the stair, but nothing more had passed between them. And here was the room, clean and swept, ready for trade.

He suspected it was her room. The chest at the bed's foot was full of women's things, gowns and shifts and ribbons and, deep down, a purse that clanked when he lifted it. There was a fair amount of copper inside, and a piece or two of silver.

He slipped a handful of pennies into it, on impulse—rare with him; he was careful of his money, since he had to make it last. But she had not laughed at him when the hour of dalliance turned into two hours of straining frustration. He could consider it a contribution to charity, and take the credit for it in the Christians' heaven.

When he returned the purse to the chest, his fingers caught at the dark cloth on the bottom. He drew it out. It smelled of mildew and something musty—candles? Incense?

It was a nun's habit. A novice's, he would guess: homespun brown rather than black, and the veil was small, hardly more than a kerchief. There was a wooden cross with it, and a pair of sandals, the soles almost worn through, as was the hem of the habit. Whoever had worn it had traveled far, through mud and briar.

He laid it carefully back where it had been, and the rest on top of it in as good order as he could, then shut the chest carefully and went back to sitting on the bed.

He was just in time. Her step sounded on the stair; she slipped through the curtain into the room. She seemed slightly surprised and not too displeased to find him still there.

"Here," she said. "Take this."

She held out a small bag on a string. It smelled of herbs and pungent spices. He recognized rosemary and rue, ginger and cloves, and something faint but sweet—rose petals?

If there was magic in it, maybe what she had said before was true: it was below the threshold of his senses, even as finely honed as they were. He put it on nonetheless, because she asked it. "My thanks," he said.

She shrugged. "Maybe it will work. Maybe it won't. It can't hurt."

"You're very kind," he said.

That made her wriggle like an awkward child. "I'm not kind, no. Things that are out of order—they make me itch. You'll find her, or she'll find you. Then I'll stop feeling that part of my left shoulderblade is too far out of reach to scratch."

His brows went up. "That is a very . . . unusual talent."

"Isn't it." It was not a question. "You had better go. Whoever she is, I doubt she'll be looking for you here."

Henry was more than ready to go. But once he had risen, he paused. "Tell me your name," he said.

Her head tilted slightly. She knew why he asked. And whatever she might say, she knew how to be kind. She answered, "Ethelfleda. My name is Ethelfleda."

"Ethelfleda," Henry said carefully. "I thank you for your help and patience." He bowed as if she had been a great lady, and left her standing there, looking much bemused.

As soon as Henry came back to the castle, he took off the bag, which was rather too pungent for his comfort. But he could not bring himself to cast it away. He thrust it into his purse instead, far down on the bottom, where it could do what good it might, without making him want to sneeze.

Then he forgot it. He would have liked to forget Ethelfleda, too, and the reason why he had left her, but there was no escaping that. The nameless woman from the dance had cursed him, knowingly or not. He would not be whole until he found her again.

He had no name or possession of hers to lay a wishing on. He had only the memory of her face. With that he conjured as best he could, willing her to be found.

That was all he could do, short of abandoning his brother's court and his duties there and riding out on errantry. He was not the kind of man who could do such a thing—unfortunate for his peace of mind and body at the moment, but there it was.

Word came in that very day, that the king was coming back; there was much to do to make his kingdom ready for him. Henry threw himself into it. It was not necessarily true that work made a man forget his troubles, but it did make them seem a little less daunting.

❋ CHAPTER 39 ❋

William came back to Britain as he had left it: running ahead of a storm. The sea was quiet enough for the crossing; the wind and rain held off, mostly, until he was safe in harbor.

"That's always the way of it," he said to Walter Tirel that night as they lay warm and dry together, listening to the wind and the rain. "Whenever I want to cross the sea, if there's a storm, it stops. Then after I'm across, it starts up again."

"God has laid a blessing on you," Walter Tirel said between nibbles of his ear. "Who was the English king who couldn't command the sea? Canute? He'd have gone mad with jealousy."

William grinned at the ceiling, while Walter Tirel worked his way down William's body, tracing it in shivers of pleasure. "I do love to be king," he said.

"And I love my king," said Walter Tirel, and set out to prove it.

It had been a golden autumn in Normandy, but England was thick with rain and fog. Nor did it let up, except to turn bitter, locking in the land with ice and snow well before All Hallows. By the time William caught up with his court in Gloucester, he was ready to settle in for a while where he could be assured of warmth and dry feet.

Robin was not in Gloucester when William first came there. He was in Somerset, looking after matters there. William doubted many people knew just what those matters were.

William was sorry not to see him, but guiltily glad, too. It had never bothered him before that there were others in his bed, and it had never seemed to trouble Robin, but this was different. It was not a few days' dalliance.

Robin would not mind, he told himself. They had been lovers seldom enough in recent years. Duty kept them apart as often as not; when they were in the same place, there always seemed to be some reason why they managed not to share a bed. Robin had married—like Walter Tirel, he had found a wealthy and advantageous match and an understanding wife. And of course he was a Guardian of Britain.

The eve of All Hallows brought with it a storm that would have been better suited to the depths of winter: bitter cold, fierce blasts of wind, and sleet that turned, as the day went on, to blinding snow. The great hall of Gloucester castle was a haven of warmth and light. The fires burned high, and William had ordered all the lamps and candles lit. Guests who might have left days ago were crowded into every cranny, kept there by days of rain and rivers running high, washing out roads and bridges.

"God help us if this goes on all winter," Henry said. He had been in a dour mood for as long as William had been back; at least now he had a reason, what with having been hall-bound for the better part of a week.

"If it tries," William said lightly enough, "I'll have a word with God."

"Take care, sire," said one of the numerous clerks and priests who were a necessary evil of courts. William could never remember which was which. This one was middle-aged as they all seemed to be, with ink-stained fingers and a tightly pursed mouth. "God takes poorly to such jests, however innocently meant."

William stared him down. It took a while. When the man finally lowered his eyes, William mustered a smile. "Well, Brother," he said, "we're all sick of one another's company. Why don't you give us a psalm—an invocation to patience."

The tight mouth tightened even further. William did not get what he had asked for. He had not expected to. He turned away from the clerk and called to the musicians who had been playing their fingers raw for days now. "Are you rested? Can you play again? Someone, give us a song!"

Someone with a loud and moderately tuneful voice was happy to oblige. William went back to his high seat and contemplated escaping altogether. His head had begun to ache.

A stir at the door caught his eye. People were coming in. They must have arrived only a little while ago: their clothes were dry but showed the marks of having been folded tightly not long before, and their hair and beards were damp. Some bore the marks of travel in cruel weather: cracked and blistered lips, windburned cheeks.

Most of them were knights whom William was pleased to see. The last to come in, he knew very well indeed. Robin FitzHaimo had come back to court.

William forgot guilt, confusion, even his pounding head. He rose, grinning like a fool. "Robin! Damn your eyes. Are you out of your mind? What were you doing, traveling in a blizzard?"

Robin had made his way through the crowd with an ease that had always seemed vaguely supernatural. He stood just below the dais, unsmiling, looking closely into William's face. "It wasn't so bad on the roads I took," he said.

"Bad enough, from the look of you all," William said. "You could have waited a day or two."

Robin's head shook. "Not this day."

William held out a hand. Robin sprang to the dais without it, but he clasped it once he was up, brief and hard.

"What's wrong?" William asked. "What happened?"

"To me," said Robin, "nothing. It was cold, that was all. The wind was fierce. We're glad to be out of it."

"I'm glad to have you here," William said.

He felt that other presence before he saw it, the warmth drawing closer, Walter Tirel's arm brushing his as the young lord came to stand beside him. It was innocent, William thought: a friend and familiar coming to see who had braved the storm.

And yet in Robin's eyes he saw the coldness, the closing of doors that had never been closed to him before. Robin was jealous after all— blackly, icily jealous.

"No," Robin said softly, reading him as that strong enchanter and long lover so often could. "You remember what I said. That was fore-seeing. Hubris—do you know what that is? It's a great leveler of kings."

"Are you threatening me?" William asked, his voice just as soft.

"Never," said Robin. "I'll protect you as I can. But what you've set in motion—none of us may be strong enough to stop it."

"What? Stop what?"

Robin shook his head, spreading his hands. "What will be will be."

"Nothing will be," said William, "but what I say will be."

"Indeed," said Robin. He sounded strangely sad. His glance shifted to Walter Tirel; he bowed slightly. "Messire."

"Messire," said Walter Tirel a little stiffly. He must be able to tell that there was something between William and the stranger—something strong.

Not as strong as what William had with him. William let his arm rest on Walter Tirel's shoulders, lightly, not gripping, simply letting them both know how things were. Walter Tirel had sense enough not to overdo it: he leaned a little on William, but that was all.

It was all Robin needed to see. He bowed with scrupulous correct-ness and turned, going back the way he had come.

William almost thought—feared—that he might leave the castle again. But he stayed in the hall for a while, moving among the courtiers. William felt every movement as if it were in his own skin. He barely re-laxed when Robin slipped out, until he was sure it was to go up to the room he had always had in this castle.

He was staying. William could breathe. He lowered his face to Wal-ter Tirel's shoulder for a moment, drinking in the scent that quickly had become so familiar.

The young lord slid a glance at him, with a question in it. "Not yet," William answered. "Soon."

Walter Tirel sighed faintly, but accepted it. He was more obedient than Robin had ever been. It was pleasant, William told himself. Restful. He needed that.

Soon was soon enough. They were all in bed not long after the sun set—dark had closed in some time before. It was cold in the royal chamber, even with a fire roaring, but Walter Tirel helped William to warm the air wonderfully.

William fell asleep blessedly quickly, but there was a price for that. He woke in the dark, hours before dawn. It could not have been much later than midnight.

The wind had died down. The snow might still be falling, but if so, it was silent. He was warm under blankets and furs, with Walter Tirel's sleeping body wrapped around his, but his nose was cold. When he blew out a breath, it puffed into mist.

The world was very still. The only sound was Walter Tirel's soft, regular breathing, and his own less composed breath, and the beating of his heart. It felt like the moment in church before the processional began, when everyone was suddenly quiet, and no one moved or spoke.

This was nothing so holy. William's bones knew it. The gate that was going to open was no sanctuary gate. What was waiting to come through was terrible. Powerful, and deadly.

It was the eve of All Hallows, when the old folk said the gates to the Otherworld opened, and the dead walked, and things worse than the dead hunted the skies. William knew those things all too well. They had almost killed him, nigh on seven years ago.

He had put them out of his mind, but in this icy silence, with no light but the dim glow of embers, there was no escaping memory. The Hunt was mounted and ready to ride. It hunted souls. None of the wandering dead was safe, and the living were mad if they ventured outside their houses.

William was safe here. There were blessings on the walls, wards laid long ago and renewed at every festival of the Old Things. That was why Robin had come back. That was why one of the Guardians was always near at such times. They were charged with William's protection, and they took that charge deeply to heart.

The last time William had been in Gloucester for an ancient festival—winter solstice, was it?—Robin had been the warm body beside him. This young lord, however beloved, was no enchanter. All he could give was his living presence.

It would do. When the gates opened and the Hunt came howling forth, William steeled himself against terror. No evil thing could pass his door, nor creeping death slip through his window.

He crossed himself, to be certain, and murmured a prayer. He did not particularly care which God or gods heard it. He meant it, wherever it happened to find an ear.

❆ CHAPTER 40 ❆

That winter, the last of the old century and the first of the new, was fully as terrible as it had threatened to be. Storm followed storm. When the snow was not piling itself halfway up the castle's towers, the sun was shining with complete absence of warmth. Poor folk froze in their houses, and beasts in the fields died of the cold. Deer were starving in the forests, and wolves hunted up to the walls of the towns.

Naturally the priests looked for something to blame. William was always their easy target, and they whipped themselves into a frenzy that winter, preaching blistering sermons from their frosty pulpits. It was a wonder some of the churches failed to catch fire—which would have been a gift, in that weather, where people struggled to find enough fuel to burn.

Old Osmund of Salisbury died that winter, at the beginning of Advent. He was not the first of the old or weak to let go, but he was a greater nuisance than most, since his place had to be filled before Rome got wind of it and tried to force its choice on the king.

There was a blessed break in the weather just after the new year. In other years it would have been reckoned a cold spell, but this winter it counted as a thaw. The sun even melted a little of the snow, and riding out was bracing rather than grueling. Better yet, the storms held off long enough for William to ride with a small, fast escort to Salisbury.

Walter Tirel rode with him—and Robin, who had kept a careful and at times distressing distance since he first came back to Gloucester. William supposed he should be glad there was no catfighting. Each kept his place and performed his duties, and stayed out of the other's way. Even on the road, where that was not so easy as in a royal castle, they managed it.

He loved them both for it, and was glad they were there as he got a good look at what the winter had done to his kingdom. Trees were down and farmsteads collapsed under the weight of snow. What seemed to be branches across the road, too often were stiff and frozen bodies of people or animals.

He sent men to offer food and shelter to those who needed it. It would not be enough, not for a whole kingdom, but even a little was something.

Salisbury was in a better state than some of the towns he had ridden through. Someone had had the sense to prepare for a hard winter: there was wood and fuel enough, and a large store of food. Livestock that had been slaughtered earlier in the winter had kept fresh in the storehouses, packed in snow.

"Who did this?" William asked after he had been taken on a tour of inspection. "Osmund?"

It was his brother Henry who answered him, rather than the clerk who had been his guide. "Bishop Osmund had the gift of foresight. I expect he foresaw his death, too."

The clerk nodded. His eyes were watery with either tears or winter rheum. Possibly both, considering how cold it was in this last of many storehouses. "He prepared well in all respects. His death, even though he foresaw it, was a great loss."

"I'm sorry he's gone," William said. His teeth were chattering; he rubbed his hands together. In spite of gloves lined with fur, they were half frozen. The thaw, such as it was, was over.

None of them was reluctant to escape to the warmth of the bishop's palace. The clerk's lips were blue. Even Henry, who seemed to keep himself warm in any weather, was moving a little stiffly.

* * *

The hall was as warm as they had hoped. William went straight to the hearth and basked in the heat. Henry chose to thaw more slowly, accepting a cup of hot spiced wine from a page and sipping it as he looked for the best place to soak up the warmth.

There were not many people in the hall this late morning. Anyone who could stay warm in bed was doing it. Rumor had it that a few of the wilder knights had braved the weather to try a hunt—though what they would find apart from frozen, starved cattle, Henry could not imagine. They were probably more interested in finding an escape from boredom.

Henry settled on a bench along the wall halfway between the door and the dais. He could see everyone from here, but not be bothered unless he wanted it. The wall was warmed somewhat by a tapestry, an intricate embroidery depicting the Tree of Jesse, with the lineage of the Lord Christ stitched on it in painstaking detail.

It reminded him faintly of a tapestry his mother and great magic had made, that had gone to her grave with her. "It's as much a part of her as any of her children," old William had said. "Let it be her shroud."

Henry would not have done that, but there was no stopping the old man. The thing had been a potent work of magic, an image of the old king's past and present and, it was said, of the world to come.

Henry could not have said if that was true. He had not been allowed to see it before it went into the tomb. That its image of the great oak tree giving birth to the world had changed constantly, adding visions even while it lost others, Henry had seen for himself. But his father had prevented anyone from seeing what had appeared on it during its maker's last illness and death.

Maybe that was a good thing. Prophecy could be perilous: the more one tried to prevent a disaster, the more likely it was to happen. But if one tried to force a triumph, that was a sure way to prevent it altogether.

Human blindness was safer. Henry made the wine last a long time—

with a tiny working on it to keep it from growing cold—and watched William be king. That was an interesting and rather surprising spectacle, because he was good at it. There were brains inside that brawn, and they had grown into the office rather well.

Noon came and went; the day waned to early dark. Clouds were gathering again, lessening the cold but bringing yet another threat of snow.

Not long after noon, while William bent over the rolls of the diocese with a handful of clerks, Henry started awake. He had fallen asleep on his bench, watching a game of knucklebones and listening to a page's soft singing.

In sleep he had dreamed. Shreds of it stayed with him. Beltane again, and *her* face.

He shook himself free of it. People were stirring; there was a babble of excitement at the door. A riding had come in: an embassy. Very strange, and quite unexpected—and all women.

"Nuns?" asked William as the babble washed up at his feet.

The squire who had been hanging about when the riders came in shook his head. He opened his mouth to speak, but William was no longer aware of him.

There were seven of them, standing in the doorway. They were wrapped in mantles the color of rain. Two wore white robes beneath them. The rest wore grey. Hoods shadowed their faces.

There was no question that they were all women. Nor was there any doubt in Henry's mind—or in his bones, either—as to who was hiding behind one of those deep hoods.

He rose, setting his cup down carefully on the bench. Through two reigns now, Cecilia had come and gone as she pleased, wearing a nun's habit although the vows she had taken were not to the Church or its God. For the first time she came to court as what she was: a Lady of the Isle of Avalon.

Henry felt as if the world had shifted on its pillars. He had slid into a doze of the spirit since his arrival in England at Easter, letting all the oddities and portents and the sense of imminence pass beneath the surface of his awareness. His spirit had been subtly and imperceptibly dulled, while he went on oblivious.

These ladies brought him into sharp and painful focus. The winter's bitterness was part of it. So was the deadness in the earth, and the sense that the air was not quite clean enough or thick enough to breathe, and—yes—the malaise in his body, too.

He found himself in motion, drifting toward the dais, somewhat behind the ladies. Cecilia did not lead them, rather to his surprise. She deferred subtly to the other lady in white, who was smaller and slighter than she, but carried herself with great dignity and a sense of deep and quiet power.

The rest of the embassy felt younger, their presence less potent. They were still strong, standing behind the greater ladies like guards behind a king.

William had risen as they approached. He had that much of the gift: he could sense the power in them. He did not look overly pleased.

"Ladies," he said as they came to a halt in front of the dais. They bowed, but it was not full royal obeisance: rather, it was the acknowledgment of equals.

Even that, Henry thought, was a great concession for those fabled enchantresses. He doubted that William appreciated the honor they were paying him.

The Lady who led them spoke in a clear and carrying voice. "Majesty. We come to you with a warning and a challenge."

William blinked. As blunt as he could be, he had seldom been as forthright as this. It said something for his wits that he was able to muster them so quickly. "Indeed? Have you a green knight whose head I must cut off?"

The Lady showed no sign of offense. "That may be," she said. "The warning is this: Unless you accept the full burden of your kingship, Britain itself will exact the price."

"And the challenge?" William asked.

"To be king of all Britain, in heart and soul, as you have long refused to be."

William's face set in an expression Henry knew too well. He had seen it in mules who felt themselves excessively put upon. "You know I will not do that."

"Even though, in refusing, you destroy your kingdom?"

William laughed, loud and long. "Does this look like destruction to you? The weather's bad, but that's an act of God. The kingdom's richer, the people are better off than they were when I was crowned. The sea goes quiet when I cross it. God's blessing is on me. With all due respect, Lady, your pagan gods are dead and gone, and their prophecies are empty wind. It's a new world. A new God rules it."

"'Pride goeth before destruction, and a haughty spirit before a fall.'" The Lady's face was not visible, but Henry heard the coolness in her voice. "I have read your Scriptures, sire. Your God suffers arrogance as poorly as mine."

"Is it arrogance when it's the truth?"

The Lady gazed up at him. He must be able to see her face within the hood: his eyes fixed on it. Even more coolly than before, she said, "You have been given great gifts and a great charge. You have squandered them both. Now comes the reckoning. There is still time to soften the blow—but that time is short."

"If you know my sister," said William with visible care, "and it seems you do, you know that I do not traffic in the things of your world. I rule men, and I rule well. If you need a king for the rest, I give you leave to make one. As long as he keeps to his side of the bargain and leaves the mortal realm alone, I'll give him no trouble."

"Would to the gods it were so simple," Cecilia said. She let fall her hood, arousing a gasp or two as some of the court recognized her. "If we could do that, believe me, we would. But we can't. One king for both—that's the law."

"Then change it," William said. "Or do you want me to?"

"This is not a mortal law," said Cecilia. "Only the Great Old Ones can break it—and they will not."

"Why?" demanded William.

"That is beyond your understanding," Cecilia said.

If she meant to provoke him, she was doing wonderfully. Henry stepped forward before William sprang down from the dais to throttle her. "Peace," he said to both of them. "Remember who you are."

"I do remember," William snarled. "*She* does not."

"Oh, no," Cecilia said. "It's you who adamantly refuse to do any such thing. More than Old Britain is going to fall, brother, and every bitter shard of it will be on your head."

The Lady laid a hand on her arm. She shook it off. Henry's was more persistent—and he was forewarned. When she struggled, he tightened his grip. "If you're going to bait the lion, sister, at least make sure he's secure in his cage. What is this destruction you're speaking of? Saxon uprisings? Magic dying?"

"Worse," Cecilia said. She had calmed somewhat, enough to seem almost her usual, carefully controlled self. "The wasteland; drowned Lyonesse: those are old stories, but none the less true for that. This is an island, and the sea is always hungry. A weak king and a false one brought the downfall of the Summer Country. A stubborn king and a prideful one may bring down the rest of Britain."

"I'll set the priests to praying," William said, "and do whatever penance they set for me. God will protect my kingdom."

"That will not be enough." It was the Lady who said it, gently but with unshakable surety. "Only the old way and the old rite will suffice— and even that may fail."

"I'll put my trust in God," William said.

He was no more to be moved than she. She sighed. "On your head be it," she said.

❊ CHAPTER 41 ❊

Cecilia would have had much more to say, but the Lady's words silenced her. It even gave William pause; but he rallied soon enough, and offered a knightly consolation. "Look; dinner's coming. It's bloody cold outside, and from the sound of it, it's storming again. Eat and drink with us, and let us lodge you for the night, or however long the storm lasts."

The Lady bowed. "You are most generous," she said, "but—"

William raised a hand. "No, no, I understand. You don't want to sully your pure selves with this rough male company. But I won't send you out into that storm of hell. There's a guesthouse with its own hall. I've got the men-at-arms bivouacked in there, but there's room enough for them elsewhere."

"We'll take it," Cecilia said over the Lady's murmured demurral. She kept her glare for her brother, but there was enough to spare for anyone else who might stand in her way. "You have our thanks."

"None needed," William said with edged graciousness. "It's simple Christian charity."

Her smile was dangerously sweet. "You'll reap the reward in heaven," she said.

The hall erupted in the ladies' wake. The squire who led them to the guesthouse and the servants who ran ahead to clear it of men and their gear would be telling the tale for days. They already had flights of doves leaping from the Ladies' hands, and both uttering prophecies that grew more dire with each repetition.

Henry barely noticed. As the ladies went out past him, he caught a faint scent: hawthorn and roses.

All his senses had leaped to the alert. The two Ladies' five attendants were shadows, cloaked figures who had stood mute and motionless while their superiors engaged in battle of words with the king. Their faces were hidden deep within their hoods.

One of them was taller than the others. She was last to leave the hall, gliding as they all did, as if she moved on air or water rather than human feet.

Hawthorn and roses. It could not be—and yet—

He slipped away from the tumult, blind and deaf to it. His hand dropped to the purse at his belt, where Ethelfleda's charm still was. Its sharp scent was faded now, but he still got a waft of it whenever he opened the purse. There was no hawthorn in that, that he knew of, but roses it had.

As quickly as he had run after the ladies, once he had come within reach of the guesthouse, his steps dragged. Men were tumbling out of it, servants squawking after them with brooms, amid a great to-do of cleaning and clearing and tidying. The ladies must have retreated to the inner reaches.

They would stay at least for the night. Henry did not need to disturb them immediately.

If he delayed, they might escape. *She* might escape. And the curse would stay on him, and he would be half a man forever.

He forced himself forward. The hall was midway in its transformation from a guardroom into a ladies' bower. The servants, recognizing him, bowed him through into the room beyond.

It was a sleeping-room, with beds along the walls, and a hearth backed against that of the hall. The ladies were there, divested of their mantles. They were human enough by firelight and lamplight: dark or brown in the way of the old blood, except for one, who stood tall and fair.

Henry was dimly aware that his sister was engaging in a fiercely polite altercation with a smaller, darker Lady. He had come in quietly enough that none of them had yet noticed him. There was ample time to be certain that yes, the fair one was she. There was no doubt of it.

The Ladies' discussion went on, growing both more heated and more rigidly courteous. As far as he cared to notice, it seemed they disagreed as to whether it was wise to stay the night under the king's power. Or was it the king's curse?

It did not matter. *She* was almost close enough to touch, frowning slightly as she listened. The others were sorting out the beds, arranging belongings, and chasing cobwebs out of the corners. *She* stood still, intent on the elder Ladies.

He had not remembered that she was so tall, or that she had so much grace. Her face was carved in ivory. Her hands were long and elegant, but there was strength in them, as in the rest of her. All too well he remembered how strong she was; how easily she had borne the weight and the urgency of him.

Her magic was damped to an ember, deep within wards. It was wise of her to be so careful, but it kept her from realizing that he was there.

He should leave. He had seen her. He could summon her, as the king's brother might, and speak to her where he held the power and not she.

He should do that. But he stayed where he was. The altercation was not going to end: two wills of equal strength had clashed, and neither would give way.

"Stay the night," he heard himself say. "Leave in the morning. Surely that's a reasonable compromise."

They all jumped like deer. It would have been rather satisfying if he had been in any state of mind to notice. He could only see *her*. The others were a shadow and a blur.

"I would think it would be reasonable," his sister said. There was a distinct acidity in her tone. "Whatever any of us foresees, it's not going to happen tonight."

The Lady sighed and spread her hands. "Now there are two against me. I see no good coming of this."

"But no ill, either," Henry said. He was letting his heart speak, which was a rarity with him; but in *her* presence, he could not do otherwise. "You must have known when you came, that this was a greater game than some of us knew. I think you need to let it play itself out."

The Lady looked him in the face. He had the sensation that she knew him a great deal better than he knew her. And yet she still seemed surprised by what she saw in him. "You," she said. "You are—"

She did not go on. She shook her head and shifted her gaze to Cecilia. "You knew," she said.

"Always," said Cecilia.

"I," said the Lady, half ruefully and half in exasperation, "did not. I could only see the other. This changes things. Perhaps a great deal."

"It gives us hope," Cecilia said.

"Maybe," said the Lady. "I still foresee what I foresee."

"So do we all," Cecilia said.

Henry was feeling very young. His mother had had such conversations, usually with his father, sometimes with Cecilia, when he was small. Later the queen had taught him enough that he understood some of what passed between his elders.

Here and now, he was too stubbornly proud to demand an explanation. He bowed stiffly instead and said, "Now that you have settled the question—whatever that is—may I have your leave to go?"

"That would probably be best," Cecilia said.

The Lady nodded. They had already dismissed him; their attention had turned away from him, back to each other.

Henry found that he was seething. But not enough to keep him there. He had found out what he needed to know—and fallen into an adders' nest of new questions. He would go away and brood, sulk a little, and try to understand what he had seen and heard.

KING'S BLOOD • 283

She followed him out. He was too deep in his fit of temper to notice until he had gone most of the way through the now clean and swept hall, and had his hand on the door. She caught him then, bringing him to an abrupt halt.

Her touch made him shiver. The part of him that had been so limp and useless was suddenly and rampantly erect.

He turned to face her. There was a flush on her ivory cheeks; her eyes were fierce. "You remember," she said.

"Do all you ladies talk in riddles?" Henry asked.

"You know," she said. "You remember. I didn't think . . ."

"What, that a man could keep track of all the women in his bed?"

"Yes," she said.

"You're honest, at least," he said. "We do keep track. I do. I remember every face and every meeting. Every name."

She did not take the bait. "All of them? Every one?"

"Every one," he said.

"Why?"

"Why would I forget?"

"You are not like the other men I know," she said.

"How many do you know?"

Her flush deepened. "Don't laugh at me."

"Believe me, lady," he said, "I am not laughing. You have haunted my sleep and waking every night and day since I met you."

That surprised her. Somehow he had not thought it would. "Do you mean that?"

"I swear on my mother's name," he said.

"Oh," she said softly, in wonder. She reached to touch his face. She did not have to reach far, since she was so nearly his own height. "I'm sorry. I didn't know. There were so many women's memories in you. I thought I'd be just one more—if I was that much."

"I have not been able to touch another woman since," he said tightly. "I haven't even wanted to, except once. And that—was humiliating."

She blinked. It seemed she did not understand. She had been a maiden, after all, living in a community of women.

Then she said, "Truly, I am sorry. I didn't put a curse on you, if that's what you've been thinking. All I laid on you was my blessing."

"That's what it was," he said. "A working. A Word."

"A prayer for your safety and a wish that I would see you again," she said. "That was all."

"It was enough," Henry said. He found he could not cling to his anger. The sight, the scent of her, made him dizzy.

"I'll take it off you," she said. "Here. Let me—"

"No." That startled both of them. "No," Henry said again. "Leave it."

"But—"

"I don't want to forget you," he said.

"If you need my working on you to remember me," she said tartly, "then maybe I'm not worth remembering."

"I didn't mean—" Henry said.

She brushed his brow and cheek with her hand. He felt something go: a tightness in the spirit, as it were.

It did not change anything. He was still captivated—exasperated, too. Annoyed. Obsessed.

He hoped she could see it. Maybe she could: she frowned at him. "Now go," she said.

"Tell me your name," he said.

Her lips set.

"Why? What don't you want me to know?"

She took his face in her hands and drew it down the little way to hers, and kissed him long and deep. She did not answer his question.

She was not going to. He, unlike his sister, knew when a battle could not be won.

He also knew how to circle around it and take it from behind. "Very well then. I'll give you a name. Mathilda—I'll call you Mathilda."

Her eyes widened. "But that's—"

"My mother is dead," he said, "and no longer in need of it. Why, are you insulted? Did I offend you?"

"Not in the slightest," she said. "It feels . . . odd. Pleasing. I like it."

"Do you mean that?"

"I always say what I mean."

"So you do," he said.

She kissed him again, even longer this time. "Thank you," she said.

That was a dismissal, he thought. But she held him back with one hand, while the other reached into her robe, drawing out something wrapped in a bit of old linen.

The scent that came from it was unmistakable. She folded the worn fabric back from a rose. It was pure and shining white, fresh and blooming as if she had plucked it but a moment before. But there was no such blossom anywhere in this place, not in the dead of winter.

She held it out to him. "Take it," she said. "Keep it. It comes from the Otherworld; it's been with me since I was a child. It has my blessing on it, but that shouldn't trouble you. When you want to remember me, it will help."

He had to take the thing: she would have dropped it otherwise. Its scent was heavenly sweet. "I always did prefer roses to hawthorn," he said.

"I, too," she said, "but for a garland, with the thorns, it would be a little too much of a sacrifice for most."

He found that he was smiling. He folded the rose on its wrappings and slipped it into his purse, next to the talisman that might have brought him to her, and might not. "Mathilda," he said: sealing the name on her.

Then he could go—not easily, but it was time.

They would meet again. He was as sure of that as he was of his own name.

❋ CHAPTER 42 ❋

Edith had expected to meet Henry—had asked to come on this embassy because of it. What she had not expected was that he would do something so simple and yet so profound as to change her name. More than that, he had named her for his mother, that great enchantress and queen.

She was still Edith to herself, but the name of Mathilda had begun to work inside her, opening parts of her that had been shut, and making some of them stronger. It was a strange working and subtly potent.

Cecilia fought to the last to confront her brother again and force him to see what he must do. But Etaine won that battle. William would only grow more intransigent, the harder they tried to compel him.

"Much like you," Etaine said gently.

Cecilia's nostrils thinned. Edith braced for the blast of magic, but Cecilia was too wise to fall into that trap. "You'll pay for that," she said.

"It will be worth the price," said Etaine serenely.

Cecilia snarled, sounding remarkably like William, but she gave way.

They left Salisbury at dawn, in still and bitter cold. Wind and snow had stopped, but the clouds were heavy and low. It would be a bitter ride, even by the straight track.

Edith almost turned and galloped back into the town. She could feel

Henry in the bishop's palace like an ember in a hearth full of ashes. He was dreaming of her.

Just as she tightened rein to turn her mare, Cecilia spoke beside her. It was nothing of consequence, but it distracted her, as no doubt Cecilia had intended.

The moment of temptation had passed. Edith was bound to the journey.

They were already out of sight of Salisbury, advancing toward the Giants' Dance. In the vicinity of so much power, straight tracks could turn strange. This one pierced the Otherworld itself rather than skimming its edges, and passed through a place of ash and burned stumps of trees.

That was so much like Edith's vision of Henry in Salisbury that she looked for the ember in the ashes, but there was none. It was all grey and lifeless: dead to the heart of things.

"Half a thousand years of Saxons," Cecilia said, still riding beside Edith, "then kings who were meant to restore Britain but squandered their inheritance instead, all in a fog of Christian holiness. Now the Christians' reckoning of years comes to a crux. A thousand years and a hundred, they calculate, since their god-man was born. To the Old Things that means nothing, but men believe in it—and men's belief has immeasurable power."

"'God created men, but men create their gods,'" Edith said. "That was in a book I read when I was in the abbey."

"The gods existed long before men," said Cecilia, "but men's faith made them strong. When that faith faded, so did they. Now even their bright country is dying."

"Do you think one man, even if he is a king, can turn the tide?" Edith asked her. "My father gave his blood to the earth, and that won seven years. Now it's worse than ever. What will we have to do, go back to the year-king? Then the season-king, the month-king, the day-king? Will there be any end to it?"

"If my brother takes the kingship in the old way, the deep way, in heart and soul, there is hope," Cecilia said. "We can help, we Guardians. So can and will every other person of power in Britain. But we must have a king to complete us. Otherwise we remain a mere mob of discrete magics."

"I'm afraid that won't be Red William," Edith said. "He doesn't believe, even when he's seen—even when it's come near to killing him. He blinds himself to the truth."

"And yet my father chose him to be king," Cecilia said. "I never knew the old man hated Britain so much."

"Maybe he didn't," said Edith. "Maybe he knew something we don't know."

"I would hope for that," Cecilia said, "but I don't know if I can believe in it."

"Faith has power," Edith said. "Remember that."

Cecilia shot her a glance, warning her against insolence, but she could hardly deny her own word, turned back on her though it might be.

It was a hard road back to the Isle, and a harder winter waiting. The Otherworld could not warm the bitter cold, for it was slowly freezing over itself. The undying grass was fading; the flowers were withered and dead.

Edith wondered if the rose was still alive somewhere near Henry—if he had even kept it. She felt in her heart that he had. So much was breaking and dying in this terrible winter, but she still dreamed of him. As often as not, the dreams could have been true: he was sleeping or feasting or sitting over wine with this lord or that.

The Isle clung to its strength. More and more of that was coming from the Ladies: the earth had little to give, and the Otherworld was in worsening straits.

By the shifting of the sun's path and the turning of the stars, winter should have been giving way to spring. The snow was still deep, rivers locked in ice. Even the lake of the Isle was frozen far out from its banks, although the island in its center rose from a ring of clear water.

One morning on her way to teach the youngest acolytes certain rites that they would need to know if winter ever broke, Edith slowed as she passed one of the cow-byres. The warm smell of cattle wafted out. There were two people inside, working and talking.

Everyone on the Isle did fair duty, from the least to the greatest. Even so, it gave Edith pause to hear Etaine and Cecilia carrying on their long debate while they scrubbed out the byre.

"We need Anselm," Etaine said. "Three of us are not enough."

"He won't come," said Cecilia. "He prayed for the king to exile him and free him from his burden—and the king gladly obliged. He'll only come back if William summons him. Then he'll come, groaning and whining and making sure the world knows what a great sacrifice he's made."

"William is not likely to call him back," said Etaine.

Cecilia sighed gustily—even Edith, outside in the snow, could hear her. "No, he is not. And we do need him. Unless . . ."

"There's no time to raise another Guardian, even if one were ready," Etaine said. "In our way we were as feckless as the king. We let one of the four pillars of Britain be sent into exile, instead of fighting to keep him where he belonged."

"Where he never wanted to be." Cecilia paused. They worked in unison for a while: pitching hay, from the sound of it. Then she said, "A king who refuses to be the true king. A Guardian who loathes his own powers and does his best to deny them, though the land itself has chosen him. Is it an omen? Is Britain telling us that it wants to die?"

"Not die, maybe," Etaine said slowly. "But change, yes. It's an ill fit, this Norman invasion, though it came to save Britain from the destruction of its old powers. Saxons still live here, still work their spells in the guise of prayer. I think . . . Britain meant them to be part of it, too. If they knew; if they knew how."

That pause had an air of quiet shock in it. "It's eating itself alive, for what? To give itself back to Alfred and his descendants?"

"To be something new. Something neither Saxon nor Norman. Something stronger than it ever was before."

"You've had a vision."

"Not a vision," Etaine said. "A feeling in my bones. What I see is a black time, and the Hunt running wild over the earth. Scouring, maybe. Cleansing."

"Burning the field to make the grass grow green." Edith heard the shudder in Cecilia's voice. "I can't believe that. I'll try to get Anselm back—if I have to abduct him again, I will. We need our Guardians at full strength, to protect against what's coming."

"Be careful," said Etaine. "Promise me that."

"Of course," Cecilia said. "But what—"

She never finished her question, nor did Edith know if she got an answer. One of the acolytes was calling, and Edith realized that she was cold to the bone. She hurried away from the byre, mincing on frozen feet.

"Why do you need a Guardian who doesn't want to be one?" Edith asked.

It was warm by the fire in the Lady's house. Cecilia was sitting close to it, stitching a linen chemise such as they all wore under their robes. She paid little attention to her work, sewing by feel: tiny, even stitches that to Edith's mind were rather remarkable.

She took her time answering, but Edith had the whole night to listen. She sat on the bench beside Cecilia and spread her hands to the blaze.

After a while Cecilia said, "It's not that we need him. It's that Britain chose him, and will not un-choose him. We can't simply depose him and set up another in his place. He's bound to his Guardianship."

"One can depose a king," Edith mused.

Cecilia did not move and showed no sign of temper, but Edith flinched from the force of her glance. "One can," she said mildly, "if one is prepared to pay the price."

"Wouldn't you be, if it would save this island?"

"What if it destroyed us all instead?"

Edith felt her temper rising. That was rare enough to surprise her a little, but not enough to make her stop it. "My father gave his life and blood and soul to keep the dark at bay. Thanks to him, your brother could go on in his merry arrogance, calling himself the blessed of heaven. That arrogance has provoked the gods. It's time he paid the price."

"And then?" said Cecilia. "Suppose he goes to the sacrifice. What then? Who will come after him?"

"That's for the gods to decree, isn't it?"

Cecilia looked her in the face. "Would you do it? Would you perform the sacrifice, if it were laid on you?"

The heat of Edith's temper turned suddenly cold. This was not a light or a casual question. Whatever she answered would have consequences. Potent ones—perhaps terrible.

"If I were given that task to perform," she said steadily, "and if I were certain that it was the only way, yes, I would do it. I would ask the gods and the great Goddess to guide my hand."

"And if it was not William whom you must sacrifice? If it was another Scots king? Or a new king, a king crowned with oak-leaves, a year-king? Would you do it then?"

Edith's belly clenched. She was dizzy and sick. But she had to say what was in her to say. "Even then," she said, "in the gods' name, I would obey."

Cecilia sat for a long moment, searching her face line by line. At last Cecilia nodded, sighing faintly as if she had been as knotted inside as Edith was. "So would I. We may have to do it—you should be prepared for that."

"Better the sacrifice than the Hunt," Edith said. "Do you think . . . ?"

Cecilia arched a brow, waiting.

Edith almost let it go, but this was a night for asking hard questions. "Do you think my father can be saved? Can his soul be freed from the Hunt?"

"It's said that once the Hunt takes a soul, it's lost forever," Cecilia said. "But it's also said that once, long and long ago, love and magic freed one of those souls from its damnation. I've not seen proof of either."

"I'll dare to hope, then," Edith said. "After all, what can it hurt?"

There were many answers to that, but Cecilia ventured none of them. The shift that she had been sewing was done. She turned it right side out and shook the wrinkles from it, and folded it carefully, tucking the needle back into her purse. She was as tidy as a housewife, and as quietly practical, too.

Edith knew better than to be deceived. Here was great power and high purpose. How cold it could be, she had just learned—as she had learned that she could share that coldness. She was royal, too, and bound to the land. For that blood and the earth that bore it, she could do whatever she must, at whatever cost.

CHAPTER 43

It snowed at Easter, that first year of the new century. The fields were still too frozen to plow, and what little greenery did creep through the snow was late and shy.

Then after Easter, at long last, the winter broke. It burst in torrents of warm rain, flooding the rivers and the lowlands and turning every road and field to mire. After the rain came sun, as hot almost as summer.

God alone knew what the harvest would be like, with such a late and bedeviled planting. There seemed to be no order or measure in the world: too cold, too wet, too hot, too dry.

At Beltane, Henry waited, hardly breathing, for a summons that never came. When the gates of the Otherworld opened, he was in bed alone, glaring at the ceiling.

He had sworn to himself that he would not do what he did then. He slid out of bed in the dark, groped his way to the chest that held his clothes, and found his purse. The faint odor of roses and rue teased his nostrils.

The rose was still alive, still blooming. He breathed in its sweet scent. Maybe it meant nothing, but he could not help but tell himself that while the rose lived, she remembered him. There was a reason why she had not sent for him—maybe to save his life, if he really had been the year-king, and there still was a sacrifice.

It was cold comfort while the spectral hounds bayed in the sky. God help any man who died tonight, or any soul who wandered out of doors.

They were still drinking in the hall here at Brampton, celebrating the new shipment of Rhenish wine. William had been even more full of himself than usual. He stopped short of taking credit for the fact that spring had come at last—with summer hot on its heels—but he was clearly pleased with himself and his world.

Henry had begun to wonder if his brother was subject to a sort of divine madness. He seemed unable to see what the world was coming to, or to remember the warnings he had been given at Salisbury. He had turned his back on what gift he had, which was to see magic. Everything about him was defiantly, blindly mortal.

Rather unfortunately for his peace of mind, Henry had no such affliction. On this night, with the sounds of song and laughter coming faintly from without and the cries of the Hunt overhead, he knew deep in his bones that they were all coming to the end of things.

"And to think," he said aloud to the darkness and the rose, "people said the world would end a hundred years ago. It seems they were somewhat off their reckoning."

Over by the wall, under the shuttered window, his room-companion stirred and mumbled. "Henry? What—"

"Nothing," Henry said. "Go back to sleep."

His nephew Richard muttered a little more, incomprehensibly, then a soft snore gave proof that he had done as he was told. He was a good lad; one of Duke Robert's bastards, who must take after his mother: he was bright-eyed and quick-witted, and he was always in the thick of things. He would have been in hall tonight, carousing with the liveliest of them, if he had not been confined to bed with the last gasp of a winter rheum.

From the sound of his snore, that had nearly run its course. Henry sniffed experimentally. No sign of it in himself. He never had been ill; it was a gift, not uncommon if one had magic.

The Hunt was rampaging through the New Forest tonight, coming back again and again to the king's hunting lodge. Henry heard the snuffling of hounds at the windows, and the trampling of hooves on the roof.

Richard never budged. He was like his father, completely without magic. Even so, Henry would have thought he could hear the tumult. His own head ached with it.

The Hunt retreated with the dawn. But it had not gone out of the world as it should have done. It was still in it, gone to ground but present in the back of his awareness: raising the hackles on his neck.

Richard was up with the sun, shaking Henry out of an uneasy doze. "Come! Up! Let's roust out the lads and get up a hunt."

Henry peered at him. Maybe it was that he stood with his back to the opened shutters and the sun streaming in, but he looked like a shadow without substance. His voice, as bright and clear as it was, sounded oddly distant.

Henry was foggy-headed from lying awake and quaking all night. That was all it was. He let his nephew haul him to his feet and pitch clothes at him, some of which he put on.

He was more awake by the time he came down to the hall. There were others up and dressed for the hunt, drinking sops of yesterday's bread in wine and yelling for the huntsmen and the hounds. The doors, like the shutters in Henry's room, were open wide to let the sun in. It was a glorious morning, a fine May Day, and although the flowers were few and feeble, the sun's warmth could hardly be faulted.

Henry thought William might come down and join them, but both he and his sweet friend Walter were still abed. There were hunters enough without those two, and Richard ahead of them all, giddy with freedom after three days of coughing and sniffling in his bed.

Henry could not seem to let go of the night. The baying of the Hunt lingered in the back of his skull. As they rode down the forest track, flickering in and out of dappled sunlight, he kept thinking he saw skeletal shapes in the shadows of branches, and corpse-lights dancing just on the edge of vision.

Delusion, that was all. There was no creature of the Otherworld in the wood this morning, no spirit of air or hob of the wood. The branches were empty of anything but birds; the flash of movement in the undergrowth was a coney or a squirrel, and once the black mask and white-tipped tail of a fox.

They were hoping for bigger game: deer, or if they were lucky, boar. The huntsmen found sign of both, but nothing fresh. One or two knights who had brought falcons were fool enough to fly them in the wood; one darted off through the trees and was gone, and the other tangled its jesses in the woven boughs.

Henry was the quickest thinker, and still an agile climber though it had been a good many years since he clambered up every tree he could get his hands and feet on. He tossed his horse's reins to the nearest rider, who happened to be Richard, pulled off his boots and thrust them into his saddlebag, and tackled the tree in which the falcon was caught.

It was an oak, and old, as old as Britain. It should have been alive with spirits, but the only living things in it were a squirrel that scolded him fiercely, and the hawk struggling in its bonds.

It was too mortal, the sunlight too ordinary. It was trying too hard.

Henry shook himself. The Hunt had hooks in his soul. He slithered out along a branch, moving more carefully the thinner it became. He might be agile, but he had a man's weight now and not a boy's.

Even as cautious as he was, the branch creaked ominously before he could come within reach of the falcon. He drew in a breath and considered giving up. But it was only a little way, and it only needed a little Word, a simple bit of working. The branch steadied.

Something else, deep in the oak's heart, came awake. Henry slipped and almost fell. The rush of terror focused him admirably. He slid one last arm-length and grasped the tangle of the jesses. Carefully but quickly, he worked them free.

The falcon had stopped its struggling when he came near. It came into his hand, warm feathers and beating heart. Its beak and talons could have torn him to shreds, but it took station peaceably on his fist.

He descended one-handed, much more slowly than he had come up. When he was low enough, he handed the falcon down to the waiting falconer and paused, resting on the lowest branch.

While he was moving, nothing had seemed strange, but now that he was still, he could feel the tingling in his body wherever it touched the tree. It was not an unpleasant sensation at all, but it was odd, like the prickle in an arm or a leg after it had gone numb and begun to wake up again.

He laid both palms against the trunk. The tingling grew stronger, almost enough to make him draw back, but he stayed where he was. Somehow, whatever it was—life, magic, awareness—was flowing both ways. The oak was becoming a part of him and he was becoming a part of it.

Deep roots sank into the ground, drawing up the earth's strength. Broad branches spread to the sky, drinking the sun. Memory flickered in the human part of him: the oak that had created itself in his mother's tapestry, and the oak of Falaise in Normandy under which his father had been conceived.

This was a different earth, a different kingdom, but it was his earth. He had been born on this island—for this island. It knew him. It welcomed him.

This broken earth, this spreading blight, was like a sickness in his own body. The compulsion to heal it somehow, work magic on it, lay his will upon it, overwhelmed him. He clung to the branch, dizzy and half blind.

But not so blind that, lifting his eyes, he could not see through woven branches, piercing veils of mist and shadow. Spectral riders waited there, and spectral hounds, motionless, silent, hollow sockets fixed on the mortal hunt.

They were hunting souls. Humans had come into their domain, and they were hungry. The taste of blood was on Henry's tongue, so rich and sweet that he knew a moment's bliss before he gagged.

He slid off the branch and swung to the ground. His horse was waiting. As he swung into the saddle, Richard grinned at him. "Good view up there?"

Henry managed a sickly smile. "Trees, as far as the eye can see."

"That's a forest for you," his nephew said. "No deer? Or boar?"

"None that I could see," said Henry.

Richard shrugged. "Let's go on, then. The wolves can't have eaten them all. Maybe we'll even find the white hart, the one who brings luck to the hunter who takes him down."

Ah, thought Henry, but what kind of luck?

He was in a troublesome mood, to be sure. He fell into the middle of the pack—foolish cowardice, but he did not want the Wild Hunt picking him off from the front or the rear. Richard, oblivious as ever, had the lead; when the hounds found a fresh scent and began to bay, he whooped with glee.

Courage came belatedly. Henry tried to push through to Richard's side, but the track was too narrow and the trees too thick. A moment ago they had grown well apart.

He let himself fall back instead, and did what he could to ward the hunt: not easy at all in motion, distracted, with what was following them and flowing along beside them. The Hunt had not taken to the air—perhaps in daylight it could not? Though what advantage that gave him, he did not know.

They mounted a hill and emerged without warning in a long open meadow, a rolling expanse of fields that had just begun to grow up here and there with saplings. This would be one of the farmsteads that old William had seized in making this forest: a larger one than many, well cleared and still marked by stone fences and ragged lines of hedge. In the distance, beside a stream, Henry saw the ruins of a mill.

The hounds were in full cry, though Henry could not see what quarry they were after. The line spread out across the field, some of the knights running past Richard, whooping and singing.

Henry peered. Something was flickering ahead of them. It might have worn a stag's shape, or that of a fox. Or it might have been a shadow horse carrying a bone-thin man with the head and antlers of a stag.

Henry set spurs to his horse's sides. The beast was not accustomed to such treatment. It bucked and twisted. Henry rode it out, but the hunt gained too much ground while he did it.

There were bows strung, arrows nocked. Richard dropped his horse's reins on its neck and stood up in the stirrups, aiming straight for the supposed stag's heart.

The horse veered around a tussock and stumbled. The arrow flew wide; the bow dropped. Richard caught at the saddle before he went tumbling after the arrow.

The apparition doubled and darted back, passing between Richard and the rest of the knights. One of them followed it with his arrow, then as it paused—directly in front of Richard—he loosed.

He must have seen a living stag. Henry saw air and delusion. The arrow passed through it without slowing or bending aside.

Richard had brought his horse to a halt and recovered himself, and was bending to peer at the foot on which the stallion had stumbled. The arrow pierced his throat and went on into the horse's shoulder.

The beast went mad with pain. Richard was dead before his body struck the ground. Between the arrow and the horse's panicked plunging, his throat was ripped asunder. The earth drank thirstily of his blood.

The shadowy Hunt moved in to take the rest of it. But Henry set himself between them and their prey. Every scrap of strength that he had, he poured into wards, protecting the body and its fragile, new-hatched soul. "No," he said. "You don't get this one. Let his blood be enough."

The Hunt hovered as if astonished, staring at him with eyes sunk deep in skull-gaunt faces. Some of those faces, he almost fancied he knew. One . . . was that Malcolm of Scots?

He shook off the distraction before it cost him his wards, and therefore his kinsman's soul. "Begone," he said. "Your hunt is done. Seek out other prey, and let us be."

The force of their resistance nearly flung him from the saddle, but he held on. He kept on staring them down. Whatever they might do to his body, his spirit would not waver.

They drew back. He braced for a feint, but it seemed their retreat was honest. They melted away into the grass and the sunlight.

CHAPTER 44

William looked down at his nephew's body. Henry and the others had brought it in, pacing slowly into the hall. They had done nothing to clean or conceal the ruin of the throat. The arrow lay on Richard's breast.

The knight who had killed him flung himself at William's feet, bawling like a bullcalf. "Sire, sire! I never meant—I was aiming at the deer— oh, before God, my soul is doomed!"

William suppressed the urge to hook a toe under the fool and roll him out of the way. He was a pious creature at the best of times; now that he had got himself in trouble, he was in open and audible torment. William had to raise his voice to be heard above the wailing and breast-beating. "Get a grip on yourself, man. Even from here I can see it was an accident."

He was not feeling anything yet. The boy had been a promising young thing. William had even had a thought, once or twice, that if he could have had a son, this would not have been a bad one. The fact he had no magic was as much in his favor as his wits or his parentage.

Now the boy was dead in a foolish accident. That was the Devil's humor. William knelt and set a sign of the cross on the cold and blood-spattered brow, and covered the blankly staring face with his own mantle. "Call the priests," he said. "Tell them to give him a proper burial."

People were staring. He was supposed to do something for them to marvel at—weep, howl, swear vengeance. He was not moved to do any of those things.

The idiot who had shot Richard was still blubbering. William hauled him up and shook him to make him stop. Priests were coming—not too many, here at the hunting lodge, but enough to take Richard away and see to him. William pulled one out of the line and said, "Take care of this man. Confess him, absolve him. Tell him it's not his fault."

That took care of that. There were still the rest of them to face. The hunters had a white, shocked look to them. The rest, who had stayed behind, were itching to do something, anything.

Not a hunt. Not after this. William chased them out to the field below the manor and put them to work doing battle exercises, mounted and afoot.

That was useful work, and strenuous. With luck it would wear them out before any of them got into trouble.

It wore William out quite nicely. An afternoon of hacking at pells and practicing with lances left him aching in every bone. It was a quiet dinner, for his court, and an early night even for the most dedicated of his hellions.

When he went up to bed, it was not Walter Tirel sitting on the stool, frowning at the banked fire. Walter Tirel had fallen over at the table after a mere two cups of wine, and William had been too tired and sore to haul him up the stairs.

Henry did not acknowledge William's presence, but William could tell he knew. "You look like a ghost," William said.

"God knows I've seen enough of them," said Henry.

"Well," said William, "that, too. But I meant, you look just like the old man."

"That old? That gross?"

William cuffed him. He barely swayed. "He wasn't always a bloated bladder. He was a fine figure of a man when he was young. You're prettier—he had that rock of a jaw, and that nose. You take after Mother there. But in this light, the way you sit, you could be the old bastard all over again."

"She used to say I was too much like him," Henry said. "Usually she meant I was surly. And too much inclined to let my magic just be, instead of learning how to use it."

"I'd say she cured you of that. Remember what they used to call you? Beauclerc—the good scholar. You always had your nose in a grimoire."

Henry smiled thinly. "I was trying to make people think it was grammar."

"Everybody knew. You'd walk through walls. Or you'd stand there staring at something no one else could see, and sparks would fly off you. Then you'd go and get a sword and hack a post to splinters."

"I still do," Henry said.

"Not today," said William. "You should have. Richard wasn't your fault, either."

"No?" For the first time Henry looked away from the fire into William's face. His eyes were bleak. "It wasn't an accident."

"Of course it was," William said. "You were there. The fool shot at a deer and hit Richard instead."

"It wasn't a deer," said Henry.

"Then what? Fox? Boar? Tree-stump?"

"It was the Horned King," Henry said, "and he knew very well what he was doing."

"You're addled," William said. "You've been brooding too long. It wasn't the—"

"There is flesh on his bones again," Henry said, "but precious little of it. He drank our nephew's blood, but he didn't get the soul. He's free in the daylight, brother, and I knew it and did nothing about it. Richard is dead because I was too much inclined to just be. I moved too late and too slow."

William's jaw had started to ache. He was clenching it. "Magic again," he said, thick in his throat. "Damned magic. It's a curse on this family."

"Britain is a curse on this family," Henry said—without bitterness, rather to William's surprise. "We're all doomed to be some part of it, even if it's to be a gadfly in Normandy."

William bared his teeth. "Yes, brother Robert's coming back from the holy war. He'll have my hide, too, for losing one of his favorite bastards."

"Give him my hide instead," Henry said, falling back into gloom again. "Yours will be forfeit soon enough. That was a warning, brother. If you go on resisting, Britain will come and take you."

"This was an ugly, foolish, wasteful accident," William said. "It was no more or less than that. God knows, it happens often enough. Our brother, this boy's namesake—you're too young to remember, but he caught an arrow the same way, and in this same forest, too. Everyone was weeping and wailing then, moaning about curses and ghostly hunters. I was there. All I saw was an archer with deer fever and a brother who made the wrong move at the wrong time."

"Someday," said Henry, "you'll stop lying to yourself. If you're lucky, you'll be alive to get some use of it. You can see what's happening in this kingdom: floods, famine, and there's rumor of pestilence in the towns. Now one of our kin is dead. *I* was there, brother. I saw the thing poor Gaulthier shot at. It was no mortal animal."

For an instant William felt himself waver—felt the trickle of credulity in the back of his mind. He shut it down. His mind was made up. He was not going to listen to any talk of magic or powers—seen or unseen.

Henry thrust without warning, sudden and deep. "You're afraid. That's what it is. You're scared to death. If you accept the whole of your kingship, if you give in to it, you could pay a higher price than you ever wanted to pay."

William clenched his fists and thrust them behind him before they pummeled that insolent young face to a pulp. "So I could. So I'll do, whether I give way to your doomsaying or not—if what you say is true.

Why shouldn't I give myself what peace of mind I can? It doesn't make any difference."

"It makes all the difference," Henry shot back. "If you face the truth, Britain can be saved. Whereas if you will not—"

"Aren't there Guardians in Britain? Aren't there powers to protect it? If this is true at all?"

"They need their king," Henry said. "Britain needs her king."

"Britain has all the king she is going to get," William said.

Henry rose. Whatever else he was, he was no fool. He knew when to let be.

He bowed stiffly. "Majesty," he said. From the sound of it, his teeth were clenched.

William refused to watch him go. It was petty, but he did not care. He had had enough of bloody magic to last him for a lifetime.

For a long while after Henry was gone, William stayed where he was. His shoulders were aching with tension. He was ready to howl at the moon.

A soft step sounded behind him. He stayed where he was. Familiar arms slid around him, and a familiar body fitted itself to his back. "God's saints!" said Walter Tirel. "You're as stiff as a board. What did your brother do to you?"

"Enough," William said. He turned in Walter Tirel's embrace. "Thank God for you. You're the only creature in England who isn't after me to be something I'm not."

"You are all I need," Walter Tirel said. He rested his head on William's shoulder and sighed.

William echoed the sigh. The tension was draining out of him little by little. Maybe in a while he would want more, but for now, this would do.

❋ CHAPTER 45 ❋

nselm's dreams had been haunted of late. He had left England
with a light heart, thanking God—albeit with a twinge of guilt—
for the exile the king had imposed on him. Once he was free of that island and the burden of office that he had never wanted, he had allowed
himself to be happy. His dreams had been of peaceful things, of his
faith and his philosophy.

But all that summer, since the feast of Pentecost, he had dreamed of
Britain and its obstreperous king. The dreams had been harmless
enough at first: visions of that wet green country, remembrances of
William at court or in one of his processions, flashes of faces familiar
and not so familiar, all in William's shadow.

As summer advanced, the dreams darkened. Strange things crept
into them, creatures of the Otherworld, dark spirits walking free in daylight. News that came from across the water must have fed his dreams;
Britain was beset with storms and famine, and after a brutal winter had
entered a fierce and unforgiving summer.

It was God's justice. Anselm could be unforgiving, too, and William
had been beyond unreasonable. No amount of Christian charity could
excuse the quarrels they had waged over matters as trivial as the training
of a knight and as vital as the reform of the Church in England. They
had struck sparks from one another like flint and steel.

He could still hear that brass bellow ordering him off the island, consigning him to perdition with the Pope he insisted on consulting, as William put it, for every damned little thing. "Isn't there anyone in England to get advice from? I'd think the Pope would get advice from you—aren't you the wisest man in Christendom? What do you take us for? Get out! Get out of my sight!"

Which Anselm had been sinfully delighted to do. He had never belonged in that court of sinners and sodomites; he had certainly never wanted to be an archbishop. What he had here in Lyons, peace and solitude and the indulgence of an archbishop who was content to hold that office, was all he had ever asked for.

He was happy. And that, of course, could not be allowed to persist. The other office he never thought of, the one that had been even less welcome and even more difficult to escape, was tormenting him with these dreams.

Britain's king had forced an archbishopric on him. Britain itself had forced him to be its Guardian. That made him, whether he would or no, a magical pillar and strong support of the hidden realm, a protector of its magics and a defender of its land and borders against powers that would destroy it.

There were three other Guardians. Every realm—or so he was told— had four. Some had more. Three were not enough.

He had tried to abdicate the office. But unlike the miter and cope of the archbishop and the estates that went with them, which William had stripped away, this Guardianship could not be laid aside by mortal will. If Britain insisted that he continue, then nothing that he did or desired made the slightest difference.

He had done what he could. His wards were stronger by far than they had been when Cecilia abducted him from his study in Bec. Dreams might pass them, but mortals could not. Magic broke against them.

They had been under siege since shortly after Beltane, if Anselm would suffer himself to contemplate that pagan festival. He was losing strength as the summer lengthened. He was old; he was not as hale as he had been.

On the night after the feast of Mary Magdalene, Anselm lay in fitful, tossing sleep. His body prickled with heat; the buzzing of insects was a constant torment. He had been ill that day, beset with coughing and fever. Night had brought little relief.

"If you would open yourself to your magic, your body would heal itself, too."

This was a new face in his dream, though not in his memory: Henry FitzWilliam, looking more like his mother than Anselm had remembered.

However much Anselm had deplored Queen Mathilda's lack of Christian faith, he had admired her greatly. Her husband had been a bully and a brute, but she was a lady of tact and discretion, and notable intelligence.

Henry had the face and the wits and a good deal of the tact. He also had his father's ruthlessness and his own distinct lack of moral rigor.

He smiled at that: in dreams, thoughts could be as clear as spoken words. "We can't all be saints," he said. "Some of us have to keep the world going, or what would become of it?"

"We should all strive to create heaven on earth," Anselm said.

Henry's smile widened to a tiger's grin. "Ah! Sanctimony. I'd thought better of you. Be honest, now. Is it not an insult to God, to be so eager to abandon the world that He has made?"

"The world is a dim and corrupted image of the truth," Anselm said.

"Careful, Father," Henry said. "Someone might hear, and brand you a heretic. Heresy is such an easy accusation these days. Even if you don't think the world was created not by God but by the Devil, would your accusers believe that?"

"Will you tempt them to accuse me?" Anselm inquired. He should not be proud of his self-control, but after all he was mortal and fallible, and this hallucination was testing him sorely.

"I?" said Henry. "Why, no, because then you would accuse me of being no Christian at all—and I'd be hard put to deny it."

That put an end to Anselm's patience. "Begone! Vanish! Get thee behind me, Satan!"

Henry laughed. He was as solid as ever behind Anselm's eyes, sprawled at ease in a tumbled bed. Anselm caught himself peering toward the limits of the dream. It seemed improbable, but as far as he could see, the notorious libertine was alone.

The libertine was dreadfully adept at reading Anselm's thoughts. "No, there's no one in bed with me tonight. There often isn't. Are you disappointed? Have I taken the fire out of Sunday's sermon? Or will you be denouncing my brother again instead?"

"I do not deliver sermons," Anselm said stiffly.

"Ah," said Henry. "Your pardon. I forgot. You are spared the burden of a public ministry. You write letters; you advise, you counsel, you exhort. You are a happy man—a man freed from any obligation but that of pleasing himself."

"You have a tongue like an adder," Anselm spat—then caught himself. But the words were spoken. He could not unspeak them.

"Britain will sink beneath the sea," Henry said, sweet and deadly. "All her people, mortal and otherwise, will go down with her. That will be your doing, my lord archbishop."

"No," said Anselm. "That, you cannot lay on me. Your intemperate, degenerate king—he will bring his kingdom down."

For the first time Henry seemed less than composed. "You are the great philosopher, the master logician. Parse this, O prince of theologians. A king who refuses to be king, a Guardian who will not guard—which is worse? Or is there any choice between them?"

"What are you, then, messire? What is Britain to you, or you to her?"

"More than she is to you, it seems," Henry said. "Do you care nothing for her? Does it not matter at all that between you and my brother she will fall?"

Anselm set his mind and heart against temptation. He crossed himself, fixing his mind on the glory of God.

"You are worse than the Saxons," Henry said. His voice was thick with disgust. "They only destroyed her piecemeal. You would cast her into the sea."

"God's will be done," Anselm said.

His heart was a fortress. Henry assailed it with all the power and knowledge he had—and those were formidable. But God was Anselm's strength.

Whatever guilt he had known, whatever hesitation might have beset him, all that was gone now. He was pure in his faith. He would not yield to the lure of pagan magic or the will of Godless sorcerers.

"Tell me," said Henry, dangerously mild. "If the king summoned you, would you go?"

Anselm's heart stopped. But it began to beat again, and he remembered how to breathe. "I am sworn to that, yes. But William will not call me back."

"Nevertheless," Henry said, "if you were to receive word from the king, you would obey it?"

"That would be my obligation," Anselm said.

"Will you swear to that?"

"I am sworn to it," said Anselm, "by the servitude that was imposed upon me."

"Indeed," said Henry, cool and dispassionate. "I wish you well of your heaven. Until you come to it, may you live the life you deserve. And if God hears me, I pray you may die as you never wished to live: as Archbishop of Canterbury."

Deep in his stronghold, walled and armored in faith, still Anselm shuddered. That prayer was as exquisitely honed a curse as Anselm had heard. He could only pray in turn that God might see fit to avert it.

Anselm would have wished to wake then, to escape further bedevilment. But his tormentors were not done with him. Having failed of the direct attack, they resorted to subtlety.

This, unlike the other, was true sleep and honest dream. And yet Anselm was keenly aware of where he was and what he was doing. His dream had the flavor of memory: of a day long ago, when he was hardly more than a boy. He had come all the way from Italy to Bec in Normandy, following a word and a dream.

And there it was in the abbey, perched on a tall stool in the schoolroom, teaching grammar to children. Anselm was young and foolish; he was disappointed. "I thought to find you teaching theology to masters," he said. He blurted out the words, abandoning all the care and thought that he had put into his rehearsals of what he would say when he met the great master.

Lanfranc finished the sentence he had been dictating, as serenely as if this stranger had never burst into his schoolroom and insulted his students to his face. Only when the last word was spoken and copied and the last question answered did he turn to Anselm.

Anselm was seething, caught between outrage and mortification. Lanfranc smiled at him, a sweet, vague smile with nothing either brilliant or inspired in it. "Good day, Brother," he said. "You were looking for someone?"

Anselm gaped at him. "What? You aren't . . . ? But they said— Where is he? Where is Master Lanfranc?"

"That is my name," Lanfranc said. "Why? Am I a terrible disappointment?"

"No!" Anselm cried. "No—no, never. It's only, I expected—"

"They always do," Lanfranc said with the hint of a sigh. "So: you're the latest prodigy from Italy. Will you forgive me if I don't ask for a demonstration of your brilliance? It's late and I've been teaching all day. I need the privy. Then I need my dinner."

Anselm had gone beyond disappointment. His dream had feet of thickest, blackest clay. He could think of nothing better to do than follow it to the privy and then to the refectory, where he ate coarse bread and drank sour ale and mortified the flesh until it matched the spirit.

In memory he had gone sulkily to bed. In dream he found himself in the chapel, kneeling in the light of the vigil-lamp, while Lanfranc celebrated Mass at the altar.

Except, he realized as it went on, it was not quite the Mass as Rome had ordained it, nor did it follow any other rite that he knew. The image above the altar, that had been hidden in shadow, came slowly clear: not Christ on his cross but the Queen of Heaven with her crown of stars and the world beneath her feet.

Lanfranc's rite invoked not the Lord but the Lady: not *Domine* but *Domina*. Anselm tried to recoil from the blasphemy, but the dream bound him. He had to endure the whole of it, all that rite of a fallen Goddess, clear to the end.

As the last twisted words died into silence, Lanfranc came down from the altar. His vestments, like the rite, were subtly perverted. They were white and gold, as if for a Mass of celebration, but instead of crosses, they were embroidered all over with the sign of the crescent moon.

Lanfranc stood over Anselm, looking down as he had in life: clear-sighted, a little wry, and indulgent of human foibles. "It is all one," he said. "You're not blind, child. You can see. What keeps you from it? What are you afraid of?"

"Damnation," Anselm said.

"Ah," said Lanfranc. "Yes, that's reasonable. Still—what is damnation? To forge a chain of foolish rules and then tangle yourself in it? To be given great gifts but also great responsibility, and to accept the one but turn your back on the other? To invoke your own will as the will of God, and to refuse the task He has laid on you, for weakness and cowardice and lack of compassion for any human thing?"

Anselm rose up in wrath. "You! Uncover yourself. Which of you is it? Henry? Cecilia? How dare you conceal your true face in this of all lies?"

"No lies," Lanfranc said. "No children of the Conqueror, either, though their frustration is jangling through the aether. Between you and William, this world never saw such a pair of stubborn fools. Pride is a sin, child. So is sloth, and anger, too. Surrender them. Offer them up. Face what God has given you to face."

Anselm set his teeth, though it made the worst of them ache. The pain was a sacrifice; in its way, it cleared his head. "God has sent me here. Whatever I do, I do it by His will."

Lanfranc was neither alive nor bound by humanity. He did not give way to frustration. But he shook his head and sighed. "Be careful of arrogance, child. Never presume to tell God what He should do."

"I do not—" Anselm began.

"Listen to yourself," Lanfranc said. "Know yourself. Tell me, child. If you could give up the power that is in you, would you do it?"

"Yes," Anselm said without an instant's hesitation. "Dear God, yes!"

"Even if there were a cost? Even if it shortened your life?"

"Then I would be in heaven all the sooner," Anselm said.

"Even," said Lanfranc, "if you were to lose the keen edge of your intelligence? Would you give it up then?"

That gave Anselm pause. "How . . . much? All of it?"

"That I can't say," Lanfranc said. "Magic weaves through all that we are. If the threads of it are taken out, there's no telling what will be left."

"My soul will remain," Anselm said steadily. "I trust in God for the rest." He paused. "Are you mocking my hopes? Or are you offering me a gift? Can it be done? If it is done, will I be free?"

"From the archbishopric," Lanfranc said, "no. From the other . . ." His hand traced ambiguity in the air. "We believe that if you surrender your magic, the Guardianship will go with it. It's never been done. There has never been a Guardian as reluctant as you."

"Or, no doubt, as Christian." Anselm bit his tongue. Arrogance had overcome him again; he had forgotten that Lanfranc too, in life, had held that office. Anselm had inherited it from him, just as he had found himself in possession of Lanfranc's archbishopric.

Lanfranc said nothing of it. He had other, no doubt greater concerns. "If you are willing," he said, "we will try. We may fail. You may lose more than you wish to give up. But we are desperate—and so, I think, are you."

Anselm was shaking with the thought of it. Fear, yes, but fevered excitement, too. To be rid of thing that had laired inside him all his life, that he had dreaded and fought and resisted like temptation—was it worth the loss of his mind's brilliance?

"If I keep my soul and its salvation," he said, "then the rest is of no consequence."

"May it be so," Lanfranc said. Or had he said, "So mote it be"?

It did not feel like anything at first. He stood in the dream, and Lanfranc stood in front of him.

Then Lanfranc laid his hand on Anselm's brow. His touch was cold. Anselm stiffened but did not recoil. He held his ground.

There was a tingling in his center, somewhere between his navel and his breastbone. The tingle turned to an itch, then to a burning. As the burning rose in intensity, the only word for it was pain.

If he had been flayed alive and rubbed in salt, he would have felt no more pain than this. He was unraveling from the soul outward. The deep threads of his self and spirit worked loose one by one.

Lanfranc had no need to breathe, but the strain was evident in his face. Even for the mighty dead, this was a great working. To take the magic from the man, but leave the man entire: the subtlety and complexity of it defied understanding.

Then the magic began to fight. Anselm had nothing to do with it. It had a will of its own, to cling to the body and sink tendrils deep in the soul.

Lanfranc worked each one free. His patience was infinite. Anselm did what he could to make it less difficult, which was terribly little; but maybe it made a difference.

Except for the pain, he felt the same. His wits were no duller. He could still shape in his head, perfect and intricate and true, his proof of the existence of God.

Magic could get no grip on that. The last of it slipped free. Lanfranc caught it, confined it. When Anselm looked up, he saw it in the gnarled hands: a white jewel netted in silver thread.

So small a thing to have troubled him so much. He rose. He felt light—almost too light. He staggered. His mind and soul were intact, he was sure of it. And yet there was something . . .

Lanfranc had slipped the captured magic out of sight. He laid his hand on Anselm's brow, tracing the shape of a blessing. Anselm reared back, but too late. That blessing was not a cross but the thin curve of the moon.

He woke rubbing his forehead as if to scour it clean. But Lanfranc's blessing had sunk beneath the skin to lie like a brand on his soul.

His unencumbered, beautiful, purely human, utterly unmagical soul.

He had won, he told himself. Britain's defenders had wielded their strongest persuasion, and taken the one thing of his that they needed. They were done with him. He would stay in Lyons; he had no intention of leaving and no need to do so—unless the king commanded him. And William, thank God, would do no such thing.

❊ CHAPTER 46 ❊

The Isle was under siege. The Wild Hunt was a plague upon Britain, and pestilence ran in its wake. Both men and cattle were sick or dying. Grain withered in the ear; fruit shriveled and blackened on the bough. Whatever escaped either blight or relentless heat succumbed to swarms of devouring locusts.

Sometimes at night, when Edith was trying to sleep, she felt the earth stirring uneasily, and heard the sea's growl. It was stalking the land; all too soon it would spring.

The chanting of the Ladies and their acolytes was a steady murmur, constant beneath the yapping and yowling of the Hunt. Three of the Guardians were here at the heart of Britain, but the fourth pillar was missing. The rest were the weaker for it.

For Edith it was a kind of torment. She kept feeling in her heart, altogether without reason, that she should be able to do something. What little she did, lending her voice to the rite and her magic to the weaving, was never enough. There was more. There had to be more. But what it was or how she would use it, she could not imagine.

They were all desperate. Some of the younger or weaker Ladies were beginning to falter. Angharad had taken ill and had to be carried off to the healers. She was carrying a Beltane child, a fact she had concealed so that she could go on defending the Isle. Now both she and the child were endangered, and the rest of them were under close scrutiny.

Edith had no such secret to keep. She had her magic and her duties, and the hope that somehow the war could be won.

She was stumbling to her bed, one early morning, having spent the night chanting life into the walls of air, when she tripped and fell. The puca squawked, skittered, and laid her ankle open with a slash of claws.

Except for the ferocious stinging in her ankle, Edith was not unhappy to be lying on grass, staring blurrily up at fading stars. The puca sprang onto her breast and glared down into her face.

She saw then why his squawk had had such a strangled sound. He had something clamped in his teeth: a pendant on a chain, it seemed to be. The jewel was netted in silver wire; it was white like moonstone, and it glowed strangely, here in the dark before dawn.

She reached up dizzily to take it before he dropped it. It felt as strange as it looked, both cold and hot, heavy and light, powerful and—

Powerful. She sat up, spilling the puca into her lap. The chain was tangled in her fingers. The jewel was singing.

She knew that song. It resonated in the earth of Britain, thrumming deep in the stone circles and whispering with the wind in the forests or across the heaths and moors. The folk of air sang it in their dances. Even the Hunt sang a discordant mockery of it, beating its rhythm on the ribs of their skeletal horses.

She closed her fingers about the jewel. The singing was as clear as ever. It was inside her—as it had always been. It was in her magic and in her blood and in her heart.

As she rose, the puca climbed to her shoulder. Its purr was part of the singing. It was satisfied. What it had wanted, what it had always meant to do, was done. Now the rest could begin.

Morning light was growing around them. Mist rose off the lake. The Ladies' chanting was losing strength. The earth felt like a thin film of ice over turbulent water.

All their labors were coming to nothing. Because, Edith thought, they were fixed on the wrong enemy. Earth and sea, even the Hunt, were not the cause of it all. They were part of it, shaped by it, but they were no more than a diversion.

Maybe she owed Sister Gunnhild more than she knew. They had studied logic together, and the science of causes. Edith had learned to see past the moment; to find her way to the place where it began.

Or maybe it was only that she had come from the place where the blight began, and knew it better than anyone here—even Cecilia, who had lived in it and made use of it but never truly been a part of it. Edith's own blood and kin had wrought this; now the whole of it was gathered into one soul and spirit.

She stood by the lake. The others were in the Lady's house, but it did not matter. They were all together wherever their bodies were. She raised her arms. The jewel swung from her right hand, catching fire as the sun rose.

In the chapel of Wilton abbey, the Abbess Christina lay prostrate. Her arms were spread in imitation of the cross. The air about her was thick and grey, as if choked with fog. The earth beneath her was as black as oblivion.

Her nuns stood in the choir, chanting the morning office. They sang the verses in Saxon.

They had lost their faces. They were a blur of black robes or grey, and blank white ovals within the veils, and empty eyes. There was nothing left of them but the voices.

It should have been a vision of hell. But through all that darkness rang a chorus of exultation. Victory was near. The abbess' heart swelled with the joy of it. Yes, the kingdom would fall—but the Normans would fall with it, and all that was stained with sin would be swept away.

Edith threw all her power against it. "No!" she cried in her strongest, clearest voice. "You will not!"

The abbess rose as no human creature could: straight up like a cross raised against a storm-wracked sky. Her face was terrible, thin skin stretched tight over the living skull. She had fasted and mortified her flesh until it was nearly gone. All that was left was the implacable will.

She smiled as if in welcome—not a sight for the fainthearted. "Edith! Sister-daughter. At last. We have been waiting for you."

Indeed. The web was spun, the trap baited. And there was Edith in her youth and strength and her trained magic, blood of the abbess' blood, with the abbess' hooks sunk deep into her and her mother's before them.

All her life she had imagined that she was free; that she had chosen the other way. And all the while, they had been waiting as the spider waits, in poisonous patience. Every moment she had spent in her mother's presence or in the abbess' had come to this: to frozen stillness and soul-deep shock, and the spirit draining out of her like blood from a wound.

She had been so proud; so full of her strength. She had brought the whole power of the Isle to this place, and given it as a gift to the one who above all would destroy it.

Henry had paused in Salisbury on an errand for his brother, conveying the royal will to a pack of quarreling barons. The barons' quarrel was settled without excessive bloodshed, and Henry was riding back slowly, reckoning the state of the kingdom as he went.

Salisbury suffered less than most, but sickness had come to it, felling the old and the very young. That particular morning, he had gone out early after a night full of strange and troubled dreams. In one of them, he had seemed to be exhorting the exiled Archbishop of Canterbury to take up his magical duties. That should have been preposterous, but he woke with the conviction that he had actually done such a thing—and Anselm had been as intransigent as the king who had exiled him.

As the sun came up, he walked the streets of the town. Even the dogs took cover after dark, in terror of the things that rode in it, hunting blood and souls. With the rising of the light, they came creeping out, with the beggars close behind them. Then came the mourners with the night's dead, to bear them to the charnel-house.

There were too many dead—and not a pleasant death, either: coughing their lungs out, choking up blood. He could hear those still living who were sick, racked with coughing, and the voices of their nurses, soothing or exhorting or gone raw with grief and fear.

The earth itself was sick. Henry dared not let down his protections: he would drain himself dry trying to heal it. Even shielded as he was, the temptation was all but irresistible.

As he approached the market square, people began to emerge from their houses. They walked warily, many with cloths over their faces to guard against the pestilence. There was little conversation; eyes met and flicked aside, then they hastened past one another. No one laughed.

There were no children. No urchins playing at mock war or pretending to hunt one another through the streets. No infants in arms; no schoolboys trooping to the cathedral for lessons. All the children were dead.

A knight learned to harden his heart. A prince was a master of it— especially if he was William Bastard's son. But to look at those faces and see no beardless boys or unbudded maidens, and to know by the twisting of his gut that the plague had taken them all, was more than even he could easily bear.

He stopped a man who would have hurried past: harried and worn, dressed in clothes that looked as if he had been in them for days. A pale and haunted-eyed younger man trotted behind him, carrying a physician's bag.

Neither of them was delighted to find his way barred by a man in mail armed with a sword. The physician might not even have paused for the sword, if Henry had not gripped his arm too tightly for escape. "Messire," he said. "Tell me the truth. Are all the children dead?"

The eyes that rested on him were weary beyond exhaustion. "Why? What difference does it make to you?"

"A great deal," Henry said, "as well it should. Without our children, what hope does any of us have?"

"Good, then," the man said sourly. "A knight with the gift of compassion. They're handing out crowns for sainthood in the cathedral, I'm sure. Why don't you go and see, and let me get back to my work. There's still a child or two left alive, whom I might be able to save."

That was insolence so breathtaking that Henry almost laughed at it. He let the man go. He received no thanks for it, but he had not been expecting any.

"Why the children of Salisbury?" he called after the retreating back. "Why not the old and the weak, too, the way it is elsewhere? What is in the earth here, or in the air?"

The physician stopped and turned, somewhat to Henry's surprise. "Believe me, messire, if I knew, I would tell you."

Henry bowed to him. "Go. Do what you can. Keep them alive."

The man looked hard at him. "Christ's bones. You do care. God will reward you, I'm sure."

"What use is heaven," Henry demanded, "if the earth is a wasteland behind me?"

The physician bowed low, and only half in mockery. Then he was gone. Henry sent a prayer after him, wrapped in a working: for strength, for skill, and for the healing of the sick.

For that he had to lower his wards—which he did without stopping to think. He was not sorry, either, though as soon as he had done it, he knew it had not been wise at all.

He reeled against the wall. Power—terror—desperation. *She* was— he saw—

Brick was rough against his cheek, still cool from the night. It was old: Roman brick, salvaged and built into this house in Salisbury. He could see through it. And there *she* was, the lady to whom he had given his mother's name.

It was not the sort of battle he was used to fighting, with men and weapons, but a battle it most certainly was—and she was losing. His eye that had been trained in combat saw quickly how it was and what he faced. All too well he remembered that dread abbess. She had found a most delectable prey, long awaited and much desired; and she was savoring it slowly.

He reached through the wall into that other place and caught hold of Mathilda's hand—for that was all he knew to call her. There was something wound in her fingers. As his own locked about it, he felt the lightning fall.

❈ CHAPTER 47 ❈

Edith was dying. Her body did not know it yet, was still standing upright, but the soul was being sucked out of her.

There was nothing she could do. The bonds had been laid on her with the water of baptism. Her mother's teaching and the abbess' tutelage had only bound her the tighter.

She was the vessel, the chosen one. She would contain all that they had wrought. Through her, the rest would fall.

Abbess Christina had given up all hope of restoring a mortal kingship. Her whole desire now was for death and destruction, and for an end to this travesty that the invaders had made of England.

Despair was potent, and seductive. Edith caught herself on the brink. She could not hold; she was not strong enough. With all her magic, all her training, all the power of the Isle that had poured into her, she still could not resist that headlong emptiness.

Something caught her hand, grinding the jewel into her palm. The pain was vivid, immediate, real. So was the warmth of human flesh, and the strength of a mortal grip.

It was a man's strength, with power behind it—magic at least the equal of hers. Even as she understood that, she knew whose magic it was. No one else fit so well into her empty places.

Henry. His name invoked his face. He was with her, side by side, hand locked in hand.

She felt the power rising. Some remote part of her quailed. It was too much—too strong. Stronger even than the greyness that was swallowing Britain. So strong that it might destroy where it meant to heal.

There was no choice. She had to take the risk. She raised the power like a sword, and struck the greyness down.

It yielded like fog. Like mist, it slipped away, only to gather its formlessness together and stand before her again, as whole as before.

There was solidity at its heart. The abbess still had mortal substance, though the malice of two dead queens was in her. She was still bound to mortality.

Henry saw it even before Edith. While she flailed to find enough magic to do she hardly knew what, he drew his sword in a blur of steel.

The air between the worlds shrieked with the agony of cold iron. The greyness swirled. The living thing in its heart turned to run, but Henry was too swift. He stepped through and inabout, into the cold air of the abbey's chapel, and thrust the blade between the fleeing shoulders.

Through their linked hands, Edith felt the force of the blow: sharp steel piercing flesh, cracking bone, transfixing the shuddering heart. Henry's feet were braced. The strength of him went deep into the earth: even this earth that had been stripped of life and spirit.

Abbess Christina twisted as she fell, wrenching the sword out of Henry's hand. The cloud about her writhed and boiled.

It had drawn the Hunt. The chapel's roof was no impediment to Edith's sight. She could see through it to a sky as grey and tormented as the fog of nothingness below.

The Hunt hovered above the abbey, waiting as it had waited when her father died. A soul was a soul, however black or corrupted—and this gathering of souls was threefold, which was a great number in the Otherworld.

Edith looked up. Amid the skeletal hunters and the milling, baying hounds, she searched for her father, but they were all shadows, with no faces that she could see.

She never even stopped to think. Henry was bending to retrieve his sword. The nuns in the choir were still chanting, but the chorus had gone somewhat ragged. Edith stood astride her aunt's body.

She was still not quite in the world. The Hunt was clear to her sight, even through stone—but stone was solid enough underfoot and in walls around her. The body beneath her was more real than any of it.

The smell of blood wreathed her, and the reek of voided entrails. But the Hunt cared little for that.

"Let them take her," Henry said.

Their hands were still linked as if bound. He had cleansed the sword somewhat on the abbess' skirts, but not yet sheathed it. His face was at once deeply familiar and profoundly strange. "This is justice," he said. "Don't stand in its way."

"You have a cold heart," said Edith.

"Is it also wise?"

The Hunt stooped even lower. For the flash of an instant Edith knew why her kinswomen had so hated all that was Norman.

This Norman was wise. And practical. And there was Britain, which had nearly fallen because of this thing beneath her feet—this creature who had spread its ruin through the whole of Britain. People were dying because of it—children were dying, their souls eaten away by the blight in the earth.

This thing had been her kin. Her enemy, yes; it would have destroyed her without a qualm. But blood was blood.

She looked up into the Huntsman's fleshless face. "Her own God will judge her," she said.

"We are her judgment," said the Huntsman.

"I think not," said Edith.

"That is twice," the Huntsman said, "that you have defied us. There is a price for it. In the end you will pay."

"I'm willing," she said steadily. "Let this one go. There's torment enough ahead for her, I'm thinking, even without your pagan damnation."

"And you call my heart cold," Henry said beside her.

That was admiration. Edith was not sure she welcomed it.

She must not let it distract her. She kept her eyes level on the Huntsman, just as she had done when she was much younger and even less wise.

He bowed to her. The fire of his eyes promised a reckoning, but she had won—again. The darkness at her feet dissipated into the earth that it had blighted, leaving the body cold.

The Hunt withdrew. The fog in the chapel melted away. Light shone through the high windows, slanting golden on the floor.

The nuns stirred and murmured. They had faces. Their eyes were alive. They stared at Edith, and at the man who stood at her back, sword drawn as if to guard her from an assault of holy women.

Edith set her hands together and bowed to them, even as she slipped sidewise out of the world.

Henry had never seen such casual power. His sister was strong, and so for that matter was he, but they were always aware of what they were. She simply was.

She was like the Old Things. She passed from world to world as he would walk from one room to the next of one of his castles—and somehow, by some magic, she had him doing it, too. She had brought him from an alley in Salisbury and herself from the gods knew where, then through her power he had taken them into Wilton abbey where it seemed all the blight had begun—and when they were done there, she stepped with him onto a greensward under misty sunlight, beside the silver glimmer of a lake.

She had brought him to the Isle of Glass, where they had met at Beltane. There were people there, standing in a circle, staring—much as the nuns had. He recognized his sister, and the Lady of the Isle, and Robin FitzHaimo.

The Guardians of Britain were gathered here to defend the isle. He was standing with his nameless lady at the fourth corner, the pillar of the east: facing the lake. And that was right and proper, and as it should be.

She lifted her hand. The jewel was still in it, but the silver was blackened and crumpled, and the stone had gone grey and dead.

Its light was inside them both. They were the fourth pillar of Britain, both of them together.

She flung the spent jewel far out over the lake. It rose in an arc, then fell in a blur of swiftness. The water closed over it. There was not even a ripple to betray where it had been.

The whole of the land sighed. Life was coming back to it. The power that had drained its strength was gone. The sun's light was clean again. He could feel the earth healing under his feet.

His sister bowed with only a faint hint of irony. "Welcome," she said, "to the heart of Britain. It seems we have a new Guardian."

"Guardians," said his Mathilda. She frowned. "It's not over yet, is it? The cause is gone, but the sickness is still there. It's mending, but too slowly."

"The blight is deep," the Lady said. "Healing needs time."

Mathilda shook her head, but she did not argue with that. She turned back to Henry. "Do you know what I've got you into?"

"I rather think I got myself into it," he said.

"Blame it on the gods," Cecilia said. She slid in between them, took a hand of each, and tugged them away from the water. "It's over. It's done. The Saxon rule—it's ended, finally; there's nothing left of it. We have a victory to celebrate."

Mathilda looked as if she might have begged to differ, but again she held her tongue. Politic as well as wise, Henry thought. He was enchanted.

The feast was hasty and some of the guests were rather late, but it was a grand celebration nonetheless. The Old Things came, one by one while the daylight lasted, but once night had fallen, they came flocking, from feys and airy spirits to the Great Ones of the Otherworld.

Henry must have danced with every female thing on the Isle. Some of them were very alluring indeed, but none was the one he wanted. She had disappeared somewhere between the feast and the dance.

At last there was a lull in the music. Even immortal musicians, it seemed, needed to rest now and then. Henry escaped before they struck up the dance again.

He found her just as he had concluded that she was not in the Isle at all, but had slipped away to God alone knew where. But there she was, close by where they had appeared that day, sitting by the lake with her knees drawn up and a striped cat curled around her feet.

He moved in quietly and sat beside her. The waves lapped softly on the shore. Faintly over the water, a night bird called.

The cat abandoned her to curl purring in Henry's lap. She astonished him with a smile.

"You weren't in the dance," he said.

"I needed to think."

He reached for her hand, just as she reached for his. It was quite different, and quite pleasant, without the jewel caught between. The cat's purr rose almost to a growl; it sprang out of his lap and disappeared into the dark.

As soon as it was gone, he forgot it in the wonder of her face. "Are you always so solemn?"

"I suppose," she said. "I can't help thinking . . . there's more to come. We've won something, but not enough."

He nodded. "The Hunt is still out there. It should have gone back where it belonged. It's still harvesting souls."

"You understand," she said. "The others, they all say it will run clean again, like a river after a flood—we only need to be patient. I don't think patience is going to help us. They've been running free for too long. They don't want to go back to order and limits and the gate only open for the great rites."

"What do they do?" Henry asked. "On the other side—what are they? What are they for?"

She frowned slightly, as if searching her memory. "They're the hunters of souls—of course. They cleanse the skies of dark spirits. Their king is a great lord of the Otherworld. He rules the Beltane rite, and restores the land from its winter death. He makes life, rather than destroying it. Even the souls he takes, or took before he was twisted, are given a just punishment."

"You should have let him take the abbess," Henry said after he had considered all the angles of that. "If he is a bringer of justice, and you refused him that, his purpose is unfulfilled. He can't go away until that is somehow undone."

"I don't believe that," she said. "She wasn't for him. Something else keeps him here. Some other task undone. Something . . ."

Her voice trailed off. Henry was strongly tempted to let his hand slide softly down her back from the white curve of her neck to her rounded buttocks.

That would have been very ill-judged. Her fingers, laced with his, were warm. She sighed and bent her head and kissed the back of his hand, then turned it palm up and kissed his palm; then the inside of his wrist, where the pulse beat quick and shallow.

He had never known a woman to do such a thing—as a man would, as he would: turn to the body's pleasure and free the mind to find answers where it would.

It was a peculiar sensation to be used so. He had to be fair: when her eyes rested on him, they saw him. She knew who and what he was, and if he knew women at all, she was quite sufficiently pleased with it.

He took the challenge. He set out to make her forget everything but him. How well he succeeded, he was not absolutely certain. But when she cried out, it was his name that burst out of her.

He was pleased out of all measure—and almost out of his own pleasure. By the gods, he was in love. It had never been like this before; never so strong.

It was the magic. They were so very like, so very well matched. The land had known. It had brought them together. Maybe it had made them for each other.

Coldhearted prince he might be, but in the aftermath of loving, wrapped in her arms as she was in his, he was as giddy as a boy—drunk with the scent and the nearness of her. Then he was glad of this night and this victory, however incomplete it might seem once the light of morning was on it.

✳ CHAPTER 48 ✳

"Well, daughter," Malcolm said. "That was cleverly done. Britain's free of the Saxon yoke now. Your mother's turning in her grave. Are you content with what you've done?"

Edith was awake, lying on the grass by the lake. Henry slept beside her. The moon was westering, the mist lying low. The last of the revel had died down some while since.

Her father was standing between Edith and the lake. His feet were grounded in mist. The rest of him was much as it had been in life. She saw no mark on him of the Wild Hunt: no naked skull or corpse-lights. He was a perfectly ordinary apparition, speaking in his familiar voice.

She was glad beyond words to see him so. Even that he seemed to be reprimanding her—he had a right, just as she had a right to say, "I am content. I've preserved this land from the jaws of the sea, and put an end to the plagues and famine."

"That you have not," Malcolm said. "It had already gone beyond the old woman in the abbey, however many souls she had living in her body. Britain may stay above the wave, but the Hunt will still ride, and the children will still die. When all the children are dead, and the old begin to fall, what will the rest do? How long will the kingdom endure?"

Any warmth that Edith had felt in her father's presence was gone. He had set in words what she knew in her bones. "What, then?" she demanded of him. "What more can we do?"

"You know," he said.

"Bind the king to Britain," she said—sighed, rather. "He won't. He flat refuses."

"This needs more than a binding," Malcolm said. "To heal the land and shut the gates of the Otherworld and restore the Hunt to its old nature and purpose—each of those is a great working."

"You need a sacrifice," Edith said. Her voice had gone flat.

"King's blood," said Malcolm. "On sacred ground with a blessed weapon, in the old way and the strong way. There is no other choice."

"Must it be a crowned king?"

Henry was awake, sitting up, and clearly focused on Malcolm. They must have met, Edith thought. Or he knew because she knew.

Malcolm took him in at leisure. "So. You're the youngest. You look like your mother."

"So they say," said Henry. "Is there an answer to my question? Do you know it?"

"It must be a true-born king of Britain," Malcolm said.

"Born to the blood?" Henry asked. "Is that what it needs?"

"It needs the blood," Malcolm said.

Henry nodded. "So it does. I can feel it. The land is in me, spirit. Will that be enough—that, and a willing sacrifice?"

"No," said Edith. She had not even been aware she was speaking until the word was out. "No, not you. You can't—"

She knew that expression. William had it when he refused to be king, Anselm when he would not be Guardian. Henry refused to be the youngest brother, the one whom no one counted, the prince who would never be king.

"They told me I was the year-king," Henry said. "The land claimed me. The power is in me. If I give it up—if I offer my life and blood and even my soul—will the kingdom be saved? Will the people live?"

"That would be a great offering," Malcolm said.

"I forbid it," said Edith. "You cannot do it, and *you*," she said fiercely to her father, "cannot accept it."

"What other choice is there?" Henry asked. He sounded resigned, as if his mind was entirely made up. "My brother won't give way. It's too much a matter of pride for him now. He's a good enough king. He'll find an heir who will do—another of Robert's bastards, or for that matter one of mine. The kingdom will do well, once the burden of magic is lifted from it."

"Britain is magic," Edith said, shaping each word with care. "You can't do this. I won't let you."

"And who are you," said Henry, "to allow or forbid?"

"She is a daughter of kings," Malcolm said before Edith could speak, "and a Lady of the Isle, and a Guardian of Britain."

Edith opened her mouth to point out that she was not yet a Lady and probably never would be, but Henry was already speaking. "If you are all that, Lady, then you know I have to do this. Who else can? There are kings in Scotland and Wales, and they're as royal as any, but this needs William Bastard's blood. Doesn't it, spirit?"

Malcolm spread his hands. "It does seem so. I only bought you seven years. William conquered this kingdom; it stands to reason that his blood would be required to save it."

"There," said Henry. "That's clear enough. What do I need to do? Is there a ritual? Does it need a consecrated weapon, or will good Norman steel do?"

He had drawn his sword, the idiot, as if he would fall on it then and there. Edith rose up in outrage and blasted it to shards.

He stood empty-handed, staring at the smoking fragments that had been a sword. She was perilously close to rendering him into the same condition. "If you must die," she said with all the control she had left, "you will do it in the proper way and in the proper time. You!" she cried to her father, "Begone! I loved you while you were alive and honor you in your death, but if you take my beloved from me, I will hound you through all the worlds."

Malcolm's ghostly brows rose. "Ah, so," he said. "So that's the way of it. Well, lad, I wish you a good fight. With this one you'll need it."

Henry opened his mouth to speak, but Malcolm was gone. They were alone in the starlight, beside the still lake. Nothing moved; apart from them, nothing breathed. The world itself had gone motionless.

Edith rounded on Henry. "Don't you dare kill yourself! Or get yourself killed, either."

"Is there any other choice?" he asked her with a touch of weariness.

"There are endless choices! I won't lose you. Do you hear me? I won't let you go."

"Even if this kingdom falls? Even then, lady?"

She shook her head. "It won't fall. I won't let that happen, either. Will you promise not to die until there truly is no other choice?"

"Yes, but—"

"Good," she said. Then she stopped. "Do I appall you?"

He blinked. "No," he said. "No, you're fascinating."

She would not ask the question that her heart was insisting she ask—that no doubt, great man for woman that he was, he was expecting. She kissed him, because there was no resisting it, and pulled him to his feet. "I'll lock you in durance vile if I have to—bear that well in mind. I'll make sure you keep your promise."

"Yes, lady," he said meekly.

She eyed him with suspicion, but he was the picture of innocence. He went willingly with her away from the lake, back toward the houses and the Ladies' protection.

Henry was enchanted—truly. But the conclusion he had come to, in spite of his promise, would not go away. He had been arriving at it, one way and another, since he set foot in England the year before. He was the one. The land had chosen him. In every way it could, it had been telling him so.

He was not afraid. Death was a door, the old religion said; and the new one, its own God knew, preached the superiority of heaven. Not to be alive again, not to see her living face, did trouble him—but who knew? He might be granted leave to haunt her.

He was as close to content as he could be, as his beautiful and imperious guide brought him to the largest of the round houses in the Isle. People were still awake there, conversing softly by firelight: the three Guardians and one or two white-gowned Ladies, and a cat that was not, by its nature, a cat at all.

Cecilia greeted them with a glance that saw a great deal—but not everything. Henry smiled as he sat beside her.

She did not smile back. The council had been grim, he could tell from their faces. He had a fair reckoning of what they had been saying, too.

His lady—because she was that; he could not deny it—was eyeing him narrowly. He would tell his sister later what he had decided. For now, there were greetings and inconsequentialities, and after a little while, they all repaired to bed for what was left of the night.

There was a bed for Henry in this house, but the lady Mathilda, having kissed him until he was dizzy, turned and slipped away. She had another house, it seemed, and another bed, to which he was not invited.

He resolved not to be offended. He knew nothing of the customs here, or the laws that might govern Ladies of the Isle. Sleep was welcome in any case, and his heart was at ease. His mind was made up.

"You have gone completely mad."

One thing Henry could say for his sister: she spoke her mind. He had had to hunt her down and find her alone, which took some doing. At last, late the following day, he followed her to one of the gardens, where she had set to hoeing weeds.

He already knew that all the Ladies did whatever needed doing, no matter how menial. A hoe was not his usual weapon, but he plied one with enthusiasm if not skill, while he told her what he had decided to do.

She heard him out—that was one of her virtues, too. When he finished, she stopped what she was doing, and looked him straight in the face, and said what she thought.

"I'm not mad," he said. "I'm called—chosen. Isn't it obvious? William won't do it. Robert isn't even in it. It can't be a woman or you'd do it—don't pretend you wouldn't. I'm the one of the sons with magic. The land is in me. I have the blood. I'm willing. What else do we need?"

"Sanity," she said promptly. "You are not meant to die a wasted death."

"Wasted!" His voice had escaped his control; she swayed in the blast of it. "What other hope is there? What else can anybody do?"

"The king can die," she said.

In the wake of those words, silence grew to fill the world. The murmur of wind and water, crying of birds, voices of people and animals, died away. The sky seemed to stoop lower, listening. The earth was breathlessly still.

"But," Henry said in that great silence, "it has to be a willing sacrifice."

"Not necessarily," she said.

"Then it's murder. No more or less."

"Or a tragic accident."

"Like Richard? Like that?"

She nodded.

He hacked a nettle to death with the hoe—taking great satisfaction in it. "So that was murder, too."

"That was the Hunt, delivering a warning. William knows the price of his intransigence. It seems he's willing to pay it."

"He has no conception of it," Henry said sharply. "He's a willful innocent."

"He's a willful idiot." She threw down her hoe and stalked to the end of the row of beans on their poles, then spun. "I'll tell you what I see," she said. "I see a rule that's gone on long enough, a king who will not do his duty, and a kingdom that will not endure much longer while he is king of it."

"You'll wield the knife, then," he said.

"I may," she said. "I'll do everything I can to keep it from drinking your heart's blood."

"Why? Am I not worthy?"

She was on him before he saw her move, bearing him back and down in pure astonishment. No one had done that to him since he was a child—and certainly not his august and much elder sister.

He lay in the furrow with beans dangling overhead and her furious face thrust into his. "You're a worse idiot than he is! Don't you know what you are—what Father meant you to be? You're the next king. That's what the land is telling you. It's chosen you. But it can't keep you, or use you, or cure itself of its sickness, until the crown passes on. Do you understand now? *He* is the year-king. You are the king hereafter."

"I'm not—"

She slapped him until his ears rang. "You of all people, I would have thought would see it from the first. What, are you blind? Robert's useless here—luckily he's the eldest; he could have Normandy, which takes care of itself. William should have been less stubborn than he was; if he had done what our father wanted him to do, he would have given you a strong kingdom that you could raise above the rest of the world. Father reckoned without the grey abbess and he reckoned without William's consummate stupidity. It seems he overestimated you, too."

"If this is the old rite," he said with difficulty: she was a substantial weight, sitting on his chest, "I have to kill him. I have to kill my brother."

"Someone does," she said. "It's been foreseen. What you two did yesterday, that began the new order. This will be the last rite of the old way: the last royal sacrifice to bind the powers of Britain. There is no escaping it. If we shrink from it, we all fail. The kingdom dies."

"Why? Why us? Why now?"

"The world changes," she said. "Even the powers change. A world is ending, even as a new one is born. We're its midwives—yes, even you; don't stare at me like that. There's blood; there's pain. There's death, and there's what lies beyond death. Then—there's a new kingdom. Briton, Saxon, Norman. All together." Her finger thrust painfully at his chest, right above the heart. "That's for you to do. You have to live. The old order has to die."

She left him there, lying in the furrow, with his head buzzing and his mind reeling in confusion. So much that he had thought he saw, or believed he knew, was all changed. The world was different. The light fell in a way he had never seen before.

To be king. To take Britain in his hand, and do what he knew must be done—the elation, the exultation of it, sent the world spinning even while he lay flat on it.

But if he was to do that, William had to die. That was why the Hunt was still free in the daylight. It was waiting for its last quarry: the blood and soul of a king.

CHAPTER 49

I won't do it," Henry said. "Find yourselves another executioner."

He had lain for a long while in the furrow before he got up and went to find the Guardians. They were waiting for him in the Lady's house, in smoky dimness that seemed black dark after the bright sunlight. Once his sight had cleared, he could see that all their faces were somber. FitzHaimo looked as sick as Henry felt.

No wonder. He was plotting his lover's death.

"This is a sacrifice," the Lady said, "a gift to the gods. It's the last royal blood they'll drink. Sacrifices hereafter will be of another kind."

"The Christians gave it up a thousand years ago," Henry said.

"So they did," said the Lady, "and their last sacrifice was the greatest of all: their god's own son."

"They laid the burden of it on the Romans," he said, "and on the Jews—not on his brother."

"Therefore his hands were clean, when he profited from it?" The Lady shook her head. "The old way was simpler. There was no sin or damnation. The king died of his free will, and the new king performed the sacrifice."

"This king will not die of his free will," Henry said.

"What if he will?" That was Mathilda. "What if he accepts his fate? Will that change anything?"

"It won't happen," said Cecilia.

"It might," Mathilda said. "He's a better man than he knows. In the end, when he sees there's no other choice, he may surprise you all."

"We can't wager on it," Cecilia said. "This has to be done. How we do it, and when—"

"Soon," FitzHaimo said. That was the sound of pain exquisitely controlled. "It must be soon."

They bowed to him. Even Henry curbed his tongue. He might have asked whether that of all people could persuade William to do what must be done, but he chose silence.

It could be cowardice. Maybe it was wisdom. They were plotting a king's death—high treason in the world Henry had grown to manhood in. Here, it was something higher and somehow cleaner. It was ritual, and sacrifice.

No wonder his father had fled this world and his brother turned his back on it. There was nothing easy or simple about it. The light was too bright; the darkness was full of terror. And it all came down on the king's shoulders, even with the pillars that were the Guardians, and all the powers that bowed to his name.

He had to leave that house, though not yet the Isle. He was not ready to face his brother and know that William was condemned, by the oldest laws and powers of Britain, to death. Above all he was not ready—nor might ever be—to carry out that sentence.

William had been keeping close to the sea that summer, keeping his eye on Normandy. The duke had to come back sooner or later, and William wanted to be within easy reach when he did. Then—who knew? Maybe they would go to war over the dukedom. Or else they would join together and conquer France.

On the first of August, which was the feast of St. Peter in Chains, stag-hunting season began. A day or two in advance of that, William brought a small company to one of his hunting lodges: Brockenhurst, that was older and smaller than Brampton, but better situated for the deer. The rest of the court stayed behind in Winchester, being dutiful.

A week or two of hunting, William was thinking as he rode back from the first day's hunt, then maybe he would take an army and head for Normandy. England had seen enough of him for a while, and he of it.

But today and tomorrow and for however long it pleased him, he was hunting the red deer in his own forest. They had shot two fine stags today—one with his arrow and one with Walter Tirel's. Walter Tirel's was much the larger, which he would never stoop to brag of, but some of the others were not so delicate.

William had fallen back a bit from the rest of the hunt. They were almost to the lodge, and he was enjoying the fine weather and the free sky too much. He was halfway tempted to go back out again. There were a few hours of daylight left—why not make use of them?

The others had venison in mind, and as much wine as they could swallow. That would not be a bad thing, either, William reflected. He stayed with them therefore, and rode into the manor's court somewhat behind the others.

They were all milling about in the tight space, made tighter by the presence of a stranger. William saw the horse first, a stocky iron-grey cob, then the rider: a dwarf with a black beard, thickset and powerful, and nigh as broad as he was tall. He looked vaguely familiar, but William could not put his finger on where he had seen the man before.

The dwarf's trade and purpose were clear to see: he had set up an anvil and small forge in the corner by the stable, and was hammering lustily at a bar of iron while a horse waited to be shod.

The horse, unlike the dwarf, was very familiar indeed: a fine bay mare with a star on her forehead and one white hoof. William looked for her master, and found him soon enough, leaning against the wall, conversing with one or two of the knights.

William felt the grin spread across his face. "FitzHaimo!" he roared. "You bloody reprobate! Where have you been?" He pushed through the crowd of men and horses, in one instance lifting a large and oblivious knight bodily out of the way.

By the time he got to Robin, he found a grin to match his. The eyes that went with it looked a little haunted, but he did not let it trouble him just then. He swept his friend into a strong embrace.

Robin's grip was just as strong—if not stronger. William's ribs creaked. They let each other go in the same moment. "I thought you'd vanished into a hollow hill," William said. "Trust you to un-vanish just in time for the stag-hunting. Would you believe it? After all the cursed weather we've had, the deer are as fat as they ever were. God is smiling again, and no mistake."

"Fat deer are a blessing," Robin said. The smith called to him just then with a question about the mare; William did not get a good look at his face.

Time enough later for that. People were calling William, too. He thumped Robin on the shoulder and brushed a kiss past his ear. "Sit with me at dinner."

Robin nodded, maybe at the smith, maybe at William. William shrugged and left him to sort out the mare's shoeing.

Robin was late to dinner, damn him, but the rest were all there, and the wine was plentiful and the venison splendid. Whatever was keeping Robin, it was not the smith—the man came in between the venison and the pigeon pie with a gift for the king: six black hunting arrows tipped with fine steel and fletched with raven's feathers. "A small token of regard," the dwarf said in his deep rumble of a voice, "and a minor tribute for a king."

William rose to accept the gift, and bowed. "My thanks, sir smith," he said. "You do beautiful work. Stay with us a while; we can use you."

"Many thanks, my lord," the smith said, bowing to the floor.

William opened his mouth to invite the dwarf to share the rest of the dinner, but he was already gone. He was agile on those thick bandy legs, and quick, too.

Indeed he did beautiful work. William had been able to see as much from a distance, but once he had the arrows in his hands, he could see how well they were made.

Walter Tirel whistled softly, leaning on William's shoulder. "These are wonderful," he said.

"Aren't they?" said William. He lifted two from the rest and pressed them into Walter Tirel's hand. "Here, take these. Not that you need any help to shoot the fattest deer in the woods, but why shouldn't the best have the best?"

Walter Tirel flushed, but he was not fool enough to refuse such a gift. He thanked William with a kiss that promised more and better for later, and sat down just as Robin finally deigned to appear in the hall.

The place that William had been keeping for Robin was occupied by Walter Tirel. Robin seemed not to mind. He found a place farther down the table and let the servant fill a plate and a cup for him. He went straight for the wine, which was not like him—but yet again, William was distracted before he could say anything about it.

It was a night for distractions. The wine was strong, and there was singing. Some of the men had to reenact the hunt, turning it into a dance, with much vaunting and laughter. When William looked again for Robin, his place was empty. His plate was still there, untouched.

William started to go after him, but there was Walter Tirel, and more wine, and a song in William's honor, that needed a clever rebuttal. And after that was Walter Tirel again, and a long, drunken, joyous night.

William dreamed that he was floating in a sea of wine. He drifted to shore: crimson sand, crimson waves, black and starless sky. He lay on the sand, his body loosed as it was after love, and as he lay there, the veins of arms and groin and throat opened. Blood spurted from them, searing scarlet in that black-and-crimson world. It covered the earth and dyed the water, and leaped up into the sky. The whole world turned the color of blood.

King's blood, he said, or thought, or sang. *Blood of kings.*

William woke with the mother of headaches, with Walter Tirel sprawled naked beside him. It was already morning: light shone through the shutters, stabbing straight through to the brain.

Robin was standing over him. William reached to pull him down, but he braced his feet; William found himself coming up instead, weak and staggering, clutching at Robin. "Christ," he muttered. "That wine was strong."

"And you drank most of a butt of it by yourself," Robin said. He half led, half carried William to the washbasin and dipped the cloth into the chill water, washing William's face and breast and arms.

By then William could stand, if not exactly steadily. He let his head fall back and his eyes fall shut, giving himself up to Robin's ministrations. Those hands had always been lighter than anyone else's, even Walter Tirel's—deft in their touch, clever at finding the places where they could give the most pleasure.

"I've missed you," William said.

"Have you?" Robin's tone held no expression. Something about it pointed directly to the man still snoring in William's bed.

"There's enough of me for both of you," William said.

Robin said nothing to that. William opened his eyes. There was no expression on Robin's face, either.

"So," said William, "what? You won't fight for your place beside me? When did you turn Christian martyr?"

"I had a dream in the night," Robin said.

He had not heard William at all. He had a look William had never seen in him before: bleak and remote.

"I dreamed," said Robin, "that you went hunting this morning while the sun was still low, and a black arrow came out of the light and pierced your heart."

William peered at him. Poor thing, he was as white as his shirt. That was as unlike him as—what? Whatever had happened yesterday, which William could not offhand remember. Something odd. Maybe a number of somethings. "Are you feeling well?" he asked. "You look awful."

"Promise me," said Robin. "Don't go hunting today. Stay here and nurse your headache. Play with your lovely boy."

"Play?" William asked. "With you? Both of you? Now that's tempting."

Robin shook his head. "Don't talk like a fool. Just promise."

"Why? Because you had a nightmare?"

"Because I had a dream, and you know what I am."

"I know what you are," William said, running his hand down the front of Robin's coat. "You're dressed to hunt. What's the matter? Afraid I'll outdo you in the woods?"

"I'm afraid you'll die in the woods," Robin snapped. "Now will you promise?"

"I won't go out this morning," William said. "I'll finish sleeping instead. Maybe get rid of this headache. Do you have a spell for that?"

"If I did," said Robin with a touch of nastiness, "I'd still let you suffer—as long as it kept you safe."

"I'm safe here," said William. "Come here. Come to bed."

Robin would not. William was too shaky to fight; he let the man go. Robin bent toward him, kissed him hard and long, and left him dizzy and reeling.

✴ CHAPTER 50 ✴

FitzHaimo was gone from the Isle. So was Cecilia, and the Lady Etaine. Somehow Henry did not think the lord and the Ladies had traveled together.

"He's gone to warn the king," Mathilda said.

"And the others?"

"You know what they went to do," she said.

He had set up a wooden Saracen in the orchard and set to hacking at it with his sword, for practice and for something to do with his body while his mind spun through its endless circles. Time was strange on the Isle. He thought he had been there for three days or maybe four. He could not be more precise than that. If he tried, his head ached abominably.

Mathilda found him there, late that morning or maybe it was afternoon. She had watched him for a long while before she spoke; he was aware of her, but he kept on with his exercises until the sweat ran down his back and sides and his arms ached every time he lifted the heavy blade and brought it round and hacked another notch in the Saracen.

Then he lowered the sword until its point rested on the grass, and looked into her eyes. Her thoughts ran on the same track as his. She answered the question he had no need to ask: where FitzHaimo had gone.

Then there was the rest of it. "They're hunting a king," he said.

She nodded. "I heard the Ladies before they went. 'The weapons are bestowed,' they said. 'The snare is laid. Now to catch the prey.'"

"But if FitzHaimo warns him," Henry said, "it will all come to nothing."

"You think so?" she said. "You know how stubborn he is. He'll laugh it off."

"They left us behind," said Henry. "Why? What are they afraid of?"

"Weakness," she said. "Betrayal. I don't know."

"I can guess," he said. He sheathed his sword and slung it behind him as he strode down to the lake to wash the sweat off.

Her eyes were a little wide, watching him. He had not been thinking of what she would see—considering that she saw more of it every night. But then he never could look at her without noticing how high and yet full her breasts were, or how narrow a waist she had, or how wonderfully her hips flared from that smallness.

It was well that the lake's water was cold, or he would have been tempted to fall on her then and there. He scrubbed himself instead, a little more fiercely maybe than strictly necessary. When he went to retrieve his clothes, he found her there with an armful of metal and leather: his riding clothes, with the shirt of mail and the rest of his weapons. She was dressed to ride herself, and how she had done that in the little time he spent on his bath, he forbore to ask.

Gods knew he had no objection. He dressed with her help, and stood while she belted his sword on him. She knelt to do that, because it was the practical thing. It did not mean anything.

Even so, when she was done he raised her to her feet and set a kiss in each palm and said, "When this is done, marry me. Be my queen."

Her face closed. "You don't even know who I am," she said.

"I know you're royal," he said. "I'm slow on the uptake, Lady, but that messenger from the dead—I remembered him finally. That was old Malcolm of Scots, and you're his daughter. Yes?"

Her head bowed. Her cheeks were slightly flushed. "Yes," she said, almost too low to hear.

He set a finger under her chin and tilted her face up. "Why didn't you want me to know?"

"Because it doesn't matter," she said. "I don't want what's between us to be a—a transaction, like buying a cow in the market."

His lips twitched. "You are a very fine heifer, and I am a somewhat battle-scarred but still presentable bull."

Her eyes sparked at that. "More than presentable! Even," she said, "if you are a damned pirate of a Norman."

He laughed, full and free. He had not laughed like that in as long as he could remember. And here they were on the edge of death or worse, preparing to either kill or save a king.

He sobered soon enough. "How?" he asked. "How did you manage to be what you are? You should have been my bitter enemy."

"I can only be what I am," she said. "I'm a Gael, too. Somehow I got all of that and none of the rest."

"The gods had a hand in it, I'm sure," Henry said. "So? Will you?"

She was not disingenuous enough to pretend she had forgotten what he asked. "If we survive this day and night," she said, "and if you still want it then . . . we'll consider it."

"No," he said. "That's not an answer. Yes or no."

He held his breath. She took her time with it; he was dizzy when she said, "Yes. If we live until tomorrow, yes."

"Even if there's blood on my hands?"

She took them in hers and inspected them front and back, with all their calluses and roughness and old scars. "You've been killing men since you were old enough to hold a sword," she said.

"Not like this."

"Like a priest in the sacrifice." She held his hands to her heart. "Whatever comes of this, I'll be beside you."

He kissed her forehead and then her lips. "There's no better army in the world," he said.

"Don't indulge me," she said. "Come; time's passing."

He was ready, but he paused a moment longer. "Your name," he said. "It's—"

"Mathilda." Her eyes were level on him. "When you give me the crown, that's the name in which I will take it."

He bowed to that. It was no wonder, he thought, that she did not want England to see another Queen Edith. But Mathilda—that was worthy of her and of the one from whom she took it.

By noon William was in a truly foul mood. He had had all the lying about he could stand. Morning was past; the sun was high. He had come here to hunt, and he would hunt. He did not need Robin FitzHaimo's permission. He was king, by God, and the king would do what the king pleased.

Some of the others were out already. Walter Tirel was ready and willing, but the rest were too lazy or hung over to move. William kicked over a bench full of them and left them in a sprawl. "I'll find the others out there, then. You all stay here and finish puking your guts out."

They snarled, but none of them was fool enough to challenge the king. William raked them with a grin and went to find his horse.

Walter Tirel was close behind him. He reached to pull the boy in, and paused for a kiss. "Did you bring the arrows?"

For answer Walter Tirel held up the quiver he was carrying. Six black hunting arrows, black-fletched, stood up amid the more ordinary peeled wood and grey or brown feathers.

"Good," said William. "Let's get moving. The day's wasting."

They had hardly gone out of sight of the lodge before they picked up fresh tracks. The weather was as glorious as it had been the day before. The tracks were clear and the path easy to follow. It was a stag from size and depth, and a big one. He had been feeding in the remains of an old orchard, where a few trees still bore stunted fruit, and the grass was rich and green.

William closed his eyes and breathed deep while his horse carried him along the stag's trail. It was good to be alive; he was not going to die. Not today and not for a long while to come.

Robin liked to fret—that was all there had been to that. There had been eruptions in the magic of Britain; William had not been able to keep from sensing them. But the earth was better now than it had been before, the magic stronger. The air was brighter. Whatever had happened, it was for the good. William needed to know no more than that.

They followed the track away from the orchard and into the wood. William led, Walter Tirel followed. There was no sign of the other hunters. William was glad. He was in the mood to hunt alone—or better than alone.

He smiled over his shoulder. Walter Tirel smiled back.

The tracks were fresher; under the branches of a beech-tree, William found droppings still faintly steaming. Behind him as he strung his bow, he heard Walter Tirel doing the same.

All the good arrows were in Walter Tirel's quiver, he thought rather wryly—but the ones he had were not bad. He slipped one from the quiver and kept it loose in his hand, guiding his horse with his knees along the freshening trail.

Henry rode with Mathilda along the straight track away from the Isle. Their departure had been almost leisurely, but urgency possessed them now. Their riding was silent, both of them focused on the place where they must go. They flickered in and out of the Otherworld, passing from supernal sunlight to mortal earth to enchanted darkness to earthly daylight.

It was a monstrously dangerous thing to do. They could be lost forever between worlds, or caught in one or the other, or hunted by powers that had no fear or care for either a Guardian or a would-be king of Britain.

There was no choice. They had to find the king before this day was ended. This was his death day; the sacrifice was prepared and the rite begun. They could hear it resonating underfoot, a chant as old as time, older even than the Giants' Dance or the Ladies of Avalon.

Henry rode up beside Mathilda and took her hand. Her eyes were fixed on the road ahead, but her fingers tightened around his. The horses' pace quickened.

The road seemed rougher. Henry dared not look down for fear of what he would see. The horses traveled these roads with uncanny ease, as if this was their native country; but even they had tensed, ears flicking nervously. Henry's stallion hunched his back; his head tossed from side to side.

Henry sat down deeper in the saddle and tightened rein. The stallion jibbed but settled somewhat. They had entered a region of mist, curling in dank tendrils around the horses' legs.

The mist had substance. It slowed the horses; they began to struggle. Henry debated the wisdom of drawing cold iron in this place. Not wise, no. He reached into the part of himself where the magic was, and drew a sword of light.

It cut through the mist like a scythe through grain. The horses, freed, sprang from wallowing trot into long-strided canter.

There was light ahead, past a swirl of darkness and stars. And there was a wall of bone and ragged flesh: hounds and riders of the Wild Hunt, barring the way back into the world.

Mathilda rode straight for them. Henry had no hands free for his earthly blade. One gripped hers; the other still held the sword of magic that he had made.

He swept it before them as they plunged through the Hunt. Hounds bayed; bones scattered. Light and air and mortal earth burst upon them. They fell in a tangle of limbs, horses and humans together.

CHAPTER 51

The scent of bruised grass filled Henry's nostrils. He sneezed. His body protested vehemently. It was rather more damaged than the grass.

Something moved under him. He groaned and disentangled himself from Mathilda.

They were both alive and apparently intact. So were the horses, apart from a broken rein or two. The beasts were grazing in a meadow surrounded by trees. The sun was halfway down the sky; the shadows had begun to lengthen.

It seemed an ordinary meadow in an ordinary forest, but Henry knew well how deceptive appearances could be. There was power here: a deep well of it, rooted in the meadow and the grove.

This was a holy place. Henry rose unsteadily, drawing strength from the earth.

Mathilda was already on her feet, and her wits were quicker than his, too. She pulled him about to face the rest of the Guardians, and behind them the eerie ranks of the Hunt.

The Hunt was all around them. The trees were full of its riders.

Mathilda ignored them. She was glaring at Robin FitzHaimo. "You warned him. He knows."

"He knows nothing," FitzHaimo said. "The words blew over him like wind. He delayed for a morning, that was all."

"Sunset is a more powerful time to die," said the Lady. "You did well."

FitzHaimo's face set. Henry almost pitied him. This was easy for no one, but for a lover it must be brutal.

Old rites were brutal. That was the way of them. FitzHaimo was part of this; he had chosen it.

So had they all. Even Henry. Though what he had chosen, he was not sure yet.

The Guardians stood at each of the four quarters of the meadow. Mathilda had slipped free of Henry's grip to take the station of the east. He stood alone near the center.

The earth balanced precisely underfoot. The sky was its perfect image overhead. The Guardians lifted up walls of air: a fortress of magic and pure will. The Hunt waited, silent, unmoving. A new soul would join them by nightfall. That was their bargain and their expectation.

Unless, thought Henry, they were restored to their old semblance and returned to the Otherworld. They did not seem to have any fear of that.

There was one gap in the circle, one opening into the shadows of the wood. Henry heard hoofbeats there: swift, light, headlong. A stag was running. Behind it, fainter but still distinct, he caught the sound of horses galloping.

The stag's trail doubled on itself. Walter Tirel slipped ahead of William, who had paused to see if the beast had leaped into the underbrush. He peered through woven branches, searching for the tines of antlers.

The stag sprang out of the trees, straight across Walter Tirel's path. His horse shied. He was standing in the stirrups to shoot; he clung to bow and saddle, but the black arrow dropped, snapping under his horse's hoof.

He cursed, then laughed, flashing a grin over his shoulder at William. The stag veered and then bolted down the track toward a distant gleam of light.

Walter Tirel whooped and spurred after it. William was oddly sluggish, but his horse was not about to be left behind. When he failed to demand a gallop, the stallion made the decision for himself.

They pounded breakneck through the trees. Through the whipping of wind and lashing of branches, he could see Walter Tirel's flying hair, and the stag beyond him, bounding higher and ever higher the closer it came to the light.

There was clear air beyond, green of grass, and the sun hanging low. The stag, out in the open, leaped and darted. Walter Tirel kept the straight path—the most wizardly thing William had ever known him to do. He had a fresh arrow in his hand, as black as the other.

It was an odd clearing, a nearly perfect circle, and the trees that ringed it were all very, very old; yet they seemed planted: oak and ash and thorn. At each quarter of the wind, William saw a standing stone. It almost looked like a hooded figure, erect and still, raising a vast edifice of magic over what must be an old holy place. It certainly had the look.

William felt strangely at ease here. His horse slowed; he let it. Magic that had been the bane of his life seemed right and proper in this place. It belonged here. And so, God knew how, did he.

Men and stag burst into the clearing together. They were blind to what was in and about it: Henry saw how they looked over Cecilia's head as if she had not been there, and stared straight through Henry where he stood in the center.

The stag veered past him, so close he felt the puff of its breath on his cheek. Walter Tirel was hot on its heels. Henry roused almost too late and hauled his horse back. Walter Tirel's light-boned chestnut skittered and shied and careened into him.

Henry's larger, heavier horse kept its feet, but the chestnut went down. Walter Tirel flew from the saddle, tucked and rolled like a tumbler.

His bow took flight, too, but with evident will and intent: straight for Henry's hand. Henry had it before he knew what he had done, and in his other hand a black arrow, stinging as it slapped into his palm.

William had drawn rein just within the walls of air. The stag stood motionless between. Henry had clearly seen it bolt past him, but there it was, halfway back the way it had come. It was real; he would have known an illusion, and that was true and mortal hide and hair and bone, heaving sides and staring eyes and moistly quivering nostrils.

Henry met William's eyes over the stag's back. William had a bow and it was strung, but he had not nocked an arrow to the string. He was waiting for Henry to shoot.

Not Henry—no. William would have been surprised to find his brother here, who had last been seen in Salisbury. Henry looked for the reflection in those eyes, and saw Walter Tirel's face.

Magic and delusion. Henry willed the king to see who faced him and why. The power in this place dragged at that will; strove to distort and twist it into more illusion. Henry set his teeth and ripped at it.

He could shoot the stag. Or any of the Guardians. Or the Huntsman himself. This arrow in his hand had such power. It was a working of the Otherworld, but its tip was mortal steel—coldest of cold iron, death to Old Things.

Death to mortals, too; it was wickedly sharp, a hunting point, meant to pierce muscle and bone of beasts heavier, thicker-skinned, and stronger than men. Henry nocked it to the string. William sat still on his red horse as if enspelled—or as if, at the last, he understood.

Once more Henry met those bright blue eyes. There was recognition in them. Acceptance? Maybe William had not come to that yet.

The earth of Britain was healing. The folk of air were stronger. But plague still ran rampant, and there was the Hunt, riddled with corruption, waiting for Henry to fail.

He could not fail. His chest was tight; his breath came hard. He raised the bow, aimed and sighted. Straight for the heart.

If the stag moved, if it came between, then so be it. Maybe Henry waited a second beyond the necessary, hoping for it. But the world had gone still.

The arrow flew. William could still escape—still throw himself aside.

But he stood as stiff as a target. Did he shift, even, to lie more surely open to the shot? Did he know—understand? At the last, was he the willing, the royal sacrifice?

God knew. Henry's powers were spent. All of them had left him with that black arrow, plunging into his brother's heart.

William reeled out of the saddle. The stag was gone. He fell headlong. The arrow twisted and snapped, tearing flesh. Heart's blood sprang.

The earth sighed. The Guardians moved. Tears were streaming down FitzHaimo's face.

The Hunt left the concealment of the trees. William's blood fed the thirsty land, but the Hunt was still dark—still stained with the blight. Henry watched it in despair. Even murder—fratricide, regicide—had not been enough. Dear gods, must it be suicide, too?

He slid from his horse's back. The bow was slack in his hand. He let it fall.

Walter Tirel was crouching there, wide-eyed and conscious and paralytic with terror. Henry had no time to spare for him.

William was not quite dead. His soul was no fool; it clung to its body in dread of the Hunt.

That was the last sacrifice. Loosing the arrow—that had been easy beside this. Henry had to pry the soul free and let the Hunt take it.

William had been an infamous sinner, arrogant, headstrong, and heedless. Many a priest and holy monk would sing hosannas to hear what damnation waited for him. So would one damned soul in the Hunt: old Malcolm grinning down, savoring the prospect. He had damned himself for this, to exact the perfect revenge.

Henry knelt beside his brother and touched his finger to the still-warm stream of blood from the wound. He raised it to his lips. It tasted of iron and sweetness and slow fire. That was life, though he would have expected a good deal more bitterness, and the salt of tears.

"If he goes willingly," he said to the dead king and the immortal Huntsman, "no one here will stop him."

"You mortals," the Huntsman said, tossing his crown of antlers. "Always you bargain. We are not merchants."

"No?" said Henry. "This isn't a negotiation. This is what will be. He chooses this—or he goes free."

"And his kingdom—the kingdom you have won—dies from the heart outward. Children first, young king. All the children, every one."

Henry steeled himself against that. It was as difficult a thing as he had ever done. He would do what he must do. No matter the cost.

He dipped his finger in blood again and drew the posts and lintel of a gate on the cooling forehead. "Out," he said. "Out and face yourself."

William's eyes opened. His voice was a breathless whisper. "Don't know how. Don't—"

"Think it," Henry said. "Make it so. Choose."

The lids fell shut. He was not going to—Henry knew it. He would resist to the last, and destroy them all.

His body shuddered. His soul sprang out of it, the very image of him to the life, straight up toward the Huntsman. He had a sword in his hand—though where he had got it, only he and the gods knew.

He grinned like a wild thing, taking them all aback—even the Huntsman; even as his incorporeal blade plunged between those bony ribs.

The world stopped. The walls of air wavered and threatened to fall.

William laughed. "Lord!" he cried. "What fools we mortals be!"

He wrenched his blade free. The Huntsman wailed like the wind through empty places. The hounds echoed him, and the army of Old Things and dead souls and spectral hunters.

Then the world changed.

The sun was all but touching the horizon—and yet darkness went away. The world was washed in a tide of light. Henry looked up into William's face, the broad grin and the hot-blue eyes and the joyous arrogance that would never change, no matter whether he was alive or dead.

The Huntsman stood behind him, utterly transformed: the Horned King, tall and strange and beautiful. His mount wore flesh; his huntsmen rode in the semblance of Great Old Ones, high lords of the Other-world, or of old kings and heroes, princes of renown, who had won this destiny for their bravery and their prowess in battle. Even the hounds were returned to the light again, great white hounds with red ears, and their eyes were full of stars.

Henry bowed to them. They bowed in return. William said, "Don't worry. I understand."

For the first time Henry felt the rush of grief, the realization that his brother was dead. Truly dead, and not to be reborn.

"But not damned," William said. "Not by my lights. Don't wallow, little brother. You've got what you were always meant to have—won fair and true, in the oldest of the old ways. It takes a king to kill a king—and to make one."

Henry bowed again, down to the ground. When he rose, the Hunt had vanished, melted into the gold-red light, taking with it William's soul. The gates of the Otherworld were shut. The walls of air had grown, swelled, expanded to encompass the whole of the isle and a good part of the sea.

"There will be no other conquest," said the Lady Etaine. "No more invaders. No such defeat, ever again."

"Amen," Henry said.

The Guardians had drawn in close. With the Hunt gone, the air was full of Old Things, so thick with them that they dimmed the sky.

Etaine bent over the fallen king's body. As Henry had done, she dipped her hand in blood. She painted Henry's face with it, a war-mask of the old time. She painted his breast and hands, and last of all his lips, whispering as she did so, incantations so strong that words were too small to hold them.

He tasted blood, still warm with the heat of life. He felt the bindings as she made them: binding him to the earth, to air and sky, to the waters of Britain; weaving him into the land, and the land into him. There was no sin or atonement, no guilt or grief. He was the king, and king's blood made it so.

She crowned him with oak and ash and the pricking of thorn. That small pain, those beads of blood, completed the sacrifice.

The rest of his consecration was waiting beyond her: hair like molten gold in the last of the light, magic clothing her in shadow and shimmer. She too was crowned with oak and ash and thorn, and her hands were reaching for his as he reached for hers.

There had been grief, pain, bitter choices—stern reminders of what it was to be a king. She was there to remind him of the rest: the strength he was to bring to his kingdom, the light he would shed upon it and the gifts of life and prosperity that he would give to it. And sons, he thought; sons and daughters to carry on the blood, so that neither the royal line nor the kingdom would wither and die.

All of that was in the meeting of hands and the smile that bloomed in both at once. Sorrow would be a long time fading; this day would haunt his dreams. But here was joy, that would always balance sorrow— and long after sorrow was forgotten, it would still be there. She would be there in all his empty places.

"You're not getting the best bargain," he said to her. "I'm too much my father's son. There are women—children—"

"I know," she said. "You can't be sure what you're getting with me, either. I haven't been raised as a proper Christian queen. If we lie and say I've been at Wilton, the Church will accuse you of abducting a nun from a convent and violating her vows. If we—"

He stopped her lips with his. "Don't think," he said. "Or talk. Not tonight. Not until tomorrow."

She drew breath to protest—he could see it in her eyes. But the pause gave her time to understand. She bowed to what she would, he hoped, see as his good sense.

The light was fading at last. They had shifted out of the world. Time had gone as fluid as water.

Somewhere in the endless stream of it, William lay newly dead. Walter Tirel whirled in a panic of grief, mind and memory all hopelessly confused. Maybe Cecilia moved to help him—or maybe to bind him to silence.

She moved too late. He scrambled up and away from all that impossible strangeness, caught a dangling rein, flung himself into the saddle of Henry's horse. He hardly seemed to notice that his own was standing within reach.

His whole world was terror: that he had been caught in a cacophony of demons, and that—above all—no one would believe what he thought he had seen. His bow, his arrow had killed the king. Maybe he had. Maybe there had been a spell on him, or madness, or delusion. He had no magic and no learning in such things. He could not know.

He did the only thing he could do. He fled—all the way to the sea and back to Normandy, safe in his own castle where he could grieve in peace.

Henry could have stopped him. He made the choice: he let him go. Whether that was good or ill, time would tell. For the moment he was only sure that it was merciful.

Time would wait—would stand still for the completion of this rite. The powers would give him a night, then fold it away and open the world again to the hour before sunset, a king dead, the rest of his hunters finding him at last; then all the alarums and the pomp and the crushing urgency of a kingship that must be taken swiftly and made secure.

This night, of which the mortal world would never know, was the fulfillment of the rite. He took the kingdom in the old way, through the body of the living Goddess. It was hers to give, and she gladly gave it, she who was twice royal, Guardian and queen.

There was no pungency of hawthorn on them tonight. The scent that wreathed about them, dizzying and sweet, was the scent of roses. Her crown bloomed with them, white roses of the Otherworld, that would never fade or die.

He opened his mouth to speak, but she silenced him. No words tonight. Nothing at all but earth and air and sky, and the warmth of bodies joined together. Then he was truly king and she was queen; and Britain, at last, was whole.

CHAPTER 52

Anselm came out of morning Mass in a small church in Lyons that he had adopted for his own, still exalted with the beauty of the rite, to find a guest waiting for him in the sacristy. It was a stranger, a man of no particular age or distinction, dressed in anonymous traveling clothes. He bowed to Anselm and clearly looked for a ring to kiss; but that was shut away in a box in Canterbury.

Anselm blessed him, which he seemed to take in good part, and waited for him to provide a name and a purpose.

The name was not forthcoming. The purpose came mercifully quickly. The man drew from his purse a folded parchment with pendant seals, and a small bag, heavy for its size.

It was almost with a sense of relief that Anselm emptied the contents into his hand. It was the ring he had just been thinking of, the archbishop's ring, with its carved amethyst and its weight of significance.

He weighed the letter in his hand, but elected to wait before he opened it. "You have a message, messire?" he asked.

The man bowed again. "I come from the king of the English," he said. "He bids you return to your duties."

Anselm drew a slow breath. His hands were not shaking: good. "Truly? William bids me return? How in the world—"

"William of England is dead," the messenger said. "Henry of England summons you home."

"Ah," said Anselm. He felt nothing yet except a certain wry inevitability. "May I ask how William died?"

"By accident, holy father. An arrow in the hunt. They say his sweet friend did it, the count from Poix. He fled as the guilty might, but the king has not pursued him. There's no blame to be laid, says the king, and no punishment to be exacted. He bids you know, holy father, that the same applies to you."

Anselm's brows rose. "Does it indeed?"

"Indeed," said the messenger. His chin tilted toward the letter. "It's all in there, holy father. I'm bidden to bring you to England. The escort is waiting. The servants will have finished packing by now. Have you any farewells to make? I can allow you an hour."

That was clear enough. Anselm had begun to shake, but only a little—and after all he was old, and he was occasionally afflicted with a palsy. "I will take that hour, messire," he said. "Will you wait for me with the escort?"

The messenger shook his head—regretfully, but that did not deter him. "I'm sorry, holy father. My orders are to stay with you until I bring you safe to the king."

"Even into the garderobe?" Anselm inquired—but stopped the man before he could answer. "No, no. That was unworthy of any of us. I won't vex your patience too far. Just give me time to get out of these vestments and offer thanks to my host for his hospitality. Will that be permitted?"

The king's messenger bowed. Anselm sighed, but he was well and truly bound by his own oath and promise. He did as he was bidden.

Kingship became Henry. Anselm had to admit that. He had an air more of his mother than of his father: more grace, fewer rough edges. And, it had to be said, more magic in him than in both of them together.

It had been a long journey by mortal ways, and hard on old bones.

Anselm's escort had done its best for him within the scope of its orders. Nevertheless, Anselm was glad to see an end of it, in the hall of Westminster that Red William had built so vauntingly high.

William had filled it with arrogance and fire. Henry suited it better. He received Anselm with meticulous formality, he in the crown and on the throne, Anselm—not quite by main force—in miter and cope.

The court was there to witness it. Most of the faces were the same, along with the more deplorable excesses of fashion, but the dissolute lolling about of the previous reign had given way with edifying speed to a more becoming dignity. This court's glitter seemed less hectic, its splendor more appropriately royal.

Anselm was beginning to have hopes of this king. He bowed with honest enough reverence. Henry returned the gesture without irony, as far as Anselm could see. "My lord archbishop," he said. "Welcome home to England."

"I thank you, majesty," Anselm said, "for your welcome and for your most attentive escort. Am I to consider myself further . . . escorted, or shall I now be free of the kingdom?"

"You are the primate of all England," Henry said with diplomatic blandness. "Your freedom is commensurate with your rank."

"Indeed," said Anselm, "majesty."

Henry rose and came down from the throne. He took Anselm's elbow, all gentle solicitude. "Ah, my lord archbishop: you're worn out. Come, we'll go somewhere more comfortable. I'll have Cook send one of his tonics—he has a masterful way with herbs."

Henry's cook was not the only masterful man in this palace. Anselm was on his way out of the hall before he could open his mouth, with the tonic ordered and the court dismissed.

The solar to which Henry half led, half carried him was airy, sunlit, and powerfully warded. Spirits came and went in exuberant freedom, but no ill thing could pass those walls.

Henry saw Anselm to a chair, which he was grateful to take, then took off his crown and laid it on the table under the window. He stood for a moment, rubbing his forehead; when he turned, his smile was crooked. "It's true what they say," he said, "about the weight of a crown."

"You bear it well," Anselm said.

"Do I?" Henry sat across from him.

The tonic arrived in a goblet of clear glass; Henry waited while Anselm sipped it. It was surprisingly good, made with herbs steeped in milk and honey; it soothed his stomach, which had been griping him since he crossed the Channel.

When Anselm had drunk the last of it and the servant had taken the cup away, Henry said, "I'm not going to apologize for snatching a sick old man out of his comfortable retirement. Canterbury needs its archbishop. You may loathe the office, but it is yours. I'll give you your council and your reform of the Church. You in return will spare me the edge of your sermons. Pursue your moral crusade as you please, but leave me and mine out of it. Do you understand me?"

"Very well, majesty," Anselm said. He was blinking like a startled rabbit: embarrassing, rather, but he could not help himself. "I will confess, sire, that I am not accustomed to being reprimanded as if I were a recalcitrant schoolboy."

"Are you not?" said Henry. "We freed you from the magic that was such a burden. You knew there was a price. Now you pay it. You pay it well and in full, and God will reward you."

"And you? What will you do to me?"

"Nothing," said Henry. "Serve Mother Church to the best of your ability, stay out of my way, and we'll get on well together. I have only one favor to ask."

"Within the bounds of the Church's law, I will grant it," Anselm said.

Henry grinned suddenly—looking half his age. He was good, Anselm thought. He could keep a man off balance even better than his father had. "Oh, it's all perfectly legal. I'm taking a queen, my lord archbishop. I want you to officiate at the wedding."

"Gladly," said Anselm without hesitation. "May I ask who is the fortunate lady?"

"That is being negotiated," Henry said.

Anselm considered what more he could say: the legions of bastards, the women in every city that Henry had lived in. He chose not to say it. This king was no more amenable to sermons than his father or brothers had been. Instead he said, "I shall pray that the lady, whoever she is, will be worthy of her office—and that you will be worthy of her."

"We will be," Henry said. "Believe me, we will."

Edgar King of Scots came roaring into London in the teeth of a northern gale. Henry had been closeted with the clerks until his brains were dribbling out his ears. He was more than glad to leave the march of crabbed figures across endless pages to indulge in a bit of kingly pageantry.

Edgar was patient enough, all things considered, but after the feast and the wine and the entertainment, he leaned toward Henry and said, "All right, out with it. What were you thinking, sending envoys to negotiate a marriage for my sister? Didn't you think that would be better done face-to-face?"

Henry shrugged. "I'm new to the game. Be patient."

"You were old to it when you were born," Edgar said. "I would be delighted to see my sister as queen of England, and well you know it. You also know that she's been God knows where for God knows how long. I certainly don't."

"I do," said Henry.

Edgar's face lit with eagerness. "You found her?"

Henry nodded.

"Where? Where is she?"

"Safe," said Henry, "and free of a nun's vows."

"You've seen her."

"I love her," Henry said bluntly. "Our good archbishop no doubt will call that a mortal sin, but there it is. Can you stand to give her to a man who can't sleep for thinking of her, and curses every day that he's apart from her?"

Edgar gaped. Then he grinned. "Now there's a damnation I can understand. Of course you can have her. There's no man I'd rather give her to."

"Would you say the same if I were still a mere count?"

"Would she?"

Henry was startled into laughter. "You do know her."

"I'm her brother," Edgar said. "So—where is she? When is the wedding?"

"Martinmas," Henry said.

Edgar narrowed his eyes. Then he nodded. "Time enough to bring the kingdom together, but not so much time as to fall into the dead of winter. That will be finishing the harvest in a grand and royal fashion." He paused. Henry watched him consider asking the first question again, then reconsider.

Wise man. There was still wine in the jar; Henry divided it between them, then lifted his cup. "To the queen of England," he said.

"And to the king who loves her," said Edgar.

When Mathilda returned to the Isle after the royal sacrifice, she had thought she would not be able to bear the separation from Henry. But there was so much to do in the healing of Britain, so many gates to shut and wounds to heal and wards to sustain within the walls of air, that she stumbled out of bed before dawn and fell over long after sunset. He was always there inside her, both memory and living presence, but her days were full to bursting. She hardly had time to yearn after him.

Summer passed into a mellow autumn. The harvest was not so stunted after all; farmers reckoned it a miracle, and so it was. England would eat this winter, though not extravagantly.

On the Day of the Dead, the gates of the Otherworld opened as they had in the old time. Even Etaine confessed to a deep unease. But the Hunt that traversed the sky was the true Hunt, terrible in its own right, but clean of either blight or corruption.

Her father was riding with it, side by side with Red William. It was fair enough vengeance, she supposed, even though the victim welcomed his fate. She could imagine them making common cause, two kings who had known the same world and died on its behalf.

She found that thought oddly comforting. It was a wild night, but no more than it should be. When before dawn the gate closed, the Hunt was all on the other side, in its due and proper order.

They were all hollow-eyed come morning. It was a bright day and warm, hinting more of summer than of winter. Mathilda stumbled out blearily for her turn in the kitchens, but when she turned in that direction, Etaine was standing in her way. "It's time," the Lady said.

Mathilda stood blinking stupidly. "Time? What—"

"Time to go," said Etaine.

Slowly light dawned. "Go? To—"

"To your king," Etaine said.

That brought Mathilda fully awake. "Now? Today?"

"In three days," said Etaine. "You've much to do before you go."

Indeed. Time that had been so slow was suddenly too swift to see. Mathilda had to stop, breathe deep, focus.

She was all too aware of Etaine's amusement. Let her laugh. Mathilda was a bride preparing for her wedding. She was entitled to her share of confusion.

❄ CHAPTER 53 ❄

On the morning that she was to depart from the Isle, Mathilda bathed for the last time in the lake. The water was cold but bracing; it cleansed her spirit as well as her body.

When she emerged into air that was warmer by far than the water, so that curls of mist danced upon it, she found her old clothes gone. Cecilia was standing on the shore with Etaine. The mantle that Cecilia carried was deep blue, and the gown in Etaine's hands was white.

Mathilda stopped short. She had no need to say what was in her mind. They knew.

"You are initiate many times over," Cecilia said.

Etaine nodded. "Guardian and queen—how can you not be Lady as well? You found your own way to it, but there's no denying that you did it. We're sending you out in full armor, with all the powers and protections that belong to us."

"You'll be needing them all," said Cecilia. "You love him, and that's well; and he's besotted with you. But he's not an easy man, and it's not an easy kingdom."

"Nor am I," Mathilda said. "I'll give as good as I get."

"So you will," Cecilia said with the flicker of a smile.

Mathilda had spoken boldly, and she had been dreaming of this for long and long. She ached for her beloved, her husband and her king.

But as she mounted the horse that was waiting for her and set out on the straight track, she began to wonder if she really was made to be a queen. All her life had been spent in houses of consecrated women. She was meant to live in sacred solitude; to serve and be obedient to God or the gods. She had no arts or skills that befit a queen.

She said nothing of this to the Ladies who rode with her—all of them but a very few who must stay to guard the Isle. She knew too well what they would say. They believed that she was born for this. So had she, until it was almost upon her. Now she was far from certain.

Henry was as restless as a leopard in a cage, and rather more chancy as to temper. He was well aware that people walked wide of him, but he could not seem to do anything about it.

The preparations for the wedding were well in train. He had given all the orders and approved all the plans. He would have done more, but his subjects made it all too clear that he was in the way. Therefore he had far more leisure to brood than he would have expected, and much too much time to dream of her.

They were only fancies, mortal dreams and not true visions. She had been closed to him since he rode away to bury his brother and be crowned king. He was beginning to wonder if she would come to him at all—if it had all been delusion, or if the woman who came to him would be some other princess altogether.

That was foolishness and he knew it, but for all his many women, he had never taken one as his queen before. Surely he could be forgiven for fretting like any common bridegroom.

In the days before the feast of St. Martin, rumors began to surface in the city. There was a great riding out of the west, they said: white Ladies and knights in strange armor, glimpsed by moonlight or met on the old roads in the deep hours of the night. The Old Things were coming to the king in London, bringing his queen.

But those were only whispers. Honest Christian men professed that the Scots king had gone to Wilton abbey to fetch his sister. He would come back with her by St. Martin's Day, or so they said. Then there would be a wedding in Westminster, and a queen to share the throne.

Both tales were true, in their fashion. Edgar had gone to meet his sister; but she was not coming from Wilton, and Henry would have been surprised if she had not come with the Ladies who had raised and protected her for so long.

It was a delicate dance, this balancing of the old world and the new. Nor was it only the old gods and the Christian God, or the world of magic and the altogether mortal world. It was Saxon and Norman, too, old invader and new. Somehow, with Mathilda's help, he had to make them all one.

On Martinmas morning, in the clear gold light of autumn that had not yet given way to the grey of winter, she came riding down the westward road. Her knights were knights of Scotland and of England, Normandy and Brittany; and if any was of other than mortal blood, the sunlight concealed him. Her ladies were all clad in white or grey, but they worked no visible magic as they rode. They seemed as mortal as they could be.

To the people who crowded along the roadside, magic or lack thereof meant little. They were full of her: her beauty, her grace, her lineage. "Alfred's daughter," they called her, crying out to her in Saxon, weeping and laughing when she answered them in the same language.

Henry waited for her outside the abbey at Westminster, standing in front of the door as a bridegroom was expected to do. His procession through the city had been brief and adequately celebrated, but he had not even tried to compare with the arrival of his queen.

If he had had his way, he would have galloped off to find her, then escaped to another world altogether, where they could be man and woman alone, with no kingdom to weigh them down. But he was too hardheaded for that. He wanted this kingdom and he wanted this queen. There was no other way to get her.

So he waited, following her progress by the sound of the people's cheering: a long, rolling wave that drew ever so slowly closer.

"They're all in love with her," Anselm said.

The archbishop was more or less resigned to his fate. Today he seemed almost cheerful. It must be a great comfort to his dourly Christian heart, to be making an honest man of an infamous sinner.

"Am I allowed to love her, too?" Henry inquired.

"It is your duty," said Anselm.

Henry shot him a glance. He did not seem to be mocking his king. "I should hope to be more than dutiful," Henry said.

Anselm let that pass by, which was as well. Henry was in no mood for a sermon.

She was closer now. He could make out words in the roar of the crowd: her name, her new one that he had given her and she had chosen to take, and snatches of blessings and prayers for her joy and prosperity.

There was still power in these conquered Saxons. Yet now it was transformed. Where it been grey and choking nothingness, now it was like a wave of light. The magic of Britain had woven with it and made it all new.

She had done it, with her bright magic and her warm heart. He could feel her now, riding slowly toward him. It was like a part of his soul come home.

Only sheer raw will kept him from bolting toward her. This was her day and her glory. He would only muddle it.

Just a little longer. His breath came hard and quick. A trickle of sweat ran down his back, under the shirt of finest linen and the cotte of cloth of gold. The crown was heavier than ever on his brow.

He endured it as he endured the lack of her: with gritted teeth and tight-strained patience.

* * *

At last, as the sun inched toward noon, she came in sight, far down the road. The crowd's roar shook the stones under his feet.

He was hardly aware of it. She rode on a white horse, shining in the sun. Her gown was of white samite shot with silver, and her mantle was of cloth of silver. Pearls and silver were woven in her hair, and on her brow was a crescent moon. The light of her was almost more than his eyes could bear.

She had not seen him yet: she was bowing to the people, listening to their voices. He would not have been at all surprised if she was trying to remember every face out of all those thousands.

At last she raised her eyes to meet his. He gasped as if at a blow. Her smile came near to felling him.

There was nothing of cold intent in it. She was simply and purely glad to see him standing there, waiting with patience gone threadbare.

Her mount danced, tossing its long white mane. Its eye caught Henry's and glinted. It was not a horse's eye at all, or anything mortal.

Her puca was still serving her, and fiercely, too. Henry had a brief vision of the mortal horse that had been meant to carry the queen to her wedding. It had survived the encounter, was even sound enough to carry the Lady Etaine, but the puca had made it very clear, very quickly, that the queen was not to greet her king on the back of any common animal.

Henry could not help but smile. The puca had yet some distance to go, but Henry had had enough of waiting. He left the abbey's door at last and ran to meet his lady—and never mind what anyone thought of such impulsiveness in a king.

Mathilda had endured the long processional because she must—and because, once she had begun it, the people's joy carried her onward. They were pleased with her, even more than pleased. They loved that she was so obviously Saxon, and yet so clearly meant to wed the Norman king. They knew her deep in their hearts, without even knowing what they knew.

They were hers, her people. She had to give them their due, no matter how eager she might be to see her beloved again.

And yet, at the end, there he was, running toward her like a reckless boy, with his crown glittering and his heavy crimson mantle abandoned on the abbey's step. She had never seen him in such splendor; but she would always know him. His face was still his, his strong square hands reaching up to lift her from the puca's back, his grey eyes no longer quite so cool as she remembered but still blessedly his.

There was a rite to celebrate, a wedding and a Mass and a coronation, but all the rite she needed was here, face-to-face under the sky, before the court and the commons of England. The folk of air had come to bless it, and the Old Things were flickering in shadows, waiting for the day to pass. They would come out after the sun had set, to dance under the moon.

They stood with her hands on his shoulders and his at her waist, as if to begin their own dance. He was grinning like a fool. She supposed that she was, too.

There was nothing for it but to kiss him. It seemed he was of the same mind. People were screaming, shouting, cheering, but they were far away.

"I gather they approve of us," Henry said.

"It does appear so," said Mathilda.

"It would be unfortunate if they didn't."

"Very," she said.

Then of course she had to kiss him again, which led to another kiss, and would have led to something else—but her gown was like armor, and his cotte was no better; and there was the matter of several thousand people watching.

"Promise me something," she said.

"Anything," said the man whom other men called the most coldly calculating and least impetuous of old William's sons.

Mathilda, of course, knew better. "Promise that no matter how heavy the crown may be or how crowded the cares of the kingdom, there will always be time for this."

"By my heart I swear it," he said, "and by the love I bear you."

"You are my heart," she said, "and my beloved."

He kissed her hands, with great restraint. Anselm was waiting with yet more words, and they were beautiful words and holy; but these were all the vows they needed, or would ever need.

Her eyes met his, and found a glint of irony there, and perfect understanding. Side by side in royal dignity—much to the delight and manifest amusement of their people, both mortal and otherwise—they presented themselves for the Church's blessing.

❈ Author's Note ❈

The story of King William II of England, called by historians William Rufus, is pure gold for the historical fantasist. There is already a core of legend around the king's death in the New Forest, but the rest falls into place with remarkable ease. I knew I had my story when I discovered in the course of research that the Scots princess Edith, later renamed Mathilda, who was to become King Henry I's queen, spent her childhood in the abbey at Wilton—some seven miles from Salisbury. The proximity of so powerful a magical site suggested the direction and focus of the rest.

Most of the events of the novel actually occurred, or are presumed to have occurred—including the debacle of William the Conqueror's death and burial, and the events surrounding William Rufus' death. Sister Gunnhild's adventure, Anselm's forced investiture, the role of Walter Tirel in William's death, even the fact that whenever William was minded to cross the English Channel, storms died down and the weather cleared for the crossing—all occurred essentially as written.

Edith of course was not known to have been a Lady of Avalon. After her escape to Scotland in 1093, she returned (or was returned) to Wilton, from which she was produced in the year 1100 to marry the new king—and yes, that wedding took place on the old Celtic festival which the Christians called Martinmas. She did indeed pay a price for whatever sins she may have committed: she died rather young, in 1118, two years before the death of her only son, William Atheling, in the tragedy of the White Ship.

As for Cecilia, daughter of William the Conqueror and sister of his sons William and Henry, she was a nun and later abbess of a convent in Caen. Her dates of birth and death are not known; she was given to the abbey in 1066 and took full vows in 1075, and became abbess in 1113. As far as we know, she never set foot in England and played little if any role in the affairs of the kingdom.

For further readings in the history of these characters and their times, see Frank Barlow, *William Rufus* (New Haven, 2000) and C. Warren Hollister, *Henry I* (New Haven, 2001).